An Innocent Eye

Also by Philip Hook

The Stonebreakers
The Island of the Dead
The Soldier in the Wheatfield

An Innocent Eye

Philip Hook

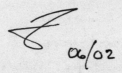

06/02

coronet

CORONET BOOKS
Hodder & Stoughton

First published in Great Britain in 2000 by Hodder and Stoughton
First published in paperback in 2001 by Hodder & Stoughton
A division of Hodder Headline

A Coronet Paperback

10 9 8 7 6 5 4 3 2 1

A CIP catalogue record for this title is available
from the British Library.

ISBN 0 340 68219 1

Typeset by Palimpsest Book Production Limited,
Polmont, Stirlingshire
Printed and bound in Great Britain by
Clays Ltd, St Ives plc.

Hodder and Stoughton
A division of Hodder Headline
338 Euston Road
London NW1 3BH

My aspens dear, whose airy cages quelled,
Quelled or quenched in leaves the leaping sun,
All felled, felled, are all felled;
   Of a fresh and following folded rank
     Not spared, not one
     That dandled a sandalled
   Shadow that swam or sank
On meadow and river and wind-wandering, weed-
   winding bank.

G.M. Hopkins, 'Binsey Poplars', 1879

Part One

PARIS

Monday, 28 June

After they had made love for the second time, Daniel Stern lay on his back and looked out of the window. It was strange that he had not registered before the oblique view across the rooftops of Paris that you caught from this angle: a landscape of parapets and skylights and aerials, with a distant glimpse of the tower of Saint Sulpice. But then his eyes had been opened to a lot of new things recently. He was seeing the world differently, from a changed perspective. This apartment, for instance, in the rue Servandoni: when he had first moved in a month ago it had struck him as an odd, angular, faintly oppressive place, hidden away up here in the eaves, all awkward rafters and unlikely dividing walls. But now he rather relished its strangeness, its seclusion. It was secure, it was a refuge. And it was inconspicuous. He particularly liked that. No one knew him here. No one knew her, either, the woman lying next to him. They were cocooned in an illusion of anonymity. Beyond care. Beyond control. Beyond redemption.

He glanced at the clock. He had to go. He calculated he must leave the apartment in another ten minutes, if he was to get to the Gare du Nord in time to catch the Eurostar. Part of him yearned to forget the train, to squander the rest of the afternoon in bed with her. It would be easy to yield to the temptation. But he knew that wasn't an option. Getting to London this afternoon was something he had to do. It was not negotiable. He reached out and stroked the skin of her long, olive-coloured arm.

'When can I see you again?' he asked.

'I can be back in Paris at the weekend.' She smiled at him sleepily.

'Will you come here, to this apartment?'

She laughed. 'Why not?'

She was as intoxicated by him as he was by her. He couldn't understand how it had happened. So quickly: this time last month neither one of them had been aware of the other's existence. It was as if their mutual attraction had been precipitated and intensified by its own improbability. By its own folly.

'I'll be waiting for you,' he assured her. He kissed her quickly and got out of bed, bending to pick his clothes up from the floor.

'But why do you have to go now?'

'I have to go to London, I told you. To a meeting.'

'What sort of meeting?'

'Don't ask. Look, it's better you don't know anything about it.'

'Why is it better? You don't own me, you cannot dictate to me these things.'

She sat up, staring at him. Angry, resentful. Still doing up the buttons of his shirt, he came to sit beside her again. 'I'm sorry,' he said. 'It's too complicated now. I'll explain everything afterwards. Just trust me: this is very, very important.'

'More important than me?'

He ran his fingers down her cheek, and shook his head. 'It's separate. A piece of business that I've got to settle.' He didn't want to tell her about it. Not now. Not yet. It wasn't right to involve her. They'd learned so much about each other so quickly; he sensed it was important to keep some things back. Particularly this.

She considered what he'd said for a moment, then pulled herself out of bed and reached for her T-shirt. 'You can be very determined, I think. When you want something.'

'You should know that by now.'

There was a brief silence between them, then she said: 'Daniel, listen. We're going to have to talk soon. Seriously. We cannot go on like this.'

'This weekend,' he assured her. 'Things will be clearer by then.' It was true: things would soon be a lot clearer, perhaps even by the end of this evening. Provided he got to the Gare du Nord in time. Provided he caught the London train. Provided he kept his appointment in the Clermont Hotel.

Out of the corner of his eye, he watched her pulling

her jeans up over her long brown legs. She had a gift for wearing clothes elegantly. Any clothes. It had been one of the first things he'd noticed about her.

He grabbed his own jacket, the green one. And the small attaché case. He was at the front door now. 'I've really got to go,' he said.

She came over and put her arms round his neck. 'Don't ring me,' she told him. 'It's too dangerous.'

'OK.' He wavered. 'So I'll see you here when?'

'Friday afternoon.'

'Friday afternoon,' he repeated. He suddenly felt sick at leaving her. Physically sick at the separation. The weekend seemed too far away. Too long to wait.

He kissed her goodbye, and she murmured into his hair: 'Jesus, Daniel! What are we doing? Are we totally crazy?'

Thinking about it as he ran down the stairwell to the street, Stern decided they probably were. He knew he was. Totally. So crazy that anything might happen.

LONDON

Monday, 28 June

'Sod's law, isn't it?' Richards observed afterwards to as many of his team as were prepared to listen. 'Bound to happen to the one wretched little bugger on the desk for the first time.'

Richards was fat and pompous, cultivating a manner intended to suggest earlier service in a good if unspecified regiment. He was fond of a drink, too, and frequently the object of his staff's derision behind his back. But it was also true that he'd been at the Clermont Hotel for twenty-three years now, reached the heights of Reception Manager, and in this instance there was general agreement that his assessment of the situation was correct. In the the guilty excitement of recent proximity to horrific events, it was comforting to find a subject of agreement. You felt bonded by the experience, moved by a subconscious craving to pull together for a while. Just until the shock wore off.

Gregory Jackson was the wretched little bugger on the desk for the first time that warm Monday afternoon. He was twenty-two, neat, personable, possessed of that patience of spirit and deftness of manner which distinguishes the natural servant, the individual born to wait upon his fellow men. He'd been tempted to train as a steward with British Airways, like his friend Terence, but because of a residual unease about flying he'd opted for a career in the hotel trade. He was good with people; indeed, seemed to relish humanity with an indiscriminate eagerness. Neatly turned out, too. You had to be at the Clermont, didn't you? Everyone knew the Clermont, Americans particularly. It was a bit of a legend, tucked away just off Berkeley Square, in the heart of London's Mayfair. It summed up all that was best about British standards of service, tradition and civilisation. To foreigners, anyway. He came on duty at four that afternoon, resplendent in the tail-coat which had been one of the secret attractions of the job. ('Here, Terence, what d'you think? Touch of the old Fred Astaires?' 'More like Ginger Rogers, dear, if you ask me'). He'd been taught the correct procedure for checking people in. How you got them to fill out a registration form if they hadn't stayed before, and took an imprint of their credit card. Well, it happened, didn't it? Even at the Clermont. People doing a bunk without settling their bills. And at £195 a night for the cheapest single room, Jackson could well imagine the temptation.

It was a busy afternoon. Almost immediately he was drawn into the thick of it, checking in a party of twenty-seven Japanese. Not a package tour, you understand. The very idea would have outraged an old hand like Richards;

such groups would never have been acceptable at the Clermont. No, these were upmarket Japanese, members of the Osaka Chamber of Commerce and their wives, in London on an official visit. Maybe they had all arrived at Heathrow on the same aircraft, and been borne into the centre of the city on the same air-conditioned bus. Maybe a block rate had been negotiated for their rooms. But a package tour, never. They talked very fast and not very intelligibly. Richards moved among them in an affable manner, paying no attention to their muffled, faintly hysterical outpourings but greeting them in an exaggeratedly plummy voice. 'Welcome to the Clermont, sir. Expeditious journey over, madam? Excellent, splendid!' Finally he withdrew to the cover of his office, pausing to address Jackson urgently out of the corner of his mouth: 'Get these ruddy Nips on out of it, pronto.'

Jackson had just assigned the last Osaka couple to a room on the seventh floor when the man in the black polo neck approached the reception desk. As Jackson told the police afterwards, there had been nothing particularly remarkable about the way he behaved; no, he hadn't seemed anxious or overexcited or in any way apprehensive. He was in his late fifties, broad-shouldered, with the sort of greying, exaggeratedly well-cared-for hair that marked him out as foreign. He was wearing dark glasses which he took off once he began to speak, revealing deep blue emotionless eyes. Jackson didn't say it to the police because they wouldn't have understood, but he'd been unnerved by those eyes: there was something hard about them. Pitiless.

But it wasn't the job of a reception clerk to note down those sort of judgments about the hotel's clients, was it? There wasn't a column for such observations on the form, no space on the computer screen. He was just there to check them in.

The guest didn't say much, but when he did speak it was in a faintly foreign accent. Spanish, maybe? Or it could have been Italian. Anyway, the man gave his name as Mr Vincent, and Jackson found the reservation on the screen, which told him that Mr Vincent had an address near Windsor and that he'd stayed at the Clermont before. Just the one night would it be, Mr Vincent? That's fine, sir. And how would he be paying?

'Cash,' he said.

Cash. Right. For a moment Jackson could not remember the correct procedure. Cash was unusual.

'In advance,' the man said. He handed over six fifty-pound notes.

'Thank you, sir,' said Jackson. 'Excuse me just one moment.'

He ducked back into the office. Richards was alone in there. 'What is it, Jackson?' he demanded, closing his desk drawer rather too abruptly. There was the clink of a bottle.

'Guest wants to pay by cash in advance. What do I do?'

'Take the money and make a receipt,' Richards told him testily.

'And the receipts are . . . ?'

'Do I have to do everything for you?' Richards lumbered over and produced one from the stationery cupboard. 'Be asking me to wipe your own arse next.'

Later that evening, when he was giving his statement to the police, Richards had to be reminded of the exchange. But he'd been delighted to confirm it. Its recounting placed him rather more centrally in the frame of action. As a figure of authority and experience to whom his juniors referred for guidance and counsel.

Jackson made out the receipt, and gave it to the guest. He completed the other formalities and handed him the key to Room 623. On the sixth floor, sir. The lift is just across the hall. Do you need help with your luggage? No? Enjoy your stay with us, Mr Vincent.

The luggage? No, as far as he remembered, there had been nothing very distinctive about it. Just the one small bag, brown he thought it was. And a black briefcase. Mr Vincent had carried them both quite easily. As he'd bent to pick them up, a ripple had passed over his back, an involuntary, faintly feral movement, like a predatory animal setting itself on the alert.

About quarter to seven Jackson first noticed the other man, the one in the green jacket. There was a temporary lull in activity at the reception desk, and glancing across the grandeur of the hotel foyer, Jackson's eye fell upon him by chance. He was a striking-looking youngish man of about thirty with quite long dark hair, and he sat on one of the Louis Quinze-style sofas reading a newspaper. But even at this distance Jackson could tell he wasn't giving the newspaper his full attention. He was tense, worried about something. Every so often he laid the newspaper aside and glanced about him, vigilant, wary; not so much looking out for someone as constantly taking his bearings, reminding himself of his surroundings like a field officer on exercise. Measuring angles. Calculating lines of exit, routes of escape. Now I'm imagining things, thought Jackson. Over-fanciful, that's me. But that was the thing about hotels, wasn't it? What made them such fascinating places to work in. All human life was there. He moved his gaze on to the table near the fireplace where a hefty woman in ill-judged orange was berating her sulky, adolescent daughter for some unknown misdemeanour over tea and cucumber sandwiches. A multitude of separate human dramas, all playing themselves out on this warm, slightly humid late June evening.

Jackson was distracted from his speculation by the arrival of a husband and wife from San Francisco with a quite prodigious number of Louis Vuitton suitcases. It took two bell-boys and a baggage cart to get them all upstairs. He checked in another two or three guests. Then he looked up and found that the man with the green jacket was actually standing at the desk. It must have been just on seven o'clock.

'Can I help you, sir?' offered Jackson.

Close to, Jackson sensed the intensity emanating from him even more strongly. He was a good-looking number, no doubt about that: wavy black hair that fell forward over his forehead, strong jaw, clear brown eyes. But preoccupied. 'Can you tell Mr Vincent that I'm here?' he said. But he spoke as if his mind were on something else, concentrating on something much more important. He frowned and stared through Jackson, as if he weren't there. Afterwards they wanted to know if he'd had an accent. Could he have been Italian too, perhaps? Jackson couldn't tell them. All you really registered with him was that he wanted something; was intent upon it. You felt a strength of will coming from him that was almost physical. As it happened, it sent a little shiver of excitement down Jackson's spine, but that was another thing he couldn't have told the police, now, could he? Not without running the risk of misinterpretation.

'Mr Vincent, sir?' The name did not immediately mean anything. Too many other distractions in between. He checked on the screen. Of course, Room 623.

Jackson lifted the house telephone and dialled the number. 'What name shall I say, sir?'

Afterwards, when he was asked to recall it, a terrible thing happened. Jackson's memory failed. You couldn't remember everything, could you? It just wasn't humanly possible. Jackson must at that point have been told the man's name, must have announced it to Mr Vincent. Because Mr Vincent had told him, 'OK, send him up.' But what was the name the visitor had given him? There had been no reason actually to write it down. So many different names in the course of a spell of duty on a hotel reception desk. Particularly one as busy as the Clermont.

You couldn't possibly be expected to recall them all. Specially not on your first day.

'I'm sorry,' he told his interrogators afterwards. 'I'd know him again if I saw him. But his name's gone.' Jackson felt as bad about that as anything that terrible day. He sensed that professionally he'd fallen short of the highest standards. Let the Clermont down. Failed to meet the ultimate challenge.

So the unknown man with his intense, preoccupied manner and his wavy black hair went up to Room 623. On the sixth floor, sir. The lift is just across the hall.

About an hour and a half later one of the members of the Osaka Chamber of Commerce who was staying in Room 624 rang down to the reception desk to register a complaint. Everyone was busy. Richards, who was passing, had to take the call. He made a performance of it, the captain on the bridge not too proud to help out below when all hands were needed on deck. A mucker-in. A team player. He shot his cuffs out and put the receiver to his ear. He'd show the youngsters how these things were done.

'And what can I do for you, Mr Hiroshiga? What's that, in the next-door room? I'm sorry, sir, but if I'm going to understand you, you're going to have to speak a little more clearly. And a fraction more slowly too, sir, if you don't mind. Right. So you're saying it's particularly loud, is it? I am so sorry about that, really I am. Now, have you tried knocking on the door yourself and asking them to turn the television down? Sometimes a direct approach is the most effective way. What's that, you've tried already? And no reply. Oh dear. You don't think they could hear you. That does sound as if it's on loud, I must say. Well, you just leave it with me, then, sir. I'll sort it out. Which neighbour is it, left or right? I see, number 623. Thank you so much for drawing this to our attention. It'll be seen to immediately. No trouble at all, sir. Goodbye.'

Richards withdrew to his office to make his next call. Fortified by a nip of something, he dialled Room 623. In his experience, people generally responded to politeness and an appeal to reason. But there was no reply. The line just kept on ringing, exacerbating Richards's temper with every unanswered trill. Bloody hell. Was it possible that a guest could go out leaving his television on that loud? He reminded himself that it was; that all things were possible with hotel guests, even at the Clermont. That times were changing and the class of people that had money enough to check into top hotels these days, even here, often left much to be desired. So he rang Hotel Security. He'd had enough. Bloody Security sat around all day doing bugger all. They could bloody well cope with it.

The man from Security was at the door to the room a matter of six minutes later. He knocked four times, with increasing vigour. Still no answer. Out here in the passageway the television was certainly audible. What were they, deaf or something? He fitted the master key in the lock and turned it. As the door swung open, the noise from the television was suddenly very loud indeed. But he didn't really notice it. Not once his attention had been distracted by Mr Vincent.

Mr Vincent lay on the floor at the end of the bed. His eyes stared sightless at the ceiling. He had been shot in the chest, and there was a lot of blood. It had spread out, a deep, darkening crimson across the carpet, like the map of some ceaselessly expanding empire.

The face of the security man discoloured to a liverish kind of green. He turned away to switch off the television. It was blaring out the canned laughter of a comedy programme. Mindless, contrived. Rising and falling in laboured paroxysms. On the edge of hysteria.

DI Grewcock walked over to the Clermont from West End Central Station in Savile Row. It took him seven minutes, along Conduit Street, Bruton Street, and across Berkeley Square. The uniform car had been first at the scene, quarter of an hour earlier. DS Chesney had followed shortly after. Getting the show on the road. Cordoning off sites: scene of the crime, likely entry and exit routes. Meanwhile Grewcock hoped the fresh air would clear his head. When he found it didn't, he lit up a Silk Cut instead. He ground it out half finished on the steps of the hotel. He felt well pissed off.

At the reception desk where he flashed his ID he was met by a fat wanker in a tail-coat. 'Are you in charge, Officer, of the investigation?'

'Yep. Which floor?'

'Sixth.' The fat man scuttled after him. 'Before you go up, might I have a word?'

Finger on the lift call-button, Grewcock turned on him. 'What is it?'

'Just to say, discreet as possible, if you please. We are the Clermont. Reputation to preserve, don't you know?'

Grewcock sensed rather than smelled the alcohol on the man's breath. It took one to know one. 'I don't care if you're bloody Buckingham Palace, mate,' he said, and got into the lift.

Chesney was already there in the room. He gestured to the corpse. 'Looks like a single shot, guv. Forensic are on their way. The Charing Cross mob.'

'Who is he?'

'Room was booked to a John Vincent.'

'And is this Vincent?'

'That's the point, guv. It is and it isn't.'

'Don't play bloody stupid games with me. Is it Vincent?'

'He's got two passports in his briefcase. One British Cayman Islands, in the name of Vincent. One Swiss. Look, it's Vincent again in the photo. But this time a different name.'

'Shit.' Grewcock's headache was worse. The Scotch an hour ago had been a mistake.

'Shall I run a check on General Database? See if there's a link with Organised Crime?'

'Why would you want to do that, Sergeant?'

'I just thought, what with the two passports, it might be relevant . . .'

Bloody smartarse. 'Do it, then.' Grewcock paused. 'And get the reception clerk up here who checked Vincent in.'

Grewcock waited for Jackson in 622. The room was empty and had been commandeered as a base of police operations. Farther along the passage, a Japanese guest and his wife were being discreetly chivvied by hotel staff out of 624 to a suite on another floor. He caught snatches of the managerial assurances that the new quarters would be even more commodious than the ones vacated. That the move was necessitated by 'technical problems' in the adjoining room. Technical problems, my arse. He sat glaring at the two passports that had come out of Vincent's briefcase, listening to the fainter, more distant sounds of the evening traffic in Berkeley Square. And wondering about access to the minibar. No key. He supposed it wouldn't look good if he forced it.

There was a knock on the door. He glanced up as Chesney showed the receptionist in from downstairs, and thought, as he took in the slim, tail-coated figure with his unctuously graceful movements, That's all I need, the queen of the bloody fairies. He asked him questions first. Got a description of the visitor who'd gone up to Vincent's room an hour before he'd been found. Got it all down first, because he guessed Jackson wouldn't be good for very much afterwards. Not once he'd seen the body.

'So this visitor, this man who asked for Vincent: did you see him leave again?'

Jackson shook his head.

'Could he have left without you seeing him pass?'

Jackson thought of the constant toing and froing of the hotel foyer, and agreed he could have. Only too easily. And then there was the exit into Mount Street. He wouldn't even have had to pass the reception desk to get out if he'd gone that way.

Grewcock snapped his notebook shut and sighed. 'Ready to take a look, then, sunshine?'

Jackson nodded.

'Just need confirmation from you that this is the man known as Vincent. The same man you checked into the hotel at approximately six p.m. this evening.'

Grewcock led him out into the passage, waited for Chesney to unlock the door, then ushered Jackson through into 623.

'Is that him? Is that Vincent?'

'That's him,' said Jackson. He was the colour of parchment.

Grewcock nodded. 'Find it upsetting, do you? The blood and all that?'

Jackson swayed, and turned to look away. It wasn't the blood. He could cope with that, he'd steeled himself for it. No, what he found much more horrible than the blood were the eyes. Staring. Still hard and emotionless, but macabrely more alive in death than in life. He mustn't look. Anywhere but at those eyes. His gaze fell on the jacket, lying in a heap on the carpet by the door. A green jacket.

'That's his jacket,' he said dully.

'Whose jacket? Vincent's?'

'No ... the other man's. The one who went up to see him. He was wearing it.'

Chesney picked it up gingerly and held it out. Its front was saturated in blood. 'Would have had to leave this behind, wouldn't he, guv? Couldn't exactly have made an inconspicuous exit wearing this.'

'Any ID in the pockets?'

Chesney felt through them carefully. 'Nothing here. He must have emptied them before he ran.'

'We'll get a description out,' said Grewcock. He felt obscurely thwarted that Jackson hadn't keeled over yet. Little pansy should have hit the deck by now. There's nothing more aggravating, when your head aches and your mouth tastes like sandpaper, than having your prejudices undermined.

'I'll check the hotel security cameras.'

Just then Grewcock's mobile rang. Urgently; insistently. He put it to his ear.

'Yep ... yep ... yep ...' There was a prolonged period of nodding and frowning as Grewcock absorbed what he was being told. 'Got you,' he said finally. 'Understood. OK, fifteen minutes. I'll wait for them here.' He clicked the mobile shut and turned on Chesney in a fury. 'So that's the end of us, then.'

'What's up?'

'We got the posers from Spring Gardens coming in.'

'Was that . . . ?'

'Your bloody call checking out the names on the passports. We've only got half the sodding Drugs Squad turning up now. Taking over, I shouldn't wonder. Sending us off to make the fucking tea.'

'So there *was* a connection,' said Chesney doggedly. 'The names must have triggered something.'

'I know how the system works, Sergeant.'

'If they're on to it that quick, he must be someone big.' Chesney indicated the corpse at the end of the bed.

'Yes, well. We'll see about that.'

'Can I go now?' asked Jackson. Quietly.

Grewcock turned on him, giving quick vent to the mass of frustration that had built up within him. 'Yep, just sod off out of it now, why don't you?'

Two of them came, in their snappy suits and natty ties. The familiar figure of DI Higgins, who thought he was Bruce Willis, and another fancy bastard who Grewcock had never met before and was barely introduced to now. This second one nodded cursorily in Grewcock's direction and announced himself as Wesson. As an afterthought to his arrival in the room. As if Grewcock was no longer relevant to proceedings. Grimly Grewcock read the body language of the interlopers. Higgins moved about a lot, hint of a swagger, but nimble like a boxer. Pleased with himself. Deferential, though, when he spoke to the other man or looked in his direction. Like a dog with his master. Wesson was taller, blond-haired. Thoughtful, giving less away. Grewcock had him down for an arrogant sod. But one interesting thing he noted: Wesson spoke with a distinct transatlantic accent. What was an American doing here, then?

Together Higgins and Wesson peered at the passports, then took up positions either side of the bed to gaze at the body. Grewcock watched their reactions. Higgins frowned, seemed about to say something, then checked himself. Instead he looked quizzically at his colleague. Waiting for him to commit to an opinion.

'No,' announced Wesson. 'It isn't him.' He paused, then added almost meditatively, 'I'll tell you who it is, though.'

'Who?'

'It's his fucking brother.'

'Christ. His brother? What's his brother doing here?'

'Whose brother?' demanded Grewcock, but they didn't seem to hear him.

'Whatever he came to do, he's not doing it any more.'

'Jesus Christ!' It was Higgins now. There was a sudden, shocked edge to his voice, a genuine surprise laced with excitement which made them all turn towards him. He'd gone over to Vincent's briefcase and was examining its contents. 'Look what we've got here. Amelga paperwork. Pages of it.'

Wesson was across the room like lightning, at Higgins's shoulder, reaching for what he'd found. Like a teacher confiscating a forbidden magazine. He stood there by the window, leafing methodically through the documentation himself. Pausing every now and then to absorb something particularly significant. For perhaps two minutes no one else spoke, sensing the momentousness of the discovery.

'Shit,' Wesson said at last. 'I think this may be it.'

'Shall I get on to Hauser in Bern?'

'Later. These need full analysis first. Jesus, Inspector: I think we finally got the slimeball.'

Grewcock's patience finally wore thin. He felt excluded from the party. 'Who? Who do you think you've got?'

Wesson didn't reply, but Higgins turned to him. Higgins was always a smug bastard. Now he was preening himself, bathing in the reflected triumph. 'This is one of the big boys, Inspector,' he explained. 'One of the very biggest.' There was no mistaking the implication: out of your league, mate.

Grewcock controlled his anger because he was curious. 'Drugs?' he persisted.

'Drugs. Murder. Among other things.'

'What's this, then?' Grewcock indicated the corpse. 'Likely to be a professional job?'

'Could be.' Higgins was non-committal. Frightened of venturing an opinion that could later be held against him. Grewcock knew the type, and despised him.

'Looks like we've got the killer's jacket here,' offered Chesney encouragingly, from over by the door.

Wesson and Higgins wheeled round to face him.

'Only there's nothing in it,' said Grewcock.

'But there is, guv, look. I found it just now. Slipped down through a hole in the pocket into the lining.'

'What is it?' Wesson looked up, interested. The boss, asserting his authority over all of them.

'A photograph.'

'A photograph? Of what?'

'Here, take a look, sir.'

Grewcock joined them. Peering at it. 'It's a bloody painting,' he said, disdain mixed in with the perplexity. 'It's a photo of a bloody painting, isn't it?'

And Stern. Where was Stern by now?

Daniel Stern had drifted away into the London evening. His emotions were almost totally numbed; if anything penetrated his consciousness in the immediate aftermath of his encounter in the hotel room, it was the flickering of a deep, slow-burning anger. Dusk was falling. By instinct, he kept moving, down the curve of Regent Street, still dense with traffic, then skirting the neon lights of Piccadilly Circus. He took an obscure comfort in the milling crowds, in the sheer mass of normality that they represented. He was minus his jacket, but it was still warm, even at 9.30, and there were plenty of other people in shirtsleeves. Plenty of other people to offer him cover. Had he thought rationally about it, he might have hugged the shadows more; but he was not rational. And that was his salvation. He just kept walking straight ahead as if nothing had happened, blending seamlessly into the evening mêlée of touts, tarts and tourists.

From Piccadilly, he cut across Leicester Square, past the fast-food stands and the big cinemas and the queues beginning to build up outside the discothèques. A few minutes later he'd edged by St Martin-in-the-Fields, negotiated the Strand, and found his way down to the river, in the lee of Charing Cross Bridge. He paused, looking about him. There were fewer people here. He walked casually forward to the embankment wall and leaned against it; a solitary figure resting his weight on his elbows, apparently contemplating the huge Ferris wheel they were constructing on the south bank to celebrate the millennium. No one saw him drop something quickly into the glutinous waters of the Thames. No one, that is, except one bleary-eyed tramp, and he was far too drunk to register whether the small metal object could have been a gun.

What followed in Stern's mind wasn't so much a decision as the gathering realisation of an irresistible necessity. London was suddenly intolerable, suffocating, calamitous; he had to get out, back to France. Now. The preservation of his own freedom was paramount, because there were things that still had to be done, important things, and, as it seemed to him then, only he could do them. And there was her, too. She also beckoned him back to Paris. What had happened this evening must not jeopardise his meeting with her on Friday. So the sooner he left England the better. OK, the last Eurostar had gone. But ferries ran through the night. All he had to do was get to a Channel port. He doubled back up Villiers Street to Charing Cross Station, where he found a train that reached Dover just before twelve. His determination strengthened. He'd always had an obstinate streak.

Only on the crossing, out there on the open sea, did his numbness partially melt and occasional feelings begin to impinge.

Like the brief surge of exhilaration he experienced as he stood on the deck of the ferry and watched the white cliffs recede into the distance beyond a foamy wash of moonlit phosphorescence. An exhilaration totally divorced from the events of his brief stay in London. An exhilaration born of running his tongue over his lips and finding the taste of her still lingering, faint but unmistakable from earlier that afternoon.

Like the first doubt, which followed soon after the elation, the first murmur of uncertainty about tonight. But he clamped down on that, instantly.

He was right, he told himself. He was doing what was right.

And to convince himself, he went back over it all. The events of the past two months. He went back to the beginning.

Part Two

NEW YORK

Tuesday, 4 May

Nat was wearing earth colours that day. He always wore earth colours. They were his statement of intellectual weight, an affirmation of seriousness: a dark brown shirt, baggy charcoal-grey trousers, and a knitted tie the shade of slimy green that plant life attains in a stagnant pond. At forty-two, fashion sense wasn't his strong point. Enthusiasm was. He was leaning forward over his desk, nodding his head eagerly. He was an oddly proportioned figure: his large, pale, egg-shaped head seemed the wrong size for his stocky, compact body. He'd taken off his spectacles, and was making little stabbing motions with them to emphasise his point. Few things animated Nat with as much enthusiasm as one of his own ideas.

'I've got a feeling about this one, Dan. It's got legs. This one will run.'

Daniel Stern leaned back in the chair opposite and contemplated the proposition. Nat was the features editor who'd given him his first break, soon after he'd arrived in New York two and a half years ago. He'd always be grateful to him for that, but it didn't give Nat permanent rights over him. And it was a measure of Daniel's subsequent journalistic success that he didn't need to accept every commission he was offered now. That he could pick and choose his assignments. 'It's been done before,' said Daniel. 'And anyway, movie moguls are essentially pretty dull people.'

'So it's been done before,' Nat said. 'I know it's been done before. That's not the point. I reckon you'll give it a new spin. Remember, all these guys are Jewish. I kind of like the Jewish mafia angle. The Jewish readership likes it too. Makes them feel good to know they own Hollywood. Powerful.'

'It's not for me, Nat.'

'Think about it.' Nat scratched himself in the area of his armpit. He always scratched himself when he was arguing. 'Your being Jewish yourself will give the piece its validation.'

'You know it's not an issue for me, all that Jewish stuff.'

'Maybe you don't see it that way right now.'

'I don't.'

'Maybe you should.'

'How do you mean?'

'Why do you think you've been a success here? Why do you get read? I'll tell you why: because most of the creative people in this town are Jewish. You feel at home here.'

It was true that he'd flourished since his arrival from London. This place stimulated him in a way that London hadn't. He enjoyed its flexibility, its energy, its premium on talent. He appreciated the way it wasn't hidebound by the absurd constrictions of the British psyche with its crabbed cynicisms and constipated prejudices (to quote one of his early articles, headlined – God forgive him – 'Why London's dying'). But was all that just because he was Jewish? Certainly, in his experience being Jewish in London tended to make you subliminally an outsider. Coming here he still felt an outsider, but this time a more exotic one: an Englishman. An English accent never hurt you in New York, so – ironically – he found himself playing on it here, despite his disaffection with the country of his birth and upbringing. Perhaps that was the key to it: to be any good, a writer should always be an outsider. The point was that here he'd found a more fulfilling outsidership. Anyway, he felt obliged to argue against Nat. 'Jews don't hold a monopoly on talent, you know,' he said.

'Come on, Dan. Take away us Jews from New York and what are you left with? Kansas City.'

Daniel laughed. 'I'm still not doing that piece, OK?'

Nat sighed, and was silent. He'd stopped scratching, which was a positive sign. It meant he probably wasn't going to argue any more, that he'd admitted defeat. Daniel got up and went to the window. He felt good that day. It was a warm spring morning with a wide blue sky strung out across Manhattan, and the leaves were fresh on the trees. He'd got up at seven and gone out jogging in Central Park.

Everything was very green and clear and clean. He'd come back to his apartment on the upper West Side feeling the sort of glowing virtue that is only given to those who take violent physical exercise before breakfast. He'd showered, then called in at the local coffee shop for bacon and eggs. Sunny side up. New York was a great place in which to be young and single and successful.

'So what else have you got for me?'

Nat consulted his file. 'I guess we're committed to this interview with Madonna when she's in town later this month. Fancy talking to Madonna?'

'How many words?'

'Two and a half, three thousand. Flesh her out a bit. Your own take.'

'Not just puff?'

'Did we ever?'

He went back to his chair and gathered up his briefcase. 'OK, I'll write that,' he said. He was suddenly impatient to be on his way.

'The thing about you, Dan,' Nat said, 'is you know what you want.'

'Is that bad?'

'I guess not. But you frighten me sometimes. When you go for something, you're just about the most single-minded guy I ever met.'

'Come on, Nat. I wouldn't exactly call you Mr Indecisive.'

'Yeah. But I'm just overcompensating for my under-lying insecurity.'

'Then perhaps that's what I'm doing, too.'

Afterwards, in the elevator, on the way down to Park Avenue, Daniel thought about it. He tended to brood on words, particularly ones applied to himself. Single-minded. What did that mean? Ambitious. Obsessive. Obstinate. Was it true? Perhaps so; it was the way he was made. He decided he didn't have a problem with it. Not then.

At street level he looked at his watch. It was 12.15 p.m.

5.15 p.m. in England.

A fine spring day here, too. An innocent afternoon.

A fifty-eight-year-old woman is driving her car along the southbound carriageway, of the M11 motorway, twenty miles from London. She is on her way home to her flat in Regent's Park from visiting a friend in Cambridge.

It happens suddenly, like all catastrophes. Without warning. Part of the load on a truck carrying timber breaks loose and spills from the back of the vehicle on to the road. The articulated lorry behind, travelling at sixty miles an hour, swerves to avoid the planks of wood bouncing on the carriageway.

The lorry veers out of control, careers across the lanes, and collides with the woman's car. The impact is massive. The car is slammed against the crash barriers and almost totally crushed, so that parts of its bodywork are found afterwards scattered over a three-hundred-yard length of the carriageway. Returning commuters stuck in stationary traffic heading north watch in horror. Some are showered with fragments of glass.

*Summoned by twelve different mobile telephone calls, the
emergency services are there within nine minutes. They need
cutting equipment to carve a way through the wreckage to
the driver. It takes fifty-five minutes to release her. They
work with less urgency for the last twenty-five. By that
time they've discovered she is dead.*

After Daniel Stern left Nat's office he took a cab to the
restaurant on 54th Street where he had a lunch date. He
paid off the driver, listening to the abrasive, pre-recorded
voice of some minor celebrity advising him to make sure
he took all his personal possessions with him as he left the
car. He switched his mobile off for the duration of lunch.
Lola, she was called. She was something in publishing, and
very good-looking. The sort of New York girl that exerted
a fascination for him: blonde, poised, perfectly presented.
She was already there when he arrived, long-legged, all
sleek surface. Let's talk, she'd said. About him doing a
book. On anything, his choice: he only had to come up
with the idea and she'd run with it.

She ate a few leaves of rocket and pecorino salad with
a stylised delicacy, touching the corner of her mouth with
a napkin after every minimalist mouthful. She took herself
very seriously indeed. She talked about concept realisation
and profit margins and interpersonal dynamics. About
a book on weaving she was packaging that was all so
ridiculous and real that it felt kind of sacred. He knew
long before she ordered the organic coffee that he couldn't
work with her. But she was good to look at.

When the check came, he paid it. Just so as there should be no misunderstanding. So that she should not feel he was in any way professionally beholden to her.

'I'll call you,' he said as they parted. 'Perhaps we could have dinner next week.'

'I'd like that.' It was the first time all lunch that he'd seen her smile.

The message was there waiting for him on his mobile when he switched it back on. He was walking down Madison Avenue when he heard it. The instruction to ring his Aunt Stephanie on a number in London. Urgently. Because there had been an accident. A terrible accident.

He had to stop walking and stand still, then lean for a moment against a shop window. He felt sick, physically sick. He knew she was dead, even before he made the call.

Because that fifty-eight-year-old woman, the one they finally pulled out from the mangled metalwork of her own car that spring afternoon just as he was leaning across to fill Lola's glass with sparkling mineral water, that was Daniel Stern's mother. The mother whom Daniel, her only son, had been unable to find time to visit since the previous November, and for four weeks had not even spoken to on the telephone.

Oh, yes: there were perfectly legitimate reasons for Stern's negligence. He was three thousand miles away, in New York. He was busy, absorbed. Meeting deadlines, interviewing people. Rejecting the Hollywood mafia in favour of the Madonna piece. Ringing his mother was something that he knew he had to do, that he knew he wanted to do, but he kept putting it off because other things came up; it was always the one task too many that got cut from the day's schedule because he was either too tired or it was too late to disturb her. That's how he rationalised it afterwards, anyway. The truth was, he had so much to do he barely thought of her. Single-minded, that was Daniel Stern. Well, you don't think of your mother all the time, do you, no matter how much you love her? Not when you're twenty-nine, and suddenly in urgent and flattering professional demand.

The memory of his lunch with Lola was all at once intolerable. He couldn't bear the fact that he'd had time enough to set up lunch dates with beautiful girls, but none to ring his own mother. And now it was all too late. Much, much too late.

Dazed, he caught a taxi back to his apartment. Presumably the sun still shone; presumably the leaves were still unfurling on the trees. But in his eye the city was disfigured, unrecognisable from this morning. A hammer blow had fallen on the smooth and glossy glass of its image, sending out a web of jagged cracks across the surface.

LONDON

Wednesday, 5 May

Dawn comes quickly flying east across the Atlantic. Sleepless and miserable, Daniel was grateful for the fast-forwarding of the night. Perhaps this was what all passages of time would be like from now on: blunt, colourless, at best mercifully abbreviated. In the grey half-light of the Economy cabin, while others stirred and moaned and snored, he sat and stared at the shuttered porthole next to him, and wondered. What would he have told her, his mother, if he'd had one more chance to speak to her before she died?

He'd have told her how much he loved her, how much she meant to him, how close he knew they'd always been, deep down; how much he appreciated her for not being the caricature Jewish mother she could so easily have become, considering he was her beloved only child; for giving him space, for not playing wounded when he didn't ring her for weeks on end (although, God knew, if she herself could just have lifted the telephone and called him once in the last four weeks during which he had neglected her, it would have spared him some of what he was going through now). And if he could have been granted that one last conversation with her, he'd have made time to talk to her about the past. Her past. About the things that, with the consummate arrogance of the child who loves his mother so much that he takes her for granted, he had never bothered to ask. Like what really mattered to her. Like what had happened to her family, and what she really felt about it. The things he might have pressed her on, the things she'd never talked about before. Perhaps because she'd wanted to shield him from them. Perhaps because he'd never really asked.

Coming home. It was grey and damp as they landed, and his mouth tasted stale. Gritty-eyed, he contemplated the place he'd made the conscious and never-regretted decision to leave two and a half years ago. There was a depressing familiarity about Heathrow, an amalgam of small, unremarkable but oddly piquant vignettes: like the typeface on the yellow public notices; like the *Sun* newspaper sticking out of the back pocket of the man in overalls; like the line of smug black cabs drawn up outside the terminal building. He found himself resenting the self-satisfied way life had gone on here, unchanging, parochial, oblivious to his absence.

He was met by Aunt Stephanie. Strictly, she wasn't his aunt, only a cousin, but she had been closer to his mother than anyone; almost an older sister, given that Stephanie's own parents had effectively brought his mother up from pretty early on.

When they first caught sight of each other in the arrivals hall, he instinctively began to run towards her, then when they got close, he paused. They both stood motionless, wordless for a brief moment of suspended time. He looked at her and saw a plump, comfortable, capable woman in her early sixties, eyes swollen and red-rimmed, her natural bossiness capsized in a sea of sadness. He saw her looking at him, and shrugging her shoulders. Impotently. Suddenly the whole thing was too awful, too unimaginably awful to go on. They were in an emotional territory without maps. There was no prescribed way for dealing with the situation.

She broke the silence. 'Danny, it's just the most terrible thing,' she said.

Up till that moment he'd had himself under a wintery control, as if the shock had frozen over his responses, held them rigid. He put his bag down on the floor of the airport concourse and they embraced.

It was the bag that did it. He caught a glimpse of it as he looked down over her shoulder, and suddenly the memory swept over him, carried him away like some irresistible tidal wave. It was the memory of another bag. Of the first time he'd ever spent a night away from home, the first time he slept over with a friend. He was seven years old, and the bag that his mother had packed for him was standing there in the hallway, neat, perfect, nothing forgotten, its contents tenderly assembled: pyjamas, toothbrush, favourite teddy bear. He'd stopped on the doorstep of their house in St John's Wood and panicked. He'd turned to her and wailed through his tears that he was frightened, that he'd miss her, that he didn't want to go after all. She'd picked up the bag and put it gently in his hand. 'Be a big boy,' she told him. 'Because it's only one night, and when you come back I'll be here for you. You know I'll always be here for you, Danny.'

I'll always be here for you. Throughout his life, she'd kept her promise. When it mattered. But where had he been at her moment of crisis? She'd had to meet that alone. He suddenly saw the scene very clearly: her frail, crushed, middle-aged body in the wreckage of the car. A shoe here. A handbag there, spilled open in the broken glass. Then he had a brief, horrific glimpse of it: the eternity of her future non-existence. And all at once he was crying, there on the airport concourse. Really crying. Huge sobs, for the first time in his adult life. Crying for his mother's loneliness. And crying for his own.

Later, in Stephanie's car on the slow drive back into central London, she said to him, 'You know something, Danny? For the first time since the divorce she was really enjoying life. She was happy. She was getting out, seeing her friends.'

His resentment flared suddenly. Why was she telling him this? Was she implying that he hadn't been close enough to his own mother to judge whether she was happy or not? Was she getting at him because she knew he hadn't called for four weeks? He opened his mouth to justify himself, but just as suddenly his anger subsided. 'I'm glad,' he said instead. Recognising in time that the only way to negotiate situations as appalling as this one was to join a conspiracy of the grieving. A conspiracy to adduce evidence – often groundless – that the person who's just died has at least died happy. There was a comfort in such delusions.

'Listen, Danny, you're staying with us, OK?' Gradually Stephanie's natural bossiness was reasserting itself, her need to control. 'You'll be very comfortable in that guest room. You've got a decent bed, king-size. And your own bathroom, of course. With power shower.'

He'd forgotten her obsession with showers, with bathrooms, with all aspects of personal hygiene. It had been a source of fond amusement to his mother. 'Your aunt believes that cleanliness is next to godliness,' she'd told him once, with her enchanting, conspiratorial smile. The smile his mother had used when he was younger to admit him to her own interior world. The smile that had been the hallmark of their intimacy, private to the two of them. Stop remembering, he told himself. Stop. Now.

'Thanks, Stephanie,' he said quietly. 'It's very good of you both to put me up. I appreciate it.'

Stephanie and her husband Stewart – a bronzed, taciturn man with an emotional existence almost entirely encompassed by the golf course – lived in a flat ten minutes away from his mother's Regent's Park block. For the time being there was no question of Daniel going there, to his mother's flat. Certainly not today, anyway.

His aunt's thoughts must have been running along the

same lines, because she said briskly: 'Let's get the funeral over first. All that other business can wait.'

All that other business: for a moment he glimpsed it. All the small details of his mother's life aggregated together in that comfortable three-bedroomed apartment overlooking the park where she'd moved when his father left her, the changing mosaic that made up the continuity of her existence. The sense of that existence abruptly terminated in mid-flow, the mosaic arbitrarily smashed. Now every little piece of it would have to be picked up, examined, and dealt with or disposed of. The cruellest pieces would be those that underlined her expectation of continuing routine. The bedside lamp she'd forgotten to switch off; the hairdressing appointment that she would no longer keep; the clock still ticking, which she'd rewound that weekend.

They arrived. He'd got out of the car and was closing the passenger door behind him when Stephanie said: 'Oh, and I've called Thérèse.'

For a moment his mind went blank. 'Thérèse?'

'Tante Thérèse. In Paris.'

'Of course.' He was still struggling to place her. He had a faint memory of a white-haired woman with fierce eyes; someone he hadn't seen for many years.

'I spoke to her yesterday evening.'

'Was she ... was she all right?'

'He's asking was she all right. Please, this is an eighty-six-year-old woman. Imagine, getting news like that. You know how ... how she felt about your mother.

But she's strong, this one, incredibly strong. She was actually talking about flying over for the funeral. Then she realised it was going to be too much even for her. But she said she would love to hear from you. Do this for me, Danny, OK? **Go and** see her. Later, when you have a moment.'

'Of course,' he **said. 'Of** course I will.'

He trudged miserably behind Stephanie to the entrance of the block. It was drizzling slightly. He glanced at his watch: only 11.15 a.m. He felt the day stretching indefinitely ahead, a misery with no discernible end.

At that stage he didn't know about Thérèse. He really didn't know. He was aware she'd been special to his mother. He was conscious that she had played some part in her very early upbringing, back in France, and as a result of that experience had formed an abiding sentimental attachment to her. But he really didn't know the full story.

43

LONDON

Thursday, 6 May

The low cloud and drizzle of yesterday had cleared, and an increasingly powerful sun radiated from a vivid blue sky. There was general agreement among those who attended the funeral that afternoon – grateful for a topic of conversation that avoided the embarrassing central issue of someone having died – that it was the hottest day of the year so far. 'Global warming,' murmured Uncle Laurie, shaking his head gloomily. 'They're all talking about it. But find me one man who knows how to stop it.' Uncle Laurie was Stephanie's brother. He hadn't changed: he moved with the same shuffling gait and his face wore the same doom-laden expression as always, funeral or no funeral.

A sleek black limousine had been hired to carry the chief mourners up to Willesden Cemetery that afternoon. Four of them squeezed awkwardly into the car, perspiring in the unexpected warmth: Stephanie in the front next to the driver, and Stewart, Daniel and Uncle Laurie in the back. They travelled in silence, apart from occasional, increasingly frenetic calls made by Stephanie on her mobile telephone: once back to the caterer ordering an extra two dozen bridge rolls for tea, another on to the cemetery checking parking arrangements. 'Of course I can't tell you how long the service will take. What am I, the rabbi?' Having something to organise was Stephanie's best therapy, Daniel could tell. He looked out of the window and all at once found himself projected back into the world of his childhood. As they negotiated the traffic north through St John's Wood he recognised the streets in which he'd been brought up: a world of Sunday afternoon walks, and surreptitious visits to the newsagent to buy sweets; of school runs, and teenage trips into the West End on the 159 bus.

They came to a halt at lights, not far from the house in Hamilton Terrace in which he'd lived the first fifteen years of his life. Daniel gazed out and found himself face to face with one of the most familiar landmarks of his childhood. There were the black iron railings which he'd always stopped to touch, either on his way to school or on his way home. Alternate railings, every morning or evening. Sixty-four in all, so thirty-two touches. If he didn't do it, there'd be bad luck. He'd fail the spelling test. Or his mother would die of pneumonia, like old Mrs Jacobs had the previous winter. The poignancy of his childish anxieties returned to him with a momentary vividness. He remembered how one evening, aged eight, he'd saved his mother's life. He'd come back home and found her ill in bed with flu. Worse, he'd forgotten his railing ritual. It was winter, but after he'd been put to bed himself he'd pulled on a jersey over his pyjamas and slipped out into the dark, leaving the back door on the latch. In the pool of strange yellow light cast by the streetlamp he did what he had to do, moved along the line touching every other one, then slunk back in unobserved. It was the most frightening experience of his life to date: he could still recall the breathless terror of the night. Two days later his mother had pronounced herself better. But it had been a close-run thing.

The car accelerated up the Edgware Road. He felt rudder-less, disorientated, disturbingly incapable of an accommodation of the past with the present. Barely forty-eight hours ago he'd been Daniel Stern, sought-after New York journalist, debating whether he could fit an interview with Madonna into his successful professional schedule. Single-minded. Ambitious. In control. Now he was catapulted back into his existence as Daniel Stern, insecure schoolboy. Who missed his mother. Who'd let his mother down by failing the railing ritual. Except that then he'd rectified the situation. Now there was no chance to put things right.

'Arnold making an appearance, is he?' inquired Laurie.

Daniel hadn't even thought. His father. Would his father come today?

'Arnold's office sent a fax,' said Stephanie frostily. 'It said he was flying in this morning from Nice.'

'In his private plane,' added Stewart.

All three of them nodded sagely. When all was said

and done, Daniel could feel them thinking, you had to
hand it to Arnold. He might have behaved deplorably
in the past, he might have proved himself a deeply
inadequate husband and a largely absentee father, but
he'd made a packet of money. And he knew how to
spend it, did things in style. Daniel normally excluded
his father from his thoughts. He was not part of his
emotional landscape. Now that he was faced with the
prospect of meeting him again, he found himself unable
to assess him in any sort of objective light. This was
the man who'd let them all down. Hurt and betrayed
his mother, and run away. Not that he hadn't been
generous afterwards. He'd made a large settlement on his
wife, and Daniel himself received a substantial monthly
allowance. But that wasn't the point, was it? Salving of
the conscience wasn't something you should be allowed
to buy with money. This wasn't just another problem
which could be resolved simply by throwing a cheque
book at it. Because Daniel had never been able to forgive
his father, he'd decided to forget him. To cut him out of
his life. His reappearance now was one more miserable
challenge to have to meet on this day of despair.

They arrived, disembarked, then filed into the hall.
The light was lower here. Austere, all shadows and
dark wood. There must have been forty or fifty people
already assembled, but he didn't take them in individually.
Friends, distant relations. His mother's bridge partners. He
followed Aunt Stephanie to their position in the front.
Then he allowed his gaze to rest momentarily upon the

coffin. It stood alone in the centre of the hall, bleak, draped in black cloth. A meaningless construction, set up like some obscure modern sculpture in a public place. Her body was in there. His mother's. Just a body, not her. A poor, mangled thing, bruised, lacerated, broken. Just a husk, no life left. Don't think of it. He closed his eyes.

The rabbi began to speak.

Afterwards, walking next to Stephanie, he led the procession that followed the coffin out into the sunlight again, to the freshly dug grave. He could smell the newly turned earth. There were more prayers, then the coffin was lowered slowly into the hole. He concentrated very hard on how neat it was, the way it just fitted. He clung on tenaciously to that geometric detail. It distracted him, held at bay the awfulness. Then he was handed a spade, bent to shovel in a quick scoop of earth, and heard the hollow reverberations as its grains sprinkled on the wooden coffin top. Just a body. Not her. Resolutely, he turned away.

Funerals are full of tortured lacunae, intervals when people stand around waiting, floundering for something suitable to say to break the silence. As they hung about in the carpark at the end of the ceremony, Daniel suddenly saw his father; caught his eye, then stood his ground so that his father had to walk over to him. The way the man moved was determined, but oddly self-conscious. Driven not so much by grief as by embarrassment.

'Daniel,' he said, offering an awkward hand.

Daniel shrugged, and shook it. 'Dad,' he said.

At least he hadn't brought his new, much younger wife with him. What was her name? Deirdre, he remembered. Hadn't she been his secretary, or his personal assistant, something like that? He could imagine what she was like: glamorous, bossy, assertive; proud of her capture, living only for her man. Exactly what his first wife, Daniel's vague, gentle and ultimately independent-minded mother, had not been for him. Daniel noticed that under Deirdre's influence his father had miraculously acquired more hair. There had been some ill-advised implant treatment since he'd last seen him. Where there had previously been a sparseness, there was now an unnatural plenitude. His father kept touching the crown of his head, as if seeking surreptitious reassurance that the growth was still in place, had not withered and died and blown away in the balmy spring breeze.

'Sad business,' observed his father.

'Very sad,' agreed Daniel.

Above, the skies were a glorious unbroken blue. It was as warm as New York. His father was perspiring extensively. The wetness extended like the U of an undervest below his collar, underneath his tie. 'Usually hell's cold here this time of the year,' he observed. 'What's going on in this damned country?'

Daniel had forgotten the exaggerated heartiness which tended to surface in his father's vocabulary when he was ill at ease. It was alien, an act. Who did it impress, this affectation of a certain sort of English good-chappery?

Perhaps his business associates. Perhaps his mistresses. But not his son.

'It's hot today, yes,' Daniel agreed again.

'Would have pleased your mother. Always liked the sun.' His father looked upwards resentfully, as if he suspected his former wife of some final act of conspiracy against him, this time with the weather itself. Luring him out in an overcoat, then making him swelter.

His limousine drew up. 'Give you a lift back to Stephanie's?' he suggested. 'Told there's a bit of grub on offer.'

'I'd better go with Stephanie. I came up with her, you see.'

His father shuffled uncomfortably, his hand on the top of the open limousine door. 'Splendid stuff,' he remarked, and slid abruptly into the back seat.

Later, after they'd all taken tea and sandwiches in Stephanie and Stewart's flat, and Uncle Laurie had held forth extensively about the imminent collapse of the financial markets, Daniel's father tried again. 'Suppose the time's come to make a move,' he said to Daniel. 'Better be heading back to the airport. Can I drop you off?'

Why not? thought Daniel suddenly. He was eager to get away. Out of Stephanie's space, away from the plumped cushions and the power shower. Now the funeral was over, he recognised he'd negotiated stage one of the process of mourning. The aching grief of the last two days wasn't going to diminish, but now he was aware of a distinct feeling that he wanted to keep moving, to get on with what had to be done. He felt in his pocket and his fingers closed around the keys that Stephanie had given him last night. He made the decision. 'Drop me at Mum's flat. I think I'm ready to start sorting out her things.'

The car eased to a halt outside the block overlooking Regent's Park. Unexpectedly, his father told the limo driver to wait and got out with Daniel, muttering that he'd like to pay his last respects to the place where his mother had lived these past five years. In part Daniel put it down to curiosity about what sort of a life she'd made for herself in his absence; but it was also some last tangle of guilt working itself out within him. Daniel recognised the phenomenon with a weary familiarity. Guilt was a commodity of which he'd become a connoisseur himself of late. As they travelled up in the lift together, father and son, he felt them joined by a common betrayal. His father had deserted her, run off with a younger woman; he'd neglected her, failed to call her for the last four weeks of her life.

Even so, Daniel's father could find almost nothing to say to him. In the few brief moments that they spent together in the flat itself the older man kept picking up odd objects – photo frames, ashtrays, a piece of Japanese jade – then putting them down again with a sort of baffled resentment that they had not proved more effective conversational stimuli. Once he rested a tentative hand on Daniel's shoulder, then withdrew it rather quickly, as if he'd overstepped the mark; as if he'd turned to the wrong page in the manual. Daniel realised then that he had never met a man of such tragic emotional inarticulacy. His father was blessed with huge wealth, an innate knack for making money, and at the same time cursed with either a complete poverty of feeling or the ability to express it. It wasn't so much a fear of intimacy as an utter ineptitude in dealing with it.

'Great stuff, Dan,' he said at the end, as he retreated to the front door. 'Look us up next time you're in Monaco. Deirdre'd be keen to meet you.'

Daniel nodded. He had no energy left to grapple with his father's inadequacies. Not on top of his own misery. Let the man fly back to his trophy wife, he thought. Let him tell her about them. If she had a formula for treating hair loss, maybe she could also recommend him one for loss of communication with his only son.

'Keep in touch, OK?' called the older man over his shoulder as he waited at the lift.

From the open door Daniel watched the cabin arrive and his father get in. Just before the doors closed, he caught a brief vignette of his father's hand beginning another quick exploratory journey up to the crown of his head. Suddenly Daniel felt sorry for him. Desperately sorry. 'You too,' he called as the machinery clanked into action and the cabin started its descent.

He wasn't sure if his father heard him.

Once he was alone, Daniel deliberately steeled himself to make a full tour of the empty apartment. Opening every door, going into every room. Even her bedroom, where her clothes still hung in the cupboard and her scent still stood on the dressing table. Next to her bed lay the book she had been reading, a Georgette Heyer, the marker set three-quarters of the way through. He was rebuilding a bridge for himself back into his mother's world. A painful bridge, but one that had to be crossed. The memories of her were everywhere. The rooms were redolent of her personality: tidy, gentle, with odd, whimsical flights of fancy. Like the ensemble of empty champagne bottles in the bathroom, each one holding an artificial rose; like the fur hat with which she'd decorated her treasured bust of Napoleon. 'Don't forget, Daniel,' she had told him once, 'I may look like a tired old Englishwoman, but underneath part of me is still French.' He spared himself nothing. In the room she used as a study, for instance, where she was fond of sitting because of its view over the park, he had a particularly vivid image of her, as she'd been the last time he'd stayed with her, back in November. He saw her looking up from her papers spread out on the table, her reading spectacles balanced on her nose. Thanking him for the cup of tea he'd brought her from the kitchen.

A cup of tea. It wobbled slightly in her hand as she reached out to take it from him. Is she getting old, he'd wondered suddenly? And now she was dead.

A little bit of him rejoiced every time memories like these gave him pain. For the next four days, as he sorted meticulously through her possessions, there were many such moments, many such poignancies. It was an atonement, the beginning of an expiation. A deliberate forcing of himself to confront the relics of his mother's life. It wasn't easy, but it was a necessary rite of passage. And in the process of torture that he intentionally inflicted upon himself by such close proximity to the texture of his mother's lost existence, he learned a number of things about her.

Things that he had not known before. Things that were about to change his life.

ROME

Sunday, 9 May

Like flotsam on an increasingly sluggish current, the taxi came to a halt still half a kilometre from the Olympic Stadium, its progress impeded and finally snagged in the thickening crowd of football fans and vehicles on the Ponte Duca d'Aosta. The driver raised his hands, and began an expression of profane frustration, hastily tempered by respect for his clerical passenger. *'Scusi, padre.'*

'Va bene,' said Father Alfonso Cambres. He paid the driver off and got out. For a moment he stood still, steadying himself in the bright sunshine. Then he began walking, uneasily at first, suddenly aware of his own incongruity in svelte but clerical black against this mass of light blue worn by the Lazio supporters; but his confidence grew as he fell into step with the jostling, raucous river of people, eddying round the stalls selling scarves, hot dogs, programmes, flowing onwards to the stadium itself. After all, why shouldn't a priest go to a Lazio game? Particularly a worldly-looking priest like Cambres. He was 65, but he still had a striking face, a strong face of noble lines and

angles illuminated by deep blue eyes, a face that could not disguise the quality of its breeding. He felt suddenly elated, caught the almost palpable expectation in the atmosphere: the convergence of many streams of people into one huge surge of emotional humanity.

The ticket had arrived three days before, at his private quarters. Addressed to him personally, but without any sort of covering note. Odd. But not unprecedented. As a priest he'd been in his time the beneficiary of various such harmless gestures of anonymous generosity, occasionally visited upon its priesthood by the faithful laity. Who knew what had prompted this particular one? Some secret guilt assuaged; some burgeoning need for God's favour, to be curried via His clergy on earth; perhaps even some obscure hope of enlisting an extra measure of divine support for Lazio's cause. So he'd gone. He liked football, but it was a long time since he'd attended a game. As a young man in the fifties, he'd had an uncle on his father's side who had been a director of Real Madrid. Then he'd been often to the Bernabeu stadium, in the days of glory when the team carried all before them. He'd barely been since, however. Still, he followed the game sufficiently to know that Lazio were doing well this season. They were top of Serie A, the champions apparent. People he met in Rome talked of the team's success. He liked success. He was drawn to it. It was both the weakness and the strength of his priesthood.

The seat was a good one, not too far back, near the halfway line. He settled himself, surreptitiously observing the young man in a leather jacket on his left, chain-smoking away the anxious minutes before kick-off. He'd forgotten how distinctive of football matches was the scent of cigarette smoke in the open air. Around the rapidly filling stadium he sensed the air of anticipation again, the compressed excitement of this mass of many thousands, all carried on the same wave of feeling. The same shared intensity of desire: to assert their territorial rights; to repel the interlopers from Milan who dared to challenge them on their home ground, to dispatch them back broken and defeated to the north. Then, as the two teams emerged on to the pitch, there arose the baying, brutal roar of the mob. Primitive; but at the same time focused, into a warlike exultation, into the celebration of a cause. This is how armies are raised, thought Cambres. This is how Crusades begin.

The game started. Fast, physical. Extraordinarily efficient; a muscular contest of highly honed skill. A white pinball ricocheted between quick-moving feet. A long, curling cross arced in from the left, became lost in a mêlée of light blue and red jerseys, then all at once emerged on a different trajectory, and before Cambres could blink it was bouncing in the rigging of the goal net and Lazio had scored. The crescendo of noise was deafening: exultant, triumphant. A goal in four minutes. It was sensational, like an electric storm or a volcanic eruption; it was ecstatic, an almost physical release; it was as close to heaven as these Lazio supporters would very likely approach here on earth.

The leather-jacketed young man on Cambres's left stood up, arms held aloft in wordless, soundless delirium. The man on his right stayed seated, but leaned across and observed, 'A good start for our boys.'

Cambres turned and smiled back, nodding in agreement. The man was not old, in his thirties, bulky, swathed in a dark overcoat. His eyes were bulbous, frog-like, behind heavy spectacles. He was sweating slightly. Suddenly he was familiar.

'We have met somewhere, haven't we?' said Cambres, also leaning closer, so that he was almost talking into his neighbour's ear. It was the only way to make himself heard over the celebrations.

'Forgive me, Father. Yes, we have,' said the other man.

'You are perhaps . . .'

'My name is Donaghy. Father Dermot Donaghy. Excuse me that this afternoon I do not wear my uniform.' Beneath his overcoat, Cambres saw that Donaghy had on a dark blue polo neck.

'But of course. I recognise you now. Are we not . . . colleagues?'

'*Pro Deo Pugnamus*,' murmured Donaghy. We fight on God's behalf. The greeting of the Pro Deo Service was exchanged only between its members. As a secret mark of mutual recognition.

'*Pro Deo Pugnamus*,' repeated Cambres automatically.

There was a renewed surge of sound as light blue shirts burst forward once again; a brief opening in the billowing wall of red, a moment's exquisite anticipation; and then a breaking wave of cascading disappointment as the ball thudded into the advertising hoardings just behind the goal. Cambres smiled and shrugged at his colleague. To indicate that the noise was too great for extended conversation now. They'd talk more in the interval.

Half-time came. Lazio had not added to their lead. The crowd's jubilation was tempered by a murmur of anxiety. Would a single goal's advantage be enough? The players, slaking their thirst from proffered bottles as they walked, disappeared to the refuge of dressing rooms. Donaghy sighed and said: 'I'm happy that you came. I feared football might not interest you.'

'Was it you, Father, who sent me the ticket?'

'It was.' Donaghy spoke staring straight ahead now, as though absorbed by some imaginary passage of play on the pitch below.

'I'm grateful, of course. But why did you single me out for such generosity?'

The other man's eyes blinked behind the moons of his spectacles. 'Because I needed to talk to you. Discreetly.'

'But now I come to think of it, our desks are no more than two offices apart.' They both worked in the Service's Secretariat. Cambres had responsibility for Pro Deo's activities in Universities. He wasn't sure quite what role Donaghy fulfilled, but he remembered having run into him two or three times on the stairs carrying files. 'You could come to me at any time.'

'You do not understand. I had to do it somewhere where I could rely on our meeting seemingly by chance. Where I knew we would not be watched.'

'What do you mean, where we would not be watched?'

'I am under surveillance.'

'You are what?'

Donaghy gave a bitter laugh. 'There. You think I'm mad, perhaps. Paranoid. But what I say is the truth. My movements are kept under observation.'

Cambres glanced quickly across at the other man's weating, anxious face. He sensed something extreme in him. Paranoia? Or desperation? Then he smiled, and put his hand on his companion's arm. He knew the power of his own smile. 'No, I don't think you are mad. But you're going to have to tell me more about all this. Let us wait for the end of the game and then go somewhere quieter, where we can talk in peace. Will you do that, Father?'

The huge crowd ebbed out of the exits and dispersed along the many rivulets by which they had converged two hours before. Milan had scored from a disputed penalty with ten minutes to go. A 1–1 draw. There was a mass sense of disappointment, of anticlimax. Less elation to the step, much shrugging of shoulders, the odd frustrated kick aimed at a drinks can in the gutter. That was football, wasn't it? Like life: moments of ecstatic elation counterbalanced by the sudden blow to the solar plexus. The two priests walked on through the crowd, in the general direction of central Rome. After about ten minutes, they found a bar not far from the river, at the top of Viale Angelico. Unremarkable. Anonymous. No one would know them here. Cambres watched Donaghy ease his bulky frame on to the seat opposite, and look surreptitiously about him. Checking for what? For whom?

'So,' said Cambres gently. 'What is this about?'

'I'll go back to the start of it all, Father.' Donaghy paused, glancing one more time over his shoulder, out of the window into the street. Then he began, in quick, breathless sentences. 'A few months ago, I met this man here in Rome. His name is di Livio and he's a journalist. He became my friend. I trust him, Father, I believe him to be reliable, a serious man writing not for cheap sensation but in order to get at the truth. He's writing a book about the workings of organised crime in modern society. How it has become totally international in its operation, a huge and dangerously powerful force for evil in our time. Do you know, by the way, what proportion of world trade is now represented by criminal transaction?'

'No?'

'Eight per cent. That's more than the entire economy of a country the size of Italy. Put it another way, one in twelve commercial transactions in the world today is dirty, involves money made in the handling of drugs or other criminal activities. It's a horrifying statistic, is it not?'

Cambres agreed it was. He couldn't see where Donaghy's narrative was leading, but already he had an inkling of unease, a presentiment of something evil undammed, running out of control.

'Di Livio showed me papers,' went on Donaghy, 'cuttings from the international press and other more confidential documents. These concerned certain individuals whose business dealings are apparently under investigation here and in the United States. They are closely connected to a Panamanian trading company called Amelga, whose American assets have recently been frozen by the authorities. Does this name perhaps mean anything to you, this company Amelga?'

Cambres shook his head. 'I do not follow financial matters,' he said. 'I have no reason to.'

Immediately Donaghy pressed into his hands a slim file of photocopied pages that he brought out from an envelope secreted in his overcoat. Cambres reached into his breast pocket for reading spectacles and glanced quickly through them. There were press stories about Grand Juries, and businessmen who'd fled tax evasion charges in the United States; and there was a CIA document marked 'Restricted, Highly Confidential' detailing the activities of Amelga SA, registered in Panama City. According to this document, there was strong suspicion that profits from American drug deals were being handled through Amelga. Laundered. Washed clean through bank accounts that Amelga controlled. Bank accounts in many different countries.

Cambres finished reading and asked, 'Yes, but how do these affairs concern you?'

'This is what I'm coming to now, this is the terrible part.' Donaghy's anxiety and outrage were expressed in a sudden movement of his arm, which upset his coffee cup. He dabbed ineptly at the spillage with a napkin, and went on. 'Di Livio told me that he was convinced that large sums of money had passed on at least two occasions from Amelga into an account in the Vatican Bank. He had no means of obtaining the confirmation himself, but he had an account reference. Father, I recognised that account reference. It was one of ours, a Pro Deo account. Of course, I said nothing. But inwardly I was most desperately concerned. In turmoil.'

Cambres sat up himself now. The other man's anxiety had communicated itself to him. If this was true, it was serious. 'What did you do?'

'You may say that at this point I should have backed off, gone no farther with di Livio. Or referred the matter to superiors within the Service. But my friend was insistent and persuasive. He said that if I cared at all for the wellbeing of our Service and our Church, I should at least check myself if these transactions had taken place, if money had been received into a Pro Deo account from this notorious Amelga. He told me that if my conscience then dictated that I could tell him nothing of what I had discovered, then so be it. But at least check it, he urged me. Check it yourself, for God's sake.

'I had the opportunity a week later. I was alone in

the office and I was able to access the account records. I wanted to be reassured, to disprove these allegations once and for all. To show that di Livio's information was mistaken and no such transactions had taken place.

'But to my horror I found everything confirmed. I found the name Amelga. I found the transfers. I have the print-outs here.' Slowly he pulled out another envelope from the folded copy of *L'Osservatore Romana* that he carried. An envelope containing sheets studded with names and figures and dates. Columns of debits and credits, withdrawals and deposits. The raw material of commerce.

'Into what account were these sums paid?' asked Cambres quietly.

'Into an account kept for the donations of the faithful.'

Cambres paused, his unease accentuated by perplexity. 'How can it work laundering criminal money by donating it to our Service?'

'Very simply, in the first case that I found. Twenty million dollars were received from Amelga. Two weeks later, nineteen million were paid out into a legitimate account in Switzerland. The difference of one million was, I assume, retained as commission. As the donation.'

'And in the second case?'

Donaghy shifted in his seat, suddenly awkward for reasons that Cambres could not immediately fathom. 'The second transaction was a little less straightforward than the first,' he admitted.

'In what way?'

'It involved the sale of an asset.'

'What asset was that?'

'If you look at this page here, you will perhaps understand.'

Cambres took the sheet and replaced his reading spectacles. What could be more absurd? Here, at a clandestine meeting in an anonymous bar, he – a priest – was poring over print-outs of secret financial transactions. And then, as he read, he felt suddenly sick. All at once he realised the intense personal significance of what he was being shown. It was as if the essence of his whole priesthood had been distilled on to this single sheet of paper. The achievement of his life's work lay before him, exposed. And hideously, viciously corrupted.

'So,' he said slowly, trying to keep his voice calm. 'The transaction involved this item.'

'Yes. I wasn't sure if you knew. In view of your connection with it.'

'I had no idea.' For a moment, Cambres felt short of breath. A murmuring about his heart. It was the shock. And the betrayal.

'You should see this also,' Donaghy went on. His outrage made him remorseless. 'Here I printed out the name and address of the ... of the ultimate beneficiary in the deal. It is the same name as one of the individuals in the press cutting. The man whom di Livio – and the authorities – are investigating.'

Cambres stared at the page in front of him. 'I cannot believe it.'

'We have to believe it. This is the proof.'

'But you haven't spoken to your journalist friend again? You haven't told di Livio?' Even now, Cambres's first anxiety was for the security of the Service. The instinct to preserve Pro Deo from scandal was deeply, ineradicably ingrained.

'Of course I have not. How could I do such a thing?' Donaghy clearly felt it, too. Whatever had happened, it would be an act of unpardonable cowardice and disloyalty to wash the Service's dirty linen in the outside world. They had both sworn sacred vows of loyalty and obedience.

'But there has been serious misconduct here. It has to be referred to the highest internal authorities.'

'That was my reaction also. But ...'

Cambres demanded urgently: 'But what?'

'It is difficult to know how to say this.'

'Tell me.'

There was incomprehension in Donaghy's eyes. And despair. 'You see, when I was alone in that office, I dared to probe a little further. There is a code in the system which indicates who had authorised these transactions.'

'And?'

'Father, it was the Prelate-General of Pro Deo, his Eminence himself. It was Cardinal Tafurel.'

They paid the bill, and stood together for a moment in the

street outside. A last desultory band of Lazio supporters trickled past them, like remnants of a defeated army.

'We should return separately,' said Donaghy.

'Is that necessary?'

'I know that people are watching me.'

'How can you know that?'

Donaghy raised his hands in frustration. 'Small things that happen.'

'What sort of things? What do you mean?'

'I hear strange noises before and after calls on my personal line. I am sure that my telephone is tapped. Also I have come back and found private papers in my room tampered with, moved from where I left them.'

Cambres struggled with the outlandishness of the idea, for a moment wanting to believe that Donaghy was after all a madman who had dreamed up his persecution, indeed imagined the whole conspiracy. 'But why do they suspect you particularly?'

'That is what I asked myself. Then, afterwards, it came to me. Any unauthorised person who accesses sensitive parts of the financial system as I did leaves a trace. I entered under my own password. Security checks would have identified me as having made enquiries into areas that did not concern me. They are vigilant about these things.'

'But why is it dangerous for *us* to be seen together?'

'I'll tell you why. Because anyone else in the Service who I am observed talking to is at risk. If I'm seen with them for any length of time without good reason, they will be tainted too.'

Donaghy was Irish. He gave the impression of a wild and impulsive man, with his impetuous, maladroit movements and passionate explosions of emotion. But there was something about him, a palpable honesty underlying his rashness, which commanded Cambres's trust and belief. And what Donaghy had told him was terrible. It sinned against the order of things, undermined the carefully constructed system of values that sustained Cambres personally in his priesthood. For a moment Cambres felt the impotence of old age; he was unmanned by frustration at events he did not understand, at situations he did not know how to fight against.

He needed to analyse it all. Quietly, in his own time. 'May I at least take with me this last page that you showed me?' he asked. 'Since it materially concerns me?'

Donaghy thought for a moment, then passed it to him. 'But be careful, Father. It's better that they do not know you have this.'

Who were they? Was there really some mysterious part of the Service that was actively keeping its own members under surveillance? Could it be that they did so with the authority of the Prelate-General, of Tafurel himself?

Cambres returned to his quarters clutching the paper that Donaghy had entrusted to him. For a while he sat at his desk, thinking. Remembering things from the past that he had for many years deliberately excluded from his mind. Trying to decide what to do now in order to reconcile that past with the present. In order to see justice done and God's will carried out.

LONDON

Tuesday, 11 May

William Bainbridge handed Daniel a cup of tea and offered him a chocolate biscuit. Bainbridge was his mother's lawyer. It was 11 a.m., and they were sitting in a panelled office in Chancery Lane.

'Um,' said Bainbridge.

The man was dried up. Not old, but prematurely aged. Emotionally constipated in a peculiarly British way. His conversation was peppered with distancing devices: uncompleted conditional sentences, impersonal pronouns, discreet recourses to the passive tense. If all else failed, he said 'Um'.

'Sympathy and condolences offered,' he mumbled. 'By the whole firm. Deeply to be regretted.'

'Thank you.'

He cleared his throat. 'If one might, under the circumstances, make a start . . .'

'Please,' said Daniel.

Bainbridge began an explanation of the duties and responsibilities of an executor. When it came to purely legal matters, his words flowed more freely. Correct, no doubt, but chronically cautious. Hedging his every observation with limiting ablative absolutes, attaching exclusions, riders and provisions. And remorselessly pompous. Daniel found his manner first irritating, then depressing.

'Your mother was the recipient of a financial settlement from your father at the time of the divorce,' confided Bainbridge with a fastidious little sniff. 'A settlement which might legitimately be described as generous.'

Of course it was generous, thought Daniel. That was what his father was good at. Using money as a substitute for emotion. Assuaging guilt by largesse.

'At this stage,' continued Bainbridge, 'precision is impossible. But it may be hazarded that the total of your mother's estate will amount to something in the area of five million pounds.'

'Five million?'

'All of which will come to you. As her sole legatee. Um.'

It was obscene. Something that he couldn't come to terms with. How could this grotesque personal enrichment result directly from the tragedy of her death? He took rapid leave of Bainbridge, as if holding the lawyer obliquely responsible for the indecency of the windfall, and travelled back on the Underground in a daze of grief. On the way, he made a decision: to get out of Stephanie's apartment. King-size bed, power shower and all. To move his things into his mother's flat, into the spare room with the wallpaper of endlessly disporting eighteenth-century shepherds and shepherdesses.

Stephanie was perplexed by his decamping, her innate need to control the lives of those around her thwarted. 'If you're sure that's what you want,' she said doubtfully. 'Personally, I'd have thought ...'

'It's what I want,' Daniel told her. Not rudely, but firmly. There were aspects of Stephanie that were beginning to suffocate him.

The act of moving into the empty flat was one more stage in the self-imposed process of confronting the loss of his mother, a significant step in the working out of the misery and the guilt. For the past few days he'd been getting rid of things, with Stephanie's help. Bagging up clothes and shoes for the charity shop. Earmarking furniture for the auctioneers. Immersing himself in his mother's surroundings and sorting through her intimate possessions answered the need he had to feel pain, to build up a bank deposit of personal suffering with which to pay off the debt that he owed her.

The debt that he owed her. In material terms, it had magnified rather than diminished after his visit to Bainbridge. He didn't want her money. He wanted her. So, once he'd settled himself in the spare room he went in even more determined pursuit of her. He followed the only trail available to him: the continued perusal of her things. Her papers, her records, her photographs. He made coffee, then sat down at her desk and went through them methodically, the files, the letters and the albums.

There were a lot of them. He hadn't realised what a hoarder of papers she had been. It was poignant to discover in what tender regard she had come to hold the past, as represented by these papers. She was a neat hoarder; that was in her character. Everything was well organised, in a series of clearly labelled files. So it was not difficult for him to track what she had been doing in recent years, to get a picture of the things that had come increasingly to occupy her. He developed a picture of her, too; a more objective one. Even through his grief, he found himself increasingly able to assess her not simply as his mother but as an independent human being. As a human being with a clear and distinctive intelligence. Odd, that, and sad: it had taken death to provide the necessary distance.

He found that what had drawn her interest so insistently back in time was not so much her own past as that of her immediate antecedents. In a way, he decided, what his mother had been experiencing was the genealogist's desire to uncover roots, to test them and thereby perhaps to stand the more securely in the present. But with his mother it wasn't a question of searching dusty European parish records in order to establish the date of birth of some obscure eighteenth-century collateral. No, it was closer than that. Something at once more understandable and more terrible. Her attention had become particularly focused on her own parents.

For the first time in his life, he made the effort of imagination to put himself in her place. To do the thing that, perhaps subconsciously, he'd always resisted, always shied away from. Perhaps because she'd always been protective of him, never made that demand on him. Never inflicted upon him the need to confront directly the wretched details of her family's tragedy.

'My real parents?' she told him when he first asked, when he was eight or nine. 'They died when I was a baby. I never knew them. I grew up with Aunt Stephanie. Her parents became my mum and dad.'

'But Mum, how did they die, your real parents?'

'They were killed in the war. Wars are terrible things. That's what happens to people in wars.'

Later, as a teenager, it had dawned upon him gradually. From history lessons. From other people's casual remarks. 'Mum,' he'd said, 'my grandparents. Your real parents. They died in a concentration camp, didn't they?'

He remembered her flinching; a perceptible physical reaction to his question. 'A place called Auschwitz,' she'd said softly.

Auschwitz. He'd heard of that, it was in the history books. He hadn't been old enough to do more than make the link, sense the piquancy of connecting your ancestors to a notorious historical event. She never talked of it again. By choice, he presumed, and he had been content to acquiesce in her silence. By tacit consent the subject had become forbidden territory to them, an area of conversational quicksand where you walked at your peril. If he analysed it at all while she was still alive, he concluded she had buried it all, resolved to inter their deaths so deep within her that she'd succeeded in sealing them off even from her own consciousness.

Now, as he went through her papers, he realised that she'd been delving again. Peering into the chasm. Confronting the fact that both her mother and her father had been murdered. Been locked up in railway trucks and sent to meet their deaths. In a place called Auschwitz.

And now Daniel himself was forced to tangle with the horror. To imagine it on her behalf. It assailed him in noxious, gaseous breaths, as if wafted into the room from the chambers of death themselves. Death, deliberately, clinically inflicted on a whole people. Oddly less terrible to bear in large numbers than in small. It wasn't the generality of the millions which rent you apart. It was the specific details of the individual ones and twos. So how much worse must it have been when those individual ones and twos had actually been your own parents? The fact that she had no memory of her mother and father, that their existences had been extinguished before she'd been old enough to register them, did not take away the horror.

But somehow she must have passed through that, come to terms with it as far as humanly possible, set it on one side. What she had achieved was a successful separation between her parents' deaths and their lives. As he read through her files, he realised that it was on to their lives that she'd exclusively shifted her focus. And of course it was natural that, when you'd never known either your mother or your father, as his own mother hadn't, your intelligent adult years should be punctuated by waves of curiosity about them. In his mother's case, the leisure of her later middle age had evidently created another such wave. He could imagine her beginning to ask herself, what were they really like, her mother and father? How did they spend their days? What were they interested in? And one of the things that she'd discovered about her father was that he'd been an art collector. It had offered her an intriguing line of research, the attempt to track down and reassemble, on paper at least, as much of his former collection as possible. She had apparently been pursuing the challenge diligently over the past two or three years, as an act of daughterly piety. When Daniel thought about it, he found it strange that she'd never mentioned it to him, disturbing that she'd never talked to him of this enterprise, which was something that clearly absorbed her. Had she decided that he wouldn't have been interested, that he was too busy with his own life? Had he really given her that impression? What sort of a son had he been to her? Mum, he thought to himself, you should have let me in. You should have let me help you.

But then again, perhaps the explanation was that it was all too private, too intimate, too delicate to talk of. That her relationship with those parents of hers whom she had never consciously met was something too fragile to be shared even with her son. That this was territory off limits to her relationship with Daniel, no matter how dearly she loved him. Quicksands again. An area where he was not to be allowed, for his own protection. And for hers.

As he picked through the fruits of her meticulous research, he could not decide of what he was more culpable: a callous distance while she was alive or an intrusion into her privacy now that she was dead. But he read on. The material that she had assembled was fascinating: letters from archives, photocopies of catalogues, ancient photographs. She had put it all together in another of her files. Through the aggregation of evidence of determined acquisition, his grandfather's passion for works of art came alive. Furniture, porcelain; and pictures. Outstandingly good paintings, by very important names. A lost museum.

Something else happened that day as he reconstructed his mother's researches and the delicate web of motivations that underlay them. Up till the moment that he came across the file on the art collection, his journalistic existence had been on hold, suppressed by what he'd had to deal with ever since that sickening message came through on his mobile as he walked down Madison Avenue. But now, half subconsciously, it was reawakened. Some professional instinct within him, working separate from but in tandem with his personal sensibilities, told him this was great copy. That this material held the seeds of a wonderful longer piece. Or a book even. Something simultaneously to honour his grandparents' achievement, and his mother's piety towards their memory. Who better to write it than Daniel himself, who might thereby in his turn honour the memory of his own mother and, more than that, if he did it well, even lay the entire sequence to rest; restore peace to the generations. Achieve closure, as Nat would probably say.

That was before he picked up the last file. The one his mother had marked simply 'Maurice and Danielle Benjamin – Personal'. Odd to call them by their names like that. As if she were deliberately trying to distance herself from them, to set them in their place not as parents but as objective historical phenomena.

He released the spring on the box file and it jumped open. There were three things in there. Objects from the past. Memorials of another world. Simultaneously distant, and extraordinarily, shockingly real.

The first was a French identity card in the name of his grandfather. Its date of issue was 20 October 1939, and its date of expiry 20 October 1942. *Délivrée par M. le Prefet*, it read, and it bore the stamp of the Prefecture of Police of the Ninth Arrondissement of Paris. At the bottom it was signed by the *'titulaire'*: Maurice Benjamin, in firm, cultured handwriting. And at the top left-hand corner there was a yellowing photograph of the man himself. Formal, immaculately brushed hair, stiff collar, perfect tie, a little toothbrush moustache. And eyes, which he suddenly recognised as being his mother's eyes: deep-set, gentle, faintly sad. But what was most shocking was the later superimposition of a larger, more violent stamp. Dominating the document. A four-letter word, in massive capitals: *JUIF*.

The second thing he came across upset him even more. It was an ancient, somewhat moth-eaten furry toy.

A bird, or a duck perhaps. Where had that come from? he wondered. It had obviously been treasured and much loved by some child. A very long time ago. What child? Suddenly he did not want to imagine the answer. Its poignancy was unbearable.

The last item in the file was a book. A book of closely written script whose title page was boldly inscribed '*Journal de Danielle Benjamin*'. The first entry was in 1939. The last, a hundred or so pages later, was dated 8 July 1942.

He picked up his grandmother's diary and began to read.

THE DIARY OF DANIELLE BENJAMIN

15 October 1939

We had four guests to dine with us last night: the Leblancs, and David Levy with his new young wife Patrice. I was worried beforehand because there has been something on Nadine's mind lately, I don't know what, and her cooking has been very unreliable. Thank God, last night she was back to her best form, the *coq au vin* was delicious, so

I was able to relax again and concentrate on the guests. Now I am going to say something unkind about the Levys. After all, what is a diary for if one cannot confide to it the things one would never dream of saying out loud? Patrice Levy is a little fluffy blonde, probably at heart well-meaning, but she strikes me as one of the most empty-headed women I have ever met. She has no conversation of her own. Her only contribution to the evening is a tinkling, vacuous laugh that makes the person speaking to her (generally male) feel he has just said something incredibly witty. Why are otherwise intelligent men so susceptible to such flattery? I leave her to Maurice and Emile Leblanc, and talk to her husband about the war. David Levy remains smug and somewhat pleased with himself, but not stupid. I say it is now six weeks that we have been in a state of hostilities with Germany, but it is a difficult war to believe in. It's a sham, nothing seems to happen. What is really the truth? I ask him. Levy should know, after all, because he is something high up in the Ministry of War.

He repeats what we have been told before, that our troops are mostly deployed underground, manning the defences built by M. Maginot. The Germans make no attack, because it would be a waste of their time and men to attempt it. Our line is impenetrable, our defences are so strong and technically sophisticated. Levy says that in his official capacity he has visited the fortifications. They are quite extraordinary, huge barriers against the enemy mounted with bomb-proof turtle-neck gun turrets; and then six or seven storeys below ground, air-conditioned galleries with railway lines, hospitals, supply rooms, etc. 'They shall not pass,' he concludes, with an unexpected and slightly ridiculous flourish. Emile and Maurice agree with him that France is secure because the enemy can never penetrate our borders. The Maginot Line is our protection, and our national territory is inviolable. When I say that this is a very comfortable theory which people believe to be true because they want it to be true, Maurice tells me that I am an impossible old cynic. Patrice gives one of her tinkling little laughs. Maurice says that militarily the declaration of war is no more than a rattling of sabres, anyway, a gambit in an elaborate game of political chess. I ask Levy for confirmation of this theory. He just purses his lips and disappears in a miasma of discreet cigar smoke.

Emile Leblanc says perhaps it is no more than logical. Today we have paintings without subjects, music without melody, novels without plots: why not wars without casualties?

This is a typical clever remark of Monsieur Leblanc. It is the first time that he has been to our house, this famous art dealer with whom Maurice and his family have done so much business over the years. I find the impression I formed of him when I first met him last winter is confirmed. I do not trust him. But it is not simply that he is a charming rogue; if that were the case I would forgive him. I like charming rogues. No, there is something disturbing about him, something dangerous. His weasel eyes regard you with a calculation, a rodent in a bow tie always seeking advantage. When they are not looking at you, those eyes, they are surreptitiously scanning the furniture, the porcelain, what is hanging on the wall. Assessing, pricing, coveting. His wife Geraldine, on the other hand, is a mystery, sitting there very still and very silent.

Then suddenly Maurice starts talking again. Maybe he has had more to drink than I thought, but he is unexpectedly voluble, there is an unfamiliar edge of emotion to his voice. Anyway, he says, there's another reason why this ridiculous war won't come to anything. People won't fight. Why not, says Emile? And Maurice replies, not now, not like that. Not after the last time. Intelligent, civilised nations do not make the same mistake twice. It would be unthinkable to inflict upon humanity such unspeakable degradations a second time. There is a shiver to his lip, which suddenly reminds me of our little Matthieu, that makes me think for one ridiculous moment that my thirty-nine-year-old husband is about to cry.

At the end of his outburst, there is an awkward little silence. Even Patrice Levy forgets to laugh. For once, it is broken by Geraldine Leblanc: 'No,' she says very seriously. 'It must not happen again.'

Later, when our guests have gone and we are undressing in the bedroom, I ask Maurice again what it was like, the last time. He is reluctant to discuss it, talking vaguely of the *crise de tristesse sombre* that everyone carried away with them from the unspeakable experience of battle. I press him, harder. I feel an impatience with him, a strange desire to hurt him, by making him confront what he refuses to talk about. Perhaps it is no more than jealousy, that he should keep secrets which he will not tell me. Look, he says finally, with that familiar air of a patient old bear baited beyond all endurance, if I told you, you would not believe me. Was it really so bad? Worse, he says. Far, far worse than you can begin to imagine.

I lie in bed wakeful, thinking about it all. I have to admit that of those at dinner this evening, only Maurice is qualified to speak of these things. Unlike Levy and Leblanc, who are both two or three years younger, Maurice actually fought in that war. He was there, he had ten weeks of it in the front line near Bethune in 1918. Before I knew him, of course. Another

Maurice, a nineteen-year-old, closer in age and outlook to our own little son Matthieu than to the man I am married to now. A consoling thought comes to me then, that if this ridiculous war ever does get worse and soldiers start being killed again, at least those dying won't be my beloved ones. In six months, Maurice will be forty, too old for call-up, and my darling little Matthieu is only five. I get out of bed and go and stand in the doorway of Matthieu's room, watching him sleeping peacefully. I suddenly feel secure again, comfortable, protected from the bad things in life. I drift off easily after that.

On the face of it, everything seems normal again this morning. Maurice leaves the apartment at 8.45, catches the Métro and – I assume – arrives at his office by 9.15. It takes more than a war to interrupt the inexorable processes of the legal system, and his practice is as busy as ever. Perhaps busier, in fact, because Maurice says that even the lazy slug Vernon is bestirring himself sufficiently to come in four days a week this month. The famous sleeping partner of the firm occasionally wakes up, it seems.

But still some uneasiness lingers with me this morning. I worry about Maurice, and I'm not sure why. He is preoccupied, not quite himself. Or is it simply that I'm the one who's jumpy, and all I'm suffering from is a hangover?

16 October 1939

A shock yesterday evening: Maurice returns from work and announces in a dull, matter-of-fact sort of voice that he has decided to sell some important items from his art collection.

I am knocked sideways. Why are you doing this? I demand. I know how much he loves his furniture and his pictures. He says he's been thinking, and perhaps there's a time coming when francs will be more valuable than furniture. He wants to take precautions, so he's resolved to sell the best things before the war depresses the market. Apparently he went at lunch-time today to the Galerie Leblanc to talk about it. Emile Leblanc is eager to buy from him, and quoted some encouraging prices, particularly for the paintings. I argue with Maurice, because I know how dear many of these objects are to his heart. Also, although I don't say this, I don't trust Leblanc, I am not happy that it should be to him that Maurice is contemplating selling. But Maurice is very determined, and gradually I allow myself to be persuaded. Part of me can also see the attraction of increasing our financial security at this uncertain time, so in the end I don't argue too long or too forcefully.

Right, he says, that's settled. But a sadness has settled upon him, nonetheless, an underlying misery.

I wonder guiltily if his decision has something indirectly to do with the conversation I forced him into after dinner two nights ago, whether it is not in some way the result of my having stirred up once more that war-induced *crise de tristesse sombre*.

Then Nadine brings Matthieu into the room, and the mood lightens. The boy runs delightedly into his father's arms. Maurice lifts him from the floor in an embrace, and murmurs to me over the boy's shoulder, 'It is better for the little one. Better for his future.' That seems to settle it.

Again I cannot sleep. I get up and wander into the salon to read a book. I run my eye over the treasures: the clocks, the bureau, the desk, the two landscapes by Sisley. I stop in front of the Degas drawing of the resting ballet dancer that Maurice's father bought at the artist's estate sale back in 1917. He must have been an extraordinary man, Maurice's father, and I am sorry that I never met him. I am fascinated by his story. He was the one who began the Benjamin family's art collection. Maurice has told me that his father arrived in Paris from Warsaw only in the 1890s, and within ten or fifteen years he'd built an extremely successful legal practice, been granted French nationality, and started buying paintings. It was a rich inheritance that Maurice received from his father: the law firm, the love of France, the art collection. I reflect that Maurice is selling part of his heritage. I look round the room again, and realise that the physical landscape of our lives will be changed without these works of art in our apartment. It will be like saying goodbye to familiar friends.

But he is doing it for Matthieu, I tell myself. After all, it is healthy for a father to love his child more than his possessions. I suddenly wish that in compensation for what my brave, sad husband is giving up I could double his paternal happiness by conceiving another baby.

What God wills, will be.

23 October 1939

The men from Leblanc come this morning to collect the paintings and objects which the gallery are buying from us. Maurice leaves me with a detailed list to supervise the operation. He makes an excuse about an important client he has to meet with the ridiculous Vernon, but I know the real reason is that he cannot bear actually to witness the process, to see his treasures going. Of course they are not nearly as dear to him as Matthieu, but they are more than friends, these things, more like members of his family to him, and he feels a bereavement. I tick them all off as they disappear through the door, down the stairs, and into the lorry that the men have waiting in the street below. Two bureaux, a table, the two best clocks; then the two Sisley landscapes, the Fantin-Latour of flowers, and the Degas. I am surprised when I see the Monet also disappearing, the one from Maurice's study. But Maurice tells me that we shall be banking almost a million francs all told from these sales. I reassure myself that this is the sensible course in these uncertain times.

I follow the men down to their lorry as they take the last load, then sign their receipt just outside Madame Balbec's room. Here a stupid thing happens. Madame Balbec, ever inquisitive, puts her nose out from behind her door. 'Ah, Madame Benjamin,' she says, 'so you're having to make disposals, are you? Hard times, even for you.' It's not just her impertinence, but also the pretentious way she phrases it that annoys me. 'Having to make disposals' indeed. I don't deign to reply to her. But just then Madame Lisieux from the apartment above comes in with her little girl. Although I don't know her at all well, I always like the look of Madame Lisieux. When she says good morning, I return the greeting and gesture to the lorry outside explaining in a loud voice for Madame Balbec's benefit that Galerie Leblanc are taking away various works of art from us simply for restoration. It is a ridiculous lie on my part, of course. Now Madame Balbec will be on the lookout from her concierge's parlour to see if they ever come back. When they don't, she'll feel she's won a little victory over me.

It is absurd to care about these things. But, upon reflection, I find that what I regret most is having involved Madame Lisieux in my little drama of bourgeois insecurity.

24 October 1939

Maurice comes home tonight with a large brown paper parcel that he has brought with him in a taxi. As he undoes the string and opens it, he smiles, half sheepish, half triumphant. It is the Monet again, the familiar landscape with the trees. He has retrieved it from the clutches of Emile Leblanc. He cannot after all bear to be parted from it. He shrugs at me with that questioning little movement of his shoulders which I recognise as a plea for my approval of his action. I laugh, and tell him I'm happy that he's got this painting back.

Maurice explains that this was the first painting that he ever bought himself, the first one that he made the conscious decision to acquire, as opposed to having inherited from his father. It is important to him. Does he think I did not know that? It was the reason I was surprised to see it leaving yesterday. I tell him that naturally I understand, that it is my favourite landscape too (this of course is a lie, but such well-intentioned untruths are the cement of any marriage). Our bank account is looking quite healthy enough, anyway, with the sale of the other items. He assures me that retaining ownership of this painting will mean we get only 75,000 francs less.

I ask him if there was a problem with Leblanc about getting it back. Maurice says no, not really, but his expression clouds over, and I can tell there was an unpleasantness. My husband is sometimes like a little boy himself, no more subtle than Matthieu in disguising his true feelings from me. My heart warms to both of them. Sometimes I feel I really do not need another child, because I am already looking after two of them.

29 November 1939

I always feel a tendency to depression in winter, and perhaps that is what is afflicting me now. The longer spans of darkness, the biting cold, they are getting me down, reducing my spirits. Today I learn that the Kellermans have a passage booked from Cherbourg next week and they are packing everything up and emigrating to New York. I think of the many friends we have lost in the past four or five years, Jewish families leaving France, sometimes even Europe, and I wonder if we should be joining them. I mention it to

Maurice this evening. He is adamantly opposed
to the idea. He says that there may be a war on,
but we are Frenchmen, that we have a duty not
to run away. Besides, everything that is familiar to
us is here, our home, the business, our way of life.
Why should we cut ourselves off from what we
have built up, throw it all away, and go and live
in a place like America that is completely alien to
us? On balance, I am persuaded by his arguments.
No doubt next spring when the sun returns I will
wonder what I was getting so worked up about.

11 January 1940

A strange incident this afternoon. As I walk home
down the rue Lafayette with an icy wind blowing
round my ears I decide to pause at a café for a
cup of coffee. Inside I am just taking my seat and
arranging my shopping when I glance at the table
next to mine. A single woman like me sits there,
her fur coat sagging about her shoulders, staring
straight ahead at the empty glass in front of her.
She looks desolate, utterly miserable. Suddenly
I recognise her, and before I can stop myself
I am leaning across saying her name. Madame
Leblanc. Geraldine. She turns to me, confused,
and fumbles with a handkerchief. Her solemn
dark eyes are red and swollen, and she mumbles
to me something about a bad cold, but I can

see that she has been crying.

I ask if I can do something for her. She shakes her head and looks away. There is an awkward silence for a time, then suddenly she turns back. My God, I hear her say through clenched teeth, men are such pigs. She spits the words out with a real venom. It is a shock to hear such violence coming from her, when I remember her as so still and quiet. I ask what's happened, and she tells me she has found out that her husband is having an affair with the wife of one of his clients. She feels utterly betrayed. I think of those weasel eyes, and suddenly I hate him for making this poor woman so miserable. I try to calm her down, to console her. It will pass, I tell her. Even the strongest marriages have their crises. He'll come back to you. Oh yes, she says, he'll come back, but that's not the point. It is the lack of compunction with which he makes love to other women. It is the lack of remorse with which he returns to me. It has happened before? I say. Of course it's happened before, she tells me, but each time the pain is no less. He comes back to me sheerly as a convenience. It is so unfair. If only his infidelities could make him as unhappy as they make me.

After a time she shakes her head, and looks at her watch. She pulls her fur back over her shoulders. She has to go.

When Maurice gets home, I decide not to tell

him. For once, it is not his business. Madame Leblanc has been talking to me in confidence, woman to woman.

13 January 1940

This morning I receive a short, very formal note from Geraldine Leblanc apologising for having imposed upon me on Wednesday and imploring me to forget the whole incident. It is in the past, and better never referred to again. A strange letter. And a very sad one, I think.

10 May 1940

I am still trying to make sense of today. The past twenty-four hours have been the most shocking I can ever remember. Last night we returned home to rue Véronique after an idyllic day on the river. It was the first warm weekend of the summer, and we took a picnic on Maurice's brother's boat up the Seine past Asnières. Matthieu adored it, and insisted on swimming, although the water was icy. He loves the water, he has become my little frog.

Then this morning at 7.45 we hear the devastating news on the radio. The Germans have invaded. Their tanks have cut through Belgium and they are already on French territory. It is extraordinary, and my first reaction is not to believe it. What about the Maginot defences,

I say to Maurice angrily, as if he is personally responsible. He tells me there is no Maginot Line along the border with Belgium. Why should there have been? Belgium are our allies; you don't build defences against your allies.

Later we hear Monsieur Raynaud addressing the nation. He tells us that German aggression will be repulsed, and that with our British allies we will stand firm. Suddenly the war that I had complained about as unreal becomes horrifically real and dangerously close. And I remember Maurice's outburst last year, that people don't fight any more, not civilised nations, not after the last time. As we sit there listening, I put my hand out to him. He squeezes it quickly, then stands up saying he must go to work. For a moment I am angry with him for seeking to normalise a situation beyond his control by blindly sticking to his own routine. But then I think, who am I to criticise? When really terrible things happen, things for which there is no prescribed response, we all find our different ways of coping.

6 June 1940

Each day now is worse than the last. It is the chaotic uncertainty into which our lives have been thrown that makes existence so difficult. No one knows what is really going on. We listen to the radio and hear stirring martial music interspersed with half-hearted and unconvincing bulletins about the strength of the resistance our troops are putting up to the invader. Everything that we are fed officially is contradicted by the anecdotes of people who know people in the know. There are any number of panicky rumours exchanged in the bars and cafés. If you believe what you hear on the streets, the truth is that our soldiers are deserting in droves in the face of the Germans' advance, that our brave British allies have abandoned us, that the enemy now control Rouen and Amiens, that in some places they are no more than sixty kilometres from Paris itself.

It is all so sudden: can it really be less than a month ago that we spent that hot and care-free weekend picnicking upriver at Asnières, still secure behind the comfortable illusion of the impenetrable Maginot defences? Oh, for those innocent days when that unpleasant man Emile Leblanc could sit at our dinner table and make clever remarks about wars without casualties.

This evening I have a terrible argument with Maurice. Look, I tell him, the time has come to get out, to leave Paris, to go south. Where? says Maurice doubtfully. Biarritz, I say. That hotel where we went to stay that August after Matthieu was born, let's go there for the summer so that we're out of all this, away from the fighting and the destruction and the refugees. It's not as if we can't afford it, for God's sake. Wasn't that exactly why we sold all those pictures and furniture? Maurice says that he can't just abandon the business. That things aren't as bad as people say. That people are exaggerating.

'Who's exaggerating?' I blaze at him. 'The refugees on the streets, are they exaggerating? The families from the north sleeping out in the squares with nothing left in the world but a couple of suitcases? Are they exaggerating?'

Maurice shrugs regretfully but repeats that we're better off staying put. Who says we're better off? I demand. Levy for one, he tells me. Levy knows. Levy works in the Ministry.

Look, Maurice goes on, defeat is an appalling ignominy for France, no one feels it more keenly than he does. But if the Germans come, the Germans come. Life will go on. We are French citizens, after all, and the enemy have no quarrel with the French people themselves. Nothing is to be gained by fleeing, by just abandoning everything and running for it.

I break down and ask him what sort of a father he is, endangering his son's safety like this? He just looks miserable, and I know I have hit home with him. He sighs and says you go, then, you take the boy. I'll join you later. It's not the answer I want to hear. Maurice is being pig-headed. It is his absurd mistrust of that ass Vernon which makes him not want to leave the business. He thinks that while he is away Vernon will make mistakes, cut him out, foul things up. The short-sightedness of it all!

8 June 1940

Now I don't know which way to turn.

The morning starts with a letter arriving from Patrice Levy wishing us farewell. As a senior civil servant, her husband is following the government in its withdrawal to Bordeaux. She is going with him, they depart in an official car today. So much for Levy knowing best about staying in Paris. For a moment I want to telephone Maurice and taunt him with the news, but I don't of course, I couldn't bear the wound his pride would sustain if I showed up his misjudgment in this way. No, I have to be strong for both of us. All of us.

The news of the Levys helps me finally decide to do it. To book seats for Matthieu and myself on the Biarritz express. To have the tickets ready, anyway, in case I decide to use them, to be prepared. I send Nadine to take Matthieu to school – although apparently only half his class is now turning up, the rest having left Paris – and set off on my own to the Gare d'Austerlitz. Three streets away I can hear already that something is wrong. There is the wrong sort of noise as

I approach, no longer the sound of traffic, but the murmuring of a huge crowd of people, of a huge crowd of anxious people. I turn a corner, and there they are, literally thousands of them, all heading for the station itself but not moving, cramming the streets around, clutching suitcases, jostling, pushing, perspiring. Two gendarmes are helping to bring out a woman who's fainted. Children are crying, voices are raised. I ask a man what is going on. They are all queueing to get on trains, he says. But there is no hope for the people massed out here. Passengers are already standing twenty deep on the platforms, fighting to board any train that leaves, regardless of its destination. At the present rate of progress, people out here won't get near a train for seven days or more, even if they have the tenacity to queue for that length of time. And who knows if there'll be any trains at all by then. Panic ripples over this mass of people like wind over a cornfield. I catch a whiff of it myself, sense the horror of being trapped in a claustrophobic place towards which a remorseless enemy is daily approaching closer. It is too late. We won't get out of here. The Levys are the lucky ones. I feel an almost debilitating sense of envy for them. Why should they get out, and not us?

Back home, I meet Madame Lisieux on the stairs. We smile at each other, as usual. But this

time I pause and say, 'You're still here, then?'
She shrugs and tells me that her husband is
a surgeon at the hospital and feels that he is
needed in Paris. It is difficult, what with her
little daughter to consider too, but she proposes
to stick it out with him. What about me? she asks.
I say that my position is the same, my husband
does not want to leave his work, so we're keeping
the family together. We both laugh, and shrug
again, as if to say, what can you do with such men?
But that moment forms a bond between us. I feel
momentarily better, because there is consolation
in being allied with the Madame Lisieuxs of this
world rather than with the Patrice Levys.

Now I am back in the apartment I resolve to
make the best of it. Not to be bitter with Maurice
about the departure of the Levys, certainly not to
admit to him what I tried to do this morning at
the Gare d'Austerlitz. And to maintain complete
normality with Matthieu, my little one, to deny
that there is anything to fear. To shield him as far
as possible from the terrible upheavals which may
be coming. After all, there is something to be said
for staying together on territory that is familiar.

10 June 1940

This morning I am visited by a tearful Patrice
Levy. After all, she did not get to Bordeaux. The

roads were so clogged with traffic — cars, refugees on foot, even deserters from the army, she says — that they were literally impassable. They had to turn back. Now I am sorry for her. I try to console her, I repeat for her all the arguments that Maurice used on me to justify staying. I find that her weeping is having an unexpectedly invigorating effect on me, it is strengthening my will. Then she says an odd, rather disturbing thing. 'Of course it will be the worse for people like us,' she wails. What does she mean? I ask. You know, for Jews, she says. The German regime is against us, they will do terrible things to us. Look at what happened in Poland. Come on, I say, people are always against the Jews. Even when they're not, the Jews imagine they are. We've made a mythology of it, a way of life. It won't be any different this time. But after she's gone, I feel an unease at what she's said. This is certainly one more cause for anxiety.

The Germans are very close now. In the distance we can hear the guns.

What God wills, will be.

14 June 1940

A curious unreality once again. Paris has been declared an open city. Its defences are abandoned. Shops are boarded up, streets are deserted. No traffic even. It is as if we are sitting with our eyes closed, flinched for some massive blow. I stand for quarter of an hour this morning just watching the square from the window. I count one pedestrian passing, one girl on a bicycle, and three dogs just scampering around joyously, as if they can't believe this new freedom of the pavements. For once, even Maurice does not go to work. Nadine has stayed at home with her mother, so it is just the three of us. I read out loud to Matthieu. Maurice sits in his study, examining papers, sifting through them, sorting them methodically, and occasionally burning odd sheets. We wait, apprehensive, yet not quite sure what it is we are waiting for.

And then it is Madame Balbec who is at the door, white-faced and breathless. They are here, she says. The Germans have come. Tanks are progressing up the Boulevard Haussmann. Columns of men are following. There has been no shooting. So far, they are behaving correctly. She sounds almost disappointed.

But who has betrayed us? she demands. France can only have fallen through treachery within. It has all been so precipitous these past few weeks, our descent into defeat, that I suddenly think that perhaps in this she is right. One day, probably many years in the future, the truth will come out. But it will be left to the generation of Matthieu's children to uncover it.

17 June 1940

We are to sign an armistice with the Germans. France has admitted defeat. Maurice and I sit together this evening listening to events unfolding on the radio. Monsieur Raynaud has resigned and Marshal Pétain – who I thought was dead – broadcasts that he is now Prime Minister. He makes a speech in a thin, high, old man's voice, punctuated at regular intervals by little coughs. He announces with a certain melodrama, 'I make a gift of myself to France to lessen her misfortune.' Poor France, to have to accept such a donation. There is something so abjectly passive about it all. I cannot stand to listen any longer and go into the kitchen.

20 June 1940

I notice how quickly Paris begins to return to normal. Shops and restaurants reopen, and today Maurice has gone back to the office. Food is a problem – there is very little available, and some sort of rationing is about to be introduced – but as you walk about the city you think how much worse it could have been. No bombs, no shelling, no snipers, no street-to-street fighting. Just a lot of big red German flags, sprouting like excrescences from familiar buildings, and signposts and

notices in German, too. Then there are the enemy
soldiers themselves, in their distinctive grey-green
uniforms, wandering about, peering at the sights
just like tourists. They are perfectly polite: there
has been none of the rape and pillage that people
like Madame Balbec were throwing up their hands
in horror at the thought of (and probably secretly
relishing, too).

But there remains an overriding passivity, a numbness in our reaction to defeat and subjugation.
Maurice shrugs and gets on with his work. People
walk by the cafés and bars unmoved by the tarts
who are already sitting there giggling with German
officers. Nadine peels precious potatoes in our
kitchen and says to me over her shoulder, 'After
all, madame, it is not so bad. They are not wild
animals. They behave correctly.'

25 June 1940

Two incidents today which bring home to me
the reality of this occupation of our city by an
alien force. This morning I find myself on the
Champs-Elysées. There is a huge march-past of
German troops. It is hard not to be impressed
by their sheer numbers, by their discipline, by
their immaculate turnout. Of course, this is the
intention, the object of the exercise, to impress
on us that we are the occupied, subjugated people,

that we are dealing with an irresistible power. A few pedestrians pause to watch from the pavement. Unexpectedly a man leans over to me and observes, 'Ah, madame, now I see where we went wrong – we've taken too many prisoners.'

I am still laughing to myself at his remark as I go down to take the Métro. The carriage is full as I board, and I have to stand. A man gets up from his seat to offer it to me, and I thank him and sit down before I realise that it is a German officer who has made the gesture. I am covered in confusion and annoyance. I feel cheapened and compromised, as though I have been tricked into some sort of collaboration.

28 June 1940

Our clocks have been moved forward by an hour, to bring us into line with Germany. When something as basic as your time is changed, it makes you realise how completely you are dominated. What more powerful symbol could you imagine of the fact that our country is now just a part of the German Empire?

5 October 1940

This afternoon Patrice Levy knocks on my door. As soon as she sits down in the salon, she bursts into tears. She is too upset at first to tell me what is the matter, then at last it comes out in sobbing, breathless bursts. Levy has lost his job, he has been dismissed from his position in the Ministry. Why? I demand. Apparently there was some poisonous law enacted two days ago called the *Statut des Juifs*. This specifically excludes Jews from the higher levels of public service. No time has been lost in enforcing it.

This comes on top of the edict last week that because we are Jewish we have to register our names at the local police station. Our identity cards have had a big stamp superimposed on them imprinting the single word '*Juif*'. In fact I cannot believe the hostility that has been orchestrated against us. Hatred and prejudice is everywhere. Every day brings some new article in the gutter press, or some new regulation to limit our lives. Certain newspapers are particularly vitriolic, carrying banner headlines that vilify us in the most horrible terms. I begin to ask myself, is this the result of pressure from our occupiers, or has the German invasion come as a convenient pretext? Was the anti-Semitism actually already there in the French soul, waiting its chance to be expressed? Those articles in the newspapers, they are not written by Germans but by Frenchmen. That is what makes them even more nauseating.

I sense that wherever we turn there are enemies,

people who want to do us down, to kick us, to hurt us. In past years we never went regularly to the synagogue, admittedly, but now we barely go at all, even though it is only five minutes away in the rue de la Victoire. Because attendance there merely draws public attention to our status, opens us up to personal attack.

Suddenly I remember a book by that American writer I met once at one of those crazy parties I used to go to in my Bohemian days before I knew Maurice, in someone's ramshackle apartment in the rue de l'Université. The writer's name was Henry Miller. He was a strange man, very wild and drunk, and what he wrote was full of obscenities. I tried his book and never finished it. One thing I remember about it, though: he used a simile about being Jewish which I didn't at the time understand, because I didn't think then that it had any relevance to my own experience as a Jew. But I went and looked it up again today:

There are people who cannot resist the desire to get into a cage with wild beasts and be mangled ... Fear makes them fearless. For the Jew the world is a cage filled with wild beasts. The door is locked and he is there without whip or revolver.

That is exactly what we are doing now, living

in a cage filled with wild beasts, unprotected by whips or revolvers. It is not so much for Maurice and myself that I fear, but for little Matthieu. What kind of an environment is this in which to bring up a child? Where will it all end?

6 October 1940

Just as I imagine that things can get no worse, they do. Last night, when Maurice came home, I told him the news of Levy's dismissal. He looked very thoughtful, but didn't say much. 'Thank God,' I encouraged him, 'that at least you're not in public service.' This evening Maurice returns, and breaks it to me. His legal practice is to be Aryanised. What does that mean, I ask, assuming in my ignorance that it is some sort of technical term peculiar to the law. It means, he says slowly, that 'Benjamin and Vernon' is to become simply 'Vernon'. Jews are no longer allowed either to practise law or to run businesses. I am being thrown out of my own premises.

I don't know which is worse: that Maurice should lose his precious family firm, or that it should pass in its entirety into the hands of that revolting slug Vernon.

'I fought for France in 1918,' says Maurice. 'I am French. Vernon never went near the front line, never held a gun, although he was of military age.

I love my country, but now I am being disowned by her. I don't understand what is happening.'

He looks miserably at me. I have never seen such desolation in his eyes. I try to buoy him up, become tough with him. Look, I say, this is the most monstrous injustice, but you're handing them a further victory if you allow yourself to be undone by it. You owe it to us, to Matthieu and me, not to be beaten. But what am I going to do, how am I going to spend my days? he asks. It is true, his work has been everything to him, it will leave a huge vacuum, but I am not going to allow that. Write a book, I say. Now you will have the leisure to do it. Amaze them all by writing a really brilliant book. He rallies slightly at this. The idea flickers, and momentarily burns. I must keep at it, to ensure that it fans into a proper flame.

21 October 1940

Hurrying towards the shops this morning – you have to be so punctual to get bread now, you cannot afford to be a moment late or there is nothing left – I see Geraldine Leblanc coming towards me, I recognise the elegant way she walks. She looks up and sees me, too. We are not far away, close enough for me to see her expression, her solemn eyes. It is the first time we've met since that sad little incident last year in the café.

And then very deliberately she crosses the street, cuts me totally.

I try to analyse why she has done it. Is it because we're Jews, no longer fit people for her to consort with in the present climate? Perhaps. But I think it is also something else, something more personal. She feels she has let me see too much of her, she wants to distance herself from me again after what happened. She feels compromised by my knowledge of her unhappiness with her husband, and resents me for it.

6 January 1941

This looks like being a long, cold and dreadful winter. The snow is piled high in the streets. Coal is in very short supply, and there is a split in the glass in the salon window through which, no matter how we tape it, the wind howls. Certainly there is no possibility of finding someone to replace the glass, that sort of service has completely broken down for us.

The Levys call on us this afternoon. They tell us there is so much snow that yesterday there was even a skiing competition at the Porte Saint Cloud. Everyone talks of only two things: the cold, and how to get enough to eat. Patrice Levy says that she spends much of the day in bed. It is the most effective way of keeping warm. She puts on a coat and makes a hot-water bottle and stays under the blankets. She also makes sure she is wearing as much gold jewellery as possible because she has read that gold is an effective conduit for heat. She is the most absurd woman.

14 June 1941

I write exactly one year on from that terrible moment when the German Army rolled into Paris. What deprivations and horrors we have got used to in the twelve months that have elapsed since. Maurice has lost his job. Matthieu has been spat at and persecuted at school. We have completely given up attending synagogue, for fear of our lives. We barely have enough to eat: for instance, our dinner this evening was made up of thin soup, a few stringy carrots, and some tiny little shavings of cheese. And yet suddenly I feel wildly, ridiculously, outrageously happy. I want to go out into the street and sing. I want to accost unknown passers-by and tell them of my good fortune.

I am pregnant.

I went to see Dr Baum at the Rothschild Hospital this afternoon and he confirmed it. After all these years of trying, suddenly we have succeeded. A little brother or sister for Matthieu is on the way.

11 September 1941

As I walk up the Boulevard des Italiens this morning, I come across a large queue of people waiting in line as if for a cinema. Then I see what the attraction is that draws them. It is an exhibition in the Palais Berlitz called '*Le Juif et La France*', advertised with a huge caricature of a grasping, evil-looking Jew trying to clutch the globe in his hands. Horrible. So people's minds are poisoned against us.

3 October 1941

Twice last night we were awakened from sleep by distant explosions in the city. They were ominous, threatening sounds, somehow magnified by the silence of the darkness. Then this morning, shortly after daybreak, there is another, louder detonation, much nearer by, followed by the sound of showering glass. Maurice goes out and discovers the terrible explanation for what we have heard. All over the city, synagogues have been blown up, culminating this morning in our own local synagogue, just round the corner in the rue de la Victoire. Curious, I go out myself to see the devastation. I crunch through the broken glass. The building is in ruins. Suddenly I want to cry at the desecration, not just of our religion, but of our community. Of us. But I hold back my tears because I feel that they would add to the triumph of the evil men who have done this. Being Jewish in Paris is increasingly like being under siege. With these sickening acts of violence I feel that a different and even more fearful phase of our lives has begun. Now the menace is not just mental but physical.

The rumour is that the Germans carried out these acts of wanton destruction, but no one is sure. Whoever is responsible, there is no shortage of Frenchmen to applaud them.

10 February 1942

This date will always live in my heart. At half past five this morning, here at the Rothschild Hospital, my little daughter Elise is born. Six hours' labour, less than with Matthieu. But I would have undergone any pain for this incomparable gift. Of course there are problems in this world into which we have brought her, serious problems. The heating is inadequate, and no one has enough food. We are surrounded by enemies. But I look at her and feel she is strong. A survivor.

This afternoon Maurice arrives with Matthieu. Maurice is distant, even now; but for a moment I see him gazing at our daughter and I do not mistake it, there is pride in his eyes. Matthieu has a little speech prepared about how much he loves his new little sister. He has such a sweet nature. I take him in my arms and tell him he will always be my first-born, my special one.

15 May 1942

I am worried about Maurice. His morale is low. It is hard for him to be so inactive. He has stopped work on his project, the book of legal history he has been trying to write. Three times in the past month, when he has disappeared into his study on the pretext of working on it, I have gone in and found him doing nothing, just staring at the wall in front of him. Today I tax him with his idleness. He says he no longer has the appetite for it, and anyway progress is impossible now that Jews are banned from all public libraries. How can he research the finer points of the Code Napoléon, whose genesis was his chosen theme, when he cannot get to any of the reference books?

Then the crying of Elise unsettles him, he has little patience, and I must work to raise his spirits. 'We are mad,' he says to me this morning. 'We are mad to have brought another little one into this world.' I tell him it is the wrong way to look at it. Perhaps this is not the ideal time to be bringing up a baby. But we've given her the gift of life. She will always be grateful to us for that. If she could speak, she would tell us she would rather have been born than not. He takes another long walk this afternoon. I do not ask him where he went. I have this sad vision of him wandering aimlessly about the streets. Most of the time, I find it difficult to reach him, he is living in a world that is beyond contact with others.

Meanwhile I am busy with the children. They bring me great joy. My Matthieu, who despite his terrible diet is growing up so fast. And my little Elise. She smiled again today. What pleasure that smile brings me.

24 May 1942

This morning Maurice goes on one of his long lonely wanderings about the streets of the city. While he is out, a strange and unexpected thing happens. There is a knock at the door, I open it, and there stands, of all people, Emile Leblanc. He smiles his weasel smile. 'Is your husband not in?' he says. He is all charm, as if we are all the best of friends, as if he last saw us two weeks ago rather than two years. 'May I come in for a moment or two? Perhaps you and I can talk.'

I am suspicious of him, but I bring him through to the salon. As he sits down I suddenly have a very vivid picture in my mind of Geraldine weeping in that café. It makes me uneasy. 'What can I do for you, Monsieur Leblanc?' I ask him.

I watch him carefully. He looks rich, prosperous. His suit is immaculate. I contrast it in my mind with the poor, darned clothes that Maurice is now reduced to. 'I thought we might talk some business,' he says.

'What sort of business?' I am still watching him. His eyes make a surreptitious tour of what we have left in this room, sizing it up. Then they come back to me, settle on me, and I suddenly have the unnerving feeling that he is appraising me too.

He says, 'You are a beautiful woman, Danielle. I had forgotten quite how beautiful you are.'

To my shame, I blush. It is a long time since I have had a compliment like that from another man, and I don't know how to respond, I can think of nothing to say. He goes on, 'Forgive me. It is just that I have a very highly developed eye for such things. It comes of handling so many fine works of art.'

I am angry now. I say: 'I know. I have heard about your famous highly developed eye from your wife.'

He laughs, and says, 'Ah! You women.' But I think that somewhere beneath his smooth and glossy surface my remark has hit home. He knows

I have seen through him, that I recognise him for what he really is.

I ask him again to tell me what this business is he wants to discuss. He adopts a serious expression and says that he understands life isn't easy for anyone at the moment, particularly not for people like us. Would we be interested in selling one or two things to him now? Like, for instance, the Monet. The picture that Maurice withheld from the original deal. Could he have another look at it, by the way? I am not sure whether to allow him to do this, but already he has got up and is making his way into the study. I follow him. He stands in front of the painting of the trees, nodding appreciatively. Then he turns round and smiles again. 'Get Maurice to telephone me,' he says.

I tell him we have no telephone. It is no longer permitted to Jews. He shrugs jauntily, and picks up his hat. 'Perhaps he would like to call on me in the gallery, then,' he says.

Maurice comes back and I tell him about what has happened. He is very angry. He calls Emile Leblanc a bloodsucker, and says he never wants anything to do with him again. When I suggest that perhaps we need the money that the Monet would provide, Maurice says that we are still adequately provided for and he would rather starve than do business with Leblanc again. On balance I am inclined to agree with him.

30 May 1942

Another quite terrible measure against us is announced by an urgent summons to the local Mairie this morning. Here we are distributed with a length of yellow material from which we are instructed to cut and sew on to our clothes a large yellow star of at least eight centimetres in diameter that must be worn whenever we go out. The official version of the Star of David, to distinguish us as Jews. All of us, I query, even my little son? How old is he, says the official, in no way embarrassed or shamed. Seven, I tell him. Then he too must wear it. And my four-month-old daughter? For a moment he looks doubtful, goes to consult his superior. He comes back frowning, as if a little disappointed. No, he announces, she is exempted. But in order to get his own back, he makes great play of charging me the regulation fifteen francs for the material, and demanding from me a textile coupon for the purchase. He calls after me as I leave that there must be strict adherence to this measure. Any failure to observe it will be punished severely.

6 June 1942

The first day of our existence as marked people. I venture out with Matthieu, our yellow stars attached to our jackets. Some people stare at us. Here and there I catch sight of others wearing the same badges. Proud though you may be about your origins, there is a sense of shame about being distinguished in this way, about being forced to differentiate yourself.

Then, this afternoon, just as I am feeling very low, something happens to raise the spirits. I receive an unexpected visit from our upstairs neighbour, Thérèse Lisieux. She knocks on the door just as I am feeding Elise. I ask her in and we sit together in the salon and talk about our children. Her daughter Céline is a year younger than Matthieu. She is an extremely sympathetic woman, probably a year or two younger than I. She is outspoken about the yellow-star regulation. You can see she feels things passionately. How would it be, she suggests, if she, who is not Jewish, took to wearing the yellow star, and so did all her other non-Jewish friends? That would soon confuse all these cretinous authorities, convince them of the absurdity of their regulations. I laugh, thinking that she is not serious. Then I realise that she is, that her mind is temporarily occupied with the practicalities of the idea. The strategy would of course achieve nothing, and only make trouble for her, but my heart goes out to her for suggesting it. And I rejoice that I have made a new friend. It is ridiculous that we should

have lived so close by for so long and never have
got to know each other properly till now.

8 June 1942

Maurice receives a letter this morning from Emile
Leblanc. He doesn't tell me about it. I only know
because I find it crumpled up in the wastepaper
basket in his study. Was it wrong of me to read
it? The truth is, Maurice is so uncommunicative at
the moment that I have to resort to these methods
in order to discover anything about what is going
on with him. My own husband. The letter repeats
Leblanc's offer to buy more pictures from us. He
is particularly anxious to buy the Monet.

Obviously there is no question of us doing
business with Leblanc, but I try to analyse why
Maurice still feels so strongly about this painting of trees tracing a curving pattern along a
riverbank. It is only paint and canvas, after all.
But, being the first work of art he ever bought
for himself, I think that it has come to symbolise
something important to him, that to lose it
now would be the final sacrifice of his self-
esteem. He has already had so much taken from
him: his business, his security, his love of his
country.

In a way, his strong feelings about this are good,
because it is invigorating for him in his present

low mood to feel strongly about anything. I shall
back him up completely in his resolve.

23 June 1942

I do not normally read the newspapers, but
today by chance I see one. I go down with
Matthieu to buy bread at the boulangerie at
the prescribed time of 4 p.m., the beginning of
the hour when we as Jews are allowed to make
purchases. Miraculously there is half a stale loaf
and a mangled croissant left. I buy them both
gratefully. No wrapping paper, so the baker gives
them to me in newspaper. When I get it home,
I glance at it. It is that despicable rag *Au Pilori*.
The headlines scream out at me and make me
sick: 'The Reality of the Jewish Peril', in large
letters. What is happening to our country?

Then I read further. I cannot stop myself. I
record now what I read printed there, for the
benefit of my grandchildren, for Matthieu and
Elise's children, so that they can understand to
what depths certain French people once sank.

Many readers ask us to which organisation
they should address themselves in order to
point out the occult activities or frauds of
the Jews. It is sufficient to post a letter or
a simple signed note to the Commissariat

Général aux Questions Juives, or failing that,
to the offices of our paper for forwarding.

I find a match, put the newspaper into the
grate and burn it. I can't afford for Maurice
to see it.

What horrifies me about all this is that there
are clearly any number of ordinary French citizens
queuing up to denounce Jews to the authorities,
working out old vendettas and prejudices in this
appalling way. I know about this Commissariat
Général aux Questions Juives. It is an organisation – shamefully French, and set up by the
government – which exists to persecute Jewish
people and confiscate their property. Thus these
denunciations are gratefully received and enthusi-
astically acted upon.

4 July 1942

Earlier this evening, just after supper, Maurice and
I have another visit from Emile Leblanc. Maurice
opens the door and tells him that there is no point
in his coming in, we have nothing more to say to
him. But Leblanc is persistent. He says we owe it
to ourselves and to our children at least to listen
to what he has to propose. There is something
different about his manner as he walks in this
time. It is more confident, more threatening, as

if his visit is a means to some violence against us. Reluctantly Maurice allows him to sit down in the salon. I do not offer him anything to drink as – to be honest – there is nothing in the apartment anyway. But I do not want him to know that.

Leblanc tells us again that he is eager to buy from us, particularly the painting by Monet. Maurice, who is standing by the fireplace, does not even deign to reply, but out of curiosity I ask what he is prepared to offer. He says perhaps forty thousand francs. Maurice spins round, suddenly animated with fury. He tells Leblanc that this is barely half the price he offered us in 1939, and that it is an insult to propose so little. How does he have the effrontery to walk into our apartment and waste our time in this way? Leblanc shrugs and says that it is a generous price under the circumstances. Under what circumstances? I ask.

Madame, he tells me, I am sure you are a realist. For people like you (he indicates Maurice and myself) it is a buyer's market. As sellers you have to realise that you are not entitled to lay down conditions.

What do you mean, people like us? storms Maurice. He is suddenly very angry indeed and voluble in a way that I have not seen for a very long time. You mean Jews, don't you? You mean you feel you have some sort of advantage over us because we are Jews. You think that you can exploit us because we are defenceless, kick us when we're down. You are not only a thief but a coward. I despise you.

Leblanc is stung by this, and turns very unpleasant. He reminds me even more of a weasel with his long pointed nose and his sharp, angry eyes. He insults us, calls us grasping Israelites. Then he says, mysteriously, that if we had any sense we would see how generous he is being with us by proceeding in the way that he is. He could perfectly well employ other means to lay hands on our picture, means that would deliver the Monet to him without our receiving a centime for it.

'What do you mean?' I ask, but a horrible suspicion has already occurred to me. I remember the existence of the Commissariat Général aux Questions Juives, and the hundreds of letters of denunciation flooding in every day. And then Leblanc gives expression to my fears. He says that there are authorities who are very interested to know of important works of art in Jewish ownership. Works of art ripe for confiscation. All it takes is a tip-off ... and the confiscating agency is a much easier organisation for him to buy from than greedy Israelites like ourselves who cannot see what's good for them.

We are beside ourselves with rage. I hold the front door open and Maurice literally pushes Leblanc out of our apartment. He is a foul and horrible man. After he has gone, we sit down, shaking. I cannot believe that this is the same person who was once with his wife a guest at our dinner table.

Maurice says that he refuses to be threatened, that he is going to make an official complaint. One French citizen cannot threaten another in this way. Leblanc has intimidated us, made demands with menaces. It is a criminal offence. He proposes to visit the local Prefecture of Police in the morning to register the accusation. I let him have his say, play out his rage, but what he proposes is just a fantasy. Who is going to listen to the protestations of a Jew these days? At best, his complaint against Leblanc will be filed away and forgotten. At worst, it will be the pretext for some further measure to be taken against us.

Two hours on, as I sit here and write, I am still angry. But I am uneasy, too. What concerns me most is that we have another enemy out there now. Another wild beast which we have no whip or revolver to control.

8 July 1942

Today Maurice did it. He went to the prefecture and registered his complaint against Leblanc. He comes back to the apartment elated, in as good spirits as I have seen him in for six months. The policeman who interviewed him was a very decent fellow, he says, and wrote down all the details. The matter will be investigated in due course. Maurice will be asked for another statement at the end of the month. He goes into his study and starts leafing through legal textbooks, checking points of law. All at once I can hear a very unfamiliar sound. Then I realise that it is him whistling. When Matthieu comes back from school, he is happy because he has won a commendation for his drawing. Elise gurgles in my arms. It's a beautiful summer's evening. Perhaps things are not so bad after all.

Daniel closed his grandmother's journal and leaned back in the chair, there at his just-dead mother's desk, rubbing his eyes with the insides of his palms. He didn't like it. In fact it made him feel sick, the way the entries came to an abrupt halt on 8 July 1942. Because he knew the horrific ending of this story. He knew what it was all leading up to. This diary made it worse. Too poignant to bear. Too vivid.

What he'd just read thrust him into a new intimacy with his long-dead grandparents. It was as if he had just met them for the first time, begun actually to appreciate them as people. He felt desperately sad. And he felt angry. In fact he was unprepared for the anger that the narrative created in him, even half a century on. His outrage swelled against the injustice of it all. Against the constant erosion of freedom, the remorseless wearing down of the spirit that Jews like his grandparents had suffered in occupied Paris. Against the evil of the people who threatened and exploited them. The petty officials, the callous tradesmen; and erstwhile friends like Emile Leblanc. Truly Paris had been a cage filled with wild beasts in which the Benjamins had been locked without whip or revolver.

Almost as a distraction, he reached across for the file his mother had labelled 'Benjamin Art Collection: Paintings'. Had she done it? he wondered. Had she succeeded in identifying the Monet, the picture that recurred throughout the narrative he had just read? The landscape with river and trees that had been his grandfather's first purchase, the one painting he had been unwilling to be separated from, right up to the end. He leafed through other photographs. There was the Degas that his grandmother had mentioned, the study of the ballet dancer that his own great-grandfather had apparently bought in the artist's estate sale back in 1917. His mother had pinned that one down, identified its present whereabouts. Today it was in a museum in California. Then he found one of the Sisleys, a river landscape gleaming in the sun. That had passed through a sale at Sotheby's New York in November 1989, because a photocopy of the page from the auction catalogue was appended. When he ran his eye down the provenance of that catalogue entry, the history of the Sisley's ownership, he saw it all laid out in sequence: Benjamin Collection,

Paris, he read, followed by Galerie Leblanc, 1939, then another French owner, and finally the American family who were the sellers in 1989.

He leafed on, and finally he came across it, towards the bottom of the file. A handsome coloured photograph of a landscape with trees, with the Monet signature unmistakable in the bottom right-hand corner. They were poplars, a sinuous line of them following the bank of a river winding away into the distance. Most of the composition was sky and tree, a dazzlingly simple procession of thin, upright trunks and swirling foliage against the clouds. Even in the photograph, you could tell how shot through with sunlight the original painting must be. How the brush strokes danced. For a moment he understood it: the attachment to this painting his grandfather must have felt. Not just because it was the first work he'd ever bought for himself. But because it was good. Exciting. Exhilarating.

Attached to the photograph were the details of the painting that his mother had assembled. There was another photocopy, this time of a page from a book that was identified in his mother's handwriting as being the Wildenstein *Catalogue Raisonné* of Monet's work. And there was the painting again, no mistake. Once again, Daniel's eye followed the provenance given. Once more it started 'Benjamin Collection, Paris'. Then 'Galerie Leblanc, 1939'. The final line read simply 'Private Collection'. Anonymous, secret, impenetrable. Because next to it, in his mother's handwriting, was a simple question mark. He did not know how far she'd gone in attempting to identify this Monet's current ownership, but she clearly hadn't succeeded.

And there was something more here. Another mystery, beyond that of the painting's present whereabouts. He ran his eye down the catalogue entry once more. Then held it on the penultimate line of provenance. 'Galerie Leblanc, 1939.'

Yes, but that was wrong, wasn't it? According to his grandmother's diary, his grandfather had retrieved the painting in 1939, borne it back home in triumph and relief, wrapped in brown paper and string. It had still been hanging in his study in the rue Véronique in July 1942. It hadn't left his collection. Leblanc might have coveted it and tried to buy it, but he hadn't succeeded. Or had he, later? But how? There was something that didn't smell good here. Something sordid, wafting rank into his nostrils half a century later.

Daniel Stern felt suddenly galvanised, even strangely elated. All his feelings of guilt had simultaneously found a focus and an outlet. He knew what he had to do now. He knew what he had to achieve. He was going to find that Monet. And he was going to uncover the truth about its history. In the process he was going to write the piece of his life, the story of his family in wartime Paris, documenting it all for posterity. As a tribute to his grandparents. In honour of his mother. And for himself, too. Here was his chance to touch the line of railings one more time. To put it all right. To redeem the debt that he owed to his past.

ROME

Friday, 14 May

Sunlight lay at an angle across the narrow, whitewashed cell, accentuating its spare stillness and illuminating the dust motes that flickered in the beam. To its solitary occupant, the room's geography was already achingly familiar. Father Alfonso Cambres could close his eyes and memorise exactly the disposition of every object contained within its four walls. There was a door at one end and a single window at the other. Beneath the window stood a small cupboard, with a knob missing from its left-hand door; against one wall was positioned a bed, against the other a chair and a table on which was placed a simple wooden crucifix. He could draw you a map of the patterns that the cracks in the plaster traced across the ceiling, tell you which pane of the window's glass had a small defect at its upper edge, pinpoint the thread that had worked loose from the coarse woollen rug that covered the bare boards of the floor.

Faintly, in the distance, Cambres caught notes in the low hum of the Roman traffic. A sharply sounded horn; an accelerating motorcycle. Life heard, but not seen. He walked over to the window and looked out; a profusion of flowers greeted him, of azalea, hibiscus and bougainvillaea against the yellow stone of the palazzo wall. But the window's promise of a vision of the outside world was illusory. It gave only on to an internal courtyard. An introverted view, a further symbol of enclosure. He contemplated the single almond tree that grew in the centre of the paved area. He was struck simultaneously by its beauty, and its futility.

He was sixty-five. And he was living in a cell. The fact that there was no physical lock on his door made it nonetheless a place of imprisonment. The lock existed just as compellingly, but in his own mind. The search for the key to release him from its restriction was what occupied him now. Exclusively, obsessively, in endless rounds of devotion and meditation. Except to attend Holy Mass each morning and to perform essential ablutions, he would not leave this room. This was his fourth day of incarceration, and the disciplined routines were already established: mental prayer; examination of the conscience; reading of the Holy Gospel; self-criticism; Holy Rosary; further examination of the conscience; recital of the Angelus or the Regina Coeli. And finally sleep. Anxious, shallow sleep.

I'm too old, he told himself at moments of extremity, for these rigours. Too old, and, to look at him, you might have added too urbane, also, for the humiliations of religious discipline, too distinguished for extended asceticism. He could have been a diplomat, perhaps. A successful diplomat from an old Spanish family, reminiscing over mellow wine at grand dinner tables. But instead he was living enclosed by these simple whitewashed walls, in self-inflicted incarceration. Trying to work it out, trying to salve something. Trying to reach some rapprochement between his conscience and the extreme demands of duty being made upon him by the Service to which he belonged. The Service to which he had devoted his priesthood. Pro Deo, it was called. On God's behalf.

He had awoken on Monday, the day after the Lazio match, in a ferment of uncertainty. The memories were agonising him, the memories of the past which up till yesterday he thought he had subdued. They kept resurfacing now, reactivated by what Father Donaghy had told him; by the piece of paper he had himself carried away from their meeting. Once that morning he lifted the telephone to call Donaghy's extension, but when a strange voice answered it, he had replaced the receiver without speaking. He was wary of alerting those who might or might not be watching. He considered sending him a note, but an absurd piece of Vatican folklore recurred to him:

Don't think
If you think, don't speak
If you think and speak, don't write
If you think and speak and write, don't sign your name
If you think and speak and write and sign your name, don't be surprised ...

At three in the afternoon, he had finally taken the step he had been postponing. Confused and exhausted, he had gone to see his confessor.

'You are troubled,' Monsignor Abello had told him. 'It is a crisis. God is testing you. But it is a crisis which you will come through strengthened.' And he had been led to this cell. For his own protection. To work out his own salvation.

It was too hot to stand any longer in the direct sunlight at the window. Cambres turned away and bent his stiffening joints to kneel in prayer in the cooler, shaded quarter of the room.

LONDON

Monday 17 May

'Mr Moran?'

'No. Who are you?'

'Daniel Stern. Is Mr Parnello Moran there?'

'He's engaged at the moment.' The woman's voice on the entryphone, despite its affectation of grandeur, had a distinct cockney accent.

'I have an appointment to see him. I rang this morning.'

'Just step back from the entryphone camera so I can take a proper butcher's at you.'

'That better?'

'My, you're a big, tall boy, aren't you? I think you'd better come on up, love.'

The lock was released and Daniel pushed his way into the stairwell. He'd found the card in among his mother's papers. Parnello Moran, Art Consultant, it had read. With an address in Jermyn Street. On the back was a handwritten note from an unidentified friend of his mother's saying 'Elise – you asked me for an intelligent and knowledgeable art dealer to help you with your research. I recommend this man.' Parnello Moran. The name had intrigued him, and he'd telephoned to arrange a meeting. But now he'd heard the voice of Mr Moran's assistant, he wasn't so sure he'd made the right decision.

She was waiting for him in the open doorway on the fourth landing. She was a bulky woman in her sixties wearing an apron, an exotic headscarf and a generous amount of lipstick. She clutched a fag-end between her thumb and forefinger. 'Knackering, them stairs,' she confided. 'Finish me off one day.'

She ushered him into the hall. There was a hatstand on which hung an extraordinary variety of headgear, from a kepi to a fez to a luridly coloured cricket cap; and a very beautiful painting of an Italian landscape at sunset resting casually against the wall on the floor.

'Is Mr Moran going to be long, do you think?'

'Nah, he'll see you now. Lazy sod's lying on the sofa in the sitting room doing bugger all. It's just you have to be a bit careful who you let in off the street these days. I was keeping me options open in case you was the VAT man.'

She opened the door into a rambling room of immense if dilapidated charm. Its walls, decorated with an ancient, stained red brocade, were hung with pictures which, even to Daniel's inexperienced eye, looked outstandingly good. In front of the marble fireplace were drawn up two ramshackle but stylish sofas. Stuffing spilled from one of them like some exotic vegetable growth. On the other was draped horizontally the long, thin form of a man smoking a pungently aromatic French cigarette.

'A gentleman to see you, Mr Moran,' announced the woman in an exaggeratedly plummy voice.

'You'll have to excuse Brenda,' said the proprietor, unwinding himself from his prone position and standing up. 'It's her John Gielgud-playing-a-butler impersonation. It's not very good, I'm afraid. I'm Parnello Moran. How do you do.'

Upright, he was even thinner and lankier than he'd seemed lying down. He had long fair hair, and eyes that drooped like a bloodhound's to give him a naturally laconic, even lugubrious expression. Daniel shook his hand. 'Daniel Stern,' he said.

'Tea?' suggested Moran, stubbing out his cigarette. 'Or why not something stronger? Let's celebrate.'

'Celebrate what?'

'I don't know. The fact that you're not the VAT man.'

Daniel reflected that it was some time since he'd celebrated anything, so he said, 'OK, why not?'

'Excellent. Brenda, there's still some champagne in the refrigerator. Bring a couple of glasses, there's a good girl.' She hobbled off, wheezing slightly, and Parnello Moran explained: 'She's a treasure, really. Used to be an actress's dresser in the West End, which accounts for her theatrical inclinations. She's my cleaning lady cum secretary cum foul-mouthed mother confessor. And when I say foul-mouthed, I mean sometimes really foul.'

'So is this your gallery?'

'I live here, actually. But yes, it's also my place of work. Where I try and sell the odd painting. To finance my disgracefully expensive lifestyle.'

'I came to see you for some advice.'

'Why don't you sit down and tell me about it?'

Daniel cleared some auction catalogues from the second sofa and lowered himself in among the excrescent stuffing. It was surprisingly comfortable. 'You're an expert on what kind of paintings?'

'A bit of everything really. As my famous compatriot Oscar Wilde once said, a little knowledge is a dangerous thing. On that basis, I suppose I'm rather dangerous.'

Brenda came back in with the champagne. Daniel took his glass, sipped, and felt suddenly light-headed. He asked: 'Do you know about Impressionist painting?'

Parnello nodded. 'Do you want to buy one or sell one?'

'Neither, I'm afraid.'

'Pity. For a moment there I had this vision of really huge amounts of money. Disgusting quantities of the stuff.'

'I'm sorry. I'd just like you to tell me about this.' He handed the photograph over. Of the Monet of trees by a river.

Parnello peered at it and raised his eyebrows slightly. 'What do you want to know?'

'You haven't seen it already, have you? I mean, my mother didn't show it to you?'

'Ah, wait a minute: your mother being Elise Stern?'

'That's right.'

'She rang ten days ago to say she would call in some time about a picture. She didn't say what it was,' Parnello paused, and looked back at him. 'So you've come instead, have you?'

Daniel suddenly felt too weary to go into all that. Too tired to activate the inevitable sequence of condolence that would follow if he explained that she had died. Instead he nodded and asked, 'Is this Monet a good one?'

'I rather think it is. Don't go away, I'll get the book. Let's see what Mr Wildenstein has to say about it.'

He was back a minute or two later with his distinctive, loping, almost apologetic stride, carrying Volume III of the *Catalogue Raisonné* of Monet's works. He sat down next to Daniel and opened it. 'I'm afraid my library doubles as my bedroom,' he explained. 'The bedroom element of it's in an appalling mess at the moment. Not for the faint-hearted. That's why I didn't ask you in there. Now where were we? Oh, yes. Poplars, 1891. Yours is one of that series.'

'Are there several versions?'

'Processions of them.' Parnello flicked through the pages and the illustrations. 'Look, twenty-four to be precise. Same line of trees, same riverbank, but painted at different times of day and in different weathers. All done that one summer of 1891. Extraordinary, aren't they? And rather sad.'

'Sad?'

'Gerard Manley Hopkins wrote a poem about a line of poplars.' He looked up, narrowed his drooping eyes, and unexpectedly began to quote:

'My aspens dear, whose airy cages quelled,/ Quelled or quenched in leaves the leaping sun,/ All felled, felled, are all felled;/ Of a fresh and following folded rank/ Not spared, not one ...'

Daniel gazed at the image again. A fresh and following folded rank. 'Yes, but Monet's poplars are still standing,' he objected.

'Not for long, that's just it. You see, soon after Monet started painting them he found out that all those wonderful trees were about to be cut down and sold as timber. So he did a deal with the local timber merchant to keep the poplars up until autumn, so he could finish. *Then* they went.'

'They were doomed, you mean?'

Parnello nodded. 'A bit of an operator, old Monet. Not above manipulating his own landscape.'

'Single-minded,' said Daniel. Thoughtfully.

Parnello picked up Daniel's photograph once more. Comparing it with the other versions of the subject in the *Catalogue Raisonné*. 'Yes, now I look at it again, yours is rather a dream, isn't it? It's got everything you want in an Impressionist painting: sunshine and sky and reflections in the water. I can imagine any number of rich Americans getting very overexcited about this. Are you *sure* it's not for sale?'

'Not that I know of. What's it worth, do you think?'

'Aha. Nothing to beat them, is there? All those noughts lined up after a dollar sign.' Parnello smiled happily. But beneath the flippancy, Daniel could see his brain calculating. Comparing, assessing. Some clever men preferred to operate behind a camouflage of foolishness. 'I seem to remember another from the series was sold by Sotheby's last year,' Parnello went on. 'Yes, there we are, that one there. Look, I pencilled in the price at the time as a reference.'

Daniel looked at the image being pointed out to him in the book. Then read what had been scribbled next to it. Incredible. 'Is that what it made?'

'That's it. Eleven million dollars. And I have to say that yours seems even a little bit better than this one. The brushwork's freer and the weather's better.' He paused, savouring it, then reached across for the champagne bottle. 'You know what? I think I'm going to have another drink. Always need a little steadying when I hit the eight-figure numbers.'

Daniel allowed him to fill his glass too. 'It's a lot of money.'

'It's Impressionism. The Holy Grail.'

'Meaning what?'

Parnello drank, and sighed. 'Call me an old cynic, but there's an awful lot of pretentious crap written about Impressionism. The earnestness of some of those academics who specialise in the subject ... talk about going very deeply into the surface of things. Because that's all Impressionism is: surface, and the light reflected off it. What Monet and his friends were trying to achieve was very simple: optical truth to nature, the immediate recording in paint of visual sensation. Not complicated at all.'

'You think Impressionism's overrated?'

'No, I'm not saying that. Just because its aims were simple, that doesn't mean they were easy to attain. And in the process, the Impressionists produced some beautiful paintings. All that gorgeous light and colour, it's lyrical to look at. But what you see is what you get. Its appeal is that it's so accessible, so easy to understand.'

Was that what had drawn his grandfather to it? wondered Daniel. Its easy accessibility, had that been what had persuaded him to make the Monet his first independent purchase? Had he been seduced by the freedom of brushstroke, the unalloyed exhilaration of a piece of nature recorded as pure visual sensation? With his immaculately brushed hair and his little toothbrush moustache, had he been the sort of man who yielded easily to such visual seduction? Daniel felt a sudden burst of curiosity about the man and his motives. His own grandfather. His own flesh and blood. What evidence did he have of him? Just his yellowing identity card, with its brutally superimposed stamp. And his passion for pictures.

'What I'm trying to find out,' he said carefully to Parnello, 'is where it is now, this painting. Unfortunately the *Catalogue Raisonné* isn't very helpful.'

'Isn't it? Let's have another look. No, you're right.

Provenance says Galerie Leblanc, 1939, then just "Private Collection". Not exactly what you'd call a mine of information.'

'Do you have any ideas?'

Parnello Moran looked troubled. 'Listen, research is rather one of my strong points. Nothing I like better than a good rootle around the archives. A bit of an addiction of mine. But with this one, I'm afraid, there's not much option. You're going to have to ask Leblanc who they sold it to.'

'What, Galerie Leblanc in Paris? Are they still in business?'

'In a big way.'

'Are they accessible?'

'It depends how you handle them. You know how the French can be when they get grand. Their delight in their own wonderfulness in unbounded. *Très snob*, and all that. You have to indulge them.'

'I'll give it a try.'

'You haven't told me why you're looking for that particular Monet.'

'I haven't, no.' Daniel still held back. The reasons for his quest were too intimate, too personal. Even though he found Parnello Moran unexpectedly sympathetic, the sadness was too fresh, the tragedy too painful to permit the intrusion of another intelligence, another sensibility. Not yet. 'I'm sorry,' he said. 'It's just a bit of private research.'

Parnello shrugged. He picked up the bottle of champagne, found it was empty, and laid it aside. He stared at it resentfuly. 'Well, I wish you good luck,' he said. 'Let me know if there's anything more I can do. And don't forget: if the painting's ever for sale, I'd certainly have a buyer for it.'

As Daniel departed, Parnello paused in the doorway, suddenly thoughtful. 'Actually, you know where Monet went wrong, don't you?' he said. 'All that business about wanting to paint exactly what you see, it's a cul-de-sac, a delusion. He said he wanted to be 'the innocent eye', the pure recorder of visual sensation. But it's not possible. Every time a picture's painted, there's got to be an artistic intervention between nature and the canvas, an element of interpretation. In the end, that's what art is.'

Daniel thought about it and said, 'So Monet was barking up the wrong tree?'

'In a way. He hadn't understood that there's no sensation without perception.'

'Everyone's eye is a bit guilty, after all.'

Parnello looked at him curiously with his strange, bloodhound eyes, then laughed. 'No need to go bringing guilt into it,' he said.

But there was, of course. Every need.

'Something's come up,' he told Nat on the telephone to New York that evening. 'A story I want to write.'

'Oh?' Nat was suspicious. 'Anything we can use?'

'Perhaps. You can see it first, anyway.'

'So what are you now? The Delphic Oracle? Care to tell me what it's about, Dan?'

He found he didn't. Not really. The whole thing had become too personal to discuss with people like Nat. He couldn't have taken any shit from Nat about his Jewishness validating this piece.

'So where are you heading now?' Nat asked.

'Paris, I think. For a while.'

'Want an apartment in Paris for the summer?'

'What sort of apartment?'

'Jarvis's. He's one of our guys over there, he wants to rent his out. It's just come up on the internal e-mail. He's off to Africa for a couple of months to do a story.'

'Where is it?'

'Wait, I'll get it up on the screen. There we are: central Paris. Sixth Arrondissement. One bedroom. Compact, it says here.'

'What's that mean?'

'I guess it means it's the kind of place you don't have to get out of bed to take a shower. Interested?'

'I might be.'

'The Paris bureau have got the keys. Call them, Dan. Mention my name.'

Why not? It was an appealing idea to base himself in Paris for a while, to get out of London. London was already depressing him. He'd had enough of Stephanie and Stewart, of the deadening correctnesses of the dried-up Bainbridge. He needed a break from the memory-laden shadows of his mother's house. He felt he'd done all he could here for the time being.

And there were people in Paris he needed to see now. Like the present-day Galerie Leblanc, with their high opinion of themselves. And like Thérèse Lisieux. He'd look her up, too. Tante Thérèse.

PARIS

Monday, 24 May

The unknown Jarvis's apartment was crammed in beneath the eaves of a tall, elegant building in rue Servandoni, a narrow street that ran down from the Luxembourg Gardens to Saint Sulpice. There was a bedroom, a bathroom, a kitchen, and a strange L-shaped reception room. It would do, decided Daniel. It was a base. A place to work. He looked down from his garret on to a group of American tourists in multicoloured shorts and anoraks, surging bravely forward clutching their maps of the city. It was raining. He didn't envy them. He was happy he was on his own. It wasn't so much that he was a loner. But Nat had been right: once set on an enterprise, Daniel was single-minded. Blinkered, almost. It was the way he was made.

His mind went back to he first time he'd ever come here to Paris. His mother had brought him. They'd stayed in the Ritz, or some other equally grand hotel. His father had sent them off, while he travelled to New York on business. 'Go and live it up a bit, Elise. Gay Paree. Take the boy with you, too. Great stuff.' Who knew what little amatorial misdemeanour his father's generosity had been compensating for? Anyway, aged ten, Daniel remembered his mother ferrying him about the sights: the Eiffel Tower, the Louvre Museum, a boat trip on the Seine.

'You know something, Danny?' she said as they chugged past the Ile de la Cité on the sightseeing boat. 'This is my homecoming. I was born here. You see, I'm really French.'

'But you don't speak French,' he said suspiciously.

'No. I left Paris when I was three. I haven't been back much since.'

'Why not?'

'All the relations I had in France had died. My family was in England, you see: Aunt Stephanie, Uncle Laurie and everyone.'

Daniel thought for a moment. 'So am I French too?'

'Half-French.'

Daniel remembered laughing. The idea had seemed quite absurd, probably some obscure grown-up joke. Neither of them had pursued it: he, because he was more concerned with persuading her into buying him an ice cream, and she ... well, who could tell with what thoughts she was already struggling, what it can have meant to her to be back in this place, in Paris, knowing everything but remembering nothing?

But as it turned out, his French ancestry manifested itself later in a marked aptitude for the language. He found he learned it easily and fluently. It had been in his blood after all. Funny, really: that he should have ended up speaking French when his French mother didn't. Or had that been another of her self-protective measures, something else she'd deliberately avoided, buried along with all the other painful secrets of her past?

The last afternoon of his first stay in Paris his mother had taken him to meet someone. On the drive there in the taxi she had seemed tense and on edge. 'Tante Thérèse is a very dear, very special person,' she explained. 'I want you to be on your best behaviour with her.'

The apartment was full of flowers and plants. Tante Thérèse had struck him as old even then, with her grey hair held up in a bun. But she had lively, searching, deep blue eyes. He'd sensed immediately she wasn't a person you could hide things from; like Miss Pickard at school, who always knew when he wasn't telling the truth. 'So you are Daniel,' she had said. 'Come here and give your aunt a kiss.' Sheepishly he had gone over to her and presented his cheek, smelling her old lady's scent. He hadn't been able to understand why, when he had gently disentangled himself from her and looked across at his mother, she was weeping. But then again his mother often cried for unfathomable reasons, in those days when she was still together with his father.

Now, twenty years on, he took another taxi across Paris to Tante Thérèse's dimly remembered apartment near the Bois de Boulogne. It smelled musty, but there were still a lot of plants. At eighty-six, she was surprisingly little changed. Her hair was completely white now, but it was still held up neatly in a bun. She walked with a stick, but she held herself upright and appraised him with the same piercing blue eyes. Her strength of will, her determination, remained palpable in everything she did.

They embraced. As Daniel put his arms around her, he sensed how frail her old body had become, just a loose arrangement of flesh and bone, in stark contrast to the vivacity of the spirit that still inhabited it. She wept a little, but then she dried her eyes with the small handkerchief that she clutched in her weathered old hand.

'It's good of you to come,' she told him. 'I'm pleased that you did. You've grown up well. You know, you have a little bit the look of your grandmother in your face.'

'Will you tell me about my grandparents?' he said.

She settled herself in her chair. 'How much do you know?'

'I know how they died,' he told her. 'And I've read my grandmother's diary. The one she kept up till July 1942.'

'Is that it?' she said. 'Is that Danielle's journal?'

He had brought it out from his briefcase and was cradling it in his lap. He reached over to put it in her hands. 'My God,' she said, examining it. Softly. Reverently. 'I last touched this book in 1945.'

'Will you tell me where you found it?' he asked her. 'You see, I need you to fill in the gaps.'

✳   ✳   ✳

What was strange and a little shameful about Paris under the German occupation, Thérèse told Daniel, was the way ordinary people continued to live ordinary lives. Superficially, not much changed in the routine of the city. Yes, food was in much shorter supply, but bread was still baked in the boulangeries; caviar could still be had in the smarter restaurants; women could still be bought, just about anywhere. If you closed your eyes to the German signposts that sprang up on the major thoroughfares, you could almost imagine the whole thing hadn't happened. Almost. If you were prepared to live and let live. And provided you weren't Jewish.

Take 16 July 1942, for instance: it was the sort of day on which, two or three years earlier, people would have been setting off on their holidays. A haze of heat spread out over Paris. It was weather for getting out of town, for Deauville or Le Touquet, for Cannes or Biarritz. For taxis to the railway station, piled high with suitcases and buckets and spades. For the laughter of excited children.

In fact, buses set out early that morning, picking up people from all quarters of the city. Many of them were children. None of them were laughing.

Thérèse Lisieux was awakened at 5.30 a.m. by one family beginning their journey. The disturbance was coming from the Benjamins' apartment, one floor below. They had a son of seven, Matthieu, a little older than Thérèse's own daughter Céline, and a baby girl, born four months earlier. Thérèse's first, somnolent reaction was to curse them for making so much noise. If Céline woke now, she would not be coaxed back to sleep. Her husband Jacques stirred uneasily next to her, swore into his moustache, and resumed snoring. There was a clattering of footsteps on the stairs, some shouting, and the sound of both Benjamin children crying. Gradually the disturbance receded. Then silence again. In the tree in the courtyard, a bird sang.

Thérèse lay there for a while, trying to make sense of it; then trying to put it from her mind. She could do neither, so she got up quietly and went to make coffee in the kitchen. Or what passed for coffee in these days of rationing and improvisation. She thought about the Benjamins. She liked Danielle Benjamin. She was the sort of woman whom Thérèse admired: strong, good-looking. Not frivolous. Maurice Benjamin, her husband, was an older, more distant figure with sad eyes. The boy was sweet: solemn, and unfailingly polite. When she met him on the stairs, he took his cap off to her.

Until quite recently, her friendship with Danielle had been no more than the acquaintanceship of neighbours: conversations in the hallway of the apartment block, exchanges about the weather, food shortages, or the vagaries of the communal plumbing system. Nothing about the important things. The things too evident, and therefore too sensitive, to be discussed. Like why the Benjamin family could no longer venture into the streets of Paris without displaying the yellow star of David sewn prominently on to their coats.

The first time she saw that star it niggled Thérèse.

One morning the previous month, she had met Danielle and young Matthieu in the Boulevard Haussmann, and thought how ridiculous it looked. Particularly huge on the little boy's breast. She felt awkward. Then ashamed. Then angry. Later that afternoon she had knocked on Danielle's door.

'Can I come in?' she said.

'Of course,' said Danielle, who had her baby in her arms. 'Come and sit down in the salon. I am just giving Elise her bottle. You don't mind, do you?'

'Not at all.'

In crossing the threshold, she was drawn into an intimacy. Through seeing where and how they lived, the disposition of their possessions, the father's battered briefcase lying across the chair, the son's toy train half hidden behind a curtain, she sensed things immediately about how they were as a family. Danielle laughed ruefully as she settled herself on a sofa and fed the teat into the baby's mouth. 'Some people say we're crazy to have had another little one now, of all times. But you can't legislate for these things, can you?'

No, agreed Thérèse, you couldn't legislate. It was ironic, really. She and Jacques had been trying for five years to produce a little brother or sister for Céline. Quite wrong to feel jealous of this woman. But she did, for a moment, and suppressed it.

'I'm sorry that the apartment has become such a mess,' went on Danielle. 'I wish I could have shown it to you in the old days.'

'It's not a mess,' protested Thérèse. 'You've got some lovely things here.' She looked about her: it was still an elegant room, with rich damask curtains at the windows and a fine mirror above the fireplace. A few pictures, too, mostly modern. But the carpet was stained and threadbare, and the upholstery sagging. An Empire clock on the table by the wall had stopped at twenty to ten. There were unrepaired cracks across two window panes.

'Just a few good things, still. But Maurice sold the best in 1939. He said he could foresee a time coming when francs would be more valuable than furniture.'

'I suppose he was right.'

For a moment Danielle allowed her bitterness to show. 'It's a pity his foresight didn't extend to getting us out too. A lot of our friends left France, you know. In time. Before the Germans came.'

'I'm sorry,' said Thérèse. 'It must be wretched for you, all these regulations.' She was aware as she spoke how pitifully inadequate her words sounded. Regulations. As if the inconvenience the Benjamins were suffering was no worse than a restricted train service. But at least she had taken a step forward. She had communicated sympathy. That was better than pretending not to see the yellow star stitched so meticulously on to the coat. Going on as if it wasn't there.

'What Maurice can't understand,' Danielle explained, 'is why they are doing all these things to us. Why they have to make our life so difficult. We are French, after all. Maurice's family has been here for fifty years. And

Maurice fought in the war, back in 1918. For his country. France was perfectly happy to accept him then.'

'It's outrageous,' Thérèse had agreed. Coming here this afternoon had reinforced it: the Benjamins were a family just like them. They lived in the same comfortable block of apartments. But for an accident of racial identity, the Benjamins could be them, in fact. Or vice versa.

'It's very hard for Maurice, you know. I try to keep his spirits up. But he's got so little to do during the day, since they stopped him working. He had a very successful legal practice, back in the old days.' Danielle laughed for a moment. She had an enchanting laugh. 'Back in the old days. Must stop saying that.'

As she'd left, an idea had struck Thérèse. 'Look,' she said, 'those stars. Where can one get hold of them? If everyone in Paris who wasn't Jewish also wore them, the whole scheme would collapse. Those cretinous authorities would have to give it up.'

Thérèse had felt better after that visit. But she was still ashamed. She had not understood until then the full extent to which her neighbours were the victims of a gathering campaign of official persecution. Danielle had explained to her in more detail the sequence of ordinances that restricted their lives. First their business activities had been prohibited, then their freedom of movement. Last August their radios, their bicycles and their telephones had been confiscated. All public parks, theatres, libraries and museums were closed to them. They were allowed to travel only in a single, crowded carriage of the Métro, and to shop at certain hours in the afternoon. And all this against an anti-Semitic campaign of unspeakable virulence being waged in the popular press. Here in Paris, the capital of civilisation, for God's sake.

She had told Jacques about it that evening when he'd come in from work. Jacques was a surgeon at the St Louis Hospital. A solid, reliable man not given to excesses of emotion: that was what had always attracted her to him, his balance and dependability as a foil to her own flights of passion. She told him of her feelings of shame when she saw the plight of the Benjamins.

Jacques nodded gravely and agreed that it was a typical Boche *grossièreté*.

'Yes, but it's worse than that, don't you see? Who's enforcing these absurd regulations, after all? Perhaps they emanate from Berlin, but it's French officials who are putting them into practice. French gendarmes, French petty bureaucrats.' She felt guilty. She was partly responsible.

'My darling,' Jacques said finally. 'It is a disgrace. One more blot on the face of France. But honestly, what can one do?'

She explained to him her scheme for making all non-Jewish citizens sew the yellow star of David on to their jackets as a gesture of protest. Even as she was speaking, she began to see the impracticalities. That made her even angrier.

'How many Jewish patients do you treat?' Thérèse's blood was up now.

'One or two.'

'I think you should be offering Jews your services free.'

'It's not as easy as that. And they have their own place. The Rothschild Hospital.'

'It's all so unfair.' That night she had shed tears of frustration. What could one do?

She poured the coffee and sat drinking it, feeling the rays of the rising sun shafting in through the kitchen window. Thinking. And finally confronting her sickening unease. What was the commotion she had heard this morning? The more she analysed it, the less she liked it. Men's voices shouting; doors slamming; the children crying; many receding footsteps on the stairs. No doubt it was one more inconvenient regulation being visited upon the unfortunate Benjamins. Some check-up on papers deliberately carried out at an hour of the day calculated to cause maximum irritation and unpleasantness. That was probably the explanation. Wasn't it?

Finally she put on her dressing gown, checked for a moment in Céline's room where her daughter still lay sleeping peacefully, and let herself quietly out of the front door of the apartment. She tiptoed softly down the stairs.

On the landing below, she paused. The Benjamins' door was firmly closed. She pushed it: locked. She knocked, twice. There was no reply. She could feel the emptiness within. Then she noticed the scrawl in chalk across the surface of the door: a series of numbers, then a tick. An official tick. As if to indicate a job carried out. She didn't like that tick. Didn't like it at all.

She hurried on down the stairs to the ground floor and tapped at the concierge's window. If anyone knew what was going on, it would be Madame Balbec. She was a clearing house for gossip, not just of the gossip of this block or street but of all Paris. She emerged grey-haired, breathless. Thérèse recognised the animation in her eyes. Excitement, tinged with fear. The same look that Madame Balbec had displayed when she'd announced the arrival in the city of the Germans in June 1940. Things were happening. Awful things. Sensational things.

'What was that terrible noise on the stairs this morning?'

'Oh, Madame Lisieux, it was horrible. So early, they came, and making such a racket.'

'Who came?'

'The gendarmes. Six of them. They had orders to take the Benjamins away.'

'All of them? The whole family?'

'All of them. They were scarcely dressed. She hardly had time to pack things for the baby. It was pitiful to hear the little ones crying. At half past five in the morning. I ask you.'

'Where did they take them?'

'They had this bus outside. There seemed to be other families on it. There were a lot of children crying.'

'Where was the bus going?'

'They wouldn't tell me. But Madame Croiset at

number forty-five, she says that they're all being taken
to the Vél. d'Hiv.'

'The Vél. D'Hiv.?'

'You know, the Vélodrome d'Hiver. The indoor
stadium on the rue Nélaton, where they have the bicycle
races.'

Thérèse ran back upstairs. We are doing these things
to these people. French gendarmes, dragging women and
children from their beds at five-thirty in the morning.
French officials, on our behalf. No time to pack properly,
even for the baby. For little Elise. She had to do something.
Take some personal action. To shake the easy acquiescence
of her countrymen in this spiral of oppression.

She let herself back into the flat and dressed quickly
in her bedroom. Jacques stirred again, but did not wake.
He had the ability to sleep deeply and at short notice,
the result of many interrupted nights on hospital duty.
When she was ready, she had to shake him to bring him
to consciousness.

'What's the time?'

'It's quarter to eight. I have to go out. Get Jeanette
to stay with Céline this morning.'

'But where are you going?'

'It's the Benjamins. They've been taken away by the
gendarmes. I've got to go and help them.'

He was sitting up now. 'Oh, my God. Taken away?
But what are you going to do?'

'I'm going to find them.' She stood up. She knew that
if she didn't keep moving she would cry and she could

not afford that. Hadn't time to allow her decision to be debilitated by tears.

'Thérèse, my darling ... don't do this. It's too dangerous.'

She turned on him, furious. Subliminally grateful for an outlet for her grief and anger. 'If you love me, just don't try and stop me. Understand?'

He got out of bed. At the door, he kissed her on the cheek. 'I do understand. I love you. Please be careful.'

No one owned a car these days. There was no petrol in Paris. It had to be carefully preserved for journeys of national importance. Like powering the buses that transported Jewish families on essential early morning trips to the Vélodrome d'Hiver. But Thérèse had a bicycle. She unlocked it in the courtyard and set off on the journey across the city to the rue Nélaton. Paris glittered in the sunshine. She crossed the Place de la Concorde. It was almost deserted. She passed the banner running almost the full length of the Chambre des Députés, blazing out its glorious message: *Deutschland Siegt an Allen Fronten.* Germany Victorious on all Fronts.

As she bicycled, she had more time to analyse her anxieties on the Benjamins' behalf. What it was exactly that she feared most for them. Danielle had told her of earlier round-ups of Jewish inhabitants of the city, series of arrests that had taken place periodically over the past year. The targets then had been poor recent immigrants, some of them lawbreakers, many of them barely speaking French, people quite different from the

Benjamins. There was apparently some sort of centre at Drancy on the outskirts of Paris where these people were held. Held, then deported to other centres in Germany. Loaded on to trains and sent to labour camps.

What if the authorities were now spreading the net wider? What if this was now to be the fate of families like the Benjamins?

She pedalled faster.

She was unprepared for the chaotic scenes that greeted her once she got to the stadium. Buses were still drawing up, spilling out their miserable human cargoes, parodies of holidaymakers on this sweltering morning, chivvied and pushed by gendarmes. They were being herded into the indoor stadium itself. Tearful mothers, wailing children, bemused and impotent fathers. Bedraggled families, some clutching suitcases, were being urged in through entrances; but iron-railinged gates were firmly locked against them at the exits.

She leaned her bicycle against an advertising hoarding and ran up to the nearest gendarme.

'Why are you doing this to these people?' she demanded. 'They've done nothing to you.'

'Move along, madame.'

'These are French citizens you're arresting.'

'I said move along.'

'Have you no shame?'

'I am carrying out official orders, madame. Now go home unless you want to get into serious trouble.'

'Cretin.'

'Right. I warned you. Show me your papers.'

Thérèse produced them, realising that getting herself arrested would not help the Benjamins. The gendarme inspected them, gave them back, and told her once more to go home. 'This is not your business, madame,' he assured her in a reasonable tone.

She moved away. Increasingly desperate, she walked slowly round the entire perimeter of the Vélodrome. At every exit point, where the gates were chained and barred, the imprisoned had gathered to plead for help through the gaps. Children separated from their parents; hysterical mothers. And an old man, his hands gripped immovably round the bars, just staring out. Not shouting, not making any noise. Just staring.

Towards the end of her second circuit of the stadium, she saw her: Danielle. At the corner, behind one of the gates, with Elise in her arms. Danielle was crying. That in itself was shocking. Danielle was not the sort of woman who cried easily, but silent tears were coursing down her cheeks. Thérèse ran towards her, shouting her name. For a moment she could not attract her attention. Then their eyes met. And Thérèse read the profundity of her despair.

They said nothing. There were no words possible. Thérèse simply made for the railings; Danielle fought her way to the front so that they could touch through the bars. Thérèse laid a hand as gently as possible on the other woman's arm. To tell her that she was ready. Although no adult or larger child could possibly have passed between them, the gaps between the iron railings at the upper level were slightly broader, and the baby just squeezed through. Thérèse took the little bundle, grasped it to her. She couldn't wait around. If she wasn't to be apprehended, if this one young life was to be saved, then she had to get away. She didn't even look back.

She abandoned her bicycle. You couldn't ride a bicycle and carry a baby at the same time. She walked quickly the length of three or four streets, anxious only to put distance between herself and the Vélodrome. Then she found a taxi, one of the horse-drawn ones that had reappeared on the streets of Paris.

The baby barely cried at all. Elise.

Back in the apartment, Jacques was waiting for her. He had delayed his departure to the hospital. He listened to her thoughtfully, his pipe clenched beneath his walrus moustache. 'Of course. You couldn't have done anything else,' he said at last.

They got out Céline's old cot that had been stored in the boxroom pending the long-yearned-for arrival of their second child. With Jeanette's help, she made it up and put Elise down in it. The baby fell asleep almost at once.

'Anyway,' she said, 'there's probably been some sort of mistake. The Benjamins will be back in a day or two, and we'll return her to them then.'

'Yes,' he agreed. 'That's what we'll do.'

No one ever heard anything of the Benjamins again.

After a week, Thérèse went down to Madame Balbec and asked to be let into the Benjamins' apartment.

Although Madame Balbec had received official instructions to keep the place sealed to everyone except the appropriate authorities, Thérèse could be forceful when she put her mind to it, and Madame Balbec duly obliged with the spare key.

What Thérèse found inside was another shock. Someone had been in and stripped the salon. The mirror was gone, and the pictures. So was the clock that had stopped at twenty to ten, and the curtains had been half torn down from their rails, so that they hung there like the sails of a shipwrecked vessel. It was the same story in the other rooms. Anything of any value had been taken.

What was she looking for? Some vestige of Elise's history and background. Something to anchor her. Some name and address of some relation, somewhere. She took a few odd letters and papers that she found in a drawer in the Benjamins' bedroom. And a book filled with handwriting that she identified as Danielle's. Perhaps they would yield some clues. And as an afterthought, she picked up from the floor of the salon a furry toy duck which she took upstairs and placed next to Elise in her new cot. As some sort of link. Some sort of memorial of the past.

Outside it had stopped raining. A limpid grey light washed the room. Thérèse sat in the shadows. Still spirited, still bolt upright. Still clutching in her contorted fingers the handkerchief with which she surreptitiously dabbed her eyes as she recounted the events that were none the less vivid for having taken place more than half a century ago.

The story continued: Thérèse and Jacques Lisieux took Stern's infant mother in for the rest of the war, looked after her as a little foster sister to their own daughter Céline. And then, after the Liberation, they had to part with her. Thérèse made contact with Danielle Benjamin's first cousin in London, Stephanie's father. She'd found his address in among the papers she retrieved from the Benjamins' apartment. He and his wife came over to collect her in the summer of 1945. Took her away by train to Calais, and then on the ferry to Dover. The route of escape which, if her parents had had their time again, they could have taken themselves in 1939. Took her away, with her few memorials of the past, the few objects that Thérèse had retrieved for her that linked her to her roots: her mother's diary; her father's identity card; the little furry duck that Thérèse had picked up from the floor of the Benjamins' ravaged apartment.

'Wasn't it hard to give her up?' Daniel demanded. Even before she replied, he realised his question was unforgivably crass.

'My little Elise?' She looked away from him, the handkerchief hovering closer to her watery blue eyes. 'It was the hardest thing I've ever done in my life.'

There was silence for a while. Daniel realised he had trespassed into a territory in his mother's emotional life where he had no rights, even as her son. The fact that his mother had never told him the full details of her relationship with Thérèse was testament to its peculiar poignancy. She must have been three years old when Stephanie's mother and father came to collect her. Old enough to feel sorrow at the parting; not old enough for the memory of her early years in Paris with the Lisieuxs to stay with her. Except perhaps subconsciously, as a formless but lingering sense of additional loss: not only had the parents she had never known been taken from her, but on top of that she had been prised from her surrogate family, too.

Daniel could not afford to dwell on it, if he wasn't going to cry himself. He didn't want to do that. Not here, in front of her. He forged on in another direction:

'Did you ever meet a man who my grandparents knew at that time, called Leblanc? Emile Leblanc?'

She thought for a moment. 'No,' she said. 'We didn't really have friends in common, your grandparents and I.'

'Do you perhaps remember a painting by Monet? The one of the poplars beside a river? Do you remember seeing it hanging in my grandparents' apartment?'

Tante Thérèse sighed and shook her head. 'I remember a clock,' she said. 'A beautiful clock that had stopped and wouldn't go again. And there were certainly pictures on the wall, but I can't remember what they were.'

She looked tired. He was about to take his leave of her when she suddenly went on, thoughtfully: 'There was one thing we could never understand afterwards, though, Jacques and I.'

'What was that?'

'Why they were taken then.'

For a moment he thought she was wandering. 'Why who was taken then?'

'The Benjamins.' She paused. Gathering the threads of memory once more. 'It was called *La Grande Rafle*, that awful thing that happened on 16 July. When all those Jewish families were arrested. But it transpired afterwards that most of the other thousands taken into the Vél. d'Hiv. that day were humble people. Recent immigrants, poor families. Not like the Benjamins. Maurice Benjamin was a fine gentleman. A respected lawyer, a man of means.'

'Why do you think the Benjamins were included?'

She frowned. 'I've thought about it a lot since. Some of the things that happened in Paris in those days were unspeakable. Perhaps your grandparents were the victims of some anonymous denunciation. Some influential person who wanted them out of the way. A professional jealousy, some old grievance. I am afraid these terrible things happened then, you see. And any Jewish family ... well, they were vulnerable.'

'Can you think of anyone in particular who might have been responsible?' Leblanc, for instance. What about Emile Leblanc?

She shook her head. 'All dead now,' she murmured. 'All too late.'

Daniel didn't press it. She was eighty-six, after all.

As he left, he took her hand in his. She looked up at him. 'The past,' she said softly. 'It's all I have. But you must go on now. Your life is in front of you.'

He kissed her forehead, then let himself out of the door.

ROME

Tuesday, 25 May

It was the beginning of the third week of Father Cambres's incarceration. Outside his window, the sun shone from a cloudless sky. In the courtyard below, as if to mock his confinement, the bougainvillaea and the hibiscus flowered in even more gorgeous profusion.

At ten-thirty, his confessor chose to come to him again. It had been almost a week since Cambres had spoken to him, and the first he knew of the visitation now was when he heard approaching footsteps along the passage, and two short, sharp knocks on the door. Then the stolid, black-robed figure of Monsignor Abello stood there on the threshold, hovering like some corpulent, dark-plumed bird. He gave Cambres a smile of greeting; a smile that was solicitous, but at the same time implacable.

'I have been praying for you,' Abello said. The words were intended as a reassurance, but implicit in them was the threat: the threat that blind conviction poses to doubt; and beyond that, the ultimate threat of authority to insubordination. Cambres raised his tired eyes towards him and regarded him dispassionately. Abello's certainty seemed momentarily enviable. Here was a man for whom all things were straighforward. For whom every issue was clearly defined in black and white.

Cambres swallowed. His voice was an unfamiliar instrument, and he was suddenly nervous of using it. 'Please come in and sit down,' he said softly, relieved that the old mellifluity had not evaporated entirely in these days of solitude and silence.

His voice. In the past he had won many victories for God with its gentle richness, exploited it ruthlessly in the persuasion of the faltering faithful to the execution of God's work. He had lived much in the world, moved among worldly people; which meant that sometimes it had been necessary to deploy worldly methods in order to achieve God's will. Pro Deo. On God's behalf. Why not? There was nothing wrong with making use of God-given advantages such as personability and persuasiveness if God's kingdom on earth might thereby be enriched. On that judiciously founded premise much of his priesthood had been based. But nonetheless, the end did not always justify the means. There was a line not to be transgressed. It was a strange thing, that boundary: he was as sure of its existence as he was unsure of its precise location in the moral landscape. But although he did not know exactly where it lay, he sensed instinctively when it had been crossed. That, after all, was why he was here now.

Abello sat on the only chair. Cambres positioned himself on the bed a little way away, facing the wall opposite rather than looking directly into the eyes of his confessor.

'I have been praying also for myself,' went on Abello. 'Praying that God should grant me the insight to clarify things for you. To relieve you of your doubts. It is a terrible challenge to be tested; but it can also be a wonderful thing, too, if you come through it strengthened by the experience.'

Tested. A priest was not like other men, reflected Cambres. His actions, his feelings, even his ailments were constantly mediated by a higher imperative. God's will. God's work. What medical opinion might in a layman call a nervous breakdown, in a priest became a crisis. A crisis of faith, perhaps. Or a crisis of obedience. And therefore a testing. Cambres spread his hands in a wordless gesture of acknowledgment of the other man's concern.

'Tell me, Father: after this period of reflection, are you still troubled?'

Troubled. Cambres considered the word. It seemed curiously inadequate as a description of what he felt. Very slowly he nodded.

'Can you tell me again: what precisely is it that troubles you?'

Cambres was silent for some time, then he sighed. That boundary again, it was as well to start there. 'There is a line,' he said at last. 'A line that has been transgressed.'

'Transgressed by whom?'

'By our Service.'

'By our Service?' Abello was like a bird again. A bird

whose territory had been challenged. He could sense the puffing up of the feathers.

Cambres sank his head into his hands, and spoke with his palms covering his eyes. 'I am sorry, but I cannot see it any other way. No doubt the motives were well intentioned, and the people concerned wished only to enhance the material interests of the Church, but they have taken a step too far. I fear they may have entered into liaisons that are ... that are ill judged.'

Abello was silent. It was almost as if he were counting to a prescribed number before speaking again. When he did so, it was more firmly. 'Listen, Father. Think back: why did you join the Service?'

He was sixty-five now. It had been thirty-seven years ago. More than half a lifetime. 'For the same reason that I joined the priesthood,' he answered. 'The better to serve God.'

'To serve God here on earth?'

'Of course.'

Cambres glanced at Abello and saw him nodding. The answer seemed to please him. Cambres was the child with his teacher. The witness being led by the expert advocate.

'Listen to me, then. In order to do God's work on earth, the Church cannot rely on its own hands alone. If we limited ourselves in this way, vowed never to accept secular assistance in our material affairs, our achievement would be impaired. God's work would suffer. One must be pragmatic.'

'Pragmatic.' Cambres mused on the term.

'Consider education. Do you not agree that to deliver to as many children as possible a full Christian education is one of our most sacred duties as a Service?'

'Certainly I agree.'

'So we must build schools? Physically construct them?'

'Of course.'

'But you would not insist that this building work be undertaken only by members of the Service, or even of the Church. For this purpose it makes sense to employ the secular construction industry.' Abello looked across at him. Encouragingly.

Cambres smiled back at him. But he knew what was coming. Abello went on, 'And if the cranes and bulldozers used happen to be the same cranes and bulldozers that have also built casinos and brothels, should we for that reason deny ourselves their employment? Of course not. They are sanctified by the purpose for which we put them to work.'

Cambres shook his head. This is all very well, he thought, this sanctification of bulldozers. But he was struggling with a problem of a different order. Evidence of a more serious complicity.

He had seen the evidence. He had seen the press cuttings and the document from the CIA. He had seen the computer print-outs, the statement relating to one of the Service's own bank accounts. He had physical possession of one page in particular. The page that had brought back events from his own past with a sudden and uncomfortable vividness. And in bringing them back in this context, simultaneously and horrifically undermined their validity.

But Cambres was aware of something else, too. That he could not admit to having seen the papers without compromising Donaghy. All he could admit to, even to his confessor, was an unease. An unease occasioned by what? he had been asked. Cambres had murmured vaguely about rumours heard by chance in the secular world. About business dealings that the Service was said to have entered into with unsuitable partners. He'd been met with obdurate denials of any sort of impropriety. And how much, anyway, Cambres wondered, did Abello know of these things? Was he merely the faithful servant, unquestioningly obedient? Who stood where in the labyrinthine organisation of the Service? With Abello he must tread carefully, walk in intricate patterns that communicated his unease without revealing the full extent of his knowledge. Without naming names. Pro Deo. On God's behalf.

To relieve the pressure of his present dialogue with Abello, Cambres decided to reverse the roles. To ask his confessor a question. He half turned on the edge of the bed, so that their eyes met briefly.

'And you, Monsignor: you are happy with the disposition of these financial matters?'

Abello sighed, and sat up straighter. 'I have made further internal enquiries on your behalf. My conclusion is that you have imperfectly understood the workings of our Service in these specialist areas. I think you must accept that you are not properly equipped to reach such an understanding.'

'But you are satisfied that . . . that those responsible are well advised, are acting properly?' Those responsible. He'd wanted to speak the name, but could not bring himself to. Help me, he was pleading to his confessor: you say it.

'Perfectly satisfied,' declared Abello.

No. No word of Tafurel. Our Service is like a furnace, thought Cambres. Those who approach it from the outside are pleasantly warmed. But we on the inside are in danger of being consumed by the flames.

Abello went on, more gently, more reasonably. 'As I say, I doubt whether you – or I, for that matter – are truly qualified to make these judgments. We must leave them in the hands of our colleagues in Christ who are expert in such fields. We must have trust in them.'

Cambres persisted. One more time. 'But you yourself, you are not troubled by any aspect of the conduct of those who lead our Service, who dictate its financial policy?'

'No,' Abello replied firmly. Unilaterally. He paused, to allow his denial maximum impact. And Cambres realised that, yet again, he had come up against the brick wall. He began to understand an uncomfortable truth: that whatever the evidence of wrong-doing he produced, it would always be denied. So long as Tafurel had authorised the transaction, no one would be able – or willing – to question it.

Abello was speaking again. Gently. Insistently. 'You know we are not just a Service fighting on God's behalf. We are also a family, joined by God's love. We care for our own. That is why it is right that you have turned inwards for help in your trouble. That's true, isn't it, Father? You have not been tempted into the disloyalty of sharing your misplaced misgivings with others ... with outsiders, who might misinterpret them?'

Cambres chose his words carefully: 'I believe, like you, that these are matters which must be resolved within the Service.'

Abello nodded, apparently satisfied. Then, insidiously, he mounted his counter-attack: 'With respect, Father, it may be helpful for you to ask yourself a question.'

'What is that?'

'Could it be that what you are suffering from here is an excess of scrupulousness?'

'An excess of scrupulousness? What do you mean?'

'Forgive me, Father, but it is fair to say that your ministry has been exercised largely among the rich and affluent?'

There was no reason why such a question should unsettle him, but it put him on the defensive nonetheless. 'I have always taken the view that the rich are as much in need of salvation as the poor,' he said. 'Perhaps even more so.'

The rich, and their needs. How well he had understood them. How skilfully he had plotted routes by which the rich might be led to salvation; plotted them, and then

persuaded suitable candidates along them. Women like
Mrs Perez.

*March in Monaco. Mink and misery. An elderly woman,
skin slackened by age then restretched by money, in an opulent
and overheated apartment. A younger Cambres austere in
clerical black, looking out from the window across the chilly
Mediterranean, relishing the magnificence of the panorama.*

'You are very lucky, Mrs Perez. It is a beautiful position
here, a lovely view.'

She shook her head in annoyance. Her crimson-painted
lips were set in a natural downturn of disaffection. 'On the
contrary, there are times when it is quite insupportable.'

'I am sorry. How can that be?'

'At the Grand Prix, for instance. This building is very
close to the route of the course. Crowds, noise; then I must
uproot, separate myself from all my beautiful things. And
in the summer: so many undesirables now. Tourists of the
lowest class. Again, I have to fly from my nest. Like a
bird.' A sudden trill of girlish laughter.

'That is hard for you, Mrs Perez.'

'No, no. Please. Not Mrs Perez. Maria.'

'Very well, Maria.'

'And I . . . well, I feel I know you too well to go on
calling you Father. Not when we are alone together like
this, enjoying each other's company. May I . . .'

'Oh, of course. Please: Alfonso.'

'So, Alfonso.' She spoke his name slowly, with an almost
sensual lingering over its syllables. 'I want you to tell me

more about the wonderful work the Service is doing now. You are aware, of course, of the long history of involvement in Pro Deo that my family has enjoyed. My uncle particularly.'

'Certainly I am aware of it.' Cambres smiled in acknowledgment and walked over to where she was sitting. 'Your uncle was one of the most generous benefactors that our Service has ever known.'

'Come and join me,' she said. 'So that I can see you properly.'

An elderly jewel-encrusted hand, fingers like lobster claws, reached out to clutch at his sleeve. As he lowered himself on to the cushion next to her, he allowed his eyes to rest for one moment on the diamond bracelet, on the huge emerald ring. Registered them, dispassionately. As a means to an end.

He said slowly: 'Our Service does extraordinarily widespread work. Few people are aware of its full extent. We do not always operate conspicuously; sometimes that is counter-productive to our purpose. But there is a particular emphasis on education. So many of the world's children need the Faith to be brought to them, are in grievous lack of it. There are so many dangers from which they need protection. From the menace of communism, for example.'

'The children,' she murmured. 'We have to win the souls of the children.'

'And of course such projects cost money. Huge amounts of money. To build schools. To send our people out to the places where they are most needed. There is a never-ending need of financial resource.'

'I wish I could offer more,' she breathed. 'All the money that Guillermo left me is tied up in investments. I have so little — how do you say it? — liquidity. But I wish to give. To support the Church. And to support you, Alfonso. To support you in your work.'

Judiciously, he moved his own hand across to touch her arm, rested his fingers on the thin flesh he could feel beneath the silk of her blouse above her elbow. For Cambres the contact was clinical, like a surgeon with a patient. A means to an end. 'There are many ways, Maria, in which you can make a sacrifice for God. There are other ways of giving.'

'Tell me.' There was an animation to her bloodshot eyes now. 'Tell me how, Alfonso.'

Of course he was aware that he was thirty-five against her seventy-five. That women found him attractive. But the fact that it affected them did not affect him. 'Perhaps there is something.' He paused thoughtfully. Then he said it: 'Some piece of jewellery, perhaps, that you no longer wear.'

She did not reply immediately to his suggestion. Indeed, when she spoke again, it was to change the subject. To rail against some shortcoming in the service she had received on a flight she had just taken from Madrid to Geneva. But a little later, when they had been through the relative merits of the various airlines, the extortionate charges of French taxi drivers for the trip to Monaco from Nice airport, and the disturbing number of Negroes one saw on the streets of the Principality these days, she sighed and exclaimed suddenly:

'Ah! My jewellery. I have so many pieces still. My late husband, he adored me, he showered me with stones. Every time he travelled abroad, he brought me back some new trinket. "Guillermo," I used to say, "how can I possibly wear all this?" It was too much, even then, when I was in my prime. He was too generous, Alfonso. He spoiled me, that husband of mine.'

Cambres smiled at her benignly. As if he could not quite see where the conversation was leading.

'I want to be part of the work that the Service does. I would like to donate some pieces. If they were acceptable.'

'Maria, this makes me very happy. I had no idea you were contemplating an act of such generosity. The Service already owes a tremendous debt of gratitude to your family. It is marvellous to feel that there is a continuation of the tradition of sacrifice in you.'

'Wait. I will go to my bedroom now. I have three or four things for you in the safe. For instance, there is a tiara. I never wear it. What use is a tiara like that to a woman of my age? And then there are two rings and a diamond bracelet. You could take them back with you to Rome tomorrow. For the children. For their education in the Faith.'

The great merit of jewellery was its easy portability. When the Perez chauffeur drove him across the border at Ventimiglia the next day, he was carrying the four items in his briefcase. He suffered a moment's uncertainty as they passed through customs, but the officers peered inside the saloon, saw the clerical collar, and waved him through. He had a small celebratory lunch at San Remo, then caught the afternoon express back to Rome.

The letter of gratitude that he wrote to her afterwards on behalf of the Service spoke of her sacrifice; of the many souls that would be saved for God by her generosity. Of her own soul's special status in the eyes of God as a result of her actions. It began 'Dear Mrs Perez', and was signed 'A. Cambres (Father), PDP'. The initials stood for 'Pro Deo Pugnamus'.

Abello was talking to him again. Gently. Coaxingly. 'I do not speak in criticism. But perhaps your proximity to worldly wealth, your exceptional knowledge of its power to corrupt, has made you oversensitive to its dangers.'

'Those dangers are very real.'

'So are the powers to resist those dangers, if God is with you.'

'Of course.'

'Think on it. Maybe you are too conscientious. Perhaps you are troubled by perils that in the ultimate analysis exist only in your own imagination.'

Abello rose to go. As he passed him on his way to the door, he put a firm hand on Cambres's shoulder.

'Thank you. I will think on it,' said Cambres, half rising. He realised he was being offered a way out. An easy exit from this cell of confinement. Here is the key of release, Abello was saying. Reach out and turn it.

But he couldn't do that. Not yet. Before he could acquiesce in such an arrangement, there were more important questions that needed to be resolved within his conscience.

PARIS

Friday, 28 May

There was an unpleasantness that morning. An incident in one of Paris's grandest art galleries. Voices were raised, and Security had to be called. A young man had to be ejected from the premises into the street. It was all handled very discreetly, though, and no one was actually hurt. Not physically, anyway.

Perhaps it wouldn't have happened if Daniel Stern hadn't woken up already angry. He hadn't slept much. He couldn't get the images out of his head. They were images of death. Of the catastrophe awaiting his grandparents, as they struggled to survive in an increasingly hostile environment, pathetically determined to hang on to their painting by Monet. Of the death that beckoned not just the adults in the family, but the boy Matthieu, too. Their son. His mother's brother. He was only seven, and they took him away as well. He was crying that morning, the little boy who swam like a frog and always took his cap off so politely to Thérèse Lisieux when she met him on the stairs.

And finally there was another, more recent death whose vividness would not give him respite: his mother's own trag-edy. He had a remorseless vision of her body lying twisted, disfigured, trapped in the mangled wreckage of her car. His mother, who'd been paying secret, valiant homage to her long-lost parents. Assembling her files. Making unkept appointments with Parnello Moran. Edging towards a reconstruction of her family's art collection. Towards the truth of what had happened to their Monet.

He set off on foot. It was a bright, clear day with a quickening breeze that blew the litter along the gutters of the Boulevard St Germain. He hoped the fresh air would clear his head. He didn't stop until he reached the Seine, where he paused for a moment, surveying the elegant spaces of the Place de la Concorde ahead, and the distant Louvre gleaming in the sun. It was no good. The beauty of Paris was no longer any comfort to him. It struck him as a mockery, a sham, like the parade in magnificent uniform of a general whose military record amounts to no more than a series of cowardly and ignominious retreats and betrayals. This place was stained, soiled by its own past. French people had done these appalling things to Jews like his grandparents. French newspapers had stoked up hatred of them. French gendarmes had forced them on to the buses, corralled them into their place of imprisonment, and finally massed them into the cattle trucks of the trains heading east. In his eyes, the city had lost its innocence.

He walked on. His appointment at Galerie Leblanc was for 10.30.

He had read up on their history, done his research. The business itself was dynastic. It had operated under the same family ownership and at the same address in the rue St Honoré since the 1870s. The present directeur, Eric Leblanc, was great grandson of the original founder, the legendary Robert Leblanc, friend of Manet and Degas, and a dealer possessed of such an intelligence and wit that even the notoriously acerbic Whistler was apparently somewhat nervous of him.

Très snob, the French called the present-day establishment. When he got there he could see why. They were very grand indeed. Galerie Leblanc made their living selling pictures, but their premises could no more be described as a shop than Maxim's could be categorised as a fast-food outlet. You entered through iron gates into a courtyard; up steps to double doors, then into a shadowy hallway hung in red damask faded to just the right degree of chic venerability. The atmosphere was palatial but discreet, understated, slightly scuffed by decades of connoisseurship; as if you had penetrated the private residence of some exquisitely tasteful aristocrat of the *ancien régime*. But Daniel was on his guard: he also knew that Galerie Leblanc had a reputation as tough, unyielding people to do business with. Iron fists in velvet gloves.

The velvet glove enveloped him as he stood for a moment in the hallway. To his left, a grand staircase swept up to the higher floors. Ahead, at an eighteenth-century desk, sat the receptionist. He was a greying, middle-aged man. Neat, dapper. Correct. He rose to greet Daniel in a movement of oddly feline grace. Daniel asked to see Monsieur Eric Leblanc. 'I called yesterday. I'm Daniel Stern.'

'Ah, Monsieur Stern. From the *New York Times*. You are expected.'

Daniel nodded. It was an extension of the truth rather than a downright lie. He'd written for the paper a couple of times last year. It was odd how even the most eminent sometimes responded to the flattery of a journalist's attention. If the bait seemed sufficiently attractive. If the prospect of an uncritically positive piece were convincingly dangled. 'The review section's running a series on the leading art dealers of the world,' he'd said on the telephone. 'I'd like to interview you because Leblanc is such a famous name, not just in Paris but across the art world.'

Leblanc was tall, rangy and bespectacled, with long, exquisitely groomed fair hair that curled over the collar of his pale blue shirt. He wore a beautifully cut grey suit and an Hermès tie. Daniel wondered how old he was and guessed early fifties, but well preserved. A skier, probably, and a frequenter of gyms. He came forward to shake Daniel's hand, moving with the sense of suppressed energy that characterises people endowed simultaneously with high levels of both intelligence and impatience.

'Please, sit down, Mr Stern.'

Daniel looked up and saw the portrait hanging behind

Leblanc. Was there a faint family resemblance? Shorter hair, and a sharper, more pointed nose than the man sitting opposite him. Small, probing, intelligent eyes. Oh, God. He recognised it then: a weasel face.

Watchful, Leblanc followed his gaze. 'My father,' he confirmed. 'Painted by Bonnard in 1937. Many leading artists tried to capture him. This, I think, was one of the most successful attempts.'

Emile Leblanc. For a moment Daniel almost lost it. All he was conscious of was a bitter, surging fury at the memory of what this man had done. But he mastered his rage. To get what he wanted here, he must continue to play a role, and play it convincingly. For as long as possible.

So he switched on the tape recorder he'd brought with him, to make it more authentic. And he began the sequence of anodyne questions that he'd prepared. About the history of the business. About Leblanc's clientèle, their exclusive image, and their current turnover. About the most expensive painting they'd ever sold. Finally, almost as an afterthought, he reached into his file and produced the photograph.

'Oh, and I wanted to ask you about this.'

'What is it?'

'A painting by Monet. The provenance is on the reverse.'

There was a brief silence as Leblanc leaned across to take the image, then sat frowning at it. He turned it over and read what was written on the back. Finally he put it down on the table, laid aside his spectacles, and contemplated Daniel. 'Why do you ask about this work particularly?' He spoke coolly, with a certain distant curiosity.

'My research team selected it at random from the many great Impressionist paintings you've sold over the years. We thought we might feature it as a typical Leblanc picture, a case history. According to the literature, you handled it in 1939.'

Leblanc paused, assessing both the painting and the proposition. 'I happen to recognise this landscape. It is of course a magnificent example, one well known to this firm since many years.' Leblanc moved his hands for emphasis. He used his hands a lot as he spoke. Daniel wondered what he'd do without them. If anything he said then would carry any sort of conviction. Any sort of credibility.

'I need a few more details about when you bought it.'

Abruptly, Leblanc stood up. For a moment, Daniel thought he was drawing the interview to a close. That this was one question too far. But instead Leblanc announced, 'If you are interested in the history of this picture, I would be happy to show you its record in this firm's archive. It may perhaps amuse you and your readership.'

Daniel followed him up another flight of stairs. Leblanc took the steps with a sudden show of athleticism, bounding away from Daniel as if releasing himself from invisible shackles. He paused on the landing to allow

Daniel to catch up, then led the way into a room shelved with rows of identical leather-bound ledgers. 'The stock books of the firm have been kept meticulously. They are rightly described as important documents in the history of art. As you probably know, many scholars are consulting them for their researches. It is always our policy to facilitate genuine scholarship.'

I do not like this man, thought Daniel. I do not like his smugness, his self-satisfaction. I do not like the way there is a little fleck of foam lodged in the corner of his mouth as he speaks.

Leblanc pulled a volume down, leafed through it, then set it on the table open at a page where a list of various pictures and the sums paid to acquire them was inscribed in fine copperplate handwriting. The last picture on the list was the Monet, clearly described as 'Poplars on the River Epte'. The measurements tallied. Everything. The entry was dated 22 October 1939.

'My father paid high prices for the time, you see. One hundred and twenty thousand francs for a Monet was not cheap.'

Daniel read across the line and found the expenditure. 'No, not cheap,' he agreed. He was delving into his memory, into the sums of money his grandmother had recorded in her diary. Identifying the discrepancy.

'But there is an explanation. You have to look at the name of the sellers of this collection. There, at the top.'

'Benjamin,' read Daniel. The anger was rising within him again. Seventy-five thousand francs. That was the price his grandmother had written in her diary as Leblanc's offer in 1939.

'You understand? A prominent Jewish family. Probably they needed the money.'

'And your firm generously supplied it.'

Daniel could not suppress the sarcasm in his tone, but Leblanc did not pick up on it. The man was absorbed now, intent upon the elaboration of his own myth. 'My father was constantly doing things for these people,' he continued. 'He was buying from them, often at inflated prices in order to help them. He felt it his duty to do what he could. Later he said to me, when he was talking about those years: *'Nous étions tous dans le même bateau. Peut-être pas dans le même cabine, mais dans le même bateau quand-même.'* Leblanc laughed. An abrupt, strangely unsympathetic laugh. A laugh like a bark.

Daniel was conscious of two alternatives confronting him. He could hit this man, punch him in the face. Now. Very hard indeed. That would be an immense relief; but it would also eliminate all possibility of further information from Leblanc. Or he could master his fury once more. Go on talking in slow, measured sentences to this smooth and despicable bastard. Go on playing the role of ingenuous, mildly sycophantic journalist. And continue to dig.

Breathing very hard, Daniel contemplated the page. 'So the Monet was bought on 22 October 1939 from these collectors, the Benjamins?'

'Exactly.'

Daniel nodded. He was leaning forward over the

table. He was aware that his hands were clenched round the table's edge in a grip of violent intensity. 'So from that moment the painting entered the gallery's stock,' he said slowly.

'Correct.'

'When was it sold on?'

'For that information, we have to check here.' Leblanc ran a well-manicured finger down the column to the right of the pictures, where various different dates were inscribed. He paused next to the Monet. 'There it is: 27 November 1942.' He turned away, reaching for another volume. 'So now it is necessary to refer to the relevant ledger entry for that time.'

'November 1942,' mused Daniel. 'Under German occupation.' It was coming a little easier now, this affectation of nothing more than journalistic interest in the unravelling of the sequence. This simulation of professional distance.

Leblanc broke away from his perusal of the records to look across at him. 'That is so. You have heard, perhaps, of the art market boom in Paris in that period?'

'Was there a boom?'

'Most certainly. Drouot, the auction house, had two years of record turnover in 1942 and '43. Why not? There was nothing else for people to spend their money on. And also very many Germans came to Paris to buy art. There was much competition. Prices rose very high.'

'A good time to be an art dealer.'

'For some, a very good time. For others it was more difficult.'

'Which were the dealers who did well?'

Leblanc stood up straight, stiffening his shoulders. Adopting an expression of sombre, high-principled regret. 'Those who were prepared to traffic with the enemy. Those who were prepared to compromise their honour.'

'Which Galerie Leblanc wasn't?' Wait for it, thought Daniel. Control yourself.

'It was my father's policy to have no commercial dealings with the occupying forces. And certainly not to benefit from – how can I put it? – the misfortunes of the Jews, whose confiscated property was on offer to be traded. Others were not so scrupulous.' He shook his head meaningfully.

There it was again: the little fleck of foam in the corner of the man's mouth. Telltale froth. Daniel struggled to retain his composure, to remain impervious, like a rock on the seashore, as this man's lies and revisions broke over him. Here was the official, sanitised version of Galerie Leblanc's war record. They were whiter than white. The truth of the Benjamin transaction had been airbrushed out of history. Daniel saw what that truth was now. Emile Leblanc had tried to buy the Monet from the Benjamins twice, once in 1939 and once in 1942. He'd failed on each occasion. But after Daniel's grandparents and their son Matthieu had been taken away to die in Auschwitz, Leblanc had somehow got his hands on the picture. There had been regular confiscations of works of art from Jewish collections, and an abandoned apartment would have offered easy pickings. Leblanc, circling like a vulture, must have swooped. Approached the agency responsible for the Monet's removal and negotiated a deal for it. Finally got his trophy. But entered the date of purchase in the stock book as October 1939, along with the other things he'd bought from the Benjamins at that point.

'So Leblanc did not do much business in the Occupation?' Daniel persisted. There was an obscure pleasure in encouraging Leblanc in his self-deception. In savouring the flagrance of the hypocrisy.

'Only deals that were completely clean. You have to look at the evidence of the ledgers. Up till 1939, transactions were running at about one volume per year. But all business from 1940 to 1945 is contained in this single ledger.' Leblanc tapped the open page in front of him. 'There it is, you see: the Monet was sold to le Vicomte Beaugard on 27 November 1942 for a hundred and twenty-five thousand francs.' He paused, frowning, calculating. 'In fact, barely a profit on the deal. But sometimes one must give up profit for principle, *non*?' He still managed to make it sound like a carefully judged commercial decision rather than an absolute moral one.

'The Vicomte Beaugard. Who was he?'

'A well-known French collector. An old client of this firm.'

'Still alive?'

Leblanc shook his head. 'He died in 1967.'

'And where is the painting now?'

Leblanc caught himself up. 'I regret, this is confidential information. I can only say that it has passed to the descendants of the Vicomte.' What Daniel wanted to know was commercially sensitive. He could sense Leblanc clamming up.

'In France?'

'No. I don't believe it is any longer in France.'

'In Europe, then?'

'Monsieur Stern, this is not information that I am at liberty to pass to you.' He let out his strange, barking laugh. 'You newspapermen are always persistent.'

Daniel walked over to the window. The curtains were beautiful, pure cream silk. And the view looked out on to a garden at the back of the building, perfectly tended, verdant with fresh spring foliage. Of course the garden was going to be perfect. It was part of the Leblanc image. They were greedy for perfection, these people. To come here was not so much to visit an art dealer as to enter a national institution. Part museum, part academy, part house of finance. Wholly distinguished. That was the image, anyway. The image sedulously projected to the rest of the world. But underneath it lay something else. Something in the past that didn't tally, that had to be concealed, disguised, rewritten.

Suddenly it was all intolerable. This papering over of evil. The lacerating injustice of the fate of his grandparents' painting. The spectacle of this man preening himself in the reflected glory of a previous generation's high-mindedness.

A high-mindedness that had never existed. Daniel had had enough. He felt the blood rushing to his head. Sometimes he got like this, he could feel it coming. He knew he was going to go for it. To blow it all. Now.

He turned back from the window and faced the man. When he spoke, he kept his voice as level and as icily cold as possible. 'Monsieur Leblanc,' he said. 'There is one thing that I do not understand. Why do you have it recorded that your gallery acquired the Monet in 1939 when it was still in the Benjamin collection in 1942?'

'What do you mean?' But Daniel had seen it. The shock. That butterfly-beat of reaction in Leblanc's eyes. That split second of horrified recognition.

'I mean that I have read the diary of Danielle Benjamin, who died in Auschwitz in early 1943. She records that the painting was still hanging in her husband's study in the rue Véronique as late as 1942. No sale actually went through in October 1939.'

'What sort of a journalist are you?' There was a sudden greyness about Leblanc's face as he spoke. It had lost all its sleekness and sheen. 'What are you writing?'

Daniel could sense the fear in the other man. A fear bordering on paralysis.

'It doesn't matter what sort of bloody journalist I am. I want to get the truth. I know the Benjamins still owned the painting in July 1942. Your gallery had possession of it by November 1942, because according to your own records you sold it then to the Vicomte Beaugard. So how did your father get hold of it?'

'I must ask you to leave. Immediately.' Leblanc reached blindly for the telephone.

'He got hold of it somehow. And it can't have been legal. I'm going to find out.'

'Security? The Archive Room, at once. Yes, an emergency.'

'What your father did to the Benjamins is disgusting, do you know that?'

'I refuse to listen to this.'

'I'll tell you something else. Emile Leblanc betrayed those people. The Benjamins were his clients and he betrayed them. Exploited them in their weakness. Read it, it's all there in Danielle Benjamin's diary. I wonder he could live with himself after that. Does it make you proud, Monsieur Leblanc, to know what your father did?'

'Here. He is insane, he's having some sort of attack. Take him out.'

The two men in leather jackets pinioned Daniel's arms, then jostled him through the door. 'You can throw me out now,' shouted Daniel over his shoulder. 'But it won't change the truth of what happened. Think about it. Bloody think about it.'

As he was bundled out of the room, the last thing Daniel heard Leblanc call after him in a thin, tense voice was: 'Naturally, all you have said is completely unacceptable.'

Unacceptable. It was a curious word to use. Particularly to a man you have just dismissed as insane.

*　　*　　*

It had come on to rain, but he kept walking because the fresh air was a relief again after the fetid atmosphere of elegant self-deceit that permeated Leblanc's premises. He followed an oddly purposeful route, down rue Matignon, and over the blustery Seine by the Pont d'Alma. Thinking. Going over it all again. He shouldn't have done it, of course. Shouldn't have lost it like that with Leblanc. It hadn't been the right way to play it. But there had been a satisfaction in shaking the man, in throwing the truth in his face. Daniel walked on round the bend of the river, checking the city map in his pocket with increasing frequency. He realised now where he was going. Realised he was looking for a particular street.

Twenty minutes later he came upon it, hiding in the shadow of the Eiffel Tower. Unremarkable enough, to the casual spectator. Just a street, to the innocent eye.

Rue Nélaton.

On one side, a modern office block, all black glass and concrete. But down the other, a line of faded nineteenth-century buildings. Yes, they were the interesting ones, because they would have been there sixty years ago. They hadn't changed. These façades were the grey and silent witnesses to the events of 16 July 1942. They'd watched the early morning buses spilling out their piteous human cargoes. Watched Thérèse Lisieux's altercation with the gendarme, observed her desperate circuit of the Vélodrome itself. They'd stood impervious as she'd made her retreat, clutching the baby. Clutching Elise. Clutching his mother.

He looked back to the other side of the road, to the modern office block. No trace of the Vél. d'Hiv. any more. Presumably that had long since been knocked down and built over. As an act of excision from history. An unspeakable episode from the past buried in the rubble. But no. Not quite suppressed. Because in the lee of the concrete and glass, hemmed in by the raised railway line of the Métro, he found a little garden with a plaque. A plaque commemorating the events of 16–17 July 1942. Listing the numbers: *4,115 enfants, 2,916 femmes, 1,129 hommes*, all imprisoned on this site, crammed like animals into the indoor stadium. Frightened, crying, desperate. Then shipped on, most of them, to their deaths in Auschwitz.

'*Passant, souviens-toi,*' the inscription exhorted. Passer-by, remember. As a mark of gratitude to those who tried to come to their aid. Who exactly had tried to come to their aid? Not many people. But Thérèse Lisieux for one. If it hadn't been for her actions that day, he wouldn't be standing here. He wouldn't be alive at all.

A bunch of long-dead flowers hung poignantly beneath the memorial tablet, garlanded with ribbons in the colours of the tricolour. On the grass below lay a couple of abandoned plastic bottles. Daniel climbed the fence and picked them up. They were unbearable lying there. Intolerably casual.

As he stood in the tiny garden of remembrance with the two plastic bottles clutched in his hand, Daniel's resolve crystallised into a single aim. He wanted justice.

He wanted that Monet back.

Not because it was rare and beautiful. He had no delusions that he was any kind of art collector. Not because it was valuable. God knew, money was the one thing that had never been lacking in his life. No, he wanted it back because it belonged to his family. It symbolised every injustice that the Benjamins had suffered over the generations; every possession stolen, every freedom denied, every act of violence visited upon them. To restore that painting to his family's ownership would be some sort of redressing of the balance; some sort of atonement for unspeakable suffering. A final release from the cage full of wild beasts. And it would be a final tribute to his mother too. An atonement for his own neglect.

He wanted restitution.

There had been other cases recently, well-publicised cases, of Jewish families getting back works of art that had been illegally expropriated from their forebears in the war. He was vaguely aware that lawyers had to get involved. Ultimately. As he turned away and began the journey back across Paris to the rue Servandoni, he thought about going to a lawyer now. It would have been a logical enough step. But Daniel Stern was not logical. Something in him, some wild, obstinate streak of independence, rebelled against the idea of dry, rational legalese being applied to this case. It wasn't a case. It was a cause. It wasn't the moment for grey men like Bainbridge to deaden its passion with their language of precedents and balances of probability, with their riders and provisions and limiting clauses. It might come to that in the end, but not yet. He wanted action. He wanted to fight. And he was going to do it all on his own. To track the picture down himself, and in the process find the clinching proof of its illegal passage from his grandparents' collection.

He was going to right the wrongs of history. Single-handed.

ROME

Monday, 31 May

It happened just before 6.45 in the evening. There was the sound of many footsteps in the passage outside. A commotion, even. Cambres knew at once that this was no ordinary visitor. Not the heavy, lone tread of Abello, his confessor. Not the softer movement of sweet, silent Sister Anna who called every Monday and Thursday to take his laundry away. There was a quick, urgent tap on the door: it was the gaunt figure of Sister Maria, breathless, awestruck, a little ahead of the rest of the party. The motorcycle outrider to the VIP.

'Father, his Eminence is on his way to see you.'

Cambres had no time to assimilate this unprecedented development. In a swirl of purple Cardinal Tafurel was upon him. A tall, thin figure with an almost ascetic face; but with an authority that went beyond the mere colour of his cassock. His presence seemed to fill the narrow room, to occupy its every extremity.

'Sit down, Father,' said Tafurel. 'Leave us, please, Tomas.'

The chaplain who had accompanied Tafurel as far as the doorway nodded and turned away, closing the door softly behind him. Cambres sank slowly on to the bed, and perched awkwardly on its edge. Tafurel remained standing, peering out of the window. He drummed his fingers momentarily on the sill; Cambres watched the episcopal ring flashing in the light of the sinking sun. Then Tafurel turned to face him. He had deep-set, watchful eyes.

'So, Father: I have been speaking about you with Monsignor Abello.' Tafurel paused; Cambres inclined his head in silent acknowledgment of his visitor's graciousness in devoting valuable time to his problems. He knew that every word he spoke now must be chosen carefully. He was not prepared to risk saying anything yet.

'Monsignor Abello is of course your confessor,' went on Tafurel. 'It would be quite improper for me to trespass on that relationship. But I am aware that your conscience is troubled. And therefore I am troubled. How could I not be anxious when a priest of your record of service to Pro Deo admits to unease? So I decided we should talk. Just you and I, before God.'

'Thank you,' said Cambres softly.

Tafurel eased himself on to the chair and drew the skirts of his cassock about him. There was a slight but perceptible increase in urgency about his manner that put Cambres on his guard. 'Will you tell me, Father, what it is exactly that is causing you this crisis?' Tafurel said. 'What is troubling your conscience?'

Here it was. The moment of ultimate confrontation. The challenge he must meet if he was to preserve the Service from evil. If he was to save his own self-respect. Cambres began slowly, feeling his way carefully forward. 'I believe that the Service, in a well-intentioned desire to increase its financial resources, has entered into certain commercial dealings with a foreign trading company called Amelga SA.' He paused to look across at Tafurel, who was nodding gently; whether in agreement or merely in indication that he understood what was being said was less clear. Cambres steeled himself and went on: 'I have heard disturbing rumours that Amelga is under investigation by the CIA. I would like to know if this is indeed the case.'

There was a moment of agonising silence. 'No,' said Tafurel quietly. 'No, it is not the case.' The denial was simple but implacable. Not so much a statement of fact as an overriding assertion of authority.

Cambres persisted: 'But it is true that the Service has disposed of an asset to these people, an asset which was a donation once given by a faithful supporter of Pro Deo?'

'If it is true, you would surely not deny to our Service the right to take such action, to raise the money necessary to do God's work?'

'Yes, but . . .'

Now Tafurel cut him short, gently but firmly. 'Listen, Father,' he said. 'I have something to put to you. This isn't really about the Service and the conduct of its financial affairs, is it?'

'What ... what is it about, then?'

'I believe it's about you. About something that you have on your conscience.'

In the distance Cambres heard Rome's traffic. Ceaseless, like a constantly murmuring sea. But another world. 'On *my* conscience?'

'Yes. Please, don't distress yourself. We are both priests, you and I, but we are both also men. Flesh and blood. Your Pro Deo ministry has been exercised among people of considerable material wealth, often of considerable personal attraction. I have great admiration for your achievements in such conditions. You have brought many souls to God – many rich and influential souls. But I want to tell you that I understand the difficulties implicit in such work.'

'Difficulties?'

'Perhaps I should say temptations, then.'

'They have been no more than ...' began Cambres.

'No.' Tafurel was remorseless. 'I understand how such a ministry's temptations might on occasion prove irresistible. Even to the most committed priest.'

Cambres closed his eyes. He sensed the pressure upon him mounting now. How Tafurel had deftly turned defence into attack. With what subtlety Cambres's weakest point was being felt out and exploited.

'I have always been sensitive to those dangers.'

'I know you have, Father. But it's precisely because of your sensitivity to those dangers that I'm concerned about you.'

'Why is that?'

'Listen to me: you have expressed reservations about certain aspects of our Service's policy in necessary areas of secular activity. Reservations that I hope you will now accept to be misguided and misinformed.'

Cambres held his breath and made a very slow movement of his head. Not quite a nod of agreement. Not yet.

'Now will you do something for me? It may be painful, but I pray that God will grant you strength enough to do it. I want you to look honestly into your own heart, and answer candidly the following question.'

Cambres looked straight ahead again; at an unevenness in the whitewashed plaster of the wall; at a small spreading pattern of hairline cracks in the surface. His left hand tightened involuntarily about the edge of the mattress.

'Are you not perhaps guilty of subconsciously transferring to the Service an accusation that could more legitimately be made against yourself? Some moment of falling short in your own personal ministry? Some moment of worldly corruption by which you were tested beyond endurance? There must have been moments of temptation in a priesthood such as yours. Intolerable moments.'

Moments of temptation. Intolerable moments. He had walked the tightrope.

There were cushions again, but this time it was high summer and they were outdoors, in a garden. A gentler, mellower sun than the Mediterranean: not Monaco now. Not Mrs Perez. No, someone altogether different from Mrs Perez. He sat on the bench, upright, exuding a certain deliberate severity, and watched his companion as she poured out tea. Watched her elegant fingers — no lobster claws here — gently caressing the rim of his cup before leaning forward to pass it to him. Then she sank back into the cushions and sighed. A dangerous languor. There was silence between them. He listened to the sounds of the garden: the buzzing of bees in and out of the roses, and the birdsong in the line of plane trees, broken suddenly by the harsh cry of the peacock on the terrace. Gradually he sensed that she was looking at him. He turned to meet her gaze. She smiled and said at last, 'Father, may I ask you something?'

'Please do.'

'Why do you have such beautiful blue eyes?' she asked with her habitual insouciance. You couldn't be angry with her. But there was an edge of something else behind the enquiry; a mystification, perhaps, a genuine quest for enlightenment. She went on: 'You know, I don't think it's right that a priest should have quite such beautiful blue eyes.'

He paused to consider the question. To give himself time. 'If I have beautiful eyes, it is only because God gave them to me. For a purpose.'

'What is that purpose?' She hovered constantly on the brink of flirtation. He sometimes speculated whether even in her prayers she didn't flirt a little with her Saviour Himself. But he knew her well enough to detect the seriousness underlying her interrogation of him, her need for spiritual sustenance.

It was that need which legitimised his presence here, made her such a rewarding subject for instruction.

'Beauty has a right use and a wrong use,' he told her. 'The true purpose of beauty is to remind us of God's sweetness and mercy. To lead sinners to God.'

Graceful hands pulling her still-lustrous hair away from her forehead. She must be — what? — fifty-two or three, but she looked much younger. Another sigh. He caught a quick breath of her scent. 'I was once a beauty, you know, Father. There was a time, not so long ago, when I had many admirers.'

'My dear, I have no doubt you still have many admirers today.'

'Ah, if you had only known me when I was younger.'

He set down his teacup, and leaned forward, letting his hand rest on her arm. This time it was not quite so clinical, no longer the entirely impersonal touch of the surgeon with his patient. There was feeling; a little electric shock of excitement as he touched her flesh. A sensation to be consigned to the category of the regrettable hazard of his occupation, to be justified by the sanctity of the ultimate goal. 'I know you now,' he said, 'and I see great beauty in you still. There are two sorts of beauty, you see, and you have been blessed with them both. There's physical beauty, but that's transient; and then there's a more lasting beauty, the beauty of the soul. You must remember that if you truly love God, your soul never stops growing more beautiful.'

'You explain things so movingly.'

'There is great goodness in you. Great capacity for your soul to grow more beautiful. Isn't that what you want?'

She was looking into herself. Serious. For a brief moment the coquette was suppressed. 'Yes,' she said. 'That's the only desire that matters now. It's going to be my salvation.'

'I pray that it will.'

'Help me, Father. What do you want me to do?'

'It is not what I want you to do. It is what God wants you to do.'

'To me, they're very much the same.' Her tone was now reflective rather than flirtatious. He decided not to obstruct the direction of the conversation by arguing with her.

'Listen,' he said. 'Sometimes what God asks you is not easy. Sometimes there is sacrifice: God asks you for sacrifice.'

'What sort of sacrifice? Tell me: I am willing.'

He heard the wind animating the trees. The sun had just sunk behind them and it was suddenly cooler. 'If you are truly willing to make sacrifices for God,' he said slowly, 'then you must start by thinking what you value most highly, and seeing if there is a way you can dedicate it to God ...'

The tightrope. Inevitably it swayed. There had been moments when he had lost his balance. Tafurel was asking him to contemplate those moments. Forcing him to. But the important thing was he'd never taken his eye off the objective. He'd always got there, reached the other side. In the end.

Dear God, he'd always got there in the end. Hadn't he?

He was vaguely aware of his own hand shaking. His gradual physical disintegration, the mounting evidence of age, held a certain objective interest but did not dismay him. Pro Deo. A life in God's service. That was its own reward. I truly believe, he told himself, that I am not guilty of the sin of vanity. He could contemplate the signs of his own decay with equanimity – the shortening breath, the murmurs in the heart. What he could not contemplate was that other, more insidious decay that was eating into the achievement of his priesthood, compromising it, undermining it. A decay for which, according to the compelling evidence of Father Donaghy, the man sitting with him in this room was substantially responsible. A decay Tafurel was not prepared to admit was happening.

He hesitated. How could he say what he really felt to Tafurel? He wanted to tell him that he understood what he was being asked, that he wished he could so easily explain away his scruples by acknowledging the fault in himself. But it was not the case: no, he wanted to say, something evil was happening, a point had been reached at which the work of the Service had lost contact with the work of God.

But instead Cambres was silent. He heard the other man draw in his breath in a long, slow sigh. Finally Tafurel spoke again. More firmly this time.

'I would be failing in my spiritual duty if I did not put one more thing to you now. Something that it may be difficult for you to accept immediately, but which I urge you to consider very seriously.'

'What is that?' Cambres's voice had sunk to a whisper. The rack of the Inquisition was a piece of distant history; but, across the centuries, he heard the turn of its screw.

'Sometimes there is an element of indulgence in a crisis of conscience. Do you not agree?'

'It is possible, certainly, but ...'

'An unhealthy pleasure in wallowing in doubt, Father. Please think about it.'

'You think my doubt is self-indulgent?'

'It is hard, I know. But there comes a point in such states of mind when the highest duty is to suppress it.'

'I should suppress my unease?'

The change in Tafurel's tempo was swift and disconcerting. He was suddenly fulminous, his words reverberating with a profound and righteous anger: 'Yes, if by its indulgent expression you are in danger of impairing the resources of the Service. Yes, if by its promiscuous dissemination you are giving succour to our enemies and reducing the power of the Service to do God's work. Remember what that work is. To fight the evil of Islam. To give Christian education to the world's children. In your self-examination, ask yourself one question: do you want it to rest upon your conscience that you have reduced the capacity of the Service to achieve these aims?'

Cambres could not reply. He was aware of Tafurel sitting still for a moment, calming the agitation of his own breathing. Reasserting his self-control. Then Tafurel stood up, and asked in a softer voice: 'Are you familiar with the Maxims of the Blessed José Maria Escriva, Father?'

'I have read them in the past.'

Tafurel reached into the folds of his cassock. 'There is one maxim which I recommend that you look up. It is Number 639. Read it, and consider it carefully.'

With an unsteady hand, Cambres took the small leather-bound book and leafed through it till he found the page he was looking for. Then he got up and walked over to the window. He stood there in the mellow Rome sunlight gazing out once more at the view that he had often contemplated in the past days. There it was: the almond tree. The introverted courtyard. The vantage point that offered no way out.

He let his eyes fall on to the page in front of him. Maxim 639 was barely a line long:

'Remain silent and you will never regret it; speak, and you often will.'

The threat was unmistakable. But so was the deal being proposed: recant and go quietly, and you will have nothing to fear.

In one way it was a breaking point; in another it was a moment of resolve, of the emergence of sudden, secret steel within him. Cambres remained staring at the short sentence for perhaps a minute. Then he took the decision. Grasped the key that was being offered him. The key to release him from his imprisonment.

He turned, and went down on his knees before

Tafurel, reaching out for the ring on the Cardinal's finger to kiss it.

'I am in error,' he said softly. 'Your Eminence has been very patient. God has opened my eyes to my own self-indulgence.'

LONDON

Monday, 7 June

'Forgive me if I look a little the worse for wear,' said Parnello Moran. His drooping eyes were particularly low-hung that morning. 'Rather a rough night last night.'

Daniel looked round the drawing room. The debris of a party: several half-drunk wineglasses, empty bottles; unemptied ashtrays. The same old stained brocade, the same peeling paintwork on the window frames, a little sadder in the harsh light of morning. The pictures on the wall looked as good as ever; except that over one frame a pink feather boa was draped, like a swag. Forgotten by one of last night's guests.

Parnello lowered himself gingerly back on to the sofa. 'I hadn't expected you to be back so soon.'

'Nor had I,' said Daniel. Not back in England. He'd come straight to Jermyn Street from Waterloo. 'I need some advice again.'

He'd spent the last seven days in Paris researching. Still angry, still bruised by his encounter with Leblanc. Reading up on the city's four years of enemy occupation.

Absorbing the background to what had happened to his grandparents, collecting material for the piece he was going to write. Reading about restitution, too. Checking recent cases of artworks being restored to Jewish families from whom they had been looted before or during the war. There were increasing numbers of them. The crucial legal point, now accepted internationally, was that any acquisition of art from a Jewish owner during the Nazi occupation of France was deemed to have taken place under duress. And therefore illegally. The transaction was invalid. It was clear enough: what he had to prove was that Leblanc had acquired the Monet after June 1940. Not in October 1939.

And then a couple of days ago he'd gone in a different direction. In search of the painting itself. He'd found an old copy of *Bottin Mondain*, the directory of the French nobility. With the help of this and various further reference books, he'd pieced it together. The late Vicomte Beaugard had indeed died in 1967. More to the point, he'd had only one child, a daughter, Gabrielle, born in 1930. She had married an English aristocrat: Edward Malpoint, 12th Lord Gascoigne, of Wenham Park, Oxfordshire. That was it. If the Benjamins' Monet had passed down the Beaugard family, as Leblanc had revealed, then this was the obvious route for it to have taken. And hadn't Leblanc let slip that the painting was no longer in France?

Parnello turned his lugubrious gaze on him and asked, 'Found the Monet?'

'I may have.'

'Coffee, Brenda!' called Parnello. 'Come on, you lazy old bat, this is an emergency.' He paused, then asked: 'Where are they, then, these famous poplars?'

If anyone could help him, Daniel had decided, it was Parnello Moran. There was something about his manner that suggested a likely familiarity with the upper reaches of English social life. 'I think they may be in the collection of Lord and Lady Gascoigne. They live somewhere called Wenham Park. Do you know them?'

Parnello frowned, and lit a cigarette. 'I know of them,' he said at last. 'I believe they have quite good pictures. But I never heard of a Monet.'

'Are they the sort of people I could ring up and ask to see their collection?'

'Definitely not.' It was the most emphatic opinion he'd ever heard Parnello offer.

'Why not?'

'I've never met them, but they're said to be prickly.'

'Prickly? In what way?'

'You know, not good form to be interested in other people's things. Unpardonable intrusion into their privacy. Traditional English prejudice against outsiders.'

Outsider. That word again. Daniel remembered why he'd left this ridiculous country for New York. He felt suddenly angry at the obstruction. Angry with the Gascoignes. Angry with Parnello, too. 'So what should I do?'

Brenda shuffled in with the coffee. Parnello poured them each a cup, laid aside his cigarette, and drank. But

Daniel knew him well enough now to see that all this was a cover. That he was thinking all the time. Concentrating. At last Parnello said, 'If you really want to get into Wenham Park, you'll have to invent a different pretext for your visit.'

'Like what?'

'Like the thing I've just remembered.' He got up with surprising alacrity and disappeared into his bedroom-cum-library. When he re-emerged some minutes later, he looked pleased with himself. He handed Daniel a piece of paper on which he'd inscribed some information. 'There you are,' he said. 'I thought it rang a bell. Lord Gascoigne's other interest in life.'

'I'm very grateful,' said Daniel as he left. 'But do you mind if I ask you something?'

'Of course not.'

'Why are you doing all this for me?'

There was a gleam in Parnello's bloodhound eyes. 'I have hunches now and then,' he said.

'What sort of hunches?'

'Just instincts. About people. And pictures. It's how I run my business.'

'That probably doesn't make you very popular with your accountant.'

Parnello brightened. 'He detests me.' He paused to stub out his cigarette. 'You see, I can't be doing with boring things like cash flows, and corporation tax, and

VAT returns. I exist for the odd, glorious deal, the one that catches my imagination because of the beauty of the picture, or the magnitude of the transaction.'

Daniel looked at him. Parnello was a curious mixture. Wild, unpredictable. An old-fashioned romantic. A man who connected Monet with Gerard Manley Hopkins. 'And what's your hunch with me?' he asked him.

'I'm intrigued by you,' Parnello replied. 'I don't know why you're looking for that Monet, but I think you're going to find it. It's a beautiful painting, and it's worth a lot of money. I smell a deal somewhere. I want to be first in line if it ever comes for sale.'

OXFORDSHIRE

Wednesday, 9 June

It was raining again as Daniel drove out of London. Warm, remorseless, early summer rain, washing the grey streets of the city, plastering prematurely fallen leaves to the pavements. He watched the endless suburbs through the regularly renewed arc of his windscreen wiper, and considered the question of guilt and innocence. His mind veered between the two polarities, as if they stood at either end of the wiper's span, measuring where on the scale he could position the actions and events with which he'd been confronted over the past month. Auschwitz. That was a pretty straightforward calculation. That came at the end of the register of absolute guilt. The people who'd driven his grandparents out of their apartment, confined them in the Vélodrome d'Hiver before loading them on to cattle trucks for the camp and their death, they could claim no innocence. Those responsible represented something close to absolute evil. Then there was his own neglect of his mother. The guilt there was less extreme, but he still felt it keenly. He had to work it out. This journey was part of the process. And now, more recently, there was Monet's eye. That was at the other end of the scale, almost totally innocent. But not quite. No sensation without perception. Ultimately knowledge was guilt.

He conjured up the image of the line of poplars, the shimmering summer landscape in whose pursuit he was now driving through the rain to Oxfordshire. Finding that painting was what mattered. Thanks to the information Parnello had given him, he was on his way. He had a foot in the door.

Daniel had telephoned Wenham Park yesterday afternoon.

'Lord Gascoigne?' he'd begun. 'My name's Daniel Stern. I hope you'll forgive me for calling you unannounced.'

'Who are you?' The voice was unexpectedly high-pitched. Aged; querulous, almost to the point of distress.

'Daniel Stern,' he repeated. He realised it was the wrong answer. To reassure Lord Gascoigne, he should have been providing a clearer map reference as to his location within the social system. What good to Lord Gascoigne was the name of an unknown North London Jew? He added, inadequately, 'I'm a writer.'

'What's that? A writer?'

'Yes, I'm just ...'

'Sure you're not a bloody art dealer?'

'Not at all, I'm ...'

'Fed up with bloody art dealers pestering me about my things.'

Parnello had been right. Daniel could see that mentioning the Monet now would not be advisable if he wanted to get to see it. 'I assure you, I'm not calling you about your art collection,' he said.

'What the devil is it, then?'

Daniel had taken a deep breath, and memorised Parnello's instructions. 'It's about Byron.'

'Byron, d'you say?'

'Yes. I'm researching a book on him, and I came across an article you wrote in the *Journal of Studies in Romanticism*, summer 1963 edition. I found it enormously interesting. I wondered if I could come and talk to you about it?'

'What? You read my article?' The softening of the tone had been perceptible even over the telephone.

'Absolutely. "A Byronic Flirtation: Two unpublished letters of October 1811."' Parnello's memory was extraordinary: before he became an art dealer, he had apparently spent three years at Cambridge studying the Romantic poets. The article, and its author's name, had stuck then. To be dislodged miraculously now, and passed on to Daniel.

'Well, I'll be jiggered. Read it, did you? Rotten bad stylist, aren't I?'

'Not at all. I found it very clearly expressed.'

'Make any sense to you?'

'A lot of sense. But it raised several questions that I'd appreciate discussing with you. In person. Would that be possible?'

There had been a pause before he answered, 'I don't see why not.'

'I'll be driving past your house tomorrow. Could I drop in?'

'Come to lunch, why don't you?' His elation peaked, then fell away almost audibly. The note of querulousness returned and, in inverse proportion to his mood, his voice rose an octave. 'But don't expect the bloody Ritz. Two million unemployed, and still can't get any staff. It's wretched here, perfectly wretched.'

If anything, it was raining even harder as Daniel swung the hired car through the gates and followed the drive about a quarter of a mile through parkland. Even under grey and watery skies the house, when he came upon it, was sublime, a Palladian masterpiece in mellow Cotswold stone. It was an effortless beauty, each elevation achieving a seemingly uncontrived perfection of proportion as if measured by some divine caliper in the eye of the architect. He parked, hurried across to the pedimented porchway and rang the bell.

He was greeted by a housekeeper, a short, tight-lipped woman. 'Lord Gascoigne's waiting for you in the drawing room,' she said.

As he followed her through, he scanned the hall-way and the stairwell for pictures. Most of them were portraits. A late-eighteenth-century gentleman and his wife: he confident, proud, imperious; she sly, crabbed and scheming. A willowy, languidly good-looking young man of a generation later. A vapidly beautiful woman of the 1920s standing full length in a garden. He glanced farther up the stairs and caught a glimpse of a dark Dutch seventeenth-century landscape. So far a typical English collection. Tasteful, predictable. But no Monet. Perhaps in the drawing room? He felt a little charge of anticipation as they approached the door.

He was shown in, and took advantage of the room's apparent emptiness to run his eyes quickly round the walls. A change of mood here, which momentarily elated him. More light, more colourful. Perhaps more French. He went up to one and saw from its label that it was by Vuillard. Good pictures. But still no Monet. And then he realised with a shock that he was not, after all, on his own. The figure of his host stood motionless at the window in the far corner of the room, staring out at the rain. He was a thin, angular man with sparse white hair. As Daniel walked towards him, he still did not turn round. His whole stance was a contortion of fury: liver-spotted fists clenched, watery blue eyes narrowed, as he watched the rain streaming from the sky.

'Oh, God!' he exclaimed with unalloyed rancour. 'Oh, God! How like you!'

It took Daniel a moment or two to realise that the man was actually addressing the deity in conversation, rather than merely invoking his name. Lord Gascoigne gave a little disgusted snort; a snort of weariness, frustration and disappointment. Infinite disappointment.

He turned to face Daniel. 'Partridges drowned. Hay's rapidly spoiling. Hurrah for the kingdom of heaven.'

'You believe that God is personally responsible for the weather?'

'If He isn't, He damned well should be. And if He is, He's making a pretty poor fist of it.' He paused, thoughtfully. 'Lot of nonsense, anyway. Humbug. Can't be doing with it. Drink?'

'Could I have vodka?' asked Daniel. He suddenly felt he needed it.

'Don't see why not.' Gascoigne moved stiffly over to the drinks tray.

While he was pouring. Daniel looked at the photographs arrayed in silver frames on the table near by. He recognised a much younger Lord Gascoigne in morning coat leaning awkwardly against a balustrade. He clasped the hand of a remarkably striking woman in a wedding dress, draped gracefully over the same balustrade. Whereas Gascoigne stood against it rigid like a ladder, she decorated it like wistaria. Lady Gascoigne was not beautiful exactly, but she had an unmistakable elegance, a style about her. An animation, too. Even in this black-and-white photograph, taken forty or fifty years ago, her eyes flared as if powered by a higher voltage than her husband's.

Fretfully, Gascoigne handed him his drink. 'Bring it through to luncheon. Just the two of us, I'm afraid.'

Lord Gascoigne's mood marginally improved in the dining room, but Daniel recognised that his host's contentment would always be a precarious state. Daniel, who had spent last night reading the summer 1963 edition of the *Journal of Studies in Romanticism*, attempted to sustain the mellowness as far as he could by conversation about Byron. It emerged that Lord Gascoigne had various Byron letters in his family's possession, some of them unpublished. There had been a brief dalliance between the poet and a wild Gascoigne forebear, a girl whose passionate disposition was later broken by half a century's monotonously respectable marriage to a High Court judge.

'Take you up afterwards,' said Gascoigne. 'To his room.'

'Byron's room?'

Gascoigne nodded. 'Great man slept there a couple of nights. In 1811. I keep the letters there, and various other bits and pieces. You might care to read through them. For your research.'

'I look forward to it. Thank you.'

'Extraordinary thing, that. Your coming across my article.'

'Lucky for me,' said Daniel. 'Do you still write?'

'Not for a long time now. Published in a couple of piddling reviews thirty years ago. You know, the sort of serious periodicals eagerly read by their contributors.'

Daniel smiled, and drained his vodka.

'"Who would write who had anything better to do?"' quoted Gascoigne. '"Actions – actions, I say!"' Gascoigne completed the poet's exclamation with a heavy irony. 'All very well for Byron. Bit more difficult when you're seventy-nine.'

Daniel asked him where his original interest in the poet had sprung from.

'Dreadful bounder, wasn't he, really?' In his quick, rueful laugh Gascoigne allowed a glimpse of his own charm to surface. 'But something in him I admire. The way he attacks life. Refuses to be short-changed.'

They ate steak and kidney pudding and drank claret. After an interval, Gascoigne became fretful again and said: 'Ring the bell, like a good fellow. It's at my wife's end of the table.'

Daniel rose and located it, taped to the underside of the rich mahogany surface. He wondered about Lady Gascoigne. Where was she? He thought of the wedding photograph: what was she like now? Almost immediately the unsmiling housekeeper brought in Stilton. Gascoigne contemplated the cheese and emitted a little grunt that Daniel guessed was as close to an expression of satisfaction as his host was ever likely to approach.

'Suffered all my life through being married to a French woman,' he confided. His tone was different now, reflective. Almost as if he were talking to himself. 'Had to live with the French cuisine. Relief to get some plain English cooking.'

'I am sure there are compensations about a French wife.'

'Such as?'

'I notice you have some very beautiful French paintings in the drawing room, for instance.'

Gascoigne regarded him suspiciously, then nodded.

But you could see him retracting into his shell. 'My wife's family things,' he said abruptly.

'She inherited them?'

'Her father fancied himself some sort of connoisseur. Pompous ass.'

'You didn't get on with your father-in-law?'

'The Vicomte united all the worst characteristics of the French male. In my humble judgment.'

Daniel went for it then. Risked it. 'I seem to remember hearing somewhere you had a Monet?' he said.

Gascoigne completely disregarded the question. He folded his napkin in front of him very deliberately, and frowned. It was not so much intentional rudeness, Daniel decided. It was more that his host suffered from chronic mental restiveness. His mind was like an old woman's sewing basket, into which he was liable to delve without warning and come up with something different to work upon. To worry at.

'You religious?' he demanded, resuming the threads of their earlier conversation.

'Sometimes,' said Daniel. He watched the other man's cheeks reddening, a network of tiny inflamed veins, like a map of the Greater London trunk road system.

'It's the sheer bloody gall of God, isn't it?' Gascoigne continued. 'When you think about it?'

'Gall?'

'Yes. Almighty, omnipotent, all-seeing. And yet He allows all these appalling things to happen. What is He, some kind of sadist?'

Daniel could sense the other man's gathering fury, and felt powerless to defuse it. 'Perhaps it's just periodic negligence?' he ventured.

Gascoigne let out a small explosion of scorn. 'Periodic negligence!' he repeated bitterly. 'World wars. Earthquakes. Cancer.'

We can all do those lists, thought Daniel. Concentration camps. Auschwitz. Random accidents on motorways.

'What's God up to?' challenged Gascoigne. He was tense, like a terrier with his ears back. A terrier who wouldn't let go. 'What's He doing allowing all this innocent slaughter? Blighter's constantly taking His eye off the ball.'

Daniel suddenly realised something. That this was an argument being rehearsed not so much for his own benefit, nor indeed even for God's. No. These shots were being directed at another, quite separate target. At someone in Gascoigne's life for whom religion had been an incomprehensible and therefore much-resented solace.

Gascoigne sighed. When he spoke again it was in a much softer, more tortured voice. 'And then Gabrielle,' he breathed. He shook his head, and looked at the table in front of him. 'Wretched thing. Utterly wretched.'

The silence was intolerable. 'Gabrielle?'

'My wife, damn it.' Lord Gascoigne was staring very hard at the salt cellar.

'Your wife.' Miserable pieces of the other man's unhappiness were falling into place.

'That's how God rewards the faithful. Some advertisement for belief in Him, eh?'

Daniel searched for some word of consolation, but could come up with nothing. Gascoigne went on, 'Agony, she suffered at the end. And half her life spent on her knees in that wretched church.'

His bony hands gripped the arms of his chair with a taut, prehensile passion. Daniel feared that at any moment the wood might splinter; and at the same time he was overwhelmed by an unexpected sympathy. Such bitterness must be exhausting, such aggression could allow no peace; here was a man for whom suffering was only rendered bearable by the ceaseless quest for someone to blame; for whom old age, far from offering a respite from the cares of the world, merely accentuated his impotence to do anything about them.

'She's still here, you know. In this house.' Gascoigne spoke more softly again, as much to himself as Daniel. 'I see her sometimes. Going into rooms just ahead of me. One evening last week, blow me if I didn't come across her at the end of the rose garden. But I can never quite catch up with her. She's always just gone when I get there.'

'I am so sorry,' murmured Daniel. He wondered how long ago Lady Gascoigne had died. Not long enough for Lord Gascoigne to reposition the bell up at his end of the table. He found that rather sad.

*　　*　　*

Half an hour later Gascoigne led Daniel up the stairs to the Byron room. Above the fireplace stood a marble bust of the poet, a romanticised image by some obscure Victorian. As Daniel inspected it, his host said: 'Always amused me, that bust. Given Byron's views on English sculpture.'

'What were they?' Daniel wondered if he ought to know. There had been no mention of them in Gascoigne's article.

'An English sculptor is no more plausible than an Egyptian skater.'

Daniel laughed, rewarded. It was the first time he had seen an expression of unalloyed pleasure cross Gascoigne's face. Short-lived, perhaps. But worth it.

Gascoigne produced a green leather-bound file, which he laid out on the desk. 'I'll leave you to it,' he said. 'Generally take a nap myself at this time of day.'

He paused at the door. Retrieving another thread. 'Monet's hanging in Gabrielle's bedroom,' he muttered, and hobbled off down the passage.

Daniel spent an hour with the letters. He felt he owed it to their owner to read them carefully, making occasional futile notes for the non-existent biographical study that he had claimed to be writing. But the truth was these pages were oddly dull. Of the three love letters to the Honourable Sybil Gascoigne that he found here, two were written from London and one from abroad. The farther from her that Byron travelled, the more mechanical and uninspired they became: Byron raking the dying embers of a passion that had already burned itself out. By the end, if you read between the lines, it was Byron railing not so much at the misery of missing his mistress as the misery of not missing her. Funny the way Daniel understood that so clearly. He remembered Holly. He'd been out with her for three months last year in New York. He'd liked Holly, but it hadn't worked. 'The trouble with you, Daniel,' she'd told him sadly, 'is you may think you want a long-term relationship, but I reckon you're just not built for one.'

He tried to imagine Byron waking up in this room. He got up and walked to the window to see what view would have greeted him. Formal gardens below. Farther on, a patchwork of fields ripening towards harvest. In the distance, a line of electricity pylons. Above, rolling grey clouds continued to merge and separate in their slow patterns of oppression. The gently taunting patter of the rain on the sill was the only sound he heard in here. Regular, incessant. Dank, English summer days. No wonder Byron had sought refuge in Italy and Greece.

Out in the corridor, Daniel paused to listen. The house was very still. Whoever had cooked lunch had long since finished in the kitchen. Somewhere Lord Gascoigne would be sleeping off the claret in dark, resentful dreams. Daniel was enveloped by the silence. He walked slowly forward, wondering which door led to Lady Gascoigne's bedroom.

He tried two handles. The first was locked. The

second opened to a deserted spare room. He advanced on the third, praying he wouldn't be disturbing his host. The fat knob turned in his hand with an unexpected smoothness.

He saw her immediately. The woman on the bed was lying on her side, facing away from him. She was completely naked. She looked back over her shoulder and regarded him for a moment, perplexed rather than shocked. She had short, dyed blond hair, and brown skin. Tanned all over, even where her buttocks swelled out from the small of her back. Without haste she laid aside the magazine she was reading, reached for a silk dressing gown and pulled it round her. Then she said, 'Don't you knock?'

'I am really sorry,' he said.

'Makes life more interesting, I suppose.'

'I'm Daniel Stern. I was here for lunch with Lord Gascoigne.'

'So you were the lunch date I couldn't face.' She stood up, knotting her dressing gown and pulling her hair back from her forehead. 'Papa told me you'd only be talking about literature. I decided to have a tray up here instead.'

'You don't like literature?'

'Not much. Not Papa's sort, anyway. My name's Sybil, by the way.' She smiled at him, a little wearily. She was older than he'd thought at first. Thirties, rather than twenties, with an air of jaded experience that produced a superficial flippancy, but an ultimate guardedness, too. From her eyes, he guessed she was more of her mother's child. But her name was unquestionably her father's choice.

'You don't live here?'

'God, no. I'm just staying for a week to keep the poor old boy company. He's been so bloody miserable since Mummy died. My summer penance. I try to cheer him up.'

'Not always easy, I imagine.'

'So you've noticed a certain tendency towards moroseness?' She laughed mirthlessly.

'I was looking for your mother's bedroom,' said Daniel. 'Will you show it to me?'

'My mother's bedroom?'

'Your father told me I could look at the Monet.' It was an extension of the truth, rather than a downright lie. The sort of thing at which journalists are rather adept.

'Oh.' She sighed. 'The Monet. You'd better come with me.'

When they reached the door, she paused before opening it. 'My father hates coming in here, you see. It causes him too much pain. But he won't have anything touched. The room has to be left exactly the way she had it when she was alive.'

Inside, it smelled musty and unaired. The curtains were drawn, creating a landscape of dark shapes and long shadows. They stood for a moment on the threshold. 'I don't come in here much myself, either,' said Sybil. 'I'm afraid it's all a bit macabre, isn't it?'

'How long ago did ... did your mother die?'

'Nearly three years.' She shrugged, and toughed it out. 'I suppose we're going to have to wait until my father croaks before it can be cleared out properly.'

She walked across and opened the curtains. The contents of the room were bathed in grey afternoon light. The ornately draped four-poster bed. The dressing table with its bottles and brushes. The sofa with a dressing gown neatly folded across its back. She shivered slightly, then said: 'It's strange, isn't it? All her things, just as she always had them. And yet I don't feel anything of her here. She's gone. It's empty.'

'And there's the picture,' said Daniel.

It hung on the wall opposite the bed. The Monet. His grandparents' painting. The one Leblanc had wanted so much that he'd perhaps been prepared to consign the Benjamins to Auschwitz in order to secure it. The painting his mother had been trying to locate when she died. For a moment Daniel's head swam. It was incongruous to see it hanging here, in the bedroom of such a quintessentially English country house. It didn't belong here. It belonged to his people. It belonged to him.

'Yes,' said Sybil. 'Mummy hung it there so she could see it first thing, when she woke up.'

He walked over to the picture. The image of the poplars was spectacular. Their thin trunks strung vertically across the landscape like flagpoles; sunlight flooded through their foliage. Pure optical sensation. Except no one's eye was entirely innocent.

What should I look for? he had demanded of Parnello. If the unthinkable happens, and I actually find myself standing in front of it; the Monet, in the Gascoignes' house. What do I need to check when I see it?

Check the condition of it, Parnello had told him. Impasto. He must look for the impasto. The brushstrokes, the way the artist has applied the paint to the canvas. Was it fresh, had it still got its edge? Could he run his finger over the surface and feel it like a relief, sense the different thicknesses of pigment? That was the first thing. Then he must get a look at the back, that was important too. See if the canvas has been relined, if it looked new. Because if relining wasn't done sensitively, it distorted the paint. A bit like a face-lift that's gone wrong, stretching the skin in unnatural directions. And he had to look at the back of the frame and the stretcher — that was the wooden structure that the canvas was tacked across. He should find dealers' stock numbers and exhibition labels there. Anything he could read he should make a note of, any numbers or stencilled letters. And then he should bring them back for Parnello to check them out.

Impasto. Right. He needed to get to the surface of the painting. He found this wasn't immediately possible because there was glass in front of the image. A thin film of dust obscured his view. He brought out a handkerchief. 'Do you mind?' he asked Sybil.

She had come over and was standing next to him

now. 'It is rather disgracefully dirty,' she said doubtfully. 'I suppose it can't do any harm.'

Daniel rubbed away a little window. Perplexed, he enlarged it. What he could make out through the glass still didn't look much like a painting. The impasto certainly wasn't there. The surface was glossy and very flat. Like a photograph. 'Does that look a bit strange to you?' he said to Sybil.

'I don't know,' she said. But her voice betrayed anxiety. She'd seen it too.

'I think we should take it down and look at the back.'

As she helped him unhook it from the wall she suddenly breathed, 'Oh, God.' As if she sensed something terrible was about to happen.

They lifted it gently to the floor. The ornate eighteenth-century-style frame seemed authentic enough. But when they turned it round, they found it enclosed no canvas, no stretcher. Just a shallow, very modern-looking board, held in place by shiny screws.

They managed to loosen them with a nail-file, then gently prise the entire backboard out of its frame. And once they could see the front without the glass, there was no doubt. No impasto, no brush strokes. No paint at all. They were looking at a large, high-quality, coloured photograph. Convincing enough under the dirty glass in this shadowy room that few people ever came into. Convincing enough, until someone looked carefully at it.

His gaze engaged Sybil's. 'Did you know this? Did you know it was a photograph?'

'Of course I bloody well didn't.' But he'd seen it there, for a moment, in her eyes: not just shock and incomprehension. Fear, too.

'When could it have happened?'

She shrugged, hopelessly. 'I don't know.' She stood there, pulling her dressing gown tighter about her. Abruptly she said, 'You'll have to excuse me.' There was a new tautness to her voice, as if a line of defence had suddenly and unexpectedly collapsed. 'Just put the painting back on the wall and shut the door after you, OK?'

'Are you all right?'

'Of course I'm all right.' But she looked very pale. 'I'm going to put some clothes on. Any objections?'

In the doorway she turned back towards him. He saw it clearly in her face then, the vulnerability that she was so anxious to conceal from him. 'He must never be told about this,' she said.

'Who?'

'Papa, of course.'

'No, all right.'

'The shock might kill him.' She paused, then added: 'No, it would be worse than that. It would be one more reason for him to go on living bitterly.'

Slowly Daniel fitted the large coloured photograph back into its frame. Labels, Parnello had told him. Look for labels and numbers. While there was obviously nothing significant on the back of the new board on which the photograph was mounted, the back of the frame was more revealing. Then the explanation came to him: the original canvas had been taken away, but the frame had been left. There were old exhibition labels attached to it. Totally authentic. And various stock numbers, one sequence stencilled, 'UNB 174', and another stencilled in blue, 'LB 12376'. He made a note of both of them before he rehung the picture. He'd take them back to Parnello, see if he could make any sense of them. He worked in a cloud of disappointment, thwarted and perplexed. Why had this much-prized painting turned out to be no more than a coloured photograph? Who had taken the real one, and when, and where was it now?

He walked across to the window to redraw the curtains, to shroud once more in darkness this sad, mysterious room with its baffling secret. On the sash Daniel noticed a comatose moth. What Gabrielle Gascoigne would have called, perhaps, *'un papillon de nuit'*. He brushed it gently with his finger to urge it into motion. The moment he touched it, it didn't fly away but suddenly crumbled. Flaked away like dust.

Daniel met Lord Gascoigne in the hall.

'Letters helpful?'

'The letters? Oh, yes, thank you. I took some very useful notes.'

'Stay to tea, won't you. It's in the drawing room.'

Lord Gascoigne led the way through, walking even

more stiffly after his nap. Sybil was already sitting there with the tea things in front of her. Dressed, she looked different. Demure, apparently poised.

'Met my daughter?'

'I have indeed.'

Sybil smiled up at them. 'Mr Stern's seen rather a lot of me, actually,' she said. She seemed recovered after the shock of their discovery in her mother's bedroom. Prepared to put on an act, at least, for her father's benefit. 'Milk with your tea, Mr Stern?'

Daniel took the cup. 'Thank you.'

'Thought I heard you in my wife's bedroom,' said Gascoigne gruffly, stirring his tea. 'Find the Monet?'

'I showed it to him, Papa,' said Sybil quickly.

There was an uneasy silence, then Gascoigne sighed and went on: 'Always her favourite, that picture. Kept it close to her. People who knew a bit about it said it was a good one. A damned good one.' He looked across at Daniel; fiercely, as if challenging him to disagree with the verdict; and at the same time pleading, appealing to him for confirmation of his wife's good taste.

He must never know, they'd agreed upstairs. Never be told the truth, that it was just a coloured photograph. Not a painting at all. That the Gascoignes had been the victims of some quite devastating scam. Someone had substituted a worthless photograph for the original Monet. An asset that should have been worth millions of pounds was actually worth nothing at all. Daniel said quietly, 'It's a very beautiful landscape.'

The strange thing was, Daniel suspected Gascoigne might have coped if it had just been the financial loss. This was not a house that would fall for want of the price of a picture, even one as valuable as the Monet. But he sensed that the pain the revelation would inflict on Lord Gascoigne wouldn't be so much about the money. It would be about the desecration of his dead wife's bedroom. The defilement of her most precious possession. The insult to her memory. It would be a grief greater than the old man could bear.

All that Daniel understood. Grief and guilt about the past: he was expert in them now.

Soon after tea, Daniel felt it was time to go. As he got up, Sybil did so too, unwinding herself from the sofa. 'Driving back to London, Mr Stern?' she asked.

He said he was.

'Could I beg a lift?'

'Of course you can.'

'You going up to town?' For a moment Gascoigne seemed perturbed. Disorientated. 'I thought you were staying with me.'

'I am staying with you. It's just that I've got that client to see in the morning in Chester Square. The American, you remember: I told you about him. Don't worry, old thing, I'll be back here tomorrow evening.'

She kissed him lightly on the cheek.

Gascoigne shrugged. 'If you must,' he said.

But as they ran through the rain to Daniel's parked car, he looked back and saw the wiry figure of Lord Gascoigne framed in the porch, raising an anxious hand in farewell. Proud. Bitter. Infinitely vulnerable.

ROME

Wednesday, 9 June

A priest, walking slowly down the Via dei Coronari towards the Piazza Navona, carrying a small suitcase. Nothing unusual, in this city of priests. Except that this one cut a particularly elegant figure in his well-tailored dark suit, with his distinguished aquiline face. The clerical collar somehow added piquancy to his ageing but unmistakable good looks. Father Cambres shuffled as he negotiated occasional obstructions in his path: a knot of chattering nuns here, a souvenir seller there; a wider detour to skirt a group of backpacked German students resting on a wall drinking Coca-Cola, all long brown legs and sweaty T-shirts. It was five in the evening, but the summer sun was still hot, and he clung to the side of the street where there was shadow. He wasn't sure who, in his mind's eye, he most resembled: a boy allowed out of school at the end of term, or a patient coming out of quarantine after an infectious disease. Or perhaps, he reflected, it was neither of these: more accurately, he was a prisoner on early release for good behaviour from a house of correction. A prisoner who'd served the minimum term. A prisoner who had seen the error of his ways.

The brightness of the sun and the noise of the traffic were a shock after the days he'd spent cut off from the outside world in the hermit-like seclusion of the Pro Deo cell of retreat. He was going home, back to his little apartment in a narrow street near the Pantheon. He looked forward to its comfort and peacefulness as a refuge after the introverted, claustrophobic existence of the tiny room overlooking the courtyard with the almond tree. He looked forward to getting back to the familiarity of his own things. His books, his pictures. His own coffee pot.

As he walked, Cambres considered his own reinvention. How he had become devious in order to achieve his release from the whitewashed cell. How he had become adept in the sort of spiritual duplicity necessary to sustain his reassumed role as the obedient soldier of Pro Deo. Expert in deploying forms of words that told his interlocutors what they wished to hear without deviating significantly from the letter of the truth.

'My conscience is eased,' he had told Abello after Tafurel's visit. 'His Eminence has explained things to me in such a way that I now see more clearly in what direction my duty lies.'

'What you say makes me glad,' Abello said. 'It is what I prayed for. So the doubts that you expressed to me have been allayed?'

'I thought very long about the element of self-indulgence that is often present in a crisis of conscience. It became clear to me that no useful purpose was being served by the expression of my doubts. That one of the weaknesses of my service as a priest has been a tendency to indulge myself.'

'You have been terribly tested,' Abello told him. 'But the experience will have strengthened you.'

Remain silent, and you will never regret it. Speak, and you often will.

He traversed the Piazza Navona, crossed the Corso Rinascimento and moments later he was there, unlocking the street door and beginning the long climb up to the third floor. It was cool in the stairwell, and he paused on the first landing to savour it and catch his breath. This apartment was the major luxury of his life; the privacy that he had bought himself twenty years ago when he'd inherited some family money. Owning it set him apart from most of his colleagues in the Service who lived in Pro Deo houses of residence, gave him independence. This was his private refuge. This, and his sister's beautiful house amid the orange groves outside Seville where he always went for four weeks each summer. Yes, he was privileged. Had he not recently confessed to Abello that one of the weaknesses of his service as a priest was a tendency to indulge himself?

He reached his own front door and turned the key in the lock. To his surprise, it was already open. He pushed inside, and there it was. The devastation. Books from his shelves scattered on the floor. The drawers from his desk pulled out and their contents spilled over the carpet. The Spanish seventeenth-century Madonna and child, his beautiful oil painting on panel, hanging askew on the wall.

The uniformed carabiniere stood in the middle of the room shifting uncomfortably, a mixture of deference and commiseration. 'It is a bad business, Father. No one has any respect any more. Had you been away for long?'

'Nearly a month,' said Cambres. 'I was ... I was on a retreat.'

'None of the neighbours seem to have heard anything. I've checked. But there probably wasn't much noise. The thief just picked the lock and helped himself. Has a lot been taken?'

'Nothing.' Cambres was perplexed. There hadn't been very much to take, but it was strange that two rather beautiful pieces of eighteenth-century silver on the table in his bedroom had been left untouched. It made him wonder why the thief had bothered.

'Videos and computer equipment, that's all they're interested in these days.'

'I don't have either.'

'No, well, the thief probably gave it up as a bad job.'

Yes, but if all he was looking for were videos and computer equipment, why rifle the desk drawers? Why go through the books on the shelves?

The answer came to him suddenly, as he stood there with the policeman. Whoever had broken in had been looking for something specific. A document, perhaps. A piece of paper. And all at once Cambres realised that what he was dealing with was something too close to home. Something too sensitive. Something he couldn't speak about to the civil authorities.

The carabiniere left soon afterwards. As he went he protested his regret once more at the incident. No effort would be spared in the fight against crime in general and the search for this criminal in particular. Presumably the speech made him feel better about it, at least.

As soon as Cambres had shut the door behind him, he went to look for it. The sheet of paper that Donaghy had given him at the Lazio game a month ago. The sheet of paper that he'd had the forethought to hide under the loose floorboard beneath the lower left foot of his bed.

They hadn't found it. It was still there. Intact.

He pulled it out, held it in his hand. There were the figures denoting such vast sums of money. Account numbers. And a name and address. Part of him rejoiced. And part of him felt very tired and frightened.

He was sixty-five, after all, and the strain was getting to him. The strain of conducting the sort of secret life into which he had been unwillingly propelled. Perhaps the simplest way out was to forget it. To give up. To plead ill health, to take retirement. To withdraw to the comfort of his sister's house, near Seville, and lose himself in the orange groves. A quiet life. But he knew his conscience would not allow him to run away now. There were too many untied strings, too many ambiguities from earlier in his priesthood remaining to be resolved. If he did not stay to put up a fight now, he feared they would all be corrupted. Then his whole priesthood would have been in vain. A force for evil, not for good.

This was the last great challenge of his life, he realised: his personal reconciliation of the present with the past. What he hadn't understood until now was the opposition that existed to his meeting that challenge. The vested interests that could not afford for him to succeed. A shadowy but implacable force was arrayed against him in his struggle; a force whose ruthlessness frightened him. If these people didn't balk at ransacking his apartment, how much farther might they be prepared to go?

Thoughtfully, he replaced the paper beneath the floorboard and pushed the bed back over it.

OXFORDSHIRE

Wednesday, 9 June

Daniel negotiated the dripping Oxfordshire lanes, uneasily aware of the restless proximity of Sybil Gascoigne in the seat at his side. He had not worked her out yet, had not got to grips with her complexities. She was difficult to approach on any terms other than her own. And the question of the Monet hung over them both, as bleak and oppressive as the rain-clouds massed above. He took comfort from the fact that driving is a legitimate excuse for not looking the person you are talking to directly in the eye.

'You work in London?' he said to her. Staring straight ahead.

'For my sins.'

'What do you do?'

'I'm an interior decorator. I've got this little business in South Kensington. Just me and a nice Sloaney assistant.'

'Going well?'

'It is rather. For the minute I've got more work than I can cope with.'

'That's very clever of you.'

She shrugged. 'Needs must. My poor pathetic husband waltzed off with some Australian bimbette five years ago. It lasted about three months, but I wasn't going to hang around waiting and moping. I had to get out. Get out and do something.'

She was an odd mixture, he reflected; not quite what she seemed. Ostensibly she fitted neatly into the familiar category of capsized divorcee: blonde, mid-thirties, slightly blowsy; loved and left stranded, beached in some desperate marital no-man's-land where the chances of happiness second time round are terminally blighted and the only weapons of self-defence are cynicism and envy. But there was more to her than that. The way she spoke of her former husband betrayed not just bitterness but an element of pity, too, as if the experience of her abandonment had convinced her not so much of the cruelty of the male sex as its hopeless inadequacy. Her cynicism was based on an unexpected strength rather than weakness, on independence rather than despair. He heard her asking. 'And what do you do, Mr Stern? How do you keep the wolf from the door?'

'A bit of writing,' he said vaguely.

He was aware of her eyeing him sceptically from the passenger seat. 'I don't know why, I had you down for an artist.'

'An artist?'

'Yes. I just wasn't quite sure which sort.'

'How many sorts are there?'

'In my experience, only two: either piss- or con-.'

He thought about it for a moment. 'I'm probably a bit of both, then.'

As they fed on to the M40, the rain had eased to a light drizzle. The red rear lights of a hundred cars snaked away ahead of him, their reflections dancing in the wet surface of the carriageway. There was some sort of obstruction farther on, roadworks or an accident. He slowed to join the procession. There was silence between them.

A few minutes later she spoke again. 'You never met my mother, did you.'

'No, I didn't.'

'I wish you had. She was very different from Papa, you know.'

He remembered the eyes in the photograph. 'Not morose?'

'Anything but. Certainly not her problem. She was great company.'

'And religious.'

Again he was aware of her turning to look at him. Quizzically this time. 'I don't know exactly what Papa has been telling you, but her faith was an enormous source of happiness to her. Religion met a genuine need in her.'

'And in you?'

'Not at all, I'm afraid. I wish it did. Looking back, I rather envy her that. Unlike poor old Papa, who resents it.'

They reached the obstruction in the road, a lorry jackknifed across two lanes. With agonising slowness, the line of vehicles squeezed through the constricting band of cones, past the flashing lights of the emergency services. For a moment he saw it, clearly: his own mother's body lying twisted on the carriageway. He stifled the image immediately. Then he heard Sybil asking: 'Why did you come today?'

'To see your father's Byron papers. I'm writing this book ...'

'No. Why did you really come?'

All at once the traffic flowed freely again and Daniel accelerated away. Then at last he came out with it. There was no longer any point in pretending. 'I was looking for the Monet,' he said.

She nodded. 'I thought so.' Then she added: 'Why?'

He told her. In short, bleak, prosaic sentences. Keeping it as matter-of-fact as possible. While he spoke, he followed the regular pattern of the windscreen wiper, took an obscure comfort in the purity of its geometry. Remembering the degrees of guilt. He told her about his grandparents in Paris and their art collection before the war. About the morning they'd been forced out of their apartment and into a bus to an indoor stadium; then later into a train that took them to Auschwitz. How Leblanc had profited from their tragedy to win possession of their Monet. How, with the help of his late mother's files, he'd traced the painting's subsequent ownership to her mother.

'I'm sorry,' she said. From the way she said it, he could hear she meant it. Now she was the one staring straight ahead. When she spoke again there was a baffled bitterness in her voice. 'And now we've gone and lost it. The bloody thing's a photograph. A *photograph.*'

And strangely he felt it again, what he'd sensed with her father: the conviction that this misery was not primarily prompted by the financial loss implicit in the Monet's disappearance. No, there was something else here. Something less easy to define. As if the discovery of its substitution stirred some long-feared and long-suppressed suspicion, some intimation of catastrophe hidden deep in the secret recesses of her own family's life.

'How could it have happened, do you think?'

'No idea at all.' But she said it just a shade too quickly for there not to have been some glimmer of a theory in her mind. Maybe not yet focused, but enough to disturb her.

He decided to pursue it himself. Out loud. 'There are various possibilities, I suppose,' he began, then paused, aware that he was treading delicate ground. 'When would have been the last time the Monet was checked properly, looked at by an expert? When your mother died, I assume.'

She sat silently for a while, smoking the last inch of her cigarette. Considering the question. Then she shook her head and said, 'No, that's just the point. It probably wasn't checked then. Papa barely allowed anyone into her room, everything had to be left as it always had been.'

'Difficult.'

'Well, you couldn't argue with him. He was her

husband, for Christ's sake. He was inconsolable. No one was going to go against his wishes.'

'So it's quite possible the original could have been removed some years ago. Before her death.'

'Stolen, you mean?'

'Yes, stolen.'

'What, the real picture taken and the photograph substituted?'

'That's it.'

It was as if the theory came as a relief. 'Yes, I suppose a thief could have broken in with the photograph already prepared and done a swap,' she speculated.

'Well,' he said, 'it could have been a break-in. Except that would imply a considerable degree of inside information. It would be more likely that the person doing the swap was an insider with a bit of time to play with.'

'A servant, you mean?'

'Could be.' He paused, suddenly wondering if she thought he suspected her of some kind of involvement in the deception. He didn't. Her shock at the revelation of the picture's status had been unfeigned. But equally there was something about all this that she wasn't telling him. Something that she knew. Something that was a source of profound unease to her. He was sure of it now. He went on, 'Did anyone in your parents' employment leave suddenly, for instance?'

She thought hard. 'No, I can't think of anyone.' Curious the way she said it: there was genuine regret in her tone.

'Well, then: is it possible your mother could have sold it secretly, and had a reproduction done so that no one would know? Was she short of money?'

Sybil sighed. 'No, you didn't know her. She wasn't like that, she wasn't short of money.'

'Perhaps someone she knew was?'

Sybil suddenly flared. 'Look, just keep your smartarse little speculations to yourself, OK? I'm telling you, you didn't know her. You didn't know her at all.'

He apologised, and wondered what nerve he'd struck. What deep-lying tenderness he had unwittingly disturbed.

He drew up outside the mews house in Queen's Gate where she lived.

'I'm going to have to sort this out, aren't I?' she said quietly. 'About the Monet.'

'Do you think you can?'

'Perhaps.'

'Is there anything I can do?'

'No. I'm going to sort it out myself.' She spoke with sudden decisiveness. Daniel knew all about that, of course. The need to do it on your own. To make amends.

He leaned over and kissed her on the cheek. She smiled back at him, but close to there was something missing. A deliberate withholding of intimacy? Or a natural deficiency in it? He thought back to the moment this afternoon when he'd first encountered her. The undulations of her body lying on the bed. The slow, unhurried way in which she'd got up and pulled on her dressing gown. An action richer in irony than enticement.

The front door of the mews house opened, and a tall, dark, loose-limbed woman stood framed for a moment in its light.

'Look, here's Romana.' Sybil's voice was altogether different, at once expectant and excited.

'Who's that?'

'Romana's Romana,' she told him happily. 'I live with her.'

Sybil was half out of the car when the woman caught sight of her. Romana strode quickly forward, put her arms round her shoulders and kissed her. Very deliberately, on the lips. Asserting possession. So there should be no misunderstanding. 'Hallo, darling,' she said. 'It's great to have you back. Who's your friend?'

'This is Daniel Stern,' said Sybil. 'He very kindly gave me a lift up from the country.'

'Hallo,' said Daniel. 'Nice to meet you.'

Romana nodded vaguely in his direction, and walked back towards the house. Daniel watched Sybil follow her, then turn and wave perfunctorily to him before the front door closed behind them.

Wearily, he put the car in gear and drove on to Regent's Park. It had been a very long day.

ROME

Thursday, 10 June

Once more, Father Cambres was travelling on foot in the heat of early evening. As he walked slowly across the broad expanse of St Peter's Square, he reflected that it would probably have been wiser to have sought the shade of the circling columns of the colonnade rather than traversing the exposed open spaces of the square while the sun was still strong. But he kept going along the course he had begun. He glanced across at the colonnade, and his eye was caught at random by a man in a yellow shirt and sunglasses also walking in the same direction as he, but progressing round the magnificent arc transcribed by the columns. Both he and the man seemed bound for the Via di Conciliazione, the wide road that linked St Peter's Square and the Vatican to the secular city of Rome. Who would get there first, Cambres or Yellow-shirt? It was the sort of abstract geometrical problem that Cambres found rather intriguing, often beguiled himself with on journeys. Yellow-shirt was probably strolling faster, but had more ground to cover.

Cambres was moving slower but over a shorter distance. He felt a little arthritic, stiff and immobile, still uncertain of himself in public after the days he'd spent cut off from the outside world.

He reflected upon his first day back in normality. Back at work. He had just attended a meeting in the Vatican on routine Pro Deo business. He wondered at the ease with which he had re-entered the benign formalities of daily Church commerce; found it impossible to link in any way the good people surrounding him at that meeting with the terrible things he had discovered within Pro Deo: the financial liaisons involving criminal money, the veiled but unmistakable menaces, the ruthless devastation visited on his apartment. What was going on in the Service? he asked himself. If there was a conspiracy, who was part of it? And how could he take action, when on the one hand the authorities denied there had been any wrongdoing and on the other his vows of obedience to the Service precluded him from seeking outside help? But he walked on, still determined. He'd taken a decision. He was on his way to keep an appointment.

Cambres had woken that morning still bruised by the violation of his apartment. Still fearful, still uncomprehending. He felt an immediate and compelling need to talk frankly to someone, to unburden himself. There was only one person to whom he could possibly do this now, he realised: Father Donaghy, the man he hadn't seen since their rendezvous at the Lazio game. So this morning he had taken a risk and rung Father Donaghy at his desk in the Secretariat. From an unfamiliar extension. When no one else was in the room.

'Can we meet?' he had demanded.

'Thank God you made contact,' Donaghy had exclaimed. Cambres had forgotten the Irishness of the man's intonation. The breathless, fretful way in which he spoke when he was anxious. 'It's vital that we meet. But we must be very, very careful, Father.'

'Where do you suggest?'

'Let's say the Caffe Greco, in the Via Condotti. This evening, at six-thirty.'

When Cambres reached the Via di Conciliazione, he was thinking about Donaghy. He was a good man, of course he was, but Cambres wished he felt more confidence in his judgment. There was a passion about him that loosened his restraint, inclined him to extremes. Cambres suspected that dealing with him meant that one had constantly to be regulating him, moderating his wilder instincts. Cambres proceeded slowly past the Castel San Angelo and along the northern bank of the Tiber. He had crossed the road to the Ponte Cavour when he turned back and suddenly glimpsed the man again. Yellow-shirt. About a hundred and fifty metres behind him. Odd. He'd completely forgotten about him. Cambres smiled to himself. He must have won the race, then. Got to the end of the colonnade first. The direct route had triumphed. But his rival must actually have stopped to do something to have fallen so far behind.

Once over the bridge, he continued along Via Tomacelli.

But something made him uneasy. Something made him look back. And there he was again. Yellow-shirt. The same distance behind. The man had stopped to look into a shop window, but he was following him. Definitely following him.

Now Cambres was worried. When he got to the end of Via Tomacelli, he didn't go straight over to the Via Condotti, but turned right into Via del Corso. After a couple of hundred metres he turned left into the Via della Vite, walked for another five minutes beside the little leather-goods shops and fashion boutiques, then turned left again, thus doubling back up to the Via Condotti. He'd paced the three sides of a square. He paused, five doors away from the Caffe Greco, feeling slightly ridiculous. The whole thing had been a false alarm, a product of his own insecurity. He'd exhausted himself because of some imagined pursuer.

Then he saw him again. About seventy metres ahead this time, up near the Piazza di Spagna. Leaning against a wall, smoking a cigarette. Almost insolent. With a perfect view of the entrance to the Caffe Greco. Go on, he seemed to be challenging Cambres. Make my day. Go in there. Go in and meet your friend.

There was no way that could happen now, of course. Frustrated, fearful and exhausted, Cambres turned back towards his apartment.

When he finally reached his own front door, with his key in the lock, he looked behind him once more. First left, then right. But there was no one. Yellow-shirt had finally disappeared. Headed him off from his rendezvous and melted away.

Upstairs in his flat he put the coffee pot on the flame and made himself an espresso. He lived on the stuff now. It steadied his nerves, since he'd given up smoking. He took it to the table by the window, sat down, and began to drink.

The past. It kept coming at him, assailing him. Allowing him no respite.

And once again he was back in another time. Sitting at another table. In front of another cup of coffee. Watching an elegant, scented hand reach out for his own.

'It is so good to have you on your own, Father.' She still called him 'Father', but there was a note of gentle mockery in the tone. Nothing at which he could take offence: it signalled only an intoxicating complicity. 'So good to have you all to myself.'

How much to risk? 'I have been looking forward to seeing you, too,' he said carefully. 'I have told you many times how lovely I find this place.'

'It gives me great pleasure to know that you like being here.'

He looked out to the terrace, and the line of plane trees beyond. Before he'd first come to England, people had warned him about the weather. How it rained all the time, and you were constantly damp. But this summer all he could remember was glorious sun and the distinctive beauty of the mellow evening light. 'I am very happy to be here,' he told her.

'You know my husband is away for three days.'

He made gently to withdraw his hand from hers but she gripped it tighter. It was very hot in the dining room this evening, even though the windows were open. He could smell the honeysuckle from the garden.

'I feel something so powerful when I am with you.'

'What do you feel?' He shouldn't have asked; he should have deflected the conversation along another line. Any other line.

'I feel a need.'

'For what?'

'A need for you.'

Need. That was the same word they had used back in Rome. There is acute need. A lack of resources. The funds of the Service must have urgent replenishment. The faithful membership of Pro Deo must gently be reminded of their duty. Particularly those lay members of the Service with wealth to spare. Ways must be found of channelling spare wealth into the places where it can do most good. You, Alfonso: you know how to handle these things. You are so good with our laity. They respond to you so well.

There was the Service's need. And there was this woman's need. He sensed a way in which the two might be used to satisfy each other. And he could be the catalyst. The orchestrator of their fusion.

'Tell me about your need,' he said.

'It is so strong, I know you must feel it too. Tell me you feel it too.'

His mouth was dry. The step had to be taken. 'I feel it too,' he said softly.

'What is it, Alfonso?'

'It is the love of God.'

She inclined her head towards him. Her hair was very close to his face. 'The love of God,' she said, 'bringing us together. You and me.'

'Bringing us together for a purpose.'

He felt her sigh. 'I know,' she murmured. 'I have not forgotten what you have told me. About making sacrifices for God. I have resolved to make the sacrifice we spoke of.'

'That makes me happy.'

'I do it for you, you know.'

'For God.'

'When I am with you, I feel it is the same thing.'

Yes, he should have denied it then as well. Corrected her. But sometimes events have their own momentum, and it is easier not to stand in their way if they are moving in a direction that is ultimately positive. Ultimately good. Remain silent and you will never regret it. Speak, and you often will.

'Show me God is pleased with me for the sacrifice I'm making. Just show me once, and I will be happy.'

Just once. The tightrope wobbled. He moved his own head closer to hers. Then his fingers reached out and touched her cheek.

LONDON

Monday, 14 June

> *The Semite is money-grubbing, greedy, scheming, subtle, sly;
> the Aryan is enthusiastic, heroic, chivalrous, disinterested,
> frank, trustful to the point of naïvety. The Semite is an
> earth-dweller, scarcely seeing beyond his present life; the
> Aryan is a son of the sky ceaselessly preoccupied with
> superior aspirations. The one lives in reality, the other in
> the ideal. The Aryan is farmer, poet, monk, and specially
> soldier; war is his true element, he goes to meet danger
> joyously, he braves death. The Semite has no creative faculty;
> not even the slightest invention has been due to a Semite. He
> can live only as a parasite in the middle of a civilisation
> that he has not made.*

It was a good quote, Daniel decided. Nauseating, but
effective. At first sight, you might have attributed it to
some Nazi theorist of the 1930s. In fact it had been written
in 1886 by a Frenchman called Edouard Drumont. Daniel
was going to start the piece on his grandparents with it.
To show what they'd been up against. To illustrate the

slimy trail of French anti-Semitism that could be traced deep into the nineteenth century, farther back even than the notorious Dreyfus case.

France. His mother's country. What a mess they'd made of it. And yet, not completely: for every Emile Leblanc there had been a Thérèse Lisieux. Would Britain have been any different if the Nazi tanks had rolled around Trafalgar Square in 1940? Probably not. The speculation depressed him. He wondered what to do now. He'd passed on to Parnello the numbers and letters he had transcribed from the back of the frame in Gabrielle Gascoigne's bedroom. Parnello had said he'd look into them. He'd parried Parnello's questions about the painting: yes, he'd seen it. Yes, it was very beautiful. No, he didn't think it was for sale. That was it now. On balance, he might as well get back to Paris to continue his research. He had no desire to hang about any longer than necessary here in his mother's bleak, half-derelict apartment, waiting for something to happen. He was actually reaching for the Eurostar timetable when his mobile rang.

'It's me,' she said. 'Sybil. Can you meet me for lunch? I've got something to show you.'

He waited for her in the restaurant. She was twenty-five minutes late. When she came in she looked tired and drawn. Older, somehow, than he remembered her. Her manner was distracted, uncommunicative, obscurely resentful. She answered his banal politenesses mostly in monosyllables; she was fine, thank you. The American client in Chester Square had been a wanker. Her father? Her father was just the same. He called the waiter and ordered them both large Bloody Marys. She drank hers frowning, chewing her lip. Then she remarked unexpectedly: 'I was remembering something in the taxi on my way here. About Monet.'

'What was that?'

'There was a certain sort of girl at school we used to call a "Monet".'

'Why did you call them that?'

'Because they were the ones that looked good at a distance, but when you got up close they were a mess.'

Daniel smiled. He'd known a few Monets in his time. He said: 'The Impressionist experts would call that the perception ruining the sensation.'

There was another troubled silence. Finally he broke it, because he could not bear the tension any longer. 'You've found out something, haven't you?' he said. 'About your mother's picture?'

She sighed, as if the whole question suddenly bored her. Then very slowly she drew from her bag an envelope, opened it, and pulled out a piece of paper. She didn't immediately hand it over to him. When she spoke, there was a harder, more bitter edge to her voice.

'I went through her things yesterday afternoon. When Papa was resting. I found this at the back of the drawer of her dressing table. I remembered that was where she always used to keep her most secret things.'

'What did you find? What is it?' He eyed the paper, which she still clutched as if uncertain whether to let him see it; whether he had done enough to deserve it.

'I didn't enjoy it, Daniel.' She spoke softly, but with a particular intensity. 'I felt like some sort of burglar in my own parents' house. Those papers had lain there undisturbed since she died. I felt like I was violating her.'

'I am sorry,' he said. But his own hand was reaching out to take it now.

'Bloody painting,' she murmured.

'Let me see it, Sybil.'

Suddenly she was venomous, almost flinging the paper at him. 'There you are,' she said. 'I hope you're bloody well satisfied.'

It didn't take him long to read. It was a document headed 'Socii Pro Deo', beneath a crest. A deed of transfer, dated Rome, September 1983, certifying that Gabrielle, Lady Gascoigne, who had full and undisputed title to the ownership of an oil painting by Claude Monet entitled *Poplars beside the River Epte*, was hereby freely and irrevocably donating it to the Service. To Pro Deo. It was signed by Sybil's mother in a firm, thick-nibbed pen. And its receipt was attested by a Father Alfonso Cambres.

He laid the paper aside. 'I suppose your mother had the copy of the painting made so that no one would know?'

She nodded. 'That's about it. A fairly successful manoeuvre, I'd say. Until you came along.'

'I hadn't realised your mother was quite so . . . quite so committed.'

'I told you, she had a need.'

'And she was close to this . . . this Father Cambres?'

She wheeled round. As if suddenly suffocating, flailing for air. 'What do you have to do to get a drink round here?'

'I'm sorry, what would you like?'

'Another Bloody Mary, OK?'

He called the waiter over. When the drink had come, he tried to make peace. 'I really appreciate your letting me see this, Sybil.'

'I'm not doing it for you,' she said miserably.

'Who, then?'

'I don't know.' She paused. 'I suppose I'm doing it for your grandparents.'

A little later she said, 'I discussed it with Romana. She agreed I should tell you.'

'How is Romana?' It was the question he should have asked earlier, along with his enquiries about her health and her business and her father. Somehow he'd been embarrassed to then.

'Oh, Romana. She's great.' She sipped her drink and added defiantly: 'I've been so lucky to find her. She makes me very happy, you know. After everything that happened.'

He was obscurely aware that she wasn't just referring

to the break-up of her marriage. To other things too. Farther back, perhaps. 'I'm glad for you,' he said.

She shrugged, then very deliberately replaced the deed in its envelope and returned it to her bag. 'Let's order some food,' she said.

The waiter appeared again, and recited an interminable list of special dishes of the day. She ordered pasta with a simple tomato sauce. But when they brought it to her she only toyed with it, and laid her fork aside with the plate still three-quarters full. After she had lit a cigarette, she said:

'I met him once.'

'Who?'

'Cambres.'

'What was he like?'

She did not immediately answer the question. 'You have to understand something about my mother,' she said, inhaling on the cigarette. She closed her eyes, as if to sharpen the memory of Lady Gascoigne; or perhaps in some way to reduce its potency. 'My mother was constantly filling the house with priests. They came in all shapes and sizes. She had a weakness for them. They'd be in and out of the place, lunch, tea, dinner. The chosen ones even got to stay with us. Do you know what she did? There was rather a beautiful old barn on the estate which she rebuilt as a chapel, and got it ... what's the word? ... consecrated, that's it. One of her tame bishops came, there was a great ceremony. She did it up a treat. It was typical of Mummy, you had to hand it to her: she always had a wonderful sense of style. I think it's the only chapel in England with moire silk curtains, velvet-upholstered pews, and a fireplace with a fender. "Why not, *chérie*?" she used to say. "I'm sure God wants us to be comfortable when we're worshipping Him." Anyway, there'd be endless Masses there. Frankly, I didn't pay much attention to them, I just let them get on with it. Occasionally if I wanted something out of my mother, I'd oblige her by attending one of her Masses. Most of the priests she had in tow were pretty unmemorable types, either intolerably unctuous or terminally taciturn.'

'And which was Cambres, unctuous or taciturn?'

'That's just it: Cambres was different.'

'How was he different?'

Her eyes flared, and he recognised the danger signals. He feared she was going to shout at him again, or perhaps clam up completely. But instead she took a deep breath and said: 'OK. If you really want to know, I'll tell you. I'll tell you how he was different. Perhaps then you'll understand what I'm on about. Perhaps then you'll realise why I am the way I am about all this.'

And it all spilled out, in a hot, sickly stream of memory, all that had happened that summer half a lifetime ago. That airless, cloudless summer, when Sybil had been eighteen, going to her first dances, and every evening the scent of the honeysuckle had wafted in through the open dining-room window in intoxicating doses.

When she'd finished, she said: 'You know, you're the only person I've ever told this to. Apart from Romana.'

✻   ✻   ✻

Later, as they stepped out of the restaurant into the afternoon sunshine, he asked her: 'Have you seen Cambres since?'

She shook her head.

'He didn't come to your mother's funeral?'

'God, that funeral. No, Cambres didn't come, although it seemed like half the priesthood of the Catholic Church was there. Even a couple of cardinals in full fancy dress. But he did send a letter when she died.'

'A letter to your father?'

'No, it was to me.'

'Where was it from?'

'An address in Rome.'

'You don't happen to . . . ?'

She put on her dark glasses as if she hadn't heard him, as if she were about to move off, but then she slipped open her bag again and pulled out a scrap of paper. 'I copied it down for you,' she said in a dull voice. 'There's even a telephone number.'

He reached out and took it from her. Gratefully. Perhaps there was a bond between them now. He wasn't the only one with unfinished business in his family's past. 'Listen,' he said, 'do you mind if I go and see him? Cambres, I mean. Simply to trace the Monet, that's all.'

'Be my guest,' she told her. 'The man hasn't entirely earned the right to be left in peace.'

An idea occurred to him. 'You don't want to come with me, do you?'

She laughed bitterly. 'What, meet Cambres again? That's a pleasure I think I'll forgo.'

'Shall I take him a message?'

She shook her head emphatically. 'Frankly, as far as I'm concerned, it's all done with. Mummy's gone. And so's the Monet. I'd rather just draw a line under it now, leave it at that. Does that make sense?'

He realised this was her way of dealing with the past. His was different. It had to be. For one thing, he didn't have a Romana in his life. 'Yes, it makes sense,' he told her.

But as they parted, she said it once more. Sharply, urgently: 'Just remember one thing, though: if Papa ever gets to know the truth about that picture, I'll never forgive you, OK?'

ROME

Tuesday, 15 June

That night, Cambres lay wakeful and irresolute in his bed. It was hot and airless, and the sounds of the city drifted in through his open window: the distant traffic, a dog barking, a lone, late clarinettist wafting sad melodies across the city's rooftops. His anguish was intensified by his failure to meet up with Donaghy in the Caffe Greco. His need to unburden himself, to talk freely with someone, was still unsatisfied. His furtive attempts to telephone Donaghy since their thwarted rendezvous had been frustrated on each occasion by someone else answering Donaghy's extension. Each time Cambres had rung off at once. He had to be careful. You never knew who might be listening. If he'd once had doubts about Donaghy's stories of covert surveillance, he'd abandoned them now. Since he'd seen the evidence of his own poor burgled flat. Since he'd realised he was being followed by the man in the yellow shirt.

He found himself more than ever incapable of deciding what was right. Something had to be done, somehow the corruption in the Service must be torn out; but he felt an instinctive revulsion at the betrayal implicit in seeking outside help. And, as he tossed about in the breathless Rome night, he could not quite suppress from his memory the reverberating words of Tafurel. Did he want it on his conscience that he had impeded the truly important work that Pro Deo was doing? Bringing a Catholic education to young people across the world. Fighting the evil influence of Islam. Guarding Catholic orthodoxy against the many forces that would challenge it. To do that, the Service needed money. Ceaseless supplies. At one particularly desperate moment, not long before four in the morning, he almost convinced himself that perhaps Tafurel and Abello were right after all. If the money flowing into Pro Deo's coffers was tainted, then perhaps indeed the purposes to which the Service put it had a miraculously cleansing effect.

Then, just as dawn broke, the dreams came, the voices whispering in his ear as he drifted into uneasy sleep. Cambres, they said, what is your game? What are you up to? You're too smooth, Cambres, your suits are too well cut, you're too good looking. What kind of priest do you think you are? Something out of a TV mini-series? What were you doing that night in England nearly twenty years ago? Look at yourself with honesty. You're no better than the rest of them, are you? You judged that the morally dubious action you took then was redeemed by the good that you calculated would emanate from it. That's exactly the way they now excuse their dealings with Amelga, that the end justifies the means. The ultimate achievement washes clean the sin. Were you any different? That night when the honeysuckle wafted in through the open dining-room doors in intoxicating doses?

Early the morning after. The sun playing through the curtains.

'Take it,' she told him. 'It's for you. I want you to have it.'

She was flushed, animated. Oddly triumphant.

'You want to give me that? The painting by Monet?'

They both looked across at it hanging on the wall opposite them. The dappled light between the poplars. The iridescent blue of the sky behind the scudding clouds. Framed, though. Boxed. To emphasise its existence as a piece of nature tamed and ensnared. Rendered an object. A thing of enormous value. But reduced to the status of a possession, a transportable, tradable, donatable thing.

'You asked for a sacrifice. The sacrifice of something that meant a lot to me. I cannot think of any possession I have that I love more than this.'

'Gabrielle, please: it is a wonderful gesture that you're making, but I insist that you remember that this donation is for God. For the Service. Not for me.'

'All right, if that's how you want it. But you know that it is given to God to commemorate us. To commemorate what you are to me.'

'To commemorate God's love manifest between us.'

He struggled to find the words to cover his own moral nakedness.

She smiled back at him, as if she saw through his posturing, recognised that these were mere semantics. They both knew what had happened here between them.

He tried to steady himself. 'If you truly want to help God's work on earth in this way, then you must do it,' he said at last. 'Make the donation. It is an act of magnificent generosity.' And he thought, there are some things that you have to say with all other faculties of the brain anaesthetised. Otherwise you will never regain your balance. Never remount the tightrope.

'I'm happy to give it,' she said, and moved up against him once more. He took her in his arms between the sheets of the bed. Ran his hand — the surgeon's hand — down her naked back. In a gesture of acknowledgment of her sacrifice.

'I suppose I have been very wicked,' she sighed luxuriously. 'I made a sort of bargain with God, came to a sort of understanding with Him. That if I made love to you, I'd give the Monet to the Service.'

There was nothing more to say, no further unravelling that he could bring to her convoluted theology. Entangled somewhere in its intricacies was a strong thread of genuine faith. To that abiding consolation he must cling. That was the justification of everything that had happened last night.

Gradually she fell into a contented sleep. The regular pattern of her breathing encouraged the anaesthesia that he strove to maintain within himself, permitting only the vague wellbeing of her animal warmth against him to register. He floated, consigning to oblivion all the uncomfortable realities of the hours just past: the unfamiliar territory of a woman's bed; the successive shocks of intimacy; the terrible pleasure of her body. He was an unusual sort of surgeon, he reflected. A surgeon who needed to anaesthetise not the patient but himself before he could perform his operations.

He could not say how long he lay floating drowsily until it happened. But when it did, it was totally unexpected and he was off his guard. Too late he heard the footsteps just outside the door. His first thought was of an intruder, because she had assured him that they were alone in the house. Paralysed, he heard the hand on the doorknob, and the husky, faintly giggling enquiry: 'Mummy, are you there? I came home after all. It was a very boring dance indeed.' The slow, inexorable creaking of the opening door. Gabrielle stirred in his arms, but did not wake. And then Sybil stood there, eighteen years old, framed in the doorway. Horrified into silence by what she came upon. For perhaps two seconds their eyes engaged. His, and hers. The eyes of the priest, and the eyes of the daughter of the woman who lay in his arms. They saw. But worse, they registered each other's seeing.

Then Sybil turned and walked away, shutting the door silently behind her. She did not speak a single word.

Gabrielle moved in his arms. 'What was that?' he heard her murmur sleepily. 'Did you hear something?'

'No.'

'Funny. I think I dreamed that someone came into the room.'

'No, you're imagining things,' he told her firmly. With

complete conviction. 'No, there was no one. No one at all.'

Here in Rome, nearly twenty years on, he awoke from his shallow sleep tense and unrefreshed. He got up slowly, eased himself into his dressing gown, then moved the bed across so that he could reach the loose floorboard. He had to confront it. The print-out that Donaghy had given him. The record of the recent sale of an asset of the Pro Deo Service, donated in 1983. The record of the sale of a Monet.

He sat wearily on the edge of the bed and gazed at the document again. The painting had been bought by Amelga SA. Eighteen months ago, for twelve million dollars. And it had entered the private collection of a man who was – according to the information that di Livio had supplied to Donaghy – the power behind Amelga. There was his name and address in Switzerland. There, in black and white before him.

He forced himself to consider the painting, the faithfully donated treasure that he had persuaded Gabrielle Gascoigne to hand over to the Service. She had given it on the understanding that, sooner or later, it might be sold and the proceeds used to carry on the good work of the Service. He had accepted it from her on that basis. He had no quarrel with the fact that it had now been turned into money. Twelve million dollars could do a lot of good, after all. But it was the circumstances of the sale that devastated him. The way the painting had been used as mere ballast in some squalid deal to launder drug money. He could see it now, understood how the process worked. The criminal with whom Pro Deo had entered into a liaison turned over to the Service large quantities of otherwise unnegotiable cash in return for a readily renegotiable asset: the painting. By reselling it at a suitable moment in the future, he would deploy the Monet as the perfect vehicle for turning his dirty money into clean.

Large sums of money were generated for the Service, true enough. But Cambres himself felt compromised. Soiled. The moral ambiguities of his acquisition of the Monet on behalf of the Service had been held in uneasy check in the years since it had happened; so long as it represented a beautiful object of enormous value freely given, the end justified the means. His own catalystic role in the transfer of ownership to the Service was purified, could even be seen positively, as the selfless performance of a necessary duty. But now the way it had been sold, the nature of the deal, the identity of the buyer, all combined to tip the moral scales against the sequence, corrupted the generosity of Gabrielle, destroyed the fragile merit of the original donation. And totally undermined his own personal position. Was that why he had entered the Church, devoted his life to God? Here was the poor, bleak epitaph to his priesthood: he'd made love to a woman in order to elicit from her a painting which had been used to facilitate the laundering of criminal money. The first sin, far from leading to God's greater glory, had merely laid the ground for another, worse sin. Without the original donation, there would have been nothing to trade with Amelga.

The players in the drama, and the different obligations that he owed to them, followed each other in tortured procession through his conscience: Gabrielle, Donaghy, Tafurel. And Sybil. The girl with her hand on the bedroom door.

He got up, dressed, and was making himself a cup of coffee when the telephone rang.

'Is Father Cambres there, please?' The voice spoke in English. It was unexpected and therefore disconcerting.

'What is it concerning . . . ?'

'Is that Father Cambres?'

'Please tell me what your business is with him.' In his new dangerous world, everything unknown was hostile. Anything unfamiliar could be a trap.

'It's about a painting by Monet that used to belong to Lady Gascoigne.'

He felt as if he had been kicked in the stomach. 'Who are you?' breathed Cambres in a lower voice.

'My name's Daniel Stern. I'm calling from London. Father Cambres?'

'Yes, I am Cambres.' There was no longer any point in denying it.

'I'm calling because I urgently need some information, and I think you may be able to help me. I want to find

out where the painting is, the Monet that used to belong
to Lady Gascoigne. You remember the painting?'

'Yes, I ... I remember it.'

'Do you still have it?'

They'd ransacked his flat. They might well have
tapped his telephone. He couldn't take the risk. 'It's not
safe to speak of this on the open line,' he said. 'Please,
I am sorry. I cannot talk to you now.'

'Father, it's urgent ... if you can't talk on the telephone, I'd very much appreciate the chance to meet.'

He was about to ring off; it was too much, too
intrusive, too problematic. But for a moment he was
curious. 'I do not quite understand. Who are you exactly?
How do you know about these things?'

'I am a friend of the Gascoigne family. Sybil gave me
your telephone number.'

Sybil.

That name. It opened a sudden chasm in front of
him. He wobbled on its brink. 'Ah,' he said at last.
'Yes, Sybil.'

'I really don't want to disturb you, but this is urgent.
If I came to Rome, could we meet?'

The trusted foundations of his life were disintegrating.
First Donaghy with his revelations. Then the four weeks
of tortured self-examination. Now the events of the past
that he thought he had bolted away secure were breaking
free, coming back to assail him. To nudge him over into
the abyss.

But he dug his heels in. Resisted. God gave him the

courage to identify where his duty lay. To recognise that he had debts to redeem.

When he spoke again, it was in a stronger voice: 'Telephone me when you get here, Mr Stern. I'll do what I can.'

ROME

Wednesday, 16 June

The Rome-bound Boeing 757 shivered as it passed through the last layer of cloud on its ascent out of Heathrow, then glided smoothly into the blue ether above. Daniel relaxed and reached for the cuttings he'd got Nat to fax him from the paper's files. Everything he could lay his hands on about the Pro Deo movement. Their background, their history, their current activities. 'So now you're an expert on the Catholic Church,' Nat had probed. 'Next thing you'll be converting, maybe?' Daniel still hadn't risen to him. The whole question remained too delicate, too sensitive. Too personal. He pulled out the sheets of paper and began to read.

The first were print-outs from the official Pro Deo website. These told him that the Pro Deo Service had started in Italy between the wars, a movement within the Roman Catholic Church founded by an Italian priest called Massimo del Vecchio with the aim of 'reinvigorating the faith'. Father del Vecchio had been a man with a vision. A saint, if you believed the official Pro Deo line.

Certainly a saint in the making: his case was up before the Vatican Committee for Beatification, the first step in the convoluted process that led ultimately to canonisation. All that was lacking was an officially accredited miracle, but his supporters were working on that. There'd been a blind girl, a butcher's daughter in a village near Parma, who'd allegedly recovered her sight after hearing him preach in 1930. Affidavits had been sworn from witnesses, statements filed by medical experts. The evidence was mounting. It was only a matter of time before it was accepted. That was the Pro Deo version, anyway.

But there was another view of del Vecchio and his movement, it seemed. A less charitable one. Daniel picked up a recent article from *La Repubblica* which gave a different slant to the Service's creation. It drew attention to the murky, fascistic origins of Pro Deo, and to the founder's frequently expressed support for Mussolini. In 1935 del Vecchio had made a speech in Florence praising Il Duce as the twentieth century's most heroic warrior for Christ. In 1936 he'd justified the invasion of Abyssinia on the grounds that a certain amount of bloodshed was a price worth paying if the Catholic message might thereby be brought to the errant heathen. After the Second World War a little doctoring of history had been necessary, a repackaging of the Service for the modern, democratic age. The original name of Milites Pro Deo, Soldiers for God, had been quietly dropped in favour of the less aggressive Socii Pro Deo, allies for God.

Daniel returned to the website print-out and read on.

The Service's manifesto declared Pro Deo's primary aim to be the invigoration of the faith. This meant that it was the duty of every member to remain vigilantly on guard against what was defined as 'dangerous tendencies', both within the Church itself and in the wider world outside. They had been rabidly anti-communist, so long as communism had flourished. Now that threat had receded they'd shifted their target. Their most militant opposition was now directed against Islam. The threat to Christian values of burgeoning fundamentalism in the East. The dangers posed by admitting a country like Turkey into the European Community.

In matters of Catholic doctrine Pro Deo were equally rigorous. A Vatican insider commented – in an article that Daniel moved on to, translated from last year's *Der Spiegel* – that Pro Deo tended to regard even Pope John Paul II as a dangerous liberal. On the other hand they were also very involved in education and health, building schools and hospitals and so forth. There seemed to be general agreement, even in pieces critical of other aspects of Pro Deo, that they'd done a lot of practical good in the third world. But the writer in *Der Spiegel* suggested that the ultimate motivation even here was Pro Deo's obsession with defeating Islam. Their horror of the Muslim hordes.

Membership of the Service was another contentious issue. No one quite knew how large it was. But membership wasn't confined to the clergy. In fact there were a lot more lay members than priests. Influential lay people, too: grand Catholic families of Italy, France and Spain were rumoured to be extensively if discreetly represented. A bit of a secret society, in a way. An article from *Fortune* magazine went farther about their covert operations. Apparently a growing element of Pro Deo was deliberately being drawn from the financial world. It was speculated that one of the agendas of the Service was to gain increasing control over Vatican finances. In order to harness them more effectively. The article concluded that, while a thorough overhaul was clearly much needed in that department of Vatican activity, the question remained as to whether the shadowy and secretive Pro Deo Service were the best people to undertake it.

Several other articles speculated about Pro Deo's enormous hidden wealth, the more lurid of them suggesting stakes in brothels in Miami and casinos in Las Vegas. Again, no one knew for sure, that was the problem. Their commercial dealings were opaque. In fact 'secret' was a word that recurred in press coverage of Pro Deo. Their membership was secret, their finances were secret, their influence was secret. 'They're the KGB of the Vatican,' maintained one critic. 'Look at the parallels: there's no accountability. It's a sort of state within a state.'

The final article that Daniel studied was an interview with the current head of the Service, the Prelate-General, Cardinal Edmondo Tafurel. A strong man. A leading conservative. He totally refuted any accusations of impropriety in Pro Deo's commercial dealings or interests, but he pointed out that occasionally a degree of discretion was called for in such matters. It should be understood that the sole aim of any financial activity undertaken by the Service was to amass maximum resources for the benefit of the Church. This was a sacred duty. What about the secrecy over membership? 'This is a wrong emphasis of interpretation,' he was quoted as saying. 'We are in no sense a secret society. We merely respect the privacy of our members.' What intrigued Daniel as much as the interview itself were the photographs that illustrated it. There was one of Tafurel. An interesting face. Striking. And yet somehow strange. He sat at his desk in a book-lined study looking into the camera with the deep, impenetrable eyes and thin, faintly smiling lips of the man who inhabits a world aligned to but not quite congruent with the one lived in by the mass of humanity. Did Cambres look like this? wondered Daniel. Was he too an obedient soldier for God? And where, he wondered, was the Monet kept now?

He imagined his grandparents' painting hanging in some private chamber of the Service's headquarters. The Service, he read, had its own independent headquarters in Rome, a very beautiful palazzo near the Borghese Gardens. There was a shot of that, too, to illustrate the Tafurel interview. You saw its courtyard, taken through a barred gate. The walls were a mass of flowering hibiscus and bougainvillaea. Apparently the palazzo had been given to Pro Deo in the 1950s by a devoted supporter. A devoted supporter, the interviewer noted, who later ended up in jail convicted of corruption charges.

❉   ❉   ❉

Daniel took a taxi from the airport and checked into the Inghilterra Hotel, all narrow passages and polished mahogany, discreetly tucked away in the web of little streets between the Via Condotti and the Spanish Steps. Opening the windows of his bedroom, he found they gave on to a tiny balcony, hung with vivid red geraniums, and echoing to the constant plashing of some nearby source of water. Across the rooftops of the city he glimpsed the cedars of the Pincio Gardens tracing a pure art nouveau pattern against the blue of the summer sky. He stood there, mobile telephone in hand, struck for a moment by the beauty of the view. Then he dialled Cambres's number.

'It's Daniel Stern, Father. I'm here in Rome now. I would very much like to come to see you.'

'This ... this is not advisable.'

'May I invite you to my hotel, then? For dinner or lunch, perhaps?'

'I cannot do that. I ... I am sorry.'

'Is there anywhere you would be comfortable for us to meet? I am at your disposal. But please, Father, I need to see you.'

There was silence again, broken finally by a sigh of exhausted acquiescence. 'Perhaps tomorrow. You should come to the Church of San Luigi dei Francesi. The Contarelli Chapel. I will be there briefly, around midday.'

ROME

Thursday, 17 June

The interior of San Luigi dei Francesi was dark after the bright sunlight outside. Cooler, too. Daniel paused at the back of the church, acclimatising himself to the shadows, breathing in the distinctive odour of the place: musty, flavoured with the accretions of ancient incense that seemed to emanate from the very stonework itself. He glanced about him for any sign of the priest who might be Cambres. What sort of a man was he looking for? he wondered. An older man, certainly. But tall or short, white-haired or balding, striking or anonymous? Would he still bear some vestiges of the attraction that had drawn Gabrielle Gascoigne so powerfully to him? He ran through all the things he wanted to ask him; all the questions to which Cambres could, if he chose, provide the answers. Most important was the whereabouts of the Monet. Was it kept hidden somewhere in Rome? What had happened to it since its clandestine acquisition in 1983? And, more practically, how might he register his family's claim to its ownership? What was the first step on the road to restitution?

Further down a side aisle three Japanese tourists, deep

in guidebooks, murmured together, then looked up and pointed, apparently at some feature of the construction of the roof. A couple of elderly women knelt devoutly in the nave. And a single nun, head bowed, shuffled out of one of the little chapels that flanked the main body of the church. No. None of them candidates to be Cambres.

He stopped for a moment, his eye caught by a plaque on a pillar immediately in front of him. A plaque dated 1731, which reminded him that this was the French church in Rome. He read:

> *Quicunque orat pro Rege Franciae*
> *Habet decem dies de indulgentia*
> *A Papa Innocentia.*

Whoever offered a prayer for the king of France was in return promised ten days' indulgence by Pope Innocent. Indulgences. Air miles, he thought. That's all this religion was. The building up of credit by devout observances and good behaviour, air miles to be used for an upgrade on the route to heaven, to the eternal reward of the after-life. A simple formula. Childishly so; surely civilisation had moved on from all that. He walked slowly down the left-hand aisle, thinking about it. He glanced into the sequence of side altars that he passed, looking for the Contarelli Chapel.

It was the last one in the row. His eye was drawn into it immediately by the painting that hung there. A large painting of such transcendent quality that he could not look away from it. On the right of it stood Christ, pointing across a room. The direction of Christ's gesture was dramatically intensified by a shaft of light across the width of the composition, illuminating the five men grouped about a table to the left. Three of the men were looking up; the two others remained absorbed by the money they were counting. One of the men looking up was actually pointing, apparently to himself. 'What, me?' he seemed to be saying. 'You're calling me?' Because that was the subject of the painting, Daniel discovered from the plaque. *The Calling of Saint Matthew.* Matthew. A good Jewish boy, as his Uncle Laurie might have observed. A tax collector. The painting achieved a sublime combination of physical grace and psychological poignancy, the expressions on the faces impassioned by breathtaking contrasts of light and shadow. He read from the explanatory label: it was the work of Caravaggio. For a moment Daniel sensed something more about this place. Something more than he had suspected. A dimension of piety, perhaps, aggregated over the centuries, like the incense ingrained into the stonework. A spiritual quality that all the manifest shortcomings of the organised Church, with its indulgences and Hail Marys and countless other absurdities, still could not quite extinguish.

Then it happened. Suddenly, without warning. The lights went out.

He felt an unexpected panic in the dark. All at once he was aware of someone else, very close to him. Another human presence. Just behind him, in his space. Menacing him. A hand was on his shoulder. He whipped round.

'Mr Stern, is that you?' The voice was unusually rich, and rather beautiful. 'Wait. It needs some coins in the slot here. I have them.'

Light returned. 'Father Cambres?'

The priest nodded, and smiled. 'Nothing is free any more, you see. Not even in church. Even the light to see Caravaggio costs money. You get three minutes for five hundred lire.'

'Cheap at the price, I think,' said Daniel.

'It is a magnificent painting,' agreed Cambres. 'In all Rome, one of the most beautiful.'

Daniel contemplated him. He was a good-looking man; distinguished, silver-haired, elegant. Yet uneasy, somehow. As if, beneath his charm, he were weighed down. Perhaps it was just that he was old and tired. The lines round his eyes spoke of exhaustion. Of batteries running low. 'It is good of you to see me,' Daniel said.

Cambres made a gracefully deprecatory movement of his hands. But he added, 'Perhaps we may sit for a moment? I am a little out of breath.'

'Of course. Are you all right? Can I get you something?'

'Don't trouble. It will pass.' Cambres lowered himself on to a chair in the nave. His hand was shaking slightly. Daniel came over to sit next to him. Cambres sighed and said. 'Please tell me, first: how is Sybil?'

Sybil. The handle engaging. The bedroom door easing open. Agonisingly slow; but gradually, implacably making

its revelation. Just wide enough to register. This man —
this priest — in bed with her mother.

'Sybil is well,' he said simply. Did Cambres know
that he knew? The idea unsettled him. 'She gave me
your telephone number, suggested I should speak to
you. You see, I have to find the Monet. The painting
of poplars that her mother ... that her mother donated
to Pro Deo.'

'What do you want with this painting?'

What did he want with it? All at once, the question
made him angry. As he replied, he couldn't repress
the bitterness in his voice: 'It once belonged to my
family. It was stolen from them. Do you understand
that, Father? Stolen.'

'Please tell me about it,' said Cambres.

There, in the shadowy chancel of San Luigi dei
Francesi, just a few yards from Caravaggio's masterpiece,
he rolled out the story. He started with Auschwitz. That
had to come first, because it was the most awful thing
that had ever happened and it had happened to his
grandparents. And he suddenly wanted to test Cambres
emotionally, to stretch him to the limit, because the man
deserved it, he needed to be punished; and also because
Cambres by virtue of his priesthood was better equipped
than ordinary people to deal with it. To deal with the
idea of the two adult Benjamins dying in misery in that
terrible place. To deal with the unspeakable notion of the
killing of little Matthieu. Seven years old. The horrific and
unforgivable calling of another, much younger Matthew.

An innocent. Totally innocent. More innocent even than Monet's famous eye.

Monet. That led him on to the painting of the poplars. He told Cambres about the way his grandparents had clung to it in Paris during the occupation. How precious it had been to them, how it had symbolised to his grandfather his own independence of judgment, his own individuality as a man. He recounted the circumstances of its theft from their apartment after they'd been arrested. How the despicable Emile Leblanc had sold it on to the father of Gabrielle Gascoigne. Which explained why the whole sequence of subsequent ownership was therefore morally invalidated. He had to have it back. For his family. For the sake of his recently dead mother. To do them all the honour they deserved. Here was a chance, just once, to rectify the wrongs of history. God help him, Daniel suddenly found he was crying. Not violently, as he had in the airport in Stephanie's arms. But just as irresistibly. Angry tears. Bitter tears. Tears that he had to wipe from his eyes with his sleeve.

He felt Cambres's hand once more on his shoulder. It rested there. They sat in silence for some moments, almost motionless like a sculpture. Then Cambres said, hoarsely, 'Will you pray with me?'

The older man leaned forward, his forehead in his hands. Daniel too bowed his head. He didn't exactly pray, but he remembered people. Concentrated on them. His grandparents, whom he'd never met. Matthieu. His mother. And then, oddly, on Gascoigne. The man for whom the Roman Catholic Church had been such a source of profound inquietude.

Finally Cambres said. 'You can't always rectify wrongs. All you can do is forgive those who have done wrong.'

Daniel looked across at him. Angry again. Incredulous. 'You're asking me to forgive the people who sent my family to Auschwitz?'

Cambres shook his head slowly. 'No, it's not for me to ask you to do that.'

'Who, then? Who have I got to forgive?'

There was silence between them. A stillness in the shadows of the church.

'I'm asking you to forgive *me*,' he said.

A little later Daniel asked, 'Do you still have the Monet?'

Cambres closed his eyes, as if the question probed an old but very deep wound. 'No, it is no longer the property of the Pro Deo Service. It was sold a little time ago.'

'Sold? Where is it?'

Cambres reached a decision. 'I'm going to tell you who owns it now,' he said. 'Under the circumstances, I see it is my duty.'

He brought out a pocket-bock and tore from it a page on which was written a name and address. As he passed it to Daniel, he added: 'Mr Stern, please listen to me. I do not know this man, I have never met him. But I urge you to be careful in your dealings with him. I believe he is dangerous. *Sensa scrupoli*. Without scruples. You understand me?'

'I understand,' said Daniel. It didn't worry him. Not then. Not by comparison with the excitement of finally identifying the Monet's owner. After all, he was a journalist. He'd met men without scruples before.

In the porch of the church, Daniel shook Cambres by the hand.

'I'm very grateful for your help Father,' he said. He paused, aware of many things. Of the trail that he had been following towards the *Poplars*, a path whose constant extensions of itself might finally be ending. Of the heat of the midday sun outside the door. Of how frail Cambres was looking. 'Do you have to go far? Can I walk with you?'

'No. Please. It is better that I leave alone.'

He spoke with a sudden urgency. But why could he not run the risk of being seen with Daniel in public? And for a moment, Daniel caught it. Clear, but inexplicable. Not just the weariness, but the fear in the older man's eyes.

ANDRISIO, SWITZERLAND

Saturday, 19 June

The road skirted the lake of Lugano, then cut between two vertiginous hillsides before entering another smaller, more isolated valley. The lake here was smaller, but more shadowy and mysterious; its waters ran still and deep and secret. Daniel kept the map spread out on the passenger seat beside him, tracking his progress towards the address written on the page torn from Father Cambres's pocket-book. He found himself climbing steadily, following a gently serpentine route up the side of a wooded mountain. Closer. Ever closer to the goal.

He had left Rome the previous morning, impatient to be on his way. He'd tried without success to find a telephone number for Dr Aldo Cressini of the Villa Loretta, Andrisio, near Lugano in Switzerland, the man whose name Cambres had slipped into his hand in San Luigi dei Francesi. So he'd decided to go there himself. Just to turn up on the man's doorstep. Why not? Ultimately he believed that if you wanted something passionately enough you got it. By your own willpower. By relying on the effort of the person you can most trust. By doing it yourself.

The girl who'd hired him a car at Lugano airport had given him a map for Andrisio and also recommended a hotel. 'The Castel San Marco,' she'd said. 'Is at the top of the mountain, just a few kilometres farther up from the village. Is very old. And very beautiful.' He'd rung ahead and booked a room. In case he had to hang around. In case Dr Cressini was not immediately tractable. He sensed that this time he was nearing the end of the trail. And if he finally found the Monet at the Villa Loretta, he was prepared to dig in. To lay protracted siege to the place. He wouldn't go home without getting what he wanted.

He swung round one more bend, and there was the roadside sign announcing the village of Andrisio. It was postcard picturesque in the sun. A church, an inn. Flowers in the window boxes around the little square. No one about: siesta time. He drove on. A kilometre farther up the mountain, he found the entrance to the villa. He pulled the car to a halt in front of the locked iron gates. Once more he smoothed out the crumpled paper with the address on it. Just to be sure. Villa Loretta. It tallied.

He got out and stretched. The view was spectacular: the lake in the valley, which he had last registered as he drove beside it, was now a sheet of turquoise glass far below. Here and there its surface glinted in the sun. Woods hurried down the slopes of the encircling hills to meet the water. This was both a beautiful location and a strategic one, he reflected. Thirty kilometres south, and you were in Italy; but here you stood on Swiss soil. Secure. Discreet. You could hide things here, if you chose. Keep them secret. It was a sanctuary beyond the reach of more intrusive jurisdictions.

Ten minutes past two. Daniel decided there was no point in hanging around. He walked to the gates and peered through. The driveway swung round so that the house was invisible from this point, hidden by trees. He reached for the bell on the gatepost and rang, keeping his finger long enough upon the button to reach the borderline separating urgency from impertinence.

There was silence for a moment. He listened to the singing of the birds in the garden. Then, suddenly, the man was there. A security guard, on the other side of the gate. Surveying him truculently through the railings.

'Yes?' he demanded.

'I've come to see Dr Cressini.'

'You have an appointment?' Daniel knew enough about security guards to recognise that this one was armed. There was a gun strapped beneath his jacket at his left breast. For a fleeting moment, he remembered Cambres's words about the owner of the property. A man *sensa scrupoli*. A dangerous man.

'I do.'

'Your name, please?' The tone was a degree more deferential. The lie had been spoken with enough authority.

'Daniel Stern.' The man rang through to the house on his mobile telephone, turning away and taking a few paces up the drive so that his conversation should be inaudible. As he came back, he was snapping the mobile shut.

'You can go through,' he said. The gates hummed and began to part.

Daniel Stern drove up to the house, trying to hide his surprise.

A Filipina maid in an immaculate white coat let him in at the front door. He paused in the hallway, looking about him. It was a grand, well-proportioned space. Ahead an elegant staircase curved away to the upper floor, beneath a large arched, light-filled window. He was led to the right, through double doors, into a spacious, very white drawing room. A light room. A rich room. A room hung with paintings.

'Mrs Cressini will join you in a minute,' the maid told him. 'Can I get you something? Coffee, perhaps?'

'Water,' he murmured. 'Just mineral water.'

His mouth was dry because he'd caught sight of it. On the long wall behind him. The Monet. The poplars winding away along the receding riverbank. His journey was at an end.

As soon as the maid had closed the door behind her, he went over to it. He knew at once he'd found it. There was no mistake this time. This was it, the original. The painting he thought he'd tracked to Lady Gascoigne's bedroom. The painting that had once hung in his grandfather's study. His grandfather's study. Another world. Another time. He ran his finger lightly over the impasto of the paint, exulting in the swirling brush stroke that caught the light filtering through the foliage. One chance; one angle of light. Blink, and it might be gone. Seven minutes, Parnello had told him: that was the maximum time Monet said that he allowed himself to paint at a stretch in his *Poplars* series. Seven minutes, to capture the evanescent effect before it changed; seven minutes, before the sunlight left a certain leaf. Had his grandfather stood like this, Daniel wondered, up close to the paint, marvelling at it? For a moment he felt a bond with him. A link. An almost physical closeness, through this painting, to a man who'd died more than half a century ago. A man with a little toothbrush moustache and immaculately brushed hair. A man with the single word *'Juif'* stamped on his identity card.

He wasn't prepared for what happened next. How could he have been, after the shock, the excitement of finding the Monet? After the anger, too, which followed immediately upon the excitement; the anger at seeing the Benjamins' picture hanging here. His family's painting. In someone else's house. It hadn't belonged in the alien Englishness of Wenham Park. It didn't belong here, either.

The double doors opened and she came in. Mrs Cressini.

He'd been expecting someone old and rich. Someone it would be easy to hate. But she was young, this woman, barely older than he was. She had shoulder-length blonde hair and she was wearing jeans and a light blue T-shirt. She had smooth, olive-coloured skin and brown eyes. She did a sort of self-caricaturing double-take as she caught sight of him.

'Who are *you*?' she said. Not hostile; more perplexed, and a little intrigued.

He told her his name was Daniel Stern. 'Oh,' she said, consulting the piece of paper she held in her hand. 'It is a mistake. I am expecting Signor Torn, not Signor Stern.'

'I'm sorry.'

'You are perhaps an expert at redesigning swimming pools?'

'I could try,' he said. 'But I don't think you'd end up with much of a pool.'

She laughed. 'I am Juliette Cressini,' she said, and held out her hand. Her accent was French rather than Italian. Her voice had a rough, husky quality that was extraordinarily attractive. 'So, if you do not know about swimming pools, why *are* you here?'

He paused, phrasing his reply carefully. 'It's about one of your paintings. About this Monet.' He turned and pointed to it.

'What do you want to know?'

'I'm doing some research. I want to know more about its history.'

'For the paintings, you must talk to my husband. Myself, I know nothing about them. He returns on Tuesday.'

He shrugged. 'OK, I can wait. I'll come back on Tuesday. I'm staying at the Castel San Marco.'

She looked at him curiously. 'Why are you interested in the history of the Monet?'

'It's research,' he repeated vaguely. He didn't want to get into this. Not yet. Not with her, anyway. 'I'm writing a book on the artist.'

'You're a writer?'

'Yes, I am.'

'I would love to do what you do.' She spoke with sudden feeling. 'What do you write? Sit down for a moment, tell me about it.'

He sensed it then. Her boredom. Her need for diversion. He lowered himself on to the sofa opposite her and told her about his life as a journalist in New York. About the magazines he'd written for. The interviews he'd done. He showed off to her. Ridiculous to show off to her. It was all wrong. Too sympathetic, too easy between them. The wrong script, the wrong conversation to be having with her. These people had taken his painting. His family's Monet. She and her husband were his adversaries. The enemy. And yet, like the first taste of alcohol after months of abstinence, close proximity to this beautiful woman made him light-headed, knocked him off balance. She was sympathetic, the way she laughed at him. And at herself. He liked being with her.

'I thought I would be a writer once,' she said. 'I studied literature in Paris. I – how do you say it, my English is so bad now – I took myself very serious. I began to write a novel.'

'What was it about?'

'It was very long and very – how you say – autobiographic.'

'What happened to it?'

'I threw it away. It was only good to read if you want to go to sleep.' She made a mock yawn, and laughed again. 'A long time ago.'

He stood up to go. He had to get out of this house, had to get away from her. Before something terrible happened.

'I'm sorry,' he said. 'About breaching your security system.'

She made a gesture with her long brown hands. 'Don't be sorry. It is the most exciting thing that's happened here all summer.'

It was there again. A tinge of bitterness beneath her flippancy. Just discernible. Like a faint cry for help on a happy summer beach.

He was aware of the heat of the afternoon. Of an airlessness in the big white room. Of her closeness, of her scent. I am going mad, he thought. I could reach out with my hands, cup her face, and kiss her on the lips. I could do it. I could do it now.

As he drove out of the gates and on up to the Castel San Marco, he concentrated on the Monet. On the triumph of having found it. On the exultation of having reached the end of a very long journey. He'd deal with her husband over it, on Tuesday. Just Aldo Cressini. He'd wait for him and have it out then. He sensed it would be better like that. Better if he didn't see her again.

ROME

Sunday, 20 June

Late afternoon: Cambres sat in the Caffe Greco with an espresso in front of him. He glanced round the familiar polished and panelled interior. Old wood and red velvet, hung with early nineteenth-century landscapes of the Roman *campagna*. It was a place of calm, redolent of the old Rome. He was waiting for Donaghy. He was early for the appointment. If he'd been followed this time, he wasn't aware of it. It wouldn't have deterred him, anyway. Not now. He'd finally steeled himself that morning, and rung Donaghy's extension. This time, he'd held on till Donaghy was found. Because he'd resolved that now they had to talk. Now risks had to be taken.

The event that had strengthened his will had been the meeting with Daniel Stern. He had been over it repeatedly in his mind in the days since. It cast a new light over everything. A hard and terrible light, as far as the history of Gabrielle's Monet was concerned. The fact that the painting had been stolen from victims of

Auschwitz added a vast and unsuspected dimension of guilt to Pro Deo's acquisition of it. Giving Daniel Stern the name and address of Aldo Cressini had been a sort of first aid to Cambres's conscience, a field dressing to the bleeding wound. Treatment of the deeper guilt would take far longer. But on the other hand, it had been a beginning. A first step in the reconstruction of his own personal understanding of right and wrong, in his agonising reconciliation of the present with the past. And a first step in the excision of the corruption from within Pro Deo itself.

Suddenly, Father Donaghy was at his shoulder. Cambres had forgotten how large and cumbersome he was. Still sweating. Still the same protuberant eyes behind the spectacles. But animated now, feverish. Not quite under control. Too big for the space allowed by the table, as though he might at any moment upset a chair or knock over a glass. Dangerous.

Donaghy arranged himself precariously over his seat. 'I was very worried about you, Father,' he said. 'Particularly when you didn't make it last time. What's been happening to you?'

Cambres, talking softly but urgently, began an account of his experiences in the weeks since they'd last met. He wasn't prepared for the cathartic relief that talking freely induced in him, and his story came out in a torrent, an irresistible stream of narrative. All the things he'd had to withhold from his confessor surged forth now, undammed. Over coffee and mineral water and then a glass of grappa, he told Donaghy everything, or almost everything; certainly far more than he had intended emerged in that intense little red velvet booth of the Caffe Greco. He told him how he'd expressed his reservations about the Service's financial activities to his confessor. How he'd been sent into enforced retreat to examine his conscience. How he'd gained release only by recanting his doubts under personal pressure from Tafurel himself. Then he told him about the break-in at his apartment, and the man in the yellow shirt who had been following him the next day. And finally, he found himself telling him about Daniel Stern. About the sad and terrible history of the Monet *Poplars*. He'd intended to keep that bit back from Donaghy, as a revelation personal only to himself. A development too complicated to explain. But out that came too, along with the rest. In fact there was only one tree of memory that the tidal wave did not uproot and spew forth now. Only one stuck fast. There was no mention for Donaghy of Gabrielle Gascoigne. No mention of the precise circumstances of the painting's donation to Pro Deo.

'It's a desperate situation,' said Donaghy, leaning forward over the table so that Cambres could see the little beads of perspiration on his forehead. 'Those within our Service who do not know what has been going on refuse to believe; and those who do know conspire together to protect themselves, to deny that there's been any wrongdoing. And worse, there is an element among the conspirators prepared to take even more extreme measures. Like your burglary. I am sorry for you, Father, but I am not surprised.'

Five weeks ago Cambres would have laughed at such an analysis. But now he knew differently. Now he was forced to agree with it.

'It's time to take action,' said Donaghy. 'You must feel the same yourself, don't you, Father? After what you've told me?'

Still Cambres held back from the final commitment. 'What do you suggest?'

Donaghy sighed. 'I have to tell you I've taken a decision,' he said. 'I took it yesterday. Everything you've just told me convinces me it was the right one.'

Cambres felt a terrible presentiment; a panic, a surge of cowardice. For a moment he wanted to run, as far from Donaghy as possible, to hide himself. To get away from what he was about to hear. 'What have you decided?'

'I have made an appointment with di Livio tomorrow afternoon.' He paused, looking away from Cambres. Staring out into the Via Condotti, where the crowds of shoppers swirled. 'I am going to show him the papers. The print-outs from the Pro Deo accounts.'

'But we cannot let this matter go outside the Service.'

'Believe me, Father, I have not taken this decision lightly. Perhaps I am doing wrong. But I do so in order to right even greater wrongs.'

Cambres was silent. In his mind's eye, he saw many things. He glimpsed again the horrified expression of Sybil Gascoigne as she stood momentarily transfixed in the slit of the half-open bedroom door. He relived the unwilling tears of Daniel Stern. Then he looked up, with a wordless spreading of his hands. To indicate his agonised agreement.

He asked Donaghy, 'What sort of man is this di Livio?'

'I think he is a good man. I trust him to do what is right.'

'But, Father, these are secrets. Secrets of the Service. We have taken vows of obedience.'

'I am sorry. But I don't believe we can allow what has been going on in our Service to continue. If this evil is allowed to flourish, it will destroy all the good that Pro Deo has ever achieved. In your heart, I think you believe that too.'

'I do, but . . .'

'If you have any doubts that what I'm proposing is right, then answer me this, Father. Honestly. Do you believe that our Church's record over the Holocaust is so snow white that we can afford to profit by one single dollar from money tainted by the blood of Auschwitz victims? Honestly, now? Can we live with that on our conscience?'

Both men's eyes engaged, then Cambres looked away. 'No. Of course we can't.' The words came out obstructed, all mellifluity strangled.

'I want to give you something,' Donaghy continued. He reached into his jacket pocket and came out with an envelope. On the envelope was written di Livio's telephone number. In the envelope was a key. A key with a metal disk attached to it on which was incised a number.

'What is that?'

'The key will open a left-luggage locker at the Tiburtina railway station here in Rome. I've deposited a duplicate set of print-outs of the relevant transactions there. For security's sake. In case ...' Donaghy shrugged, looking slightly foolish. They both realised that the sentence was difficult to complete. An absurd conversation for two priests to be having. It might have been comic if it hadn't been so appalling.

Cambres took the envelope and its contents. He could not think of any reason to refuse, but he accepted it with reluctance. Its possession widened still further the already disturbing dimensions of his new, clandestine world. Unwillingly he had been propelled into an unfamiliar existence of secrets and dissimulation, a life in which, because truth was no longer the automatic currency, you had to be constantly on your guard as to what you said and did. To remember what you'd told to whom. His sister's orange groves suddenly seemed a desperately tempting refuge.

Ill at ease, he took his leave of Donaghy and walked slowly back through the broiling city to his quarters. He didn't even look behind him to see if he was followed. Somehow it no longer mattered.

ANDRISIO

Monday, 21 June

It was six in the evening. From the balcony of his room in the Castel San Marco, Daniel watched the shadows lengthening across the valley below. It had been a long forty-eight hours of waiting. He'd written a little and read. And thought a lot, too.

The telephone rang. Daniel got up, grateful for the distraction. It was the reception desk downstairs.

'Mr Stern, there is a visitor for you.'

'Who is it?'

'It is a lady, Mr Stern. She will not give her name. But she says you will know her. It is about redesigning her swimming pool.'

He ran down the stairs, surprised by the intensity of his own excitement. He found her sitting at a table on the terrace. When she saw him, she smiled, and shrugged her shoulders. As if to say, Well, really, what can one do?

'It's good to see you again.'

'I was passing by,' she explained. 'I thought I would check how is the great writer.'

'Stagnating,' he said. 'What about a drink?'

'That would be nice.'

When the waiter had brought the glasses, he raised his to her and said, 'So. Tell me your life story.'

She hesitated. 'It is not very much that you demand to know, is it?'

'With me,' he said, 'it's all or nothing.'

She shook her head and laughed. 'I can believe that,' she said.

But bit by bit he encouraged it out of her. About her childhood in Normandy, about her studies in Paris. How she'd got her first job working for an advertising agency in Milan. How in Milan she'd met Aldo Cressini and five years ago she'd married him. 'He is older, you see. He had been married before. He was very rich, very charming. I was very young.' She shrugged again. Helplessly. From the expressiveness of that single gesture, Daniel began to piece it together. How the familiar bargain – the older man's power and money in exchange for her youth and beauty – had gradually failed for her. How she strove to combat her restlessness.

'And now?' he asked. 'What do you do each day?'

She looked away from him, across the valley to the distant mountain-tops. 'Oh, I am busy,' she said. 'Busy with many things.'

He suddenly wanted to make her confront her boredom. Admit to her loneliness. 'Yes, but tell me, I'm interested. What did you do yesterday, for instance?'

'Yesterday?' She thought about it carefully. 'I went to Mass, in Andrisio.'

'To Mass?'

'You are surprised? You are not Catholic?'

'No,' he said. 'I'm Jewish.'

She regarded him, intrigued. 'I do not know well any Jews. But people say that *au fond* we are similar, Jews and Catholics. Because our beliefs are strong.'

'Strong, but different.'

'In what way, different?'

'Look,' he told her, 'I'm not religious, I'm not practising, but I do know that in the Jewish faith you obey the laws of God for their own sake. Not because you hope to ingratiate yourself with your Maker and build up your reward in some afterlife.' He told her about the inscription on the tablet in San Luigi dei Francesi.

She shook her head. Animated. 'No more indulgences now,' she said. 'What Jews and Catholics do is the same thing, I think. In the end we both obey God's will because to do so makes us happy.'

Daniel thought of Gabrielle Gascoigne. Her religion had made her happy. But so, perhaps, had Father Cambres, when he came into her bed. Should he tell Juliette Cressini about that? Part of him wanted to, found the idea obliquely exciting.

'And what about sin?' he asked.

'What about it?'

'I mean, doesn't a Catholic gain absolution by confession?'

'Yes, if he truly repents of his sin.'

'It all seems too easy, the slate wiped clean like that.'

'Whereas you, you prefer to stay with your guilt, *non?*'

He looked up at her. She was laughing at him. He laughed too. 'Fatal to start a Jew on the subject of guilt,' he said. 'I apologise. We've become rather serious.'

'No, I enjoy this conversation. Arguing about philosophy and religion. It reminds me again of my student days.'

He suggested she should stay and have some dinner with him. She hesitated.

'Just a little pasta. Why not?' he persisted.

'You can be very determined, I think.'

'I'm sorry. Us writers. We really don't know how to behave in company. It's because we spend too much time alone with ourselves.'

'Very well,' she said. 'Just a little pasta.'

Later he walked her out to where her car was parked. It was almost dark. 'I'll call tomorrow,' he told her. 'To make an appointment to see your husband about the Monet.'

She stood for a moment by the open door of the car. Very still. Looking at him. He was aware of his own heart beating, very fast. He tried to prevent it happening, he fought against it. But all at once there was no alternative. Like with Leblanc in the Archive Room, he felt it coming. He was going to do it. Blow it all. Now. He moved towards her and kissed her. Hard. On the lips.

She broke away and hit him even harder on the cheek.

'*Merde!*' she said. Just that. Then she got into the car, and drove away.

ROME

Tuesday, 22 June

Cambres decided not to go to the Secretariat that morning. He could not face the charade of a day's work in the offices at Pro Deo's headquarters, sitting there writing letters, compiling reports, apportioning resources, all the time knowing that yesterday Father Donaghy would have taken the terrible step that he'd been proposing. Would have kept his appointment with di Livio. Divulged to an outsider the secrets of the Service's accounts. Cambres's awareness of his own complicity was better nursed here, on his own, in the privacy of his flat. So he called in to say he was sick. A touch of flu, you understand, a gastric complaint. No, not serious, he had no need of a doctor. Just rest; he'd be back in a day or two.

Perhaps it was simply cowardice that paralysed him, a deficiency in courage that now prevented him from ringing Donaghy direct. To see how the meeting had gone, to find out what exactly di Livio was planning to do with the information that had been entrusted to him. Perhaps it was an instinct for self-preservation that held Cambres back, a shameful desire to distance himself from the anguish and the turmoil that would be unleashed. What, me? No, I wasn't there, I was at home in bed. I had a stomach upset. It was nothing to do with me.

But it was everything to do with him, wasn't it? He'd been the one who'd made the first betrayal. He'd offered information to Daniel Stern, passed him Cressini's name and address. Aldo Cressini, friend and benefactor of Pro Deo, buyer of Gabrielle's Monet, the man whose identity was secret information. Sensitive information. Cambres had set the precedent, when in his compassion he had pointed Stern in the direction of the Villa Loretta, Andrisio. And after that he had not stood in the way of Donaghy taking this latest, most drastic step of all. In the end, perhaps he'd even encouraged it.

He held in his hand the envelope that Donaghy had given him on Sunday. The envelope containing the key, with di Livio's telephone number written on it. He pulled out his bed once more, dislodged the loose floorboard, and deposited the envelope in the hiding place. He thought fondly of the cool shade of his sister's orange groves, where it was his pleasure to sit in the late afternoon and read. He'd be there soon, in her farmhouse outside Seville. Far from all this. Far from the doubt and the care and the fear. Give me strength, O Lord, he prayed. Give me strength to do what is right. Give me strength to see this through.

ANDRISIO

Tuesday, 22 June

'So,' said Aldo Cressini. 'My wife tells me you are writing a book.'

They were sitting in the same big, white drawing room where Daniel had sat with her three days ago, but it was just Daniel and Cressini now. Looking across at the same sinuous line of poplars, hanging on the wall opposite the fireplace. 'I am, about Monet,' said Daniel. He'd judged it better to preserve his cover. For the time being. 'In fact, I have done quite a lot of research on your painting.'

He studied Cressini. With even more curiosity now than he would have shown three days ago: this was not only the illicit owner of the Monet, this was the husband of Juliette. The man had a hard face. It was framed by beautifully kempt grey hair, but that could not disguise its vestigial brutality. He was in his early sixties, guessed Daniel, which made him thirty years older than her. And yet, looking at him, the gap in their ages did not seem so stark. What narrowed it was money, the emollience of wealth. Cressini looked rich, his house looked rich, and his wife looked rich. This shared familiarity with luxury and comfort gave them a certain similarity. Distanced her from Daniel. On the surface, at least. Daniel wondered where she was this morning. He hadn't seen her. He touched his own cheek. The memory of where she had hit him yesterday was still fresh. Still tender. Still not understood.

'It is of course a masterpiece,' Cressini said. He got up from his chair and walked over to the painting itself. Daniel joined him, and they both stood in front of it for a moment. The recession of the trees created a sinuous movement across the surface of the picture. The sweep of its curves was exciting. Daniel caught it once more: the artist's sheer exhilaration in front of nature. So did Cressini, perhaps. He raised a large and coarsened hand to the painting; then, with an action simultaneously awkward and infinitely possessive, he stroked the frame. Caressed it. Asserting his pride in the Monet's ownership. And yet limiting it, pinning it down like a captured butterfly; defining its existence simply as a thing.

'It's a beautiful painting,' agreed Daniel. A beautiful painting that belonged to his family. That had been stolen from Maurice Benjamin's study in July 1942. That was hanging here under false pretences.

Cressini lit a small cigar and turned to face him. When he spoke again, it was with sudden, barely suppressed violence. 'So now you tell me something. How the fuck did you know it was here?'

*　　*　　*

'You have finished?' said Cressini a little later. 'This is all you have for me?'

What more did the man want? Daniel had fed him Auschwitz, the Vélodrome d'Hiver, the looting of the abandoned apartment. The subsequent passage of the painting from Gabrielle Gascoigne to Pro Deo. The evidence of the diary. The testimony of Thérèse Lisieux. He'd prepared a file of it all, with photographs and photocopies. Press cuttings of other successful Jewish claims for the restitution of looted works of art. 'I would have thought it was enough,' said Daniel.

'Enough for what?'

'Enough to establish my family's claim to the Monet.'

Cressini laughed. Said nothing, just laughed.

'I have a file here for you. Of the facts.' Daniel reached over to pass it to him, but Cressini put it aside without looking at it. Put it aside, and stared very intently at Daniel.

'So, my friend. What is it exactly that you want from me?'

Daniel was angry now. He was not this man's friend. 'I want my family's picture back,' he said simply.

Cressini nodded. Patronisingly. As if Daniel were a child. 'I have to tell you, Mr Stern: there is no chance of that happening. I own the painting now. I bought it legitimately. I paid a lot of money for it.'

Daniel's fury was rising. He wanted to shake Cressini.

Activate some lever to destabilise his confidence, under-mine his arrogance. 'And I have to tell you something, Dr Cressini,' he said. 'Something perhaps you haven't thought through. Regardless of the ultimate strength of my family's case, once this claim is in the public domain, your Monet will become a totally unnegotiable asset. No one will buy it with a restitution claim hanging over it.'

There was silence. Cressini started to say something, then checked himself. 'If you put it like that,' he said carefully, 'the necessity to resolve the matter becomes of course more pressing. To settle it once and for all.'

'Exactly what I'm saying.'

'So you must excuse me for a moment. I have to make a telephone call.'

Left alone, Daniel stood up. He was shaking slightly after the intensity of the exchange. But he felt better. He'd enjoyed jolting Cressini. He walked over to the window. He noticed a number of framed photographs on a table, and picked one up. It showed Cressini bowing solemnly before the Pope. The Pontiff's hands were outstretched towards him in a gesture of blessing. Of absolution. He picked up another. In this one Cressini stood much more intimately with a tall, thin man dressed in the purple of a cardinal's cassock. Both smiled, as if amused by a shared joke. Complicit. Daniel looked closer, and suddenly recognised the face of the man in purple. Of course, from Nat's press cuttings: Cardinal Edmondo Tafurel. The Prelate-General of Pro Deo. He felt the interlocking of the pieces. The links in the chain that bound all the players together. Be careful, Cambres had warned him. This man, this Cressini: he is *sensa scrupoli*. He is dangerous.

When Cressini came back into the room he was smiling. His mood had changed. Mellower. Affable, even.

'So,' he said, lighting another cigar. 'I have spoken with my lawyer. He's going to look at it, give his opinion on the question. Allow us a few days, OK? Then we'll come back to you.'

'When?'

'Early next week. Where will you be?'

'In Paris,' Daniel told him. 'Or perhaps in London. You have both my numbers in the file.'

'We'll call you. On Monday.' His whole manner was now more reasonable. 'Don't worry, we shall work something out. A solution. You are right, it is in no one's interests to leave it hanging over us.'

Daniel acquiesced. He had no reason not to believe the man. After all, the justice of his family's claim on the painting was self-evident.

In the hall, as he was leaving, he was suddenly aware of a movement on the sweeping staircase. A figure coming down. It was Juliette. Cool. Distant. But her eyes were sad.

'*Carissima*,' said Cressini. His whole expression softened, but Daniel noticed there was simultaneously a little flicker of anguish. 'Of course, you know Mr Stern. He is just leaving.'

She nodded briefly in Daniel's direction, then went on speaking to Cressini. 'I have to go out,' she said.

Daniel watched Cressini's reaction. From the fleeting pain in the older man's eyes, he had an intimation of the relationship between them. Cressini was a powerful and ruthless bully, but he worshipped this woman. She was his weakness, his Achilles' heel, the only way he could be hurt. And his growing inability to communicate with her was tearing him apart. 'Will you be long?' he asked her.

'An hour or two.' She opened the door. 'I'll see Mr Stern to his car.'

Daniel followed her out. He wondered what she was going to say. Remonstrate with him, perhaps. Complain again about his behaviour of yesterday. She had every right to do so. He'd blown it, hadn't he? Overstepped the mark. Perhaps he should say something now. Apologise to her, try and smooth things over. He was on the point of it, but as soon as they were alone it was she who spoke first. 'Where do you go now?' she asked him.

'Back to Paris, I suppose. To do some more work on the book.'

Round the corner, where he had parked his hired car, she turned to him quickly and put something in his hand. A card. 'What's this?'

'It's my mobile number. Call me from Paris. God forgive me, but I've been thinking about you all night.'

ROME

Wednesday, 23 June

Cambres made coffee and sat drinking it, staring out of the window of his flat. He watched a woman opposite laboriously stringing out washing along a line on her balcony. The morning sun was hot, and there was a light breeze today from the direction of the sea. Good drying weather. He reflected it was now two days since Donaghy's appointment with di Livio. What was done was done. There could be no going back now. Perhaps there was even an oblique comfort in the knowledge that Pro Deo's dirty washing – like his neighbour's – was also finally in the public domain.

He thought about a second espresso, but decided against it. It might well be the coffee that was making his hand shake so. Or perhaps it was the uncertainty that was beginning to get to him. It was no good, he decided, going on in this state of deliberate ignorance. He couldn't bear it any longer. He found he now needed to know what had happened. Needed to talk once more to Donaghy. If you have helped a man sharpen the axe with which he proposes to cut through the trunk of a massive tree, you need to know his progress. So you are not caught underneath it when it finally falls.

He dialled Father Donaghy's office extension in Pro Deo's headquarters. The line rang for some time before it was answered by an unfamiliar voice. Momentary cowardice almost persuaded Cambres to put the receiver down again, but he decided to risk it. Calling Donaghy was not in itself a criminal offence. Besides, he was suddenly anxious not just to know the outcome of Donaghy's meeting with di Livio, but about Donaghy him-self. The man was so impetuous. He hoped he hadn't exposed himself to unnecessary danger.

'Is Father Donaghy there, please?'

The pause gave it away. The pause in which he could sense the speaker searching for the right words. 'I am very sorry. You haven't heard the bad news about Father Donaghy?'

'Bad news?' Cambres felt not just fear, but the edge of panic.

'Who's that speaking, please?'

'Father Cambres. *Pro Deo pugnamus.*'

'*Pro Deo pugnamus.*' A moment's further hesitation, then: 'Well, Father, it's all very tragic. Father Donaghy had a massive heart attack. He never regained consciousness. We're still in a state of shock here, as you may imagine.'

'A heart attack? When was this?'

'Three nights ago. We heard on Monday morning.'

Cambres replaced the receiver and sat for a moment staring at the wall in front of him. Calculating. Three nights ago: that meant the night after they'd met in the Caffe Greco. The night before Donaghy's appointment with di Livio, the appointment he couldn't therefore have kept. A massive heart attack. A sudden, massive heart attack. It was hard to believe: had Donaghy any history of cardiac trouble? He was a young man, in his thirties. A little overweight, perhaps, and short of breath sometimes. But the impression Donaghy had always made on him had been one of tremendous life and energy. Cambres felt sick at the untimely termination of all that. He felt horror at the suspicions mounting within him. And once again he felt very, very alone.

PARIS

Saturday, 26 June

Daniel waited for her. In his apartment up beneath the eaves in the rue Servandoni, pacing the tiny rooms. It was a hot evening, and he kept the windows open. Every time he heard a car in the little street below, he peered out, in case it was her taxi.

Almost as soon as he had arrived back here from Andrisio, he had rung her. Just a line of eleven digits she'd left with him, written hastily in felt tip. But written by her. He'd savoured each curl of the pen round the fat zeros, analysed the firm downward thrusts of the vertical lines, indulged in elaborate speculations about the intricacies of her character on the meagre evidence of the way she constructed her fours. He was fascinated by her, obsessed. He couldn't put from his mind those last words she'd said to him. *God forgive me, but I've been thinking about you all night.*

'Thank God, it's you.' From the intensity of the relief in her tone when she'd answered his call, he'd known for sure that they'd crossed a boundary. Passed into territory from which there was no going back.

'I'm coming to Paris,' she had told him. 'On Saturday. To see my mother. You will still be there?'

When she finally reached the rue Servandoni that evening, it was on foot, not by taxi. Thus he wasn't aware of her arrival until he heard the bell ringing and found her standing outside his door at the top of the stairwell. He could not quite believe that it was happening. She looked even more beautiful than he remembered.

'Don't worry,' she said, leaning forward to kiss him on the cheek, 'I do not hit you this time.'

'That's a relief.'

She gave her shrug again. The shrug that said, it's terrible, but what can one do? She had the most expressive shoulders he had ever seen.

He took her for dinner at the bistro round the corner. It was still warm, and they ate outside. They drank a bottle of wine and gradually she told him things. About her marriage. About her unhappiness. About the way Cressini would not leave her alone, checked up on her the whole time, was neurotic about losing her. Coming to visit her mother here in Paris was one of the few pretexts that gave her the chance to travel alone. 'I am not his wife,' she told him. 'I am his prisoner.'

'Your husband,' Daniel asked her, 'what exactly does he do?' He knew that Cressini's world encompassed Pro Deo, and Monet, and the making of a lot of money. But how he did that was not clear. Except that Cambres had been at pains to warn him that Cressini was without scruple. A dangerous man. Daniel was curious as to how much she knew.

'Business,' she said. 'Always business. He owns much property, I think. Not just in Europe but in America also. But these are the things that he does not talk to me about.'

I still have some business with him, he was on the point of telling her. With your husband. Serious business. Unfinished business. But he decided to keep it from her. To keep it separate. To disentangle the two strands of obsession in his life. What good would it do for her to know, for him to rehearse to her all the sad details of his grandparents' tragedy? Not yet. It was too big an additional force to add to the emotional dynamic that already existed between them.

Later she returned to the Monet. 'Did you get from him what you were seeking?' she asked him. 'About the painting, for your research?'

'Up to a point,' he said.

'Sometimes he tells to me that he loves that Monet.'

'And does he love it, do you think?'

'Perhaps, in a way. He is proud to own it. To show it off.'

Daniel remembered the awkward, possessive gesture. The coarse hand caressing the frame. 'Yes,' he said. 'I can believe that.'

'Perhaps he feels about me a bit the same way,' she said. For a moment, Daniel saw a flicker of residual tenderness in her eyes. She didn't hate Cressini. But she was suffocated by him. Had to get away.

She came back up to the apartment with him.

'I couldn't stop thinking about you, either,' Daniel told her.

'I know,' she said. 'We're crazy, aren't we?'

He kissed her properly. 'Crazy.'

'I feel like a schoolgirl again,' she giggled in her husky, infinitely sexy voice. 'I told my mother not to wait up because I might be staying the night with a friend.'

The next morning, he was woken by the telephone ringing. He felt her body lying against him, warm and somnolent. He got up and went to the receiver. Standing there naked.

'Cressini,' said the voice at the other end. 'My lawyer will see you tomorrow, in London. Clermont Hotel at seven p.m. He has a proposal to make. Ask for Mr Vincent.'

Daniel stared across at her. Mrs Aldo Cressini. Stirring softly in his bed. Keep them separate, he told himself. The one has no bearing on the other. But before he replied he reached across and covered himself with a towel.

'I'll be there,' he said. 'Seven o'clock at the Clermont Hotel.'

ROME

Monday, 28 June

That morning, in the private chapel of Pro Deo head-quarters, there was a requiem Mass for Father Dermot Donaghy. It was an opportunity for the Service to pay its last respects to one of their own. To give thanks for the life of an obedient soldier. To pray for his soul. Cambres attended, sad and wary; but curious, too. He looked about him. There was his confessor, Abello; stalwart, faintly combative, still the bird with its feathers puffed up to see off challengers of Service orthodoxy. And Cardinal Tafurel. The Prelate-General himself. Cambres watched Tafurel surreptitiously through his fingers as he prayed. Tafurel knelt, straight-backed, at his stall. Thin, determined. A leader of men. An imposer of his will on others. Only God knew how easy his Eminence's conscience lay within him. Only God knew the truth about Father Donaghy's death. Perhaps the man had really suffered from a coronary condition. Perhaps.

Cambres remembered the first time he'd spoken to him, up in the seething crowd of the Olympic Stadium.

The eager way he'd leaned across to him. The genuineness of his outrage. He'd been a good man. Then Cambres bent his own head in prayer too. He prayed for the soul of Father Donaghy, who had died determined to do his duty. His body was to be flown back to Ireland, to the village in Cork which he'd left fifteen years ago to come to Rome. He prayed for the people who would receive back his remains. His grieving mother and his brother, his aunt and his uncle, his five little nephews and nieces. And finally Cambres prayed for himself. For guidance. For help to make the right decision.

When Cambres came out of the chapel at the end of Mass, nodding distant greetings to his colleagues as they dispersed in the sunshine, he knew the time had come. His resolve had hardened. There was still something he had to do. Something he owed to the dead priest's memory.

He made the call from a public telephone box a little later that afternoon. A public telephone box just off the Via del Corso. Where the traffic was busy. Where there was a constant stream of pedestrians Where no one would pay much attention to an anonymous priest on the telephone.

'Signor di Livio?'

'Yes.'

'My name is Father Alfonso Cambres. I am ... I was a friend of Father Donaghy.'

'Father Donaghy, yes, of course. I was very sorry to hear the news about him.'

'It was a great loss for us all. He was still such a young

man.' Cambres paused and glanced about him. Checking on passers-by. On anyone loitering too near the booth. When he spoke again it was in a quieter voice but with more urgency: 'I'm telephoning you now because I believe that you had an appointment with Father Donaghy the day after he died.'

'I did, yes.'

'And I think there was certain ... certain information that he was going to pass to you at that meeting.'

If the other man's interest quickened, it was not perceptible on the telephone. Di Livio's voice remained calm. 'There was, but I never received it,' he said.

'I think I can help you. If you still need the information, that is.'

'I do need it, very much indeed, Father.'

Cambres paused. How could he be sure about di Livio? How could he be certain that he was honest and reliable, a suitable person to be entrusted with these terrible secrets? He must see him, talk to him, make his own assessment of the man before he finally allowed him access to them. Before he finally handed him the axe that would bring the whole tree down.

'Then meet me at the Tiburtina railway station tomorrow morning,' he said. 'Eleven o'clock. By the left-luggage lockers, at platform thirteen.'

LONDON

Monday, 28 June

At first Daniel dozed on the train. His somnolence had a sensual undertow, as if part of him were still back there in bed with her, in the seclusion of the apartment. The taste of her, her scent, the feel of her skin still lingered with him. *Jesus, Daniel, what are we doing? Are we totally crazy?*

Then, in order to focus himself, to concentrate his mind, he brought it out again: the photograph of the Monet. The original one, which he'd taken from his mother's file. It was a little battered now, but he kept it with him as some sort of talisman, a reminder of the challenge he had set himself, the duty he owed to his people. A symbol of the redemption of his family's suffering that the painting's reacquisition would achieve. Well, he'd listen to what Cressini's legal adviser had to say. Under what terms the restitution of the painting to his family could be brokered. Then it might be time to bring in his own lawyers, to tie up the details. Perhaps he wasn't going to get his picture back today, but there was every chance he was going to take a big step forward. The righteousness of his claim was self-evident, Daniel believed, even to a bully like Cressini. Ultimately the man, however unscrupulous, would have to come to terms with it. The fact of this meeting having been set up at all was testament to the necessity.

He sat and stared at the photograph, and gradually, swaying slightly with the motion of the speeding train, he began to dream again. The image began to dissolve, to separate itself from its function as a representation of nature and to exist simply as an abstract design. The foliage of the trees, receding away into the distance along the edge of the twisting river, formed a sinuous 'S' across the picture space, broken by the strong vertical lines of the straight trunks of the foremost poplars. For a brief moment, he achieved it: sensation without perception. All he saw were coloured shapes. Vision drained of knowledge. Perhaps that was what he should strive to attain with her, too, the same suspension of perception: just the sensation of Juliette as a beautiful woman. Not the knowledge of her as the wife of Aldo Cressini. Passion drained of guilt. Love in a vacuum.

Thoughtfully, he picked the photograph of the painting up and put it away. Into his inner breast pocket. The one that had the hole in the lining.

At Waterloo he caught a taxi. He reached the Clermont early and hung around the hotel foyer for a while. Then, a minute or two after the hour, he was announced and went up to Vincent's room.

Something was wrong. He sensed it the moment he stepped through the door of Room 623. He didn't like the atmosphere. Didn't like the man who greeted him in his shirtsleeves. Vincent had a veneer of smoothness, but Daniel recognised in him even more starkly the animal quality that was evident in Cressini. A grossness. Literally, a brutality.

'Who are you exactly?' Daniel asked him.

'In London I go under the name of Vincent. I am legal adviser to Aldo Cressini. I also happen to be his brother. Drink?'

Daniel Stern refused. It was a hot day and he was thirsty, but he found he didn't want to drink with this man. Didn't want to share anything with him. Cressini's brother poured himself something from the minibar. It could have been Scotch. He asked Daniel to take a seat. It was a big room, and Daniel found a chair as far away from him as possible, over by the bed. He remembered the warning Father Cambres had given him. With this man, he began to understand the priest's concern. Whatever Mr Vincent did – opening a door, uncapping a bottle, loosening his tie – the movement carried an undertone of violence, an intimation of menace.

Daniel's unease expressed itself in a gathering impatience. He didn't want this meeting to go on any longer than it had to. 'So I assume you've had a chance to consider my family's claim on the Monet,' he said.

'We looked at it.'

'And?'

'And what?'

'What are you going to do for me about this painting?'

The man turned on him then. 'I'll tell you what we're going to do for you, my friend.' He spoke with a kind of relish. Spoiling for a fight. 'We're going to do fuck all.'

The words took some time to sink in. 'What do you mean?'

Mr Vincent cradled his drink and smiled. As if he were enjoying himself. 'We've looked at the evidence in this case, and you know something? I almost feel sorry for you. You've got nothing. Nothing that carries any weight in a court of law. That file you gave to us, it's garbage. It's a nothing file. So you know what I did with it? I threw it away. Shredded it.'

Stern was in shock. But he said, 'You're forgetting the diary, my grandmother's diary.'

'That diary?' The man was laughing at him. 'Some hysterical woman scribbling her fantasies in a notebook. I'll tell you something for free: you're wasting your time if all you've got's the diary. You might as well give up and go home.'

'The evidence is that the Monet was stolen from my grandparents,' repeated Daniel doggedly. 'In 1942. Before they were sent off to die in Auschwitz.'

'What do you want from me with your sob stories?'

'You can't dismiss that diary.'

The other man narrowed his eyes and nodded. 'You know what I think? I think you made that diary up yourself, forged it. It's the kind of thing you people do, isn't it?'

You people. Daniel kept a grip on himself. 'I'm telling you, the diary is genuine.'

'Hysterical garbage. Forget it. Let me tell you something: we've had it all checked out. That evidence is nothing, not compared to the cast-iron proof of the Galerie Leblanc stock number.'

'What stock number?'

'The one on the back of my brother's painting. We've checked it with Leblanc's archives, and it all ties up. They bought the painting in 1939.'

'Yes, but ...'

'Hey, read my lips. They bought the painting in 1939.'

Daniel began to explain, reasonably, logically, about the discrepancy. How it must have arisen. How Galerie Leblanc were in it too, trying to rewrite history. But Vincent cut in, no longer listening to him. 'You know nothing,' he said. His amusement was gone now, his anger rising. 'I'll tell you what you are: you're ignorant Jewish scum.'

Strange that Daniel should remember now something his father had once told him. A piece of lore of the business jungle. The kind of practical wisdom that Arnold Stern dealt in, intelligence gathered from the front line of commercial warfare. Once an opponent starts abusing you, he told Daniel, be happy. Because you're winning, kid. It's an admission of the weakness of his ground, not its strength. No man whose case is castiron wastes breath on abusing his adversary.

The rage of Cressini's brother was horrific, like a huge dam breaking, like a fire suddenly flaring out of control: 'You make me sick, you Jewish scum. You think you can get away with anything nowadays. You and your fucking Holocaust. The best thing that ever happened to you, wasn't it, that fucking Holocaust? People like you have been exploiting it ever since. Getting rich on it.'

You can only take so much. Everyone has their breaking point. Here was this bastard saying the unspeakable. Accusing him of exploiting the suffering of his own people. And calling his grandmother a liar. A hysterical liar. His mother's mother. The one they dragged away to Auschwitz with her husband and her little crying son. Laying into Daniel himself was one thing, he knew how to handle that, but what right had this heap of shit to abuse her? That was unforgivable.

Stern controlled himself enough to get some words out. Still rational, still logical, 'All this doesn't change what I told your brother, you know,' he said. 'Whatever you think of my family's case, once this claim is out in public, your Monet will become a totally unrealisable asset. No one will buy it with a restitution claim hanging over it.'

There was a brief silence. Daniel sensed that what he'd just said had finally made an impact. But simultaneously triggered something unforeseen. Something dangerous. Cressini's brother looked at him for a moment. Daniel had never seen such hatred coming out of a man's eyes as he did then. A virulent malignancy directed against him personally, sharpened by an antipathy as irrational as it was deeply rooted. An antipathy for his whole race. Mr Vincent nodded, very slowly. 'OK, Jewish smart-ass scum.' He said that slowly, too. Everything was in a kind of slow motion now.

The man stood up. The next thing he did was strange. He switched the television on. Loudly. After that he reached behind him, picked something up, and came towards Daniel. It was a small metal object, with a barrel.

Daniel saw it then. With that crystalline clarity that the slowing of the action created. From the Cressinis' point of view, the consequence of what he had said about the restitution claim was entirely logical. From now on, so long as Daniel was about, Aldo Cressini's asset was unnegotiable. The brother was going to have to take Daniel out. Eliminate him. Maybe that had been the intention all along. Maybe all this talk about stock numbers and diaries had just been a preamble; a charade. And the noise of the television was going to drown the noise of the shooting.

Daniel got up from his chair. He felt many things at that moment, but most of all he felt a wild, surging fury of his own. An answering rage. If this bastard killed him, it would mean they'd won. The people who'd sent his grandparents to Auschwitz would have won another victory from beyond the grave; the people who'd stolen their Monet would have triumphed too. The legitimacy of its ownership would go unchallenged for ever. And he'd be one more dead Jew to add to the list. Like his grandparents and their little son. Like his mother, half a century on, mangled in the wreckage of her car. It was the injustice of it all. The flagrant unfairness. The cycle of oppression must be broken.

The man was still coming towards him. Maybe he expected Daniel to run, to try to get away. Maybe he expected him to collapse on the floor, to whimper for mercy. Maybe he just wasn't expecting what Daniel did next.

Daniel went for him. Threw himself at him. Vincent was strong, but Daniel was momentarily stronger. He managed to grab the hand that held the gun. Twist its barrel away. Anywhere away from his own body.

He didn't know how it went off. Whose pressure finally triggered it. Perhaps it was some involuntary convulsion of Vincent's. Or perhaps Daniel did it himself. He hadn't intended to; but perhaps he wanted to, which in the end amounted to the same thing. He heard the shot, but did not immediately recognise it for what it was. Sensation without perception. Muffled, oddly indistinct. Then he knew. Something terrible had happened. For a split second, Daniel wondered if he himself had taken the bullet, whether he was in some curious state of anaesthetised suspension of pain, whether he would very shortly collapse and lose consciousness. But the next thing he registered was the other man's body giving a slight shiver, an obscene little parody of sexual pleasure, then going limp.

He fell forward, against Daniel. Daniel let him slide down slowly to the floor. He stepped back. There was a lot of blood. A terrible lot of blood.

Daniel Stern went a little crazy then. Not much registered with him, except the horror of it. And an absolute compulsion to get away from that horror. He looked down and saw the blood all over his jacket. He tore it off, but something must have been going on in his brain, because he pulled out his wallet and personal things before he abandoned it there. Then he grabbed his attaché case and ran. He just had to get away. He wasn't aware of what he'd done, not consciously. All he felt was the flickering, slow-burning anger. He concentrated on the simple things now, the sheer mechanics of movement. He shut the door after him and walked down the passage to the lift. He pressed the button and when the lift came he descended to the ground floor. Here he walked out of the hotel. By the secondary entrance, into Mount Street. He just kept walking, in his shirtsleeves. Right across Berkeley Square and Bond Street, and on to Regent Street. Then down to Piccadilly.

As he crossed Leicester Square, he happened to put his hand in his pocket. It tightened round a heavy metal object that he didn't recognise. It was then that he realised that he must have brought the gun away with him. He registered it distantly, as a problem. But a problem with a solution. So he continued on to Charing Cross, and the river.

Part Three

PARIS

Tuesday, 29 June

Daniel Stern was still angry. But now he was tired, and a little bit afraid.

This train: why did it keep stopping? Not just at a string of deserted stations with unfamiliar names, but also suddenly, arbitrarily, on empty stretches of track. Long, unexplained phases of immobility, as dawn broke and the midsummer sun rose slowly, spreading its milky pink light over the dull Normandy countryside. This was a flat and depressing landscape, punctuated by squat farm buildings and distant villages clustered round prosaic church spires. It was a god-forsaken time to be awake. A young man and a girl were arguing several compartments farther up. American backpackers. Their voices rose and fell as they quarrelled over itineraries and dollar exchange rates. Over what time this bloody train was going to reach Paris. Never, at this rate. Why couldn't they shut up, just give it a rest?

No, don't go to sleep. Dangerous to go to sleep. Must

stay alert, on guard, otherwise ... Otherwise what? No, don't think about it. Jesus, that blood. So much of it. The body slumped on the floor at the end of the bed. The green and yellow pattern of the carpet. Green and yellow squares, overlaid with a swelling crimson. Bastard. Him or you. The brutal, primal look in the man's eye as he came for you. The horror of the realisation that another human being was intent on taking your life. It could just as well have been your own blood oozing across that carpet. Just as well been you left lying there dead, impervious to the blaring television.

That left Aldo Cressini. He was still out there. Evil. Cold-blooded. He sent his brother to kill you. To *kill* you. When, by all the standards of moral right, he should have been finding ways to compensate you for your family's loss, he sent his brother to eliminate you. To wipe you out. And those words. Such words. You prayed you'd never hear such words again. You felt sick when you thought of them, the unspeakable things about Jews and the Holocaust. The insults to the memory of your grandparents; and, therefore, to your mother's memory too. Your grandmother and her diary: just the scribbling of some hysterical woman, he'd called it. These were the unforgivable things. These were the things that made you want to be back there in that hotel room. Pulling the trigger yourself. Intending to this time, pulling the trigger harder. A tooth for a tooth. An eye for an eye. An eye for an innocent eye.

You're on the run now. A hunted animal. Somewhere, not so far back, people are on your trail, tracking you, pursuing you. The police. Cressini's men. There's always the option of turning yourself in, of course. Because you've done nothing wrong. Nothing of which you won't ultimately be able to prove your innocence, with a lawyer good enough to show it was only self-defence. Easy. But not yet. The point is, you're not running because you're guilty. You're running to buy yourself time. You're ahead of the game, you're still in control; you've still got the time to do the things that need to be done. Once they're seen to, then you can give yourself up, sort it all out. On your own terms.

There was unfinished business to be settled. There were gaps to be filled in. You know the truth of it, but others still have to be convinced. You know the truth of what happened to the Monet, you believe implicitly in the evidence of your grandmother's diaries, in the guilt of Leblanc. What could be more compelling evidence of the validity of your family's claim on Cressini's painting than the fact that they tried to kill you? But the case isn't watertight. You've found nothing. Cressini's brother taunted you last night. Nothing that carries any weight in a court of law. Maybe the bastard had been right. Bainbridge again, the dried-up lawyer in Chancery Lane, suffocating with caution: weighing the evidence, calculating precedents, tacking on riders and provisos. And shaking his head. 'Not enough here, Mr Stern. Not enough to prove your case beyond all reasonable doubt.' You need that final proof; it's out there somewhere. Somewhere, there's something in an archive, some record, some witness whose evidence as to the Monet's wartime ownership will be conclusive. You cannot, must not, rest until you track it down. Only you can be trusted to do it. Only you want it enough. Get that proof, nail the guilty men. Beyond any doubt. And get the picture back. Then, and only then, you give yourself up. OK?

And there's her. There's Juliette. She's coming to you on Friday.

If you hand yourself over to the authorities now, one thing's for sure: you won't make that rendezvous. She won't find you when she comes up there to the apartment beneath the eaves. Your joint refuge, at the top of the last flight of stairs. Beyond control. Beyond care. If you turn yourself in now, maybe you'll never see her again. She'll ring the bell and there'll be no reply. That would be unbearable. That would make life meaningless. Buy the time till Friday, at least. Have one more night with her. Juliette.

The brakes locked and the wheels screamed on the rails. Another stop. Daniel shivered. He suddenly felt cold without his jacket.

Beauvais. The train started filling up with early morning commuters. Sleepy-looking men and women, mostly silent, except for a couple of girls who giggled and chattered in a corner as they put on their make-up in little mirrors and brushed out their hair. Daniel sat up straighter, edgy, on his guard again now that he was surrounded by people. They're looking at you. There's something strange about you. They can see the blood on your hands. A darkening crimson stain on the side of your shirt. All at once he felt oddly light-headed, slightly drunk. Keep a grip on yourself. It's the hunger, of course: you haven't eaten a proper meal since lunch-time yesterday. That, and the lack of sleep.

At the Gare du Nord, he was watchful as he reached the end of the platform. Watching for the watchers. But no official hand was laid on his shoulder. No one drew him quietly aside. Not yet. He relaxed a notch. He was still ahead of the game. In celebration he peeled off into the buffet and had coffee, two croissants, then a *croque monsieur*. After that he felt better. Better, but still on edge. It was the height of the rush hour, and he had to queue for twenty minutes to get a taxi. As he waited, he heard a police car siren. Closer. And closer still. Suddenly he wanted to run. This was it, they were coming for him. British police, French police: they would be working together now. He braced himself, flinched. Then the sound receded into the distance. His heart was still beating like a bird in a trap.

As soon as he reached his apartment, he locked the door after him, then walked quickly through each room. Living room, kitchen, bedroom, bathroom. Checking. First for signs of her: less than twenty-four hours ago they'd been alone together here. Laughing together, drinking coffee, making love. He buried his face in the pillow and caught the scent of her again. And checking for other things, too. Less definable things, but he'd know them when he saw them. Like a threatened animal, he felt his senses heightened, his antennae primed. Don't let your guard slip.

He went back into the bathroom and ran the shower. He stripped, and meticulously placed every item of clothing he'd been wearing into a black plastic rubbish sack from the kitchenette. Even his shoes. He secured it, and put it out ready for the communal garbage bin downstairs. Then he stepped under the hot water. Ah, that's good. Let it run over you. Now, soap every square centimetre of your body. Work the lather into your scalp, scrub your nails. No blood. Not the minutest splash, not the tiniest particle should remain. Wash yourself clean. Purify yourself.

Wrapped in a towel, he walked over to the bedroom window and looked out at the rooftops. He found himself measuring the distance he would have to jump to make his escape to the next building. If they came for him before he was ready.

What was happening to him? Perhaps over the past two months he'd been sinking gradually into a pit of madness. Perhaps sitting holed up here like some hunter's prey was the natural culmination of it all. He sensed the threats on all sides. Now he was like his grandmother. Now he too was locked in a cage of wild beasts without a whip or revolver. The revolver. He'd dropped that into the river. Deep into the swirling water of the Thames. He began to regret not having it any more.

ROME

Tuesday, 29 June

Di Livio got there fifteen minutes early. He wanted to stake out the ground in advance. To be prepared. He stood on the concourse at the end of the platform, near the magazine stall, within view of the row of left-luggage lockers. Watching. Waiting. Inventing things to do, pretexts for hanging around. He bought a copy of *La Gazzetta dello Sport* and leafed through its familiar pink pages. Some big cycle race had ended in controversy. There were accusations that the winner had used performance-enhancing drugs. Naughty boy. Disqualification might follow. Or it might not. Depending on how rich the winner's sponsors were. Typical of this bloody country. Everyone could be bought. At a price. Meanwhile Inter Milan were planning to spend sixty billion lira on an Argentinian striker. Sixty billion lira. That was one hell of a lot of money. How could any player be worth that much? You could buy a whole town with that kind of cash. Certainly several police forces and most of the judiciary. Or, if you were so inclined, sixty billion lira would acquire you just over two hundred and twenty kilos of best Colombian heroin, at current street prices. Just to put it in perspective.

He folded the newspaper and drank a Coca-Cola from the refreshment stand next door, which used up a bit more time. After the Coca-Cola he smoked a cigarette. He shouldn't have done that, not this early in the day. He was trying to quit. Luisa would be horrified if she knew. But when your life involved spending as much time waiting as his did, sometimes a cigarette was an irresistible compensation. Sometimes you earned it.

Waiting. He was trained for it, of course, it was part of his job. Ninety per cent of it, if you analysed this current case. You had to be patient, prepared to play the long game. He'd been waiting months for this particular prize, one way and another. Not literally standing around, like he was now, but generally biding his time. Not hurrying things. Playing a role. For the priest's benefit, pretending to be a journalist. Wheedling, cajoling, persuading, when the opportunity arose; sowing seeds of trust, then pausing, standing away a little, giving the confidence a chance to strengthen and grow. Waiting again. Getting closer, then farther away, then closer once more. Last week, he thought he'd got there with Donaghy, finally made the breakthrough. Everything had been in place. It had had the smell of success. I'm in, he'd told himself. I've done it. All those weeks talking to the man, building his trust, have come good. Then, suddenly, no more Donaghy. Disaster. In desperation he'd telephoned the number the priest had given him. The guy had died of a heart attack, he'd been told. *Morte improvvisa — da infarta miocardico acuto.* Jesus. Just what the hell was going on?

Now, just as suddenly, this new priest, this Cambres, had come through. Out of the blue. What was his game? Did he smell right? Di Livio would judge that very shortly. But the prize Cambres potentially brought with him was worth going to any lengths to secure.

Just before eleven he took up position so that he could see the road outside through the open entrance to the station, but still maintain surveillance of the luggage lockers. The luggage lockers were the meeting point. But where would this priest arrive from? Di Livio's attention was diverted by a train pulling in at platform twelve, all slamming doors, people shouting, and a quick surge of emerging travellers hurrying past him. Perhaps that was it, that was how Cambres would get here: he watched intently for a priest among the arriving passengers. There was a group of youths in T-shirts, a pair of nuns, a woman in her fifties dressed up like she was eighteen. The surge slowed to a trickle. No. No priest. He returned his gaze casually to the street outside. A line of parked cars: a van double-parked, making a delivery to the pizzeria opposite.

And at six minutes past he saw him, on the far pavement, moving slowly. Elderly man, carried himself well, smartly cut suit. Clerical collar. No mistake, that was him. He'd bet money on it.

Cambres stopped at the kerb, trying to cross to the station entrance. He took two diffident steps forward.

His view was blocked by the parked van. As di Livio watched, he heard the sudden roar of the gunned engine of a car, somewhere off his field of vision to the left. Approaching, obliquely threatening. Cambres took two more shuffling paces into the roadway itself. Car noise, to the left, accelerating. The priest stood for a split second, bemused, transfixed. Then, with a hideous inevitability, he was hit. A woman screamed. And the elegant black suit was lying crumpled in the roadway.

Di Livio ran out. He could still just see the car. It was speeding away to the right. A dark blue Fiat, registration number no longer discernible. He bent over the priest. The old boy was still alive at least, murmuring incoherently, a thin line of blood dribbling from his mouth, like the line of a road on a map. Di Livio pulled out his mobile telephone and called for an ambulance. Police and ambulance. Red alert. Maximum urgency.

He was joined by three or four others. Passers-by. Anxious. Concerned. Outraged. 'Did you see that? The bastard didn't even stop.'

'And a priest, too. There's no respect any more.'

'Some bloody junkie, most likely, drugged up to the eyeballs.'

One said she was a nurse, and began to make the old man a little more comfortable. Covered him with a coat. 'In shock,' she said. 'I think he may have broken his leg. But his pulse is still strong. Really, it's a miracle he's still alive.'

Di Livio nodded. He looked about him. And then

he noticed it, on the tarmac, four or five metres away. A very small envelope, just lying there, near the gutter. Small, sealed, containing something a little bit bulky. He rose from his haunches and walked over to check what it was.

It had a series of numbers on it. Familiar numbers. Jesus Christ, it was di Livio's own telephone number. The priest must have had it in his hand. Been clutching it, ready to pass over to him at their meeting. Another thirty centimetres to the right, and it would probably have slid down the drain.

Very casually, without drawing attention to himself, di Livio bent over to pick it up. No one noticed. They were all massing round Cambres, more and more of them. Gesticulating. Working each other up to new levels of citizenly outrage.

He slit the envelope open. Inside was a key, attached to a disc. On the disc was incised 'Tiburtina, no. 224'. He edged away, back into the station, back to the line of left-luggage lockers.

He found a bench a little way off, there on the station concourse. He sat down and read through them carefully, print-out by print-out, clutching the pages in his lap. He knew pretty soon that they were what they'd all been waiting for, that this was the breakthrough. He reached for his mobile and called immediately. It was insecure, of course, he shouldn't have done it, but when you lay hands on something that you've been tracking night and day for more than six months, when all the late evenings and the fruitless enquiries and Luisa's complaints about your inattentiveness finally pay off, perhaps you're entitled to a lapse.

'Put me on to Wesson,' he said to the voice that answered. 'Tell him it's Codename Sunflower. Tell him we've got a result.'

After he'd delivered his message, he walked back into the street, secreting the file of papers that he'd extracted from the locker in his rolled-up *Gazzetta dello Sport*. The ambulance was there. The priest was being lifted gently on to a stretcher. He approached one of the paramedics, and flashed ID at him.

'How's he doing?'

The man looked up, registered the badge and nodded deferentially. 'Heart's OK,' he said. 'He'll live.'

PARIS

Wednesday, 30 June

For the second day running, Daniel Stern arrived at the Archives Nationales, and impatiently negotiated the elaborate entry procedures. Showing his passport and entry card; stowing his personal effects into a see-through plastic bag; finding the pencil that was the only permitted writing material in the Salles de Consultations. Come on, come on. He knew what he had to look at now. At a set of records kept under the reference number AJ 38. Yesterday he'd come straight here from rue Servandoni, gritty-eyed after his sleepless night, and discovered that there were over six thousand boxes under that number. They mostly comprised the records of the Commissariat Général aux Questions Juives, the French government organisation that had overseen the Jewish 'problem' during the Occupation. Page upon page, dossier upon dossier, report upon report. They all stank, every one of them. They were rank with the odour of betrayal. Of cowardice and jealousy and persecution. Of petty bureaucrats saving their own skins, of the vindictive kicking of men too weak to fight back. 'I have the honour to draw your attention,' read one anonymous letter of denunciation written to the Commissariat in a neat, efficient hand, 'for whatever useful purposes it may serve, to the fact that an apartment at 57 *bis* Boulevard Rochechouart, belonging to the Jew Gresalmer, contains very fine furniture.' The Jew Gresalmer; the Jew Benjamin. Interchangeable. Revolting. Daniel saw how it must all have happened.

But he still needed the specific evidence in the case of his grandparents. So, like some cleaner of drains, he had to don protective clothing once more today and go down there, down into the sewers. Wallow in it. Search among the stench until he found what he needed. Some reference to the Benjamins. Some reference to their art collection. He must nail down the final proof of his grandparents' continuing ownership of the Monet. Show that as late as 1942 it had still been hanging in Maurice Benjamin's study. Perhaps in the process he might even come across some explanation as to why they'd been part of the horrendous events of 16 July 1942. Why their names had been included on the lists for *La Grande Rafle*.

He recognised the girl at the desk in the Salles des Consultations. She was the same one from yesterday.

'Back again?' She smiled at him. She wore spectacles, and had an odd little pointed face.

He nodded and smiled back. Look normal. Keep control. He was still moving in a strange, disorientated world, oddly lit, oddly angled, familiar objects unfamiliarly perceived. Even after nine hours' sleep last night. Nine hours' sleep with the chest of drawers wedged against the front door of the apartment, and the bedroom window ajar to the rooftops in case he had to make a run for it that way. Don't let your mind wander. Just keep a grip. Focus your attention on the single task in hand. Not the blood. Not the man's body shuddering; sliding down you on to the hotel carpet. Concentrate. Forget all that. You're just a writer doing some research.

'The same boxes as before?'

No. Not the same boxes. He'd finished with those yesterday. He'd finished with AJ 38-5940, lists of art collections seized from Jews, years 1940–42. He'd finished with AJ 38-6, denunciations and complaints against Jews, years 1941–44. He'd finished with AJ 38-7, lists of Jewish lawyers arrested on 31 August 1941. There'd been nothing there for him. Nothing under Benjamin.

'Today I need these boxes please, mademoiselle.' His voice sounded all right; she wasn't looking at him oddly. No blood still spattered on his fingers, no crimson stain still sunk into his sleeve. She inspected the numbers on the paper he passed to her. AJ 38-3807, Denunciations and Demands for the Acquisition of Jewish Goods (Surnames A–Be). And AJ 38-156, Dossiers on Individual Jews (Correspondence, various; Surnames Bas–Ben).

She looked at her screen, then back at him gravely. 'These I will order up for you. But I have to warn you, monsieur, about the strikes today.'

'Strikes?'

'Industrial action on the Métro. Only a few trains

are running. We are very short-staffed, we must close at midday.'

Bloody strikes. Bloody country. Still conspiring to prevent him getting to the truth. Taunting him. Offering him the evidence; then denying him the opportunity to study it properly. He took a seat at a desk and waited for his boxes to arrive. There was a terrible sense of time running out.

An hour and a half later, he found it. Just like that. One of the references that he was looking for. Not concealed in any way. Just a straightforward typewritten record. In Dossiers on Individual Jews (Bas–Ben), under Benjamin. He marvelled at the French bureaucratic mind: the need to register everything so diligently, in total conformity with the regulations. Even when what was recorded was so shameful. So compromising. In the merciless hindsight of history.

The folder jumped out at him. Surname Benjamin, first names Maurice Jacob. Age forty-two. Race *Juif*. An address in the rue Véronique. Its only enclosure was a record from the police Prefecture of the Ninth Arrondissement dated July 1942. There was even a case number appended. Utterly correct, this clerk at the prefecture. Missing nothing out. Filling in every box. Monsieur Benjamin had applied in person at the prefecture on the morning of 8 July. Appeared dressed up in his best suit, in order to file a complaint. An allegation of intimidation and molestation. An allegation against another French citizen. A Monsieur Emile Leblanc, of rue St Honoré.

It tied in sweetly with the diary. Danielle Benjamin had recorded her husband's report to the authorities about Emile Leblanc's behaviour. His complaint about Leblanc's harassment of them, Leblanc's hounding of them to sell him the Monet at an unfairly low price. And now here was corroboration: Maurice Benjamin had filed his complaint. On 8 July 1942. It had been a quixotic, hopelessly doomed attempt to achieve justice. But Maurice had made it, apparently still maintaining a blind and pathetic trust in the efficacy of the old ways, the sacrosanctity of proven legal processes. He couldn't see the irony of seeking redress from that same regime which for the past two years had done nothing but enact measures oppressing and discriminating against him and his race.

Daniel read on. And then it hit him, one more time. The tragic futility of his grandfather's efforts. Because a further prefecture report was attached. On the progress of the action. Monsieur Benjamin had apparently been asked by the police for a second statement. He had failed to provide it. In the absence of this second statement, the proceedings had lapsed. There had been deemed no case to answer on the part of Emile Leblanc. Straightforward, you would have thought. Until you saw the date on which application had been made to Monsieur Benjamin for this further statement: 23 July. It was hardly surprising that he had failed to respond. He hadn't been at home. No one had been at home. By that time they had all passed on from temporary detainment in the Vélodrome d'Hiver.

By then they were incarcerated in some prison camp. Perhaps the one at Drancy. Awaiting onward shipment east. To a place called Auschwitz.

'No, Mr Stern, not quite enough.' He could hear the lawyer Bainbridge's voice echoing its pessimistic refrain. 'What you have found is evidence of a dispute between Mr Benjamin and Mr Leblanc in July 1942. The complaint mentions intimidation and molestation, but it doesn't specifically mention the Monet. It doesn't in itself, therefore, prove that the Monet was still in Mr Benjamin's possession at this time.'

Jesus. It was in there somewhere. The final proof. He reached for the second box.

'Monsieur, I am afraid we are closing now.' It was the girl from the counter, calling over to him. 'Perhaps you will continue tomorrow? We are open at nine.'

He got up slowly and went across to her, handing her back the card he had had to fill in to gain access to the material. Cards, forms, records. The French loved them. But had they somewhere kept the ones that counted, the ones he really needed? He'd have to wait until tomorrow now to resume his search.

He walked back to the apartment. Down the rue des Archives, across the Seine and past Notre Dame, then on towards the Luxembourg Gardens and the rue Servandoni. The fresh air cleared his head a little. Enough to encourage him. He'd made progress today. There'd be more tomorrow. Hang on in there. And, apart from anything else, what a piece was going to emerge at the end of all this. What a story he was going to write. A book, even. A bloody marvellous book. As he strode up the Boulevard St Michel, he reached for the mobile phone in his attaché case. He flicked it open. Just checking. There was one message flashing. He had to ring Parnello Moran in London. He pushed the telephone shut again. He'd do it when he was home.

He was waiting for the lift in the hallway of the apartment building when Madame Albert's door opened and the concierge herself waddled out. This was a rare event, to see her vertical. Normally she sat immobile in her room, eyes glued to the soap on the TV screen, either chain-smoking or prising chocolate into her mouth. Sometimes both.

'*Bonjour, monsieur,*' she said conversationally.

'*Bonjour, madame,*' said Daniel. He'd introduced himself as Jarvis's tenant when he'd first moved in last month. Beyond that, he'd avoided extended contact. His instinct told him that once begun conversation with her would be difficult to terminate.

She looked at him slyly. 'Your friends are waiting for you,' she said.

'My friends? What friends?'

'A couple of fellers, didn't give their names.' She paused to light the cigarette she had just put between her lips. 'They said you were expecting them. They said they'd go on up and wait for you.'

'In my apartment?'

'They said you wouldn't mind.'

'How were they going to get in?'

'They said you'd given them a key.'

'I had? How long ago did they arrive?'

'Fifteen, twenty minutes.'

He felt a surge of pure, clear fear. Like ice in his gut.

'Excuse me, monsieur. I hope I haven't spoilt their little surprise.'

'Don't worry about it.' He paused, then flapped at his pockets. '*Merde!* Out of cigarettes. I'll just nip round the corner.'

He turned and ran back out of the door. Outside, he didn't stop running. Up the narrow rue Servandoni, to the junction with rue de Vaugirard. There was a free taxi just passing. He hailed it and jumped in. 'Where to, monsieur?' asked the driver.

Daniel checked his jacket pocket: wallet, yes. Thank God, passport too.

'Charles de Gaulle airport,' he said.

'Traffic's solid out there. Bloody strike, and there's been an accident.'

'Orly, then. But quickly. I'm already late.'

LONDON

Wednesday, 30 June

'We want to go in for him,' said Wesson firmly. 'Now.'

The room was bleak and white and characterless. Its only decoration was a framed photograph on the wall of the President of the United States. The chairs were made of tubular steel and the table at which they sat had a Formica top. There was a view from the window of Grosvenor Square, but as Wesson looked out at it, he felt hermetically sealed up here, in a different world, as if the people and the cars he could see in the street below were just a film playing on a screen and bore no relation to him.

'For Sunflower?' Avery frowned. He was a very thin grey man in a very white shirt who had a surprisingly deep voice.

'For Sunflower. There'll never be a better moment.' Wesson paused. Generally he was against displays of emotion. Emotion only complicated matters, got in the way of progress. Emotion was a bit like alcohol: it was a weakness, an escape from reality, not an engagement with it. It rendered reasoning imprecise and decisions unreliable. OK, he knew his attitude made people dismiss him as cold and impenetrable, as a machine, but he could live with that perception of himself. He found it better to repress, to stifle, to control. And the thing about machines was that they were efficient. They got things done. Still, he permitted himself a brief smile now, in the general direction of Avery and DI Higgins, who were both sitting at the table with him. A brief smile, too, in the direction of the microphone on the table-top that simultaneously patched them into Washington and to Hauser in Bern. 'We've got him now. In my view. We've got the bastard.'

'Got the bastard,' echoed Higgins. He was good at repeating other people's opinions.

'Is that your reading of the tea leaves, Ben?' said the disembodied voice from Washington to Avery. Wesson wasn't even sure who the voice belonged to, but it was someone pretty big. Sunflower's status demanded it. A final decision at the highest level.

Avery frowned again, and sucked air through his teeth in a little tune. 'I've had a chance to make an initial evaluation of the evidence.' He spoke slowly, picking out words gingerly as if they were unexploded bombs. 'On the face of it, there are compelling aspects to this new material.'

Jesus, thought Wesson. Compelling aspects. These legal experts were unbelievable.

'We got to get this one right, guys,' said Washington.

'We got to make damn sure that when we go in for him this sonofabitch doesn't have a crack to slip through. Mostly, you only get one chance.'

You don't need to tell me that, thought Wesson. I've seen it happen. I've seen eighteen months' work disappear straight down the pan because the scumbag in the dock had a clever lawyer and our guys had missed a tiny technicality. You don't need to tell me how that feels, when the slimeball who's guilty as hell walks away unpunished. Putting his finger up at you. Free to go back to peddling his poison on the streets of the cities, free to go back to making his millions by exploiting the weak and the young and the desperate. But this one's ready now. This one's watertight. And this one hasn't just been eighteen months' work. This one's been the best part of four years. Four years out of my life, shuttling back and forth between Washington and London, Miami and Milan. Not to mention the trips to hell-holes like Panama and Bogotá. Building, slowly building. Amassing evidence. I wouldn't be recommending going in now if I felt there was a danger of throwing it all away. If I didn't feel we were ready.

'Let's take it piece by piece,' continued Washington. The guy's voice carried authority, even faceless, even coming through to them out of the odd little amplifier on the table. 'Run it all past me one more time: Monday night, Enzo Cressini, Sunflower's brother and business associate, gets shot dead in a London hotel room. Correct?'

'Correct.' Wesson suppressed the weariness in his

tone. The impatience. The sense of wasting valuable time.

'Any developments on who shot him? Do we know that yet?'

Wesson sighed. He'd checked in with Grewcock first thing that morning. 'No new leads. Description of the suspect's been circulated, no positive sightings. Investigating officer tells me the jacket left at the scene of the crime is of United States manufacture, one of twenty-two thousand sold last year. But otherwise nothing.'

'Except for the photograph,' added Higgins, 'in the lining.'

'Photograph? What photograph?' There was sudden interest in the voice from Washington. Apparently that detail had been omitted from his briefing.

'A photograph of a painting, found in the jacket,' Wesson explained. Inwardly he cursed Higgins for bringing it up. An irrelevant distraction. Just Higgins needing to make a contribution, and choosing the wrong pretext at the wrong moment.

'What kind of a painting?'

'A painting of a river and trees. Unlikely to be significant.'

'Kind of odd, though. Who painted it?'

'I'll have the investigating officer check that out. But on balance our view is the killing's probably a contract job. Internal feuding between rival criminal organisations. Bad break for Enzo Cressini. Good break for us.'

'The contents of Enzo Cressini's briefcase, Ben. How do you assess the quality of that material? As evidence?'

Avery sucked through his teeth again. It was an infuriating habit, thought Wesson. 'I would say that it gives us eighty-five, ninety per cent of what we need,' Avery suggested. 'On its own, not quite enough.'

Wesson broke in. Not impatiently, but firmly: 'What di Livio got yesterday filled in those gaps. It's all there now.'

'All there now,' agreed Higgins. Sensing his last observation had overstepped the mark. Trying to retrieve the situation.

They both looked at Avery, who remained silent. Thoughtful, but silent.

'Hold it there for a moment,' said Washington. 'Di Livio's evidence came from the priest, right? In Rome?'

'The priest provided access to print-outs from secret Vatican bank accounts.'

'Genuine?'

'One hundred per cent. They've been checked out.'

'And the priest? How's the smell-test on the priest?'

'Someone tried to prevent him getting to us, ran him down in a car. He's in hospital with a broken leg. You can't get much more reliable than that.'

'So what exactly do the print-outs tell us?'

'They tie them all up. All the payments, coming in and going out. Most important, taken in conjunction with the contents of Enzo Cressini's briefcase, they link Amelga to Sunflower. Irrefutably.'

'You have to appreciate something.' The voice from Washington had taken on an ominous change of tone. 'This whole case raises issues.'

Issues. There were always issues. 'How do you mean?' demanded Wesson.

'We're entering a problematic political dimension. There's the wider diplomatic question of United States relations with the Holy See to be considered. Delicate ground. Can't just go wading in here.'

Wesson's private view was that if Catholic organisations had allowed their accounts to be used for money laundering, then they should be liable for the consequences just like anybody else; that the Holy See ought to be responsible for and capable of sorting out its own mess. But he didn't express it. Experience had taught him that the politics were best left to other people. Instead he said: 'We'd still like to move sooner rather than later. We could be missing the opportunity to take out one of the biggest players in the world.'

'What do you propose?'

'The warrants are ready for Gratsos and Hersch. We could pull them in immediately. As a first step.'

'Gratsos and Hersch?'

'Sunflower's subordinates. Those guys know where the bodies are buried.'

'Where are they?' asked Washington.

'They're both in Rome this afternoon, as it happens. Under surveillance. It's an ideal moment.'

'And Sunflower himself?'

'He's at home in Andrisio. Likely to stay there a while. They've got a family funeral to organise.'

'Andrisio? That Italy or Switzerland?'

'Switzerland,' said Avery. Grimly.

'Switzerland,' confirmed Wesson, trying to stay upbeat. 'That's why I patched in Hauser. Inspector Hauser of the Swiss Serious Crime Division.'

'Good morning from Bern,' said the microphone in a heavy Schweiz-Deutsch accent.

'Inspector, how long would a Swiss warrant take? Bearing in mind the serious nature of the charges?'

'Under the circumstances, the Federal Prosecutor's Office might be persuaded to move a little quicker than usual. Particularly in view of the fact that certain preliminaries are already in place. I would say approximately thirty-six hours.'

Wesson was calculating. It was midday now. 'So tomorrow night we could go in for him. Maybe dawn the day after tomorrow. If we set things moving at once.' He liked the sound of it. He liked going in for someone like Sunflower under cover of darkness.

'What's your view, Ben? Do we run with it?'

A further suck through the teeth, followed by a shrug of the shoulders. Invisible, of course, to Washington. 'I guess I'm comfortable if you are,' said Avery at last. To the amplifier. Batting it back for the final decision.

There was an agonising silence. Shit, thought Wesson. We've lost him. The line's gone dead. He was about to reach forward to get the secure operator to reconnect them when the voice suddenly came through again. With heavy resignation. 'OK, I'll square the diplomats, this once. But do me a favour, guys, don't screw up on this one. For Christ's sake, nail the sonofabitch.'

Wesson got up from his chair. He allowed himself a fractionally longer smile than he had intended. He glanced out of the window. The people and cars still milled round Grosvenor Square, busy, preoccupied, oblivious. They still seemed a long way off.

ZURICH

Wednesday, 30 June

Sitting on the edge of the bed, in this strange hotel by this strange lake in this strange country, Daniel dialled the number. As it rang, he looked out across the water in which distant lights were reflected. Dusk was falling. It was rather beautiful. Then suddenly, miraculously, he heard her voice. Husky, unmistakable:

'Si?'

'Juliette. It's me.'

'Oh, my God.' There was a pause, then she said with a kind of desperation: 'You shouldn't be calling. It's dangerous.'

'I had to. I had to tell you I can't meet you this weekend. I've had to leave Paris.'

'That ... no, we cannot meet. It's impossible for me too. I cannot move from this place.'

'Where are you?'

'Andrisio. At the villa. It is terrible here, bad things have been happening.'

'What? Tell me.'

'It's Aldo's brother, Enzo. He has been killed, I am not sure how, they do not tell me. All Aldo says is that he needs me here, by his side.'

The killing's separate, he told himself. Nothing to do with her. Nothing to do with us. 'I want to see you, Juliette. I have to.'

'I want to see you too, my darling. But Aldo won't let me go. I cannot leave him. I am frightened for him. He is like a crazy man. At one moment he is very silent, clinging to me. The next he is shouting, he is threatening to kill people himself.'

'Are you all right?'

'I'm OK. One thing you should know: Aldo, he will never hurt me.'

'Promise me you'll call me. If things get worse, or if you need me for anything. Promise me.'

'OK, I call you. But where are *you?*'

For a brief moment, he couldn't remember. It was getting to him now. He was on the edge of losing control. With a supreme effort of will, he pulled himself together. 'Zurich,' he said. 'Hotel Baur-au-Lac. I'm in Zurich.'

'I have to go,' she said. 'I hear him coming. All my love.'

He'd come here by chance. It had been the next flight on which a ticket had been available, once he'd reached Orly airport that afternoon. The Air France girl had checked him through. 'Run, Monsieur Stern. They are holding the gate.' Seventy minutes after getting into the taxi in the rue de Vaugirard, he'd been airborne. Then

Zurich. Safe. Swiss. Anonymous. A pause to buy a few basic necessities, underwear, a shirt, a toothbrush, at the airport shop. Then another taxi and this hotel. Expensive, comfortable. A room with a view over the lake. Another refuge. He was still free. Still just ahead of the game.

He clicked the mobile telephone off. It was still flashing: one message waiting. Must still be Parnello Moran. Waiting to be rung back. Jesus, give me a break for a moment. I need to think first.

Who had they been, the two men waiting for him in his apartment in the rue Servandoni? Don't worry, they'd told Madame Albert. We'll go on up. We have a key. Not police. No, police would not have handled it like that. Police would have arrested him in the street. Or, thwarted at the apartment, would have had the resources to watch the airports, to pull him in at the departure gate. More likely they were Cressini's men. Ruthless men. But needing to move more discreetly. Hunting him stealthily. To finish the job that Enzo Cressini had attempted and failed. He got up, walked across to the hotel-room door and drew the chain across it.

MILAN

Wednesday, 30 June

The driver was there waiting for him as Wesson hurried through customs at Linate airport. Wesson submitted his bag to the man's outstretched hand and asked, 'How long's the run up to Andrisio?'

'Two hours.' The man paused, then smiled a slow Swiss grin. 'Maybe one hour forty-five. If we don't stick too close to Italian speed restrictions.'

Wesson disregarded the pleasantry. 'Inspector Hauser and dI Higgins arrived already?'

'Yes, sir. Got there about six.'

It was almost dark, but the evening was still warm. The lights of the airport illuminated the night, an unearthly fluorescent city sprung up magically in the black plain of Piedmont. As Wesson settled himself in the back seat, his telephone rang. It was di Livio. He could tell at once from di Livio's tone of voice that there'd been developments. Things had happened. The guy was Latin, and overexcitable.

'It's all done,' di Livio assured him.

'Successful?'

'*Sì, del tutto.* Both of our friends have been pulled in. Gratsos and Hersch.'

'They gave no trouble?'

'No trouble. They were not expecting us. Signor Gratsos was entertaining a lady friend in his apartment. You cannot run very far when you have no trousers on. And Signor Hersch, he was finishing his lunch in a very expensive restaurant off the Via Veneto. We were very considerate. We gave him a chance to pay his bill before we introduced ourselves.'

'They talking?'

'Sure they're talking.' Di Livio was breathless with the good news. 'Gratsos particularly. He's ready to do a deal. I have him downstairs, I'm going back to him now. Looks like when he come across it's "ciao, baby" for Sunflower.'

'Like the sound of that,' admitted Wesson gruffly. 'Keep me posted.'

Wesson sighed, and clicked his portable shut. But he frowned as they accelerated on to the *autostrada* signposted Como and Lugano. He was always wary of things when they went too well.

ZURICH

Thursday, 1 July

Daniel awoke, sweating and fearful, in the Hotel Baur-au-Lac. He was close to breaking point. He knew he could not go on much longer. Not like this. Not on his own. Not on the run, forever looking behind him, shunning open spaces, chaining his door at night. He reached across to check his mobile telephone for messages. Only then did he remember that he still hadn't called Parnello Moran. Only then did he do it.

It was Brenda who answered.

'He's away,' she informed Daniel. 'God knows where. Might be Amsterdam. He was talking about viewing some sale over there. Most likely holed up with some Dutch bit down that red-light district. But good thing you rang, 'cause he particularly asked me to fax you something. Got a number where you are, have you?'

Daniel had a machine in his room, as it happened.

The message came through three minutes later. The message which changed everything.

Dear Daniel,

Here it is at last, the fruit of my research on the two stock numbers that you left with me from the back of the frame on your 'airy-caged' Monet. I'm sorry it's taken a bit of time. You'll see why when you read on. But I think you'll agree it's all worth waiting for.

The first stock number you found was the sequence 'LB 12376', stencilled in blue. This is a stock number of the Galerie Leblanc, Paris. Such numbers were appended to all works of art that have passed through the Gallery's hands, running in sequence from the Gallery's beginning (LB 001 = October 1881) through to 1961, when they changed their system. This means it's possible to tell from each stock number the specific time when the work of art concerned was acquired by the Gallery. According to the provenance recorded in the Catalogue Raisonné, *this Monet was bought by the Gallery in 1939. One assumed therefore that the stock number 'LB 12376' referred to that purchase. But when I applied to them for information about the number 'LB 12376', they refused to release any details. They stonewalled me with some story about their records for that time being rebound and therefore unavailable. Suspicious, wouldn't you say?*

I had an idea. I decided to check other known instances of similar Galerie Leblanc stock numbers, and consulted various museum catalogues to see if I could find any pictures with provenances that recorded them to have been in Leblanc's hands at about that time. I struck lucky. I discovered that a Fragonard portrait now in the Louvre entered the Galerie

Leblanc's possession in May 1942 under 'LB 12347'. On the other hand, the number on a portrait by Delacroix (now in the Chicago Art Institute) which was acquired by Leblanc in September 1942 is 'LB 12378' — only two numbers later than the one on the back of the frame of your Monet. These two dates act as *termini post* and *ante quem*, so we can be safe in concluding that 'LB 12376' became the property of the Leblanc Gallery between May and September 1942, in all probability very close to the latter.

Interesting, isn't it? It means that while Leblanc may have had the Monet in 1939, they seem to have acquired it again in 1942.

But the second stock number you gave me to look into is even more of a revelation. It reads 'UNB 174'. At first I thought it might be some collector's mark: you know, UNB being the initials of the collector. U.N. Benjamin, perhaps? But no. After checking with some good friends of mine in Berlin, I realise that it is something very different, and a lot less pleasant. This is not a collector's mark. It is a stock number issued by the Einsatzstab Reichsleiter Rosenberg (ERR), the agency set up by the Nazis to expedite the confiscation of works of art from French private collections (largely Jewish) during the occupation of France. I have succeeded in running checks on 'UNB 174' in the National Archives, Washington, and the German State Archives in Berlin, where most of the original ERR records are held.

Guess what? Ever meticulous, the Germans diligently filled in record cards for most of the works of art they looted. A record card for 'UNB 174' actually exists. Even better,

it refers to a landscape by Monet confiscated by the ERR
in July 1942. UNB stands for 'Unbekannt', meaning
of unknown previous ownership, but within the box on the
card where information about previous ownership was to be
recorded the name 'Benjamin' has been handwritten, together
with a question mark.

It gets better: on the same ERR card (of which my
friends in Berlin have sent me a photocopy) it is recorded
that the picture under this number was actually disposed
of to Galerie Leblanc. You won't believe this, but Leblanc
took it in exchange for a painting by Boucher acquired from
them by the ERR on behalf of the Reischsmarschal himself.
On behalf of Hermann Goering. So, whatever Leblanc may
claim now about their wartime record, here is documentary
evidence of their having traded with the enemy. That will
teach the bastards to be so smug.

Not that all this does me much good. I had this hunch that
once you'd found this famous Monet, I'd get the opportunity
to sell it and make a disgustingly large amount of money in
commission. Unfortunately, as the above shows, its wartime
history is too chequered for it to be saleable at all on the
international market.

Let's talk, anyway, when you have a moment. Meanwhile
all best,

P.M.

It was the most beautiful piece of paper Daniel had
ever seen.

He held it in his hands, and marvelled at it. There

in his Zurich hotel room with its view out over the milky lake. He marvelled at Parnello Moran, too, for what he'd succeeded in uncovering. This was vindication, vindication for all of them. For his grandparents, for his mother. For himself.

The Cressinis had pretended to argue legalities. Absurd for such people to argue legalities. But here was the final collapse of their case for the legitimate ownership of the painting. The stock number with which Enzo Cressini had taunted him in the Clermont Hotel, the one found on the back of the painting itself which constituted Cressini's cast-iron proof of valid acquisition, showed only that the Monet was in the Galerie Leblanc's care in October 1939. For a day and a night, before Maurice Benjamin retrieved it. What the Cressinis hadn't known was that the damning later Leblanc stock number was stencilled on the back of the original frame. The frame that had become separated from the painting. The frame that had stayed in Lady Gascoigne's bedroom.

And as for Leblanc, the craven hypocrisy of the man was suddenly and conclusively exposed. It was all going to come out now, all the squalid details. What his father had really been up to in the war, the business he'd done with the enemy after all. With Goering himself, in fact. 'Yes, Reichsmarschal. No, Reichsmarschal. The Boucher? A magnificent choice, Reichsmarschal.' The subsequent doctoring of the Gallery archives: that could be proved, too. After Daniel had written his piece about his grandparents, after their story had been syndicated in every major news magazine in the world, there wouldn't be much left of the Leblancs, either father or son. Here was Maurice Benjamin's posthumous revenge on his tormentors. And here was Maurice Benjamin's grandson to orchestrate it.

Now. Now was the moment to head back to London. To go to the lawyers. Forget Bainbridge and his constipations. Just engage the best, the hottest shots in town. To get Daniel off the murder charge. And to institute proceedings for the restitution of his family's Monet. With evidence like this, he couldn't lose now, could he?

He was light-headed as he lifted the telephone to call down to reception. He could have sworn that as he dialled his intention was simply to book a seat on the next flight to London. But he heard his own voice saying something quite different.

Asking for the train times to Lugano.

ANDRISIO

Thursday, 1 July

This was the final act in the madness of Daniel Stern. To be drawn back here to Andrisio, to the place of greatest danger, a moth beckoned on by the irresistible light of the flame. As the train left Zurich and headed south through the Alps, part of his brain registered the risk to which he was voluntarily exposing himself. He had it all now, he had the proof that his grandfather's Monet had been stolen in 1942. Expropriated by the ERR, and illicitly acquired by Galerie Leblanc. He didn't need to make this journey: from here on, everything could be conducted by the lawyers. As he reached Lugano and once more hired a car, he reflected on the foolhardiness of returning to the very doorstep of a man who might well be trying to kill him. A man whose brother he had unintentionally done to death in a London hotel room. A man who had most likely already sent two assassins to find him in his flat in Paris. But as he drove the familiar route round the lake of Lugano and into the farther, more shadowy valley, part of him exulted. He was getting closer. Closer to her. To Juliette. He had to see her, one more time. One more time before he finally gave himself up. Began the tortuous legal process to achieve his own exoneration from a murder charge, and the restitution to his family of their stolen painting.

It was six in the evening as he turned the sharp bend into the village of Andrisio itself. The weather had been overcast as he'd left Zurich, but here the sun had broken through and the square with its window boxes was as picturesque as he remembered it, like something from a tourist brochure. And yet oddly quiet. The café by the church was empty. There was no one out in the open. Uneasy, he drew the car to a halt for a moment. Then he glimpsed it: a slow movement in the far corner of the square. Another vehicle, easing forward, like a sleek green insect dislodged from its lair. He read the markings across its side: *Polizei*. Two uniformed officers within, alert, observing him. Daniel saw one of them speaking a few words into his radio, perhaps passing on the registration number of the hired car. Checking out his details. As casually as possible, Daniel put his own car into gear again and drove on. Calmly, not too fast. Out of the square. In the direction of the Villa Loretta.

Round the second bend, he was caught. Straight into a police roadblock. It happened too quickly for him to take avoiding action. An officer in a green leather jacket and dark glasses was already flagging him down. He drew up with a sickening sense of resignation. It was all over now. Strange that they should finally catch up with him here, of all places. How had they known he was coming? Who had been tracking his movements? There was no point in running now. A little wearily, he wound down the window and heard the policeman asking for his passport. He handed it over, and waited to be told to get out. To stand with his hands against the car and his legs apart. He'd seen enough arrests on the streets of New York. He knew how these things were done.

But suddenly the script was wrong. The document was being closed and handed back to him. He wasn't being manhandled out of the vehicle, told to lie on the tarmac. 'You are on holiday, signor?' the voice was asking him.

Daniel agreed that he was.

'Where do you go?'

He thought quickly. 'To the Castel San Marco Hotel,' he said.

The policeman nodded. 'Please do not halt your car in the next eight hundred metres. This is a security zone.'

'Right. A security zone.' He spoke as if it were the most natural thing in the world. He paused, then asked: 'What's going on exactly?'

'Please drive on now,' said the policeman, walking away.

As he passed the entrance to the Villa Loretta he slowed down slightly and saw them. The two armed paramilitaries on the other side of the road. Intent, concentrated, eyes trained on the locked iron gates. Who were they waiting for? One thing was for sure: no one was going in or out of those gates without their say-so.

Then, four hundred metres farther on, he came to a second roadblock. The policemen manning it checked his registration number, nodded, waved him on through. Jesus. What was going on here? The villa was under surveillance. More accurately, under siege. Why? Juliette: as far as he was aware, she was in there. With him, with Cressini. One thing you should know, she had told him. Aldo, he will never harm me. He prayed to God she was right.

He negotiated the steep incline of the road up to the Castel San Marco, then pulled into the hotel carpark. He reached for his telephone, and dialled her mobile number. Hell. It was switched to answerphone. He didn't leave a message.

He checked into the hotel. There seemed no alternative. 'Welcome back, Signor Stern,' said the man at the desk. 'It is a pleasure that you return to us so soon.'

Daniel went out to the terrace and ordered a drink. The view across the valley was breathtakingly lovely, the distant mountain-tops liquefying in the evening light. He remembered how he'd come down the stairs here ten days ago and found her waiting for him. Smiling at him. Shrugging, as if to say, What can one do?

'What's going on in Andrisio today?' he asked the waiter. 'The place is crawling with police.'

The waiter frowned. 'They do not say, signor.'

'How long have they been there?'

'The roadblocks were set up at midday.'

'But who are they after, who are they trying to catch?'

'It is perhaps just an exercise, signor,' the waiter said. But they both knew it wasn't.

Wesson looked at his watch: 8 p.m. The light faded earlier up here in the mountains.

'Jesus Christ!' he said. 'What's keeping your people, Hauser?'

He got up from his chair and walked to the window. Past the row of desks, and the incongruous line of children's artwork pinned to the wall. It was the first week of the holidays and they'd commandeered Andrisio's village school as their centre of operations.

'I have just come off the line with the Federal Prosecutor's Office.' Hauser was defensive. 'The warrant will be here just after midnight. It is only a two-hour delay.'

'Goddamn bureaucracy. I don't like it, this hanging around.'

'He's in there. He can't get away,' said Hauser. But Wesson noticed he was sweating rather more than usual.

'Like a rat in a trap,' added Higgins. Helpfully.

Wesson considered the situation. Up to a point, the process was going according to plan. Gratsos and Hersch had been picked up in Rome yesterday. Under a little pressure, Gratsos had indicated his willingness to do a deal. To give evidence against Cressini. He had been talking some more today, become voluble, in fact. About many things: about jobs he'd had to organise, for instance. Surveillance, burglaries, intimidations. Yeah the running down of an elderly priest, that too. But he'd only been acting on orders. His revelations implicated a couple of high-ups in the Vatican, as well. In it up to their necks, it seemed. Wesson had passed that news on to Washington a few hours ago on the secure line. What a can of worms, Washington had observed. But some deft diplomatic pressure in Rome had now ensured the Vatican's cautious co-operation with the Sunflower prosecution. The requisite details from Vatican bank accounts were to be made available. Discreetly. It was going to lead to some fairly seismic upheavals in the Pro Deo organisation, Washington had confided to Wesson. But then maybe those guys had it coming. There'd be a substantial amount of debris secreted under the Vatican carpet, Washington opined. In Washington's experience, that was where those priests stowed most of their embarrassing fallen masonry.

Either way, the sonofabitch in the Villa Loretta surely couldn't wriggle free now. The place was surrounded. If he tried to run before midnight, they'd pull him in. But it would be preferable to play it by the book. To do it with all the papers in order. Leaving no crack for the bastard to insinuate himself through later. No legal technicality for his lawyers to exploit. Still, Wesson felt uneasy. The longer they waited here on full alert, the more scope there was for something to go wrong. Wesson couldn't quite put his finger on what that might be. But something.

'The moment we get that paperwork, we go in, OK?' said Wesson. 'I mean instantly.'

Hauser and Higgins nodded their agreement. Wesson sighed, and looked up at the paintings done by the pupils of Andrisio village school. For a moment his eye rested on one of a sunflower under a blue sky. He was inclined to interpret that as a good omen.

Daniel had dinner alone in the Castel San Marco restaurant. There was nothing else to do. Later, around 10.30, he tried her number again. And that was the time she answered.

'Oh, my God,' she said. 'Where are you?'

'Very close by. I had to see you. Can you talk?'

'For a moment.' Her voice was dull with exhaustion. Still husky, but oddly lifeless. 'He's downstairs, I think.'

'Where are you?'

'I'm in the bedroom. It's been terrible here.'

'What's going on? The police are everywhere round the villa.'

'Aldo says there's some trouble to do with his business. He says his lawyers will sort it out. But he is very strange today.'

'Strange?'

'First he shouts and he breaks things. Then he goes very silent and depressed. Once he was crying, I think. I have never seen him crying before.'

'It's not safe for you to be in there. I'm going to come and get you out. Now. Tonight.'

'No, Daniel.'

'I'm going to try.'

'It's not possible. Leave it. Perhaps tomorrow.' Her voice was fading.

'Juliette. Talk to me. Are you all right?'

'I'm very, very tired. I've taken two sleeping pills. I'm going to crash out now, there's nothing more to be done. Tomorrow, Daniel. It will be better tomorrow. It is too dangerous to talk more now.'

Daniel needed fresh air. He couldn't stay inside any longer, he was getting claustrophobic. He walked out into the castle courtyard, and looked up at the clear night sky and the stars. It was colder now, but the full moon flooded the landscape with a silver radiance. He set off out of the gate, not really thinking where he was going but needing to keep moving. Doing something. Gradually the lights of the castle disappeared behind him as he followed the gently serpentine descent of the road. Ahead it would wind its way on towards Andrisio below. If he stayed on this route there'd be roadblocks sooner or later. That wasn't what he wanted. So when he came across the bridle-path that led more directly and steeply downwards, he struck off on to it.

Alone on the side of the mountain, shrouded in the shadows, he lost his sense of time. As he walked, he thought. Went back over it all again. Remembered the gentleness of his mother's smile. Pictured her as a baby, clasped in the arms of Thérèse Lisieux as she hurried away from the horror of the rue Nélaton. I'm nearly there, Mum, he told her. I've finished it for you. I've found the Monet you were looking for. I'm going to get it back for us. And I'm sorry I never rang all those weeks. But years ago, I touched them. The thirty-two alternate railings. I went out into the night on my own and touched them all for you.

He was out on his own in the night again now. Another night, another world. But the same sense of obscure menace in the darkness; of mystery and uncertainty. He was moving through a wood, his footsteps cushioned by pine needles. In a break in the trees, he paused and gazed out across the valley to the dark mass of mountain-tops on the other side. It was strange: the moonlight hung on the treetops like blue cobweb, lending the landscape an enchantment, an unreality. Then he looked down, and all at once there it was, laid out beneath him: the Villa Loretta, its grounds surrounded by the greystone perimeter wall. From this vantage point, the landscape lay at a vertiginous angle, and the property itself looked deceptively small. Daniel sensed it again: the dangerous enchantment. The unreality. Nature suddenly redefined in a new perspective. Nothing was quite the same any more; nothing was quite what it seemed.

Invisible from here, at the villa gateway, men were waiting and watching. Armed men, eyes trained on their target. He imagined the net tightening about the place. Daniel glanced at his watch. It was twenty-five to twelve.

She must be asleep now. In her bedroom drugged with sleeping pills. And what of Cressini? He was a bad man, and the police were coming in for him. Was he asleep too? Or was he restlessly pacing the villa, sensing his entrapment? Those locked iron gates: had his haven become his prison?

As Daniel stood and gazed, the peace of the landscape was shattered by a sudden whirling thwock-thwocking noise, echoing across the valley. Getting closer and louder every moment. There it was: Daniel's eye caught it in the distance. A Swiss Army helicopter, advancing like some monstrous insect of the night. It banked as it traced two very deliberate circles around the area of the Villa Loretta, strafing its grounds and surroundings with a powerful searchlight, intensifying the illumination of the moon. Like an animal hiding from a predator, Daniel stepped back quickly into the protection of the pine trees, anxious to avoid being caught, exposed in the raking beam. Then, with equal abruptness, the helicopter disappeared back the way it had come, into the folds of the valley's darkness.

The heavy stuff, thought Daniel. A very bad man indeed. The sort of man who sent his brother to kill people who got in his way. A very bad man, with a very beautiful wife. And a very beautiful painting by Monet hanging on his wall.

Jesus, what was that now?

Now there were footsteps on the pine needles, shockingly close. The rustling of a human being moving through the undergrowth. The crackle of a short-wave radio. Daniel crouched down at once behind a tree trunk, very still, his heart beating faster. The man passed him about five metres away. Uniformed. Jesus, another policeman. Part of the tightening net, patrolling approaches to the villa. Daniel watched him pause and look furtively about him. Then the man gently lowered himself to the ground, scrabbled with a packet, and lit a cigarette. It had obviously been a long day. Silently, Daniel backed away. Then, tracing a wide arc round the resting guard, he moved on through the trees. Closing in. Closing in on the Villa Loretta.

A hundred metres farther on he stopped, to look down at the house again. Checking his bearings. Keeping it in sight. And at once he saw it. Something wrong. Something horrendously wrong. From two downstairs windows at the rear, smoke was billowing out. Billowing out, like cotton wool.

Daniel Stern ran then. He ran oblivious to the policeman he'd just skirted. Oblivious to his cover. Oblivious to everything except the smoke. Crashing between the trees and rocks, and over two fences. At the perimeter wall he barely broke stride, but jumped, grasped the top, and pulled himself up. He swung his legs over awkwardly, tearing his trousers, and falling into a pile of grass cuttings on the other side. He picked himself up, sprinted over the lawn, past the swimming pool, and reached the house itself. The fire seemed to be downstairs, and it was spreading. There was smoke seeping out from four rear windows now.

He stood there for a split second of suspended horror, shaking his head in disbelief. He had to get in. His whole life, his whole being, depended upon saving what was in there. He ran along the side of the house to a rear entrance.

The door was locked. But he saw a spade lying against the wall. He grabbed it and smashed the glass panel. He reached through and released the catch. Inside, his eyes watered in the acrid atmosphere, but he felt his way along the passage till he emerged in the large hall. It was difficult to tell exactly where the source of the fire was, but smoke swirled thicker here, making him cough.

Then he heard it. Unmistakable, very loud and shocking. A gunshot. Very near, in a next-door room.

He followed the direction of the sound. Opened the door and found himself in an unfamiliar room. Don't let it be her. Please don't let it be her.

Thank God. It was the man's body lying on the floor by the desk. Aldo Cressini. The intensity of the relief held the horror in check. Cressini had put a bullet through his own head. Just at the point where his elegant silver hair curled over his ear. Quickly. Efficiently. Not her. Thank God, not her. The blood down the man's neck was still oozing fresh, and his gloved hand still grasped the gun, but there was nothing to be done for him now. That was Aldo Cressini for you. He would not have made a mistake with something like that.

Daniel ran back into the hall. The painting. The *Poplars*. He started in the direction of the double doors ahead. And then he paused. It must have been for less than a second. But it was there: a quick beat of indecision.

The beat in a man's life that defines him. Quick in time, but fathomless in its resonance.

Beyond those double doors hung the Monet. His family's Monet, the object whose restitution had come to dominate his life. Now morally, legally, irrefutably the property of the Benjamins once more. This was it, this was what he'd come for. In that split second, he saw it all again: the agony of his grandparents, the betrayal of Emile Leblanc, the poignant groping of his mother towards the truth. He saw Lord Gascoigne, the painting a symbol of his wife's unfaithfulness, of his daughter's loss of innocence. And he saw Alfonso Cambres too. Sometimes you can't right wrongs, Cambres had said. Sometimes all you can do is forgive the wrongdoers. And then he saw the painting itself. That sinuous 'S' receding across the summer sky. A record of one man's sublime artistry. Yes, a symbol of something beyond itself, more than mere paint and canvas. But in the end, an object. He recalled the awkward, hugely possessive gesture of Aldo Cressini as he stroked the painting's frame. In the end, a thing.

He wavered. Then he saw Jews. Millions of Jews, burning. Human beings, dead. Line upon charred line of them.

No. No more death. No more bodies. People, not things. People, not symbols. Nothing he could do with the Monet would bring his mother back. Still less his

grandparents. He veered left. Away. Away from the drawing room. Away from the picture. Away from the object
whose repossession had obsessed him. Up the curving
stairway to the first-floor landing. Every step that he
took was an emancipation. A release from obsession,
from guilt. Tears were pouring from his eyes and he
was gasping for air, but it wasn't just the gathering smoke
that was making him cry: there was relief and elation and
hope in those tears too. He reached the landing and ran
on along the passage, throwing open doorways to empty
bedrooms. Calling it out loud. Calling her name.

Through the final door, he found her. She was lying in
her bed, coughing weakly, torpid with sleep. Stern got her
up, exhorting her to consciousness. Her body. As he put his
arm round her and touched her skin beneath her thin white
nightgown, he felt a stirring of desire, a quick sensual shaft
of memory of her lying in his bed in the rue Servandoni.
'Come on,' he said. 'We've got to move.' He tried to lead
her back down the passage in the direction of the stairs, but
the smoke was now too thick to make any headway. She
coughed rackingly. Her frame convulsed with the effort.

Half carrying her, he retreated into the bedroom
and looked about him. The windows, the long French
windows. He threw them open. Thank God, there was a
balcony. He stumbled out, dragging her with him. Peering
over the balustrade down to the driveway below, Daniel
saw that there were men running. Uniformed men. Cars.
Flashing lights. Ambulances and a fire engine. He called
out for help.

He passed her gently over the balustrade, lowering her weakened body carefully into the upstretched arms of four policemen. He followed. More hands reached up to help him down. Someone put a blanket round him. Only as he was led away was he suddenly aware of the intense heat. Only then did he register that most of the lower part of the house was now on fire. That it made an eerie noise as it burned. A noise like rushing wind. Only then did he register that his own clothes were singed and that his hand hurt like hell.

He was the moth who'd flown too close to the flame.

ANDRISIO

Friday, 2 July

Daniel sat on a bench in the garden of the Villa Loretta. He felt oddly happy.

His eyes were still watering and his throat felt raw. The palm of his hand throbbed like hell. Some doctor had just bandaged it up, all clean white lint and brisk Swiss competence. It had got burned back there in the house, but he couldn't remember how. Funny how in an extreme crisis pain does not register; it only comes through afterwards, when things are calmer, when you have time to think. His clothes were blackened with smoke, and the right knee of his jeans was torn. He contemplated the flapping denim: yes, that had happened as he threw himself over the perimeter wall. Round about him, he heard the sounds of the emergency services mopping up. There'd been a lot of damage, but the fire was all but out now. Under control. An acrid scent still lingered in his nostrils, but now what he smelled was the aftermath of burning: a mixture of damp smoke and charred timbers, of scorched fabric and blistered paint.

Above, the Swiss Army helicopter made one final pass, its searchlight sweeping over the devastation, then retreated again, like some ravening bird denied its prey. He looked at his watch. Ten past one. Before too long, dawn would be breaking over the mountains.

A figure loomed in front of him, swaying slightly, hands clenched in the pockets of his flak jacket. A tall, muscular figure. Fit, early forties, with close-cropped fairish hair. 'Name's Wesson,' he said. 'DEA.'

'DEA?'

'United States Drug Enforcement Agency. You up to answering a few questions?'

'Of course.'

'Name?'

'Stern. Daniel Stern.' He was too tired to do anything but wait to see if it registered. If it brought the whole house of cards down on top of him. But if it made any impression on Wesson, he showed no reaction.

'Mind telling me what you were doing in the house when it went up in flames?'

'I wasn't in there. I just happened to get there first. I saw the smoke.'

'You saw the smoke?'

'I happened to be passing.'

'Passing?'

'Going for a walk.'

'Jesus,' said Wesson, shaking his head. Perhaps reaching certain conclusions about his Swiss colleagues and their ability to organise security cordons. 'But you know them? The Cressinis?'

He paused. Thinking it out. 'I'm a friend of Mrs Cressini.'

Wesson opened his mouth to ask another question, but closed it again. He was suddenly distracted by something happening outside Daniel's field of vision. 'There he goes,' he said softly. Speaking almost to himself.

Daniel followed the direction of his gaze and saw two white-coated ambulance men carrying a black shape between them. A shape in a shiny body-bag. They moved efficiently. Clinically. As if they were manoeuvring a quantity of washing. 'Cressini?' he asked. He remembered the line of fresh blood oozing from the man's ear. Just below his elegantly waved grey hair.

Wesson nodded. His whole stance exuded frustration and resentment. 'Was the bastard dead when you got in there?'

'He'd just done it. I heard the gun go off.'

'It's unbelievable,' Wesson mused. 'If the sonofabitch couldn't have it, nobody else was going to. Sets fire to his own goddamn house, then shoots himself. Taking it all with him.'

'Unbelievable.' But perhaps not unheard of. Sardanapalus, remembered Daniel, the Assyrian king: hadn't he tried to do something similar? Piled all his possessions on his own funeral pyre? Strange that should come back to him now.

'Bastard,' said Wesson. Venomously. He took it

personally, Daniel could see that. He also sensed that Wesson was the sort of man for whom the expression of such feeling was an unusual event. It came out strangled, deep-felt. There was an odd, almost embarrassed silence between them.

After a moment or two Daniel asked, 'No one got to the Monet, I suppose?' But he knew the answer already.

'The Monet?'

'There was a painting by Monet in the drawing room.'

'A painting?' For a moment it seemed as though some faint echo had sounded in Wesson's memory.

They turned to look. It was clear that the drawing room was the most devastated area of the house, where the fire had done most damage. Wesson said, 'There'd be nothing left of it. Not in there. What kind of value was it?'

'Twelve million dollars.'

'Jesus.' Wesson shook his head, savouring the sum of money. 'Twelve million dollars, up in smoke.' It was almost as if its enormity were some sort of comfort. A distraction from his own disappointment.

Daniel wondered about it then. Asked himself the question that had been lingering on the margin of his consciousness: if he'd gone for it, taken the double doors rather than the stairs, would he have been in time to get the canvas off the wall? Could he have saved it, smuggled it out through the smoke, thrown it through a window, perhaps? He allowed himself a moment's wistful remembrance of the picture, its canvas now no more than ashes, its frame and stretcher perhaps a few shards of smouldering wood. The poplars that Monet had once saved from being felled for firewood had met their originally intended fate. They'd burned. '*Of a fresh and following folded rank not spared, not one . . .*' But the painting was a thing, wasn't it? Just a thing. And in the end, the speculation was pointless. Irrelevant. Daniel Stern had made his choice. He'd headed upstairs, not straight ahead. He'd gone for life, not death; for the present, not the past. He'd taken the decision of his own free will. He was the only one who could have taken it; who'd earned the right to take it. Strange, how he could contemplate it all so peacefully. How the anguish and the raging had been stilled.

'Callous bastard, leaving his wife asleep upstairs,' observed Wesson. As an afterthought.

Daniel asked, 'Have they taken her away?'

'The ambulance left an hour ago.'

'She'll be OK, won't she?'

'Smoke inhalation. Not serious, the paramedics said. Lucky you got in there when you did.'

Daniel thought about it for a moment. 'You see, she wasn't just a thing,' he said.

But Wesson wasn't listening any more. Wesson was already walking off in the direction of his car.

ROME

Monday, 5 July

'There have been financial irregularities. Serious irregularities, Father.'

Abello sat awkwardly on the chair next to Cambres's bed. In his hands he twisted a copy of *L'Osservatore Romana*. It was faintly disturbing, reflected Cambres, to listen to your confessor's own confessions. Abello's perplexed, heavy-jowled face was frowning down at him. Cambres looked away. Out of the window of his hospital room, out across the rooftops of the city towards distant trees. He still felt bruised and shaken. Any movement was painful. His leg was encased in plaster which irritated his skin almost unbearably in the heat. But he was alive. And a heavy burden had been lifted from his shoulders. He could not resist saying it now, to Abello: 'So there was substance to my anxieties after all.'

'You are owed an apology, without question.' Abello paused. He wasn't enjoying this conversation, but to his credit he was here having it. The man had not ducked his responsibilities. 'You must believe me, Father,' he continued, 'I had no idea that matters had gone so far wrong. That our accounts had suffered this external infiltration. It is appalling to what depths unscrupulous people will stoop.' Unscrupulous. That was the word Cambres remembered he had used himself to Daniel Stern, to warn him about Aldo Cressini. *Sensa scrupoli.* There was an extraordinary story in the paper today about Cressini having died in a fire at his house in Switzerland. If that was true, then God have mercy on his soul. But what about Stern? He prayed that Daniel Stern was all right. Wherever he was now.

'There are still things that worry me about this terrible business,' said Cambres, turning his head back to face Abello. 'Forgive me, may I talk to you about them? Candidly?'

'Of course.' But Abello was no longer meeting his gaze.

'I know about these transactions. I know that they were all carried out under the authority of his Eminence himself. But why? I don't understand how he, of all people, can have countenanced them.'

Abello sighed, and stared very hard at the grapes on the bedside table. The grapes he had just brought with him. 'His Eminence is very hard upon himself in this matter,' he said slowly. 'I can tell you, in confidence, that he is standing down as Prelate-General. He blames himself for what has happened. This decision that he has taken is an extremely honourable one, because the truth is that he must have been grievously deceived by some very evil men. It is a sad day.'

'A sad day,' agreed Cambres. But he wasn't satisfied.

'The fact remains,' he persisted, 'that it was under his Eminence's own personal authority that these deals went through. Father Donaghy told me. Father Donaghy saw the secret coding.'

Abello looked tortured. 'That may be so. But — how can I put it, Father? — perhaps this is information better not shared with the outside world.'

'Better? Better for whom?'

'Better for the Service. Better for the Church.'

'But in the end, you would agree it is a matter for my own conscience.'

'Yes.' The admission was wrung out of him. 'In the end I would agree.'

There was silence. Cambres watched the fan in the ceiling which turned irregularly in the afternoon heat. Surged, then fell away. Surged, then fell away. Like a body's pulse. Cambres asked, 'Was there a proper doctor's certificate obtained after Father Donaghy's heart attack?'

Again, Abello did not meet his eye. 'It is being looked into. A second examination of the body, by an independent doctor. Just to be sure.'

Cambres nodded. He found he spent more and more time lying here thinking about his sister's orange groves. He would soon be among them, to recuperate, resting in their sweet-scented shade. It was all arranged. The prospect filled his heart with joy: peace after torment, the refuge after the storm. Once ensconced there this time, he suspected he might never come back to Rome.

He was tired. And he was old. And perhaps he'd earned his rest. Almost. But there was one more thing still to be done. One more matter to broach, before he could retreat there with his conscience salved. The most important matter of all.

Slowly but clearly, he explained it to Abello. He had thought it all out over the past few days. Agonised over it, the anguish in his mind a counterpoint to the distress in his body. He'd decided what must happen. There could be no negotiation. It was the only way to excise the corruption. To redeem the past.

'I understand what you're saying,' said Abello when he'd finished. 'But of course I cannot guarantee ...'

'What should also be taken into account,' interrupted Cambres, 'is my own conscience in this matter.'

'What exactly are you saying?'

'We discussed just now a sensitive question which you agreed could only be resolved by my consulting my own conscience. I think that you should convey to those within the Service who now decide such strategies that, if this proposal of mine were adopted, my conscience would be eased.'

'Eased?' said Abello softly. 'Or cleared?'

'Only God could clear it.' Cambres shifted his weight uncomfortably in the bed, then relaxed as he seemed to find an easier position. 'But I think that the Service could rely on the matter remaining private between my Maker and myself. If they did what I recommend.'

LONDON

Monday, 13 December

The first day of winter. There was ice on the pavements of Jermyn Street, and a light sprinkling of snow. Parnello Moran's drawing room was warm after the cold, clear morning outside. Parnello ran a perplexed hand through his long fair hair and frowned at Daniel Stern. 'So my hunch was wrong,' he said. 'About you and that Monet.'

'Not entirely. I did *find* the painting, at least.'

'But it will never come for sale now.'

'I'm afraid not.' Daniel had just told him the truth about the poplars. About Lady Gascoigne's donation. About the Monet's ultimate fate. Daniel felt he owed Parnello that much. After all he'd done.

Parnello shrugged and smiled ruefully. 'I'm not infallible, you see.'

'Nor am I,' said Daniel. 'I've done some pretty stupid things. Given my lawyers a fair amount of grief these past few months. Thank God, it's all been sorted out now.'

There was silence for a while. Parnello stared into the fire. Finally he said: 'Not that it's relevant any more, but I see Lord Gascoigne died last week.'

'I know.' Sybil had told him on Sunday. Telephoned him. The death had been a double release: Gascoigne from his torture, and Daniel from his obligation of silence. That was why Daniel was here now, speaking more freely to Parnello. And why he could push ahead with the publication of his book, too. That book. It was going to be a hell of a story. But he didn't want to talk about it yet, not to anyone, even Parnello. He didn't want to diminish the impact of the bombshell he was about to explode. On Leblanc, particularly. That detonation would be a sweet revenge.

'Bloody Mary?' suggested Parnello.

Daniel shook his head. 'I've got to be on my way.' He pulled on his coat and moved towards the door. He was late for lunch. He felt the excitement again, the anticipation: she'd be waiting for him in the restaurant on St James's Street. Juliette.

'By the way, seen the *Herald Tribune* today?'

'No.'

Parnello put the folded newspaper in his hand. 'There's an article on page five that might interest you.' He paused. 'Just another hunch.'

Daniel read it as he hurried along Jermyn Street.

CATHOLIC ORGANISATION GIVES $12 MILLION TO HOLOCAUST CHARITIES

Rome, UPI. The Pro Deo Organisation, a movement within the Roman Catholic Church, today
announced a $12 million donation to benefit
various Holocaust charities. A Pro Deo spokes-
man said that the money was the bequest of an
anonymous supporter. The intention was both to
commemorate those who lost their lives in the single most terrible act of genocide of the twentieth
century, and to build a stronger bridge between
the worldwide Catholic and Jewish communities.
The Holocaust Foundation praised the donation
as 'exceptionally generous'.

Daniel finished the short piece, then gazed at the
photograph above it. Two dignitaries of the Pro Deo
Service were shown shaking hands with representatives
of the Jewish charities. Everyone was smiling. In the
background was a face he thought he recognised. A face
with a more pensive expression. The face of an elegant
elderly priest with a distinguished aquiline nose.

Perhaps it was Alfonso Cambres. Perhaps it wasn't.
He couldn't quite be sure.